SHADOWED MEMORIES

OTHER BOOKS IN THE BATTLES OF DESTINY SERIES:

The editor said
"If you don't
write sex scenes
then you're
through."

⟨⟩

I said,
"Okay, then
I'm through."

For over 21 years, author Al Lacy wrote for leading publishers Bantam, Dell and Doubleday, using his gifts as a storyteller to write books that would financially support his greatest passion: traveling around the country as an evangelist, leading people to salvation in Christ.

With 47 best-selling novels written under pseudonyms, Al's success as an author was clear. But when faced with pressure to add sex and profanity to his books, he refused—choosing instead to take a stand for his beliefs.

That decision led one of the country's best Western and historical fiction authors to the Christian bookseller's market, where he has launched the exciting new *Battles of Destiny* Civil War series and *The Journeys of the Stranger* with Multnomah Books.

Here is Al Lacy's incredible story, told in his own inspiring words.

Q: How did you get started as an author?
AL: It all goes back to my call to preach. I pastored for several years before I went into full-time evangelism. The church I pastored had fantastic growth, and I didn't want to leave it. But it's hard to explain how God works. It's like being in love…you can't really explain it, but you know it's there.

I didn't want to be gone for weeks on end like an evangelist has to do. But God made it so plain. I've been doing preaching in churches around the country for 21 years now.

The problem is, there are a lot of expenses in evangelism that I never dreamed of. Some of the small churches can't pay anything, but I go anyway.

> It's hard to explain how God works. It's like being in love… you can't really explain it, but you know it's there.

I feel that I should do that—help the young ones get on their feet and go. But that means I wasn't putting anything away for retirement.

I thought,

"What else can I do and travel at the same time?" Then I was inspired by my wife. She said, "Well, you've read Westerns and historical books all of your life. You've talked about writing. Why don't you try writing one?" So I sat down and I wrote a Western novel called *Dead Man's Noose*.

Q: How did you first get published?

AL: I sent *Dead Man's Noose* to a few publishers. Most didn't even answer me. But one wrote back and said, "You're going about this all wrong. You have to have an agent."

So I prayed about that. I said, "Lord, I need the right agent." Then one day when I was flying, I read in the back of a magazine about an agent who was trying to find new writers. I contacted him, he read *Dead Man's Noose*, and he loved it. We signed a contract, and six weeks later, the book was sold.

I wrote several books for that publisher. Then my first editor left, and the new editor said, "I love your work. Your stories are exciting and captivating. But I want some sex scenes in here."

I told him that I don't write sex scenes. He said, "If you don't, then you're through. I said, "Okay, then I'm through."

> **I will not give in. I have standards. They are based on the Bible, and I won't break them.**

He probably thought I would give in. But I will not give in. I have standards. They are based on the Bible, and I won't break them.

After that, I worked for other publishers. But the problem continued over the years. I would get a new editor, and my book would come out with a few cuss words in it. I would call them and say, "Hey, I didn't put those words in there. I don't want that kind of language in there." Several books would go by, and everything would be fine. And then a new editor would come along, and—ZAP—out would come another.

It broke my heart that my publishing career seemed to be coming to an end, but I wasn't going to bend. God blessed me in that. Just a year ago, a pastor friend asked me, "Have you ever thought about writing for a Christian publisher?" He introduced me to Questar Publishers and Multnomah Books. And so the story goes...

Q: How do you find the time to write?

AL: The fiction series, traveling, preparing for sermons...it just takes a lot of discipline. And I don't watch a lot of television. Football season is rough on me. I love football. Writing takes a little midnight oil some times. But when you love it like I do, it's easy. I love to create stories, almost as much as I love to preach. I am amazed that I get paid to do the two things I love to do the most: preach and write. What a blessing!

....

Football season is rough on me. I love football.

Al Lacy *is the author of over fifty titles with over 2.8 million copies in print. He lives in Littleton, Colorado, with his wife JoAnna when he's not on the road "winning souls."*

BATTLES OF DESTINY

SHADOWED MEMORIES

AL LACY

SHADOWED MEMORIES

© 1994 by Lew A. Lacy

published by Multnomah Books
a part of the Questar publishing family

Edited by Rodney L. Morris
Cover design by David Uttley
Cover illustration by Phil Boatwright

International Standard Book Number: 0-88070-657-0
Printed in the United States of America.

For information:
Questar Publishers, Inc.
Post Office Box 1720
Sisters, Oregon 97759

94 95 96 97 98 99 00 01 02 03— 10 9 8 7 6 5 4 3 2 1

To Dick and Pete,
my very special sons-in-law.
The Lord has blessed me in many ways.
If you want to see two of my greatest blessings,
take a look in the nearest mirror.
I love you both more than you will ever know.

The Western Theater, Winter-Spring 1862

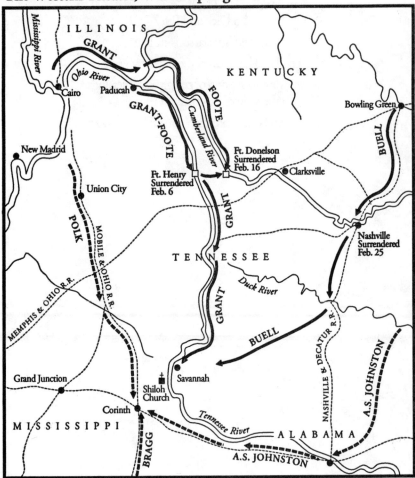

The Battle of Shiloh—April 6, 1862

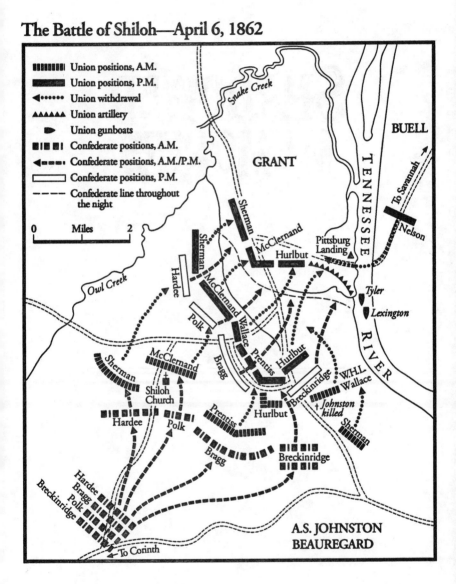

Union positions, A.M.
Union positions, P.M.
Union withdrawal
Union artillery
Union gunboats
Confederate positions, A.M.
Confederate positions, A.M./P.M.
Confederate positions, P.M.
Confederate line throughout the night

0   Miles   2

Snake Creek

BUELL

GRANT

TENNESSEE

To Savannah

Nelson

Sherman

McClernand

Hurlbut

Pittsburg Landing

Sherman

Hardee

McClernand

Owl Creek

Polk

Wallace

Prentiss

Hurlbut

Tyler

Lexington

RIVER

Sherman

McClernand

Shiloh Church

Bragg

Breckinridge

W.H.L. Wallace

Johnston killed

Hardee

Polk

Prentiss

Hurlbut

Sherman

Bragg

Breckinridge

Hardee
Bragg
Polk
Breckinridge

To Corinth

A.S. JOHNSTON
BEAUREGARD

The Battle of Shiloh—April 7, 1862

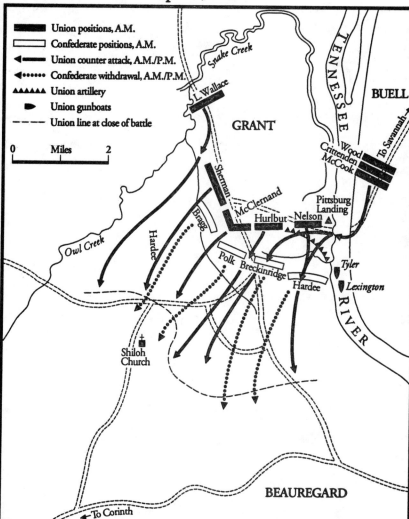

Union positions, A.M.
Confederate positions, A.M.
Union counter attack, A.M./P.M.
Confederate withdrawal, A.M./P.M.
Union artillery
Union gunboats
Union line at close of battle

0   Miles   2

Snake Creek

L. Wallace

GRANT

TENNESSEE

BUELL

To Savannah

Wood
Crittenden
McCook

Sherman

McClernand

Pittsburg
Landing

Bragg

Hurlbut

Nelson

Owl Creek

Hardee

Polk   Breckinridge

Hardee

Tyler

Lexington

Shiloh
Church

RIVER

BEAUREGARD

To Corinth

PROLOGUE

⭐

Just as the Potomac, the Shenandoah, the Rappahannock, and the York Rivers shaped the Civil War in the eastern theater, so it was with the Mississippi, the Ohio, the Cumberland, and the Tennessee Rivers in the west.

At the outset of the war, Major General Albert Sidney Johnston commanded the entire Confederate Department of the West, which took in all of Tennessee, Missouri, Arkansas, western Mississippi, and the Indian country farther west.

The Union command, however, was divided. Major General John C. Fremont, with his headquarters at St. Louis, Missouri, commanded the huge Department of the West, reaching from the Mississippi River to the Rocky Mountains, and on the east side of the Mississippi, southern Illinois and all of Kentucky west of the Cumberland River. Major General Robert Anderson of Fort Sumter fame commanded the Federal Department of the Cumberland, with central and eastern Kentucky and all of Tennessee as its potential maneuvering area.

Fremont gained fame in his early manhood as an explorer. Upon entering the U.S. Army, he became an officer in the Corps of Engineers. A controversial figure in the conquest of California and the Mexican War, he later became a politician, and in 1856 he was the first presidential candidate of the Republican Party. He owed his rank and command, not to his sketchy military experience, but to his political clout.

Of a different mold, Johnston was a West Pointer who had distinguished himself as a leader in the Texas War for Independence, and later in the Mexican War. He also had experience as an Indian fighter, and had commanded the U.S. Army expedition of 1857-58 against the rebellious Mormons in Utah.

Within a month after the Battle of First Bull Run in July 1861, both the Federals and the Confederates were massing large forces of militia on the borders of "neutral" Kentucky. By the end of August 1861, some sixty-five thousand Union troops were camped along the Ohio River in Illinois, Indiana, and Ohio while forty-five thousand Confederate troops were concentrated in northern Tennessee.

Newly promoted Brigadier General Ulysses S. Grant was appointed by President Abraham Lincoln on August 30 to command Federal forces in southern Illinois and southeastern Missouri, a part of Fremont's jurisdiction. Grant, an 1843 graduate of West Point, had distinguished himself for heroism in the Mexican War, and had then resigned from the army in 1854 to pursue a civilian career.

A respected merchant in Galena, Illinois, when the Civil War broke out, Grant immediately offered his services to the state. He was soon assigned command of an Illinois regiment with the rank of colonel.

Born Hyram Ulysses Grant, he received a congressional appointment to the West Point Military Academy and entered school in the fall of 1839. A clerical error on his appointment papers identified him as Ulysses Simpson Grant. The young cadet liked Ulysses Simpson better than Hyram Ulysses, so he left it alone. Later, at the battle of Fort Donelson (as depicted in this volume), the initials "U.S." proved to be a hook upon which to hang a new and admiring title: *Un*conditional *S*urrender Grant.

Wearing the new brigadier general insignias on his uniform, Grant arrived at his command headquarters on the Mississippi River at Cairo, Illinois, on September 3, 1861. That same day Johnston ordered his subordinate, Major General Leonidas Polk, to seize key points in western Kentucky. On September 4, Grant learned of the movement of Polk's troops into Columbus, Kentucky, just eighteen miles south of Cairo on the east bank of the Mississippi. Grant realized that a major objective of both Union and Confederate forces was control of the Mississippi.

Cairo, at the southern tip of Illinois, was a critical point because it stood at the junction of the Ohio and Mississippi Rivers. It was also the place where Illinois met the key border states of Missouri and Kentucky. Cairo's significance as a base for future Union operations was further enhanced by two major geographical spots nearby.

Less than forty miles upriver, east of Cairo, the Tennessee River flowed into the Ohio at Paducah, Kentucky. The Tennessee, rising far to the east in the mountains of southwest Virginia, swept nearly a thousand miles on a wide arc through the heart of the Confederacy. It provided a natural water highway between the critically important points of the South and the great agricultural regions of the North.

Just as important was the Cumberland River, also flowing into the Ohio, and forming a snake-like concentric arc with that of the Tennessee, flowing through Nashville. At the town of Dover, in western Tennessee, the Cumberland and Tennessee Rivers were only twelve miles apart. From that point to the Ohio, they flowed in parallel, never less than three nor more than twelve miles separating them.

General Johnston recognized the strategic position of the two rivers and ordered two Confederate forts constructed—Fort Henry on the Tennessee, and twelve miles across the mucky lowlands to the east, Fort Donelson on the Cumberland.

While construction was under way during the next four months, there were skirmishes between the Yankees and the Rebels along the banks of the rivers. It soon became evident that major battles were in the offing. By New Year's Day, 1862, some five thousand Confederate troops manned Forts Henry and Donelson under the command of Brigadier

General Lloyd Tilghman.

Telegraph lines were strung between the two forts so there could be instant communication between General Tilghman—who headquartered at Fort Henry—and Brigadier General Simon Buckner, who was his officer-in-charge at Fort Donelson.

During those same four months, two major command changes occurred in the Union ranks. General Robert Anderson became seriously ill and was replaced by Brigadier General Don Carlos Buell, who had distinguished himself in both the Seminole War and the Mexican War. In Missouri, General John C. Fremont was proving to be incompetent. He was relieved of his command by President Lincoln and replaced by Major General Henry Halleck, a brilliant, tough-minded, abrasive veteran of the Mexican War.

Though January was bitter cold, there were more skirmishes between the two factions. General Grant concluded that sooner or later he was going to have to deal with the forces at Forts Henry and Donelson, since they served as watchdogs over the two strategic rivers. Grant consulted Flag Officer Andrew H. Foote, commander of the Union Navy flotilla of river gunboats in General Halleck's Department of the Missouri. As a result, on January 28, 1862, Halleck received similar telegraph messages from Grant and Foote. Grant's message said briefly, "With your permission, I will take my seventeen thousand troops and attack Fort Henry and establish a camp there for Union forces. When Fort Henry is secure, I will do the same with Fort Donelson."

Foote's message to Halleck endorsed Grant's proposal and expressed his readiness to support the move.

The next day, Halleck received a telegram from Washington, informing him that Confederate General P.G.T. Beauregard was leaving Manassas (where he had been since the Battle of Bull Run) and heading for Kentucky, taking fifteen regiments with him.

Halleck decided to strike a heavy blow against the Confederate strongholds before Beauregard and his regiments arrived. Unaware that the information about Beauregard was false, Halleck telegraphed Grant on January 30, telling him to make his move on Fort Henry as soon as possible. Halleck also began to seek reinforcements for Grant. At the same time, he commanded Buell to make demonstrations and diversions to keep Johnston from further reinforcing western Kentucky.

Grant informed Halleck of plans he and Foote had prepared for moving his Union troops down the Ohio, Cumberland, and Tennessee Rivers by steamboat. Grant and Foote agreed that they would have the troops at Fort Henry's door, ready to attack, by Wednesday morning, February 5. General Halleck wired back his consent, encouraging them to make quick work of it. When Fort Henry was secured, Halleck would decide when to attack Fort Donelson.

Little did the military leaders on both sides realize that the Fort Henry-Fort Donelson conflicts would become the prelude to one of the Civil War's bloodiest battles on April 6-7, 1862, at Shiloh, Tennessee. The Shiloh battle would end in a draw, with nearly twenty thousand casualties.

CHAPTER ONE

✦

The light of the full moon lay like silver on the carpet of crusted snow and ice that covered the fields all around him. Lying on an icy knoll, rifle in hand, he turtled into his upturned collar and let a shudder crawl over his body. The night wind sliced through his gray wool overcoat like knives, sending chills all the way to the center of his bones.

There was a warmth within him, however, that the winter's cold could never quench. As a loyal Union soldier and marksman, he had been sent by the Federal Office of Intelligence in Washington to do a job. He was to kill as many Confederate officers as possible. The thrill of what his successful task could mean to the Union cause kept a flame burning in his soul.

His intended victim on this frigid Tennessee night was Confederate Colonel Nelson Parker, who was on his way from Fort Henry to Fort Donelson under cover of night to join Brigadier General Simon Buckner. Brigadier General Lloyd Tilghman, who commanded both forts from his headquarters at Fort Henry, had given in to Buckner's oft-repeated request for a colonel to serve under him, since his previous colonel had recently been sent to

Nashville. Since Tilghman had two colonels at Fort Henry, Buckner felt he deserved one of them.

The assassin chuckled to himself. Here he was, dressed in a gray uniform, neatly inserted into the ranks of the Rebels, and they didn't suspect a thing. He thought back to earlier in the day when he happened to be passing the telegraph room inside Fort Donelson as General Tilghman's wire was coming in. The corporal who manned the telegraph key at the time had just written down Tilghman's message when a wire from Major General Albert Sidney Johnston started coming through from Johnston's headquarters at Nashville.

While busily writing down the Johnston message, the corporal had handed the assassin the slip of paper and asked him to carry it at once to General Buckner. While moving toward the general's quarters, he had read the message:

31 January, 1862
Brigadier General Simon Bolivar Buckner
Fort Donelson

At your request am assigning Colonel Nelson Parker to your command. Because of daily skirmishes with Union forces, Parker and escorts will ride at night. Will arrive Fort Donelson app. 9:00 P.M. Escorts will return at once.

Brigadier General Lloyd Tilghman

The Yankee impostor delivered the telegram to Buckner and rejoiced at his good fortune. He was scheduled to be among the four hundred men going into town that evening. General Buckner was allowing his soldiers to spend an evening in Dover in rotations of four hundred per night. Most made the rounds between the town's six taverns. Though Buckner did not allow them to drink alcoholic beverages, they enjoyed the time away from the fort.

Dover, like Fort Donelson, was on the west bank of the Cumberland River, barely three-and-a-half miles south of the fort.

Twelve miles due west of Donelson stood Fort Henry on the east bank of the Tennessee River.

The assassin glanced in the direction of Fort Henry, then did a panorama of the wooded hills to the east and north, marked only by the spiderweb tracery of dark-shadowed, naked oaks and dogwoods, their skeletal shapes bent to the wind.

The Cumberland River was broad where it flowed beneath the towering fort, and its wind-ruffled waters reflected the silver hue of the moon. There was no sign of life in the woods or fields. Some three miles to the southeast lay Dover, where lantern light glistened from the windows of houses.

He had no idea how many men would make up Colonel Parker's escort, but with the weapon in his hands, he could knock Parker out of the saddle at eight hundred yards. If there were no more than four or five men in the group, he could take them all out before they knew what hit them. If there were more, and he had to make a run for it, there were plenty of places to hide. Besides, the soldiers in the convoy would think a bunch of Yankees had set up an ambush. Not knowing how many Yankees might be out here, they would high-tail it for Fort Donelson.

The assassin's rifle lay in the Y-shaped crotches of two small tree limbs he had positioned solidly in the ice. Parker and his escorts would have to ride across the fields north of him in order to cross the Cumberland at its lowest spot before beginning their climb up the steep, winding path to Fort Donelson. Their course would place them in the crosshairs of his new telescopic sight.

Not long after he had joined the Confederate army at Nashville, he was assigned to General Buckner's brigade. When it was known that Buckner and his men were being sent to the newly built fort, the Confederate army outfitted them with brand new .58 caliber Spencer repeater rifles. Buckner's men were the only Confederate soldiers to receive the Spencers, which had an accuracy range of eight hundred yards and a magazine that held eight rounds. By rapidly changing magazines, an expert rifleman could fire up to twenty-one rounds a minute. The Confederate army had fitted the Spencers with specially developed sights, but the assassin had replaced the government-issue sight for this occasion with his own German-built sight, a full-length brass tube that provided twenty-power vision. The challenge was to hold the rifle steady enough to cope with so much magnification. The assassin's Y-shaped tree limbs solved that problem.

Suddenly movement on the moonstruck land caught his eye. Riders coming from the northwest. Had to be Parker and his escorts. Shouldering the rifle, he peered through the sight. It was Parker, all right, and there were only five men with him. They didn't know it, but they had seen their last sunrise.

The killer estimated them to be about fifteen hundred yards out. They were in a trot, and would be within range soon. A thrill slithered down him, and suddenly his body felt warm. The only cold he could feel was in his hands, and he cupped them now close to his mouth. Putting his right eye to the scope again, he caressed the long barrel and whispered, "C'mon, you rotten Rebs. Just a little closer, and you'll be shaking hands with the devil."

The riders-in-gray seemed to be moving in slow-motion, but finally they were within the Spencer's range. He sighted in on the rider in the lead, following his movement. His finger rested comfortably on the trigger. The silvery fields lay in absolute stillness. A silence of death hovered over the snow-laden earth as the crosshairs locked on Colonel Nelson Parker's chest.

He squeezed the trigger. The cartridge exploded and the wooden stock kicked against his shoulder.

Some eight hundred yards across the wintry Tennessee landscape, the Confederate colonel was unaware that death was in flight. He would never hear the shot as it echoed over the frozen turf.

The assassin witnessed the impact through crystal-sharp

German glass. He saw the fleeting amazement on Parker's moon-lit face as his hat flew off when the bullet tore through his chest. The colonel twisted in the saddle, then fell gracelessly from his horse's back.

Instant panic sent two escorts from their saddles to attend to the fallen officer. The other three brought up their rifles and fired in the direction the shot had come from. The killer knew he was safely out of their range and calmly returned fire as fast as he could. Within fifteen seconds, the three who had remained in their saddles were lying dead. The other two had flattened themselves on the cold ground, conversing excitedly.

The killer's elevated position gave him the advantage. Though the Rebel soldiers lay flat, he had no problem bringing them into focus through the scope. Taking careful aim, he put a bullet through the one on his left. The other one, realizing he was now alone, scrambled to his feet and dashed for his horse. He had his left foot in the stirrup and was swinging the other leg upward when the assassin's bullet plowed into his back. He arched in pain and fell backward to the ground, never to move again.

On his feet, rifle in hand, the killer ran toward Dover, leaning into the wind. When he reached the outskirts, he ducked into the shadow of a small barn and removed his telescope from the Spencer. From the lining of his overcoat, he took the government rifle sight and fitted it back in place. He then slipped the German sight into the lining and walked casually onto the main street toward the Cumberland Tavern.

The place was alive with piano music and Confederate soldiers laughing and joking as they sipped their coffee and sarsaparilla. Citizens of Dover drank and laughed with them. Unnoticed, the killer slipped off his coat, hung it on a wall peg, and leaned his rifle against the wall. He moved slowly through the place, studying faces, and decided to move on. He would find the men he had come to town with.

He checked out two other places before he spotted his friends in the Two Rivers Tavern. Had he found any greater excitement touring the other taverns? He said he had not, then ordered a sarsaparilla and sat down among the men-in-gray.

Some of the men of Dover were discussing the war situation with the soldiers. The hated Yankees had set up camp just north of Fort Henry, and word was that General Ulysses S. Grant had left his headquarters eighty-five miles northeast of Cairo, Illinois, and was going to set up a temporary headquarters somewhere near Dover. The five thousand Confederate troops in Forts Henry and Donelson were bracing themselves for the assault they knew was coming. These visits to town would soon come to an end.

Among the civilians was a big farmer named Clarence Clubson. Twenty-two years of age, Clubson stood six-five and had bull-like shoulders, a pillar of a neck, deep chest, and arms like tree trunks. "Club" was known for his fighting prowess and hair-trigger temper. The men of Dover and the surrounding farming country feared him, and always gave him a wide berth.

Club had a booming voice to match his mountainous body. His face was blunt, with wide-set hazel eyes and a broad nose. He had a tangled mass of straw-colored hair that rarely saw a comb.

Club bore within him a vehement hatred for Yankees. When General Grant was mentioned, Club rose to his feet and began smacking a meaty fist into an open palm. Everyone in the place grew quiet. Club swore, then boomed, "I'd like to know just where that stinkin' Useless S. Grant plans on settin' up his headquarters! Just gimme three minutes with that bearded skunk, and I'll tear his head off!"

A young man with twisted legs sat in a chair holding a pair of crutches. "Club," he said, "if Linda Lee heard you swear like that, she'd drop you like a hot potato. You know she don't cotton to foul language."

"Yeah," spoke up an elderly man with no teeth, "and neither does the rest of her family. If you're gonna marry into the Claiborne family, Club, you're gonna have to clean up your mouth and start goin' to church."

Club ran his gaze between the two men and grunted, "What Linda Lee don't know ain't gonna hurt her none. I get mad, and when I do, I cuss. I just don't do it around her or her family. As for goin' to church, we'll see about that once't Linda Lee and me are hitched up."

"I'm not too sure you'll get hitched up," the young man said, "unless you make the family think you're a Christian. And you ain't gonna do that without bein' in church when the doors are open."

Everybody in and around Dover knew that Linda Lee Claiborne was not in love with Club. She had no intentions of marrying him, though she always treated him kindly. Linda Lee had even told Club in her gracious manner that she would not marry him, but he would not accept it. He was sure she loved him and would eventually marry him.

"Aw, Linda Lee wouldn't care so much about this church business if her ma and Hannah Rose weren't such hounddogs about it," Club said.

"Pardon me, Mr. Clubson, but could I ask you a question?" a young Rebel private asked.

"Sure, soldier."

"I don't mean any offense, mind you, but from the looks of you, I'd say you're about the biggest, strongest feller in these parts."

"Ain't no 'about' about it," Club growled. "I am the biggest and strongest. Ain't nobody gonna challenge that."

"Well, what's bothering me is how come you're not in a Confederate uniform?"

Club set steady eyes on him. "There's nothin' I'd like better, private. Nothin'. But my pa died just before the war started last year, and there's nobody to run the farm. The crops I raise are goin' to the Confederate army for food. I tried to enlist, but they told me I could best serve the Confederacy by raisin' corn and cabbage and such and sendin' 'em to the troops. So that's what I'm doin'. 'Sides that, I'm takin' care of the Claiborne place so's Linda Lee's brothers can fight."

"What's there to do at the Claiborne place, Club?" another man asked. "I mean, besides just keepin' the buildin's and fences in good repair? Other than their wagon team, they ain't got no animals."

"Well, you're right...that's about all there is to it. But somebody's got to do the stuff them women can't handle."

"I bet you wouldn't spend so much time at the Claiborne place if you weren't in love with Linda Lee," another man laughed. "When are you and Linda Lee gonna tie the knot, Club?"

The elderly man flashed a toothless grin at the others, winked, and said, "From what I've been hearin', there ain't gonna be no knot between that beautiful girl and Club. Seems she's been seein' a couple other fellas."

"Oh, no she ain't!" Club snarled. "I took care of Luke Smith and Harry Binder both! Beat 'em to a pulp. They wouldn't dare go near Linda Lee again. 'Sides, I happen to know that both of them are in the army somewhere in eastern Tennessee. Chattanooga, I think."

"I ain't talkin' about Luke and Harry. I'm talkin' about them two boys from Fort Donelson."

Club's neck turned red and the color rose to his face. "I don't know about any boys from the fort. Who are they? When have they been here?"

"You talkin' about those two young corporals, Abe?" asked Wally Speck, one of the Claiborne's neighbors.

"Yeah. Come to think of it, I did hear that they're both corporals."

"They've been visitin' Hannah Rose, not Linda Lee."

"You sure about that?"

"Positive. I was in the general store 'bout a month ago when those two came in. Hannah Rose was there, and they struck up a conversation. Taller one introduced himself as Jim Lynch, and the other one called himself Lanny Perkins. When Hannah Rose left the store, I heard both of 'em arguin' 'bout which one was gonna date her first. Since then I've seen her with Perkins four or five times. They ain't interested in Linda Lee, I can say that for sure."

A scowl rode Clubson's brow. "Well, they better not be. Any man shows interest in my gal will get hisself beat to a pulp." He went to a peg on the nearest wall and retrieved his coat and hat. "Milkin' time comes early, boys. See y'all later."

When Club was gone, Speck said, "I feel sorry for the big brute. He's so blinded with love, he cain't see that pretty little Linda Lee ain't never gonna marry him."

"Guess he'll figure it out someday," sighed one of the others.

Abe Smalley shook his head and said, "Tell you who I feel sorry for. That's the guy Linda Lee falls in love with. Club'll probably kill 'im."

No one said anything for some time after that. Then one of the sergeants glanced at the clock on the wall and said, "Well, my military comrades, it's gettin' late. Time we were makin' our way back to the fort."

"Colonel Parker oughtta be there by now," one of the soldiers said. "I'm sure glad General Tilghman is letting us have him."

The assassin felt a warmth spring up in his chest and spread pleasantly through his body. Other Rebel soldiers spoke of their admiration for Parker, and how pleased they were that he was becoming part of the command force at Fort Donelson. The man who had shot Parker only an hour before grinned to himself as he slipped into his coat, feeling the telescopic sight in its lining.

At Fort Donelson, General Buckner was sitting behind his desk in the rock-walled room he called his office. Seated in front of him were Captains Waldon McGuire, Eric Donaldson, and Britt Claiborne. Two lanterns burned overhead.

Buckner, in his early fifties, was a West Point graduate and a long-time friend of General Grant. A colonel in the regular U.S. Army before the Civil War, he had trained five thousand militiamen in Kentucky. Some of those men were now with him at Fort Donelson.

A stern-faced man with a thick head of salt-and-pepper hair, Buckner wore a droopy mustache and had a pair of wide-set, piercing gray eyes. At the moment, those eyes were resting on the pocketwatch in the palm of his hand. "This isn't like General Tilghman or Colonel Parker. It's almost ten-thirty. I don't like the smell of this."

There was a knock at the door.

"Come!" called Buckner.

The door squeaked open, and the face of Corporal Darrell Tomberlin appeared. "I'm sorry, General, but I can't get any response. They must have the telegraph key turned off at Fort Henry."

"All right. Thank you, Corporal."

"Anything else I can do, sir?"

"Not at the moment."

"Yes, sir." The door clicked shut, and Tomberlin was gone.

Worry etched itself on Buckner's face. Rising, he said, "Captain Claiborne, I want you to take a platoon of men and ride to Fort Henry. I must know what's going on."

All three captains stood up.

"Sir?" said Donaldson.

"Yes?"

"May I suggest that Captain McGuire and I go with Captain Claiborne, and that the platoon be at least fifty men? I just don't trust those blue-bellies. I hate to say it, but maybe...maybe they ambushed Colonel Parker and his escorts. If they did, and they're still hanging around out there, we'll need enough men to repel another ambush."

The lines in Buckner's brow deepened. Wiping a palm across his mouth, he replied, "An ambush doesn't make sense, Captain. It's colder than blue blazes out there. The Yankees would have no way of knowing that Colonel Parker was riding here tonight. It would be impossible for them to plan an ambush. I seriously doubt they'd be patrolling, just waiting for some gray uniforms to show up in the moonlight. The whole reason General Tilghman planned to send Parker at night was to eliminate any chance of him running into some Yankees."

"I agree, sir," Donaldson replied. "My first thought was ambush, but you're right, that isn't likely. But I see the concern in your eyes. What do you think may have happened to Parker?"

"We know that General Grant has plans to move his headquarters to somewhere in this area," Buckner said. "It crossed my mind that possibly he decided to make his move at night...and just maybe his troops and Colonel Parker's group stumbled onto each other."

"If anything has happened to Colonel Parker, sir," Claiborne said, "it would more than likely be just what you described. I hope not. I hope it'll turn out that for some reason, Parker and his escorts couldn't leave Fort Henry as scheduled, and that there's something wrong with the telegraph so General Tilghman can't get a message to us."

"I hope you're right," breathed Buckner. Turning to Donaldson, he said, "I appreciate your willingness to go with Captain Claiborne, and I'm sure Captain McGuire is just as willing, but I don't dare risk all three of my captains on one venture." Shifting his gaze to Claiborne, he proceeded. "Captain, take Lieutenant Benson, your brother William, and two other sergeants, along with fifty troops. Ride to Fort Henry as fast as you can. I've got to know if something has happened. Should you get there and find that everything's all right, and that their telegraph key was merely shut off, wire me immediately. I'll see that Corporal Tomberlin keeps our line open. Otherwise, I'll be anxiously waiting for your return with whatever news you can give me."

"I'm on my way, sir," Claiborne said as he hurried to the door.

CHAPTER TWO

✦

Clouds were scudding in from the north and periodically covering the moon as Captain Britt Claiborne watched his men saddle their horses. Beside him were Lieutenant Blythe Benson and Sergeants William Claiborne, Cliff Nolan, and Jed Masters.

At twenty-eight, Britt Claiborne was the oldest of the Claiborne brothers, and stood the tallest. He was six-three and weighed a slender two hundred pounds. William was twenty-six, stood an even six feet, and weighed the same as his older brother. Their youngest brother Robert (who had recently been promoted to corporal) was twenty-three and of the same build as William. There was a strong family resemblance among the three brothers.

Wind gusts flung ice crystals in the faces of the men-in-gray as they made ready. Captain Claiborne tugged at his hatbrim and gave the command for the platoon to mount up. Sentries on the walls bent their heads into the wind and watched as the fifty-five men rode down the gentle slope and turned due west, leaving the fort and the river behind.

After riding for no more than a quarter-hour, Lieutenant

Benson raised a gloved hand and pointed directly in front of them. "Look, Captain! Horses! Looks like five or six of them huddled together out there."

The moon was shining without hindrance at the moment. Claiborne could make them out clearly. He also saw dark forms scattered about on the white, frozen turf. His heart quickened pace as he said, "Looks like bodies on the ground!"

"You're right, sir. I...I'm afraid it's Colonel Parker and his escort."

Captain Claiborne put his mount to a gallop, and the platoon followed his lead. As they drew up, hooves scattering snow and ice, the captain slid from his saddle and shouted, "Heads up, men! There's been an ambush here! Form a circle and keep a lookout! Lieutenant, you and Sergeant Claiborne dismount and come with me."

Sergeants Nolan and Masters took charge of the remaining troops and led them into a circle around the six bodies scattered on the snow. Kneeling beside Parker, the captain found the bullet hole in his coat. Shaking his head, he spoke above the wind and said, "Right through the heart. There's hardly any blood. He probably died instantly. Let's check the others."

As they checked on the last dead man, the captain said, "This was no ordinary ambush, gentlemen. If there had been even a squad of Yankees in on this, each man would have several bullets in him. All of these poor men took a single bullet. Looks like the work of a lone sharpshooter to me."

"Yeah," Benson said, "a sharpshooter with a repeater rifle."

"But why would a Yankee sharpshooter be out here in these fields at night?" William asked. "There's no way he could have known that Colonel Parker and these men were coming from Fort Henry. I mean...a man doesn't just load up his rifle and go for a ride in this kind of weather, hoping to run onto some enemy soldiers."

"You're right," Britt nodded, stomping circulation to his feet. "It's got me puzzled, too."

"Maybe if we can find where the sharpshooter was firing from, we can learn something," Benson said. "You know...maybe some footprints in the snow that'll tell us where he came from, or where he went."

"We need to do that all right, Lieutenant, but it'll have to wait till morning." Britt said, looking skyward.

The other two looked at the moon and saw that it was about to go behind a cloud bank that reached all the way to the northern horizon and was spreading south.

"You're right," Benson agreed. "Let's get these bodies back to the fort. General Buckner will be biting his nails if he doesn't hear from us soon."

Thirty minutes later, Captain Claiborne and Lieutenant Benson sat in General Buckner's office and reported what they had found. Stunned, Buckner sat back in his chair and sighed. "I hate this. It's tragic to lose those five escorts, but its double tragic to lose an excellent officer like Colonel Parker. We really needed him here."

"Would you like for me to ride to Fort Henry and inform General Tilghman of this, sir?" Claiborne asked. "I could take a few men for safety's sake and be back in less than three hours."

"No," Buckner replied, shaking his head. "We can send a wire to him in the morning. General Tilghman's learning about it tonight wouldn't change anything, except to rob him of a night's sleep."

"I'll have Captain McGuire see to the burial detail," Buckner said. "I want you gentlemen to take the same group you had tonight first thing in the morning and see what you can learn about the sharpshooter. Mystery to me why a man would be out there at that time of night in this kind of weather."

Morning came with dismal, low-hanging clouds that looked loaded with snow. The wind had died down some when Captain Claiborne led his platoon out of the fort. Returning to where they had found the bodies, they stayed close together in case of an ambush and rode in a wide circle, searching for clues.

After some two hours in the wintry cold, the captain decided it was of no use. The man who had cut down Colonel Parker and his escorts had managed to leave no trace of himself. Turning to Lieutenant Benson, Claiborne said, "We're wasting our time. This circle has us more than six hundred yards from where we found the dead men. I'm sure those Yankees don't have rifles or gunsights any better than ours. The sharpshooter had to have been inside this range, especially since he was shooting at night. We might as well get on back to the fort."

"We've seen a lot of hoofprints in the snow, Captain," Benson said. "Maybe the guy did his shooting from astride his horse. Maybe he never even touched ground."

"I thought of that, but no matter how good the man is with a rifle, I doubt he'd try to take out six men from the back of his horse. Doesn't allow for a steady aim."

"How else you going to explain it?"

"I can't, but I know enough about shooting a rifle that when you need precision, you find a way to brace yourself or your gun. We've found no footprints around any of the trees out here, and..."

Claiborne's attention was drawn to a wagon moving their direction from Dover. It was about a hundred yards away, but he recognized Louie Metcalf and his wife, Elsie. Their farm was some five miles north of town.

"Captain, sir, what's our next move?" Sergeant Nolan asked.

"Lieutenant Benson and I were just discussing that, Sergeant. We've made our search just about as far as is sensible. Even if the sharpshooter had a gun that could shoot from beyond this distance, the most up-to-date gunsight couldn't give him the kind of accuracy he had last night. Somehow he managed to kill six soldiers and get away without a trace."

"He'd have to be some kind of spook to do that, wouldn't he, sir?" asked one of the men. "Seems to me a mortal man, no matter how careful he was, would have to leave some signs that he was there."

"Well, if he was a spook, he sure was an accurate one," the captain said. "I hate to leave this thing a mystery, but we've done all we can do. Let's head back to the fort. General Buckner isn't going to be happy with my report, but I don't know any other option."

Claiborne saw that Metcalf and his wife were drawing near. They recognized him and drew their wagon to a halt. "Hello, Britt," Metcalf said. "You fellas on some kind of patrol?"

The captain touched his hat, smiled at Elsie, and said, "Good morning, Mrs. Metcalf. And good morning to you, Louie. No, this isn't a patrol, it's a search party."

"A search party? What are you searching for?"

"Long story. Six of our soldiers were riding from Fort Henry to Fort Donelson last night, and somebody gunned them down."

"Yankees ambush 'em?"

"More like one Yankee with a repeater rifle. General Buckner sent us out to see if we could find where he did the shooting from—maybe find some tracks that would tell us which direction he came from and where he headed once his killing was done. We've made a series of circles trying to come up with something, but with no luck. I figure by now we're past the point he could've done the shooting from."

"Wait a minute!" Louie exclaimed. "That's it, Elsie! That's what those two tree limbs were for!"

"What are you talking about?" Claiborne asked.

"Elsie and I noticed a couple of broken tree limbs stuck in the ice on top of a knoll back toward town as we were drivin' in earlier this mornin'. I'd bet my bottom dollar that's where your sharpshooter did his shootin'. The way those limbs are standin' there, they'd make a perfect cradle for a long-range rifle."

The captain cast a glance in that direction. "How far is the knoll from here?"

"Oh, couple hundred yards or so," said Louie, twisting around on the wagon seat and pointing. "Look over to the right of that clump of trees just north of the road. See it?"

Claiborne's gaze followed the farmer's finger and settled on the snow-covered mound. "Yes, but...that would make it some eight hundred yards. Man would have to have some kind of gunsight to shoot as accurately as he did from that distance, even if he had one of those new Spencer .58s we just got. The gunsights on those Spencers aren't that accurate."

"Seems to me it would take one of those new telescopic sights like they have over in Europe, Captain," Sergeant Masters said. "S'pose the Federals got their hands on some of those?"

"I hope not. If they have, we're going to have real sniper trouble. Let's take a look at the knoll."

The captain thanked Louie Metcalf and led his men at a gallop toward the knoll. When they hauled up at the base of the mound, every eye was fastened on the two Y-shaped tree limbs pointing toward the murky sky.

Before leaving his saddle, Captain Claiborne said, "Everybody stay mounted. Lieutenant Benson and I will investigate."

When Claiborne and Benson reached the top, they knew Louie Metcalf was right. Scattered in the snow were six spent .58 caliber shells.

Claiborne squatted down and looked northward, following the sharpshooter's sight line. "This is it, Lieutenant. Some Yankee marksman laid in wait right here and took out Parker and his men."

"Then he had to know they were coming, sir. But how?"

"Only one explanation. Somehow the Yankees have tapped into our telegraph lines."

"But why wouldn't they have sent at least a squad for the ambush? Seems to me that would be playing it safe. I mean...sending one man to take out six could have gotten him killed."

"Well, maybe it was gambling a little to send one man, but he must've been sure he could take out Parker and his group."

Sergeant William Claiborne's voice carried through the cold air. "So what did you find, Captain?"

The captain glanced at his brother, then said to Benson, "I want to see if we can pick up some tracks around here. That killer was no spook—he came from somewhere and went somewhere."

Returning to his men, Britt Claiborne told them what they had found and showed them the spent cartridges. He also explained the conclusion he and Benson had drawn.

Puzzled and amazed, the Rebel soldiers dismounted and began the search for footprints. The wind had blown loose snow and ice crystals over the field, but it took only minutes for them to find the assassin's fading prints. They were amazed to discover that the man had come from the direction of Dover and had returned the same way.

Following slowly on horseback, they traced his steps all the way to a small barn, where they found evidence that he stood at least for a short time, then proceeded directly into town. As they neared the main street, they lost his trail. People on the street gawked at the cluster of mounted soldiers as they made a half-circle around their leader.

"Gentlemen, we've got a puzzling situation here," Captain Claiborne said. "Last night four hundred Fort Donelson men were in town at the same time this sharpshooter cut down Colonel

Parker and his escorts. Now, we find that he came from Dover and returned to Dover. I can only draw one conclusion."

"It's a sickening conclusion, sir," Sergeant Masters said. "It looks like we've got a killer in our midst."

"My guess is that he was at least dressed in Confederate gray. That way, he could come into town along with all the others, then slip away unnoticed and do his killing. When he was finished, he came back, slipped in amongst the rest, and nobody was the wiser."

William Claiborne glanced northward and growled, "And the dirty rat is up there at the fort this minute."

"Sir," said Sergeant Nolan, "how are we going to catch this guy? He's either a Rebel turned traitor or a Yankee plant. Either way, he can kill again just about any time he wants to."

"Well, we can narrow the field," one of the men said, "by finding out which men came to town last night."

"That wouldn't prove much," Captain Claiborne replied. "With twenty-five hundred men in the fort, it wouldn't have been hard for any one to slip out of the fort with the four hundred and come back with them, unnoticed. Our assassin wouldn't have to have been one of the four hundred given permission to come into town."

"Then it could be just about anybody in the fort," said Sergeant Claiborne.

"I can vouch for Captains McGuire and Donaldson," Britt said, "but that's about it. The four hundred were back in the fort before I assembled you men, so none of you are exempt from suspicion either unless you can verify that you were in the fort from immediately after supper until the time we rode out on our search. So you're right, it could be just about anybody."

General Buckner's features were completely drained of color. His mouth turned downward and his head slowly shook back and forth. "Captain," he said with constricted throat, "this is bad news...very bad news."

"I hate to be the bearer of it, sir," Britt Claiborne said as he sat across the desk from his commanding officer. "Even when we eliminate the men who can verify they were in the fort all evening, we'll still have quite a number who can't. As I see it, we could even have more than one enemy amongst us. If that's the case, they would lie for the assassin."

Buckner rubbed the back of his neck, staring vacantly at the desk top. "The ramifications of this are mind-boggling, Captain. As you said, this could be a case of treason or infiltration. There's no way at this point to know which it is, or how many are involved. We've got five captains, seventeen lieutenants, and well over twenty-four hundred enlisted men, and any one of them could be the killer."

"Well, I know it's not either one of my brothers, sir. They're not enemy agents, that's for sure. They're both good shots, but they couldn't have done what that assassin did without a telescopic sight like they've developed in Europe. I can tell you for sure, neither William nor Robert have a gunsight like that."

"I'm sure you're right, Captain, but whatever investigation is done here, everybody within these walls except you, Captains McGuire and Donaldson, and myself will be suspect until the killer is ferreted out."

"So what do you plan to do?"

"First thing is to wire General Tilghman and let him know about Colonel Parker. I haven't done that yet because I wanted to wait and see if you came back with any pertinent information about the ambush. General Tilghman will make the decision on what to do once he has all the information."

Rising, Captain Claiborne picked up his hat off the chair next to him and said, "Well, sir, I'll get out of your way so you can get the message sent to General Tilghman. I, uh, told the men who went with me to keep this under their hats until further notice. It's going to be difficult because the troops are already asking what we found. Do you want them to keep their lips sealed?"

Sighing, Buckner rose from his chair. "Tell you what, Captain. Let me get the message sent to General Tilghman, then we'll call assembly in the yard. I'll address all of them at that time. Why don't you go ahead and spread the word. We'll assemble at—" Buckner paused to look at his wall clock; it was nearly noon. "We'll assemble after lunch, at one-thirty."

"Yes, sir," Claiborne nodded, turning toward the door.

Suddenly they heard the sound of rapidly approaching footsteps, followed by a hard knock on the door. "General Buckner! It's Captain McGuire, sir! I need to see you immediately!"

Buckner motioned for Claiborne to open the door.

When the door was swung wide, Captain Waldon McGuire met Claiborne's curious gaze, then looked past him to Buckner and gasped, "General, sir, it's Captain Frank Sullivan! He's been stabbed to death!"

The words hit Buckner like a whip. Blood pounded in his head as he rounded the desk. "Where is he?"

"A couple of men found him down by the armory, sir. Just outside the door. There's a bayonet in his back."

A large crowd of soldiers gathered around the armory door as Buckner, McGuire, and Claiborne drew up on the run. Charging ahead, McGuire shouted, "Clear a path, men! General's here!"

Fort Donelson had no physician, but medical corpsman Dwight Murdock was kneeling over the lifeless form. Sullivan lay face down with the bayonet protruding from his back. Corporal Murdock looked up and said, "The bayonet went right through his heart, General Buckner. I didn't pull it out because I wanted you and the other officers to see him the way he was found."

"Who found him?" Buckner asked.

"Private Stine and myself, sir," said a young corporal. "My name is Hank Lynch. We were just passing by here when we saw him."

Buckner nodded, then looked at Murdock. "Any idea how long he's been dead?"

The killer stood in the tight crowd and thought, I could tell you, Buckner, if I wanted to. It's been exactly thirteen minutes.

"Not very long, sir. I'd say by his body temperature, not more than fifteen minutes."

Buckner looked around at his men and said grimly, "I want an assembly of all personnel in the yard in five minutes. The only men excluded are the watchmen. Those who aren't close enough to hear what I say will be given the message by the chief officer of their unit as soon as I'm through."

The sky was spitting snow as General Buckner stood in the bed of a wagon and addressed his men. Mincing no words, the rough-and-ready general told the fort personnel every detail of Captain Claiborne's report. A pall of gloom seemed to descend over the crowd as they realized that at least one man in their midst was a heartless killer. It was worse to think that the killer might also have accomplices.

Buckner explained that he would be wiring this information immediately to General Tilghman. He would await Tilghman's decision about what to do.

A soldier raised his hand. "General, sir?"

"Yes, Sergeant Weathers."

"What kind of precautions should we take until this thing is cleared up and the guilty man is caught?"

Buckner's mouth turned down and he stroked his droopy mustache. "All I can say is that no man should be anywhere in this fort alone. If we have more than one killer in our midst, even that might not be enough. But right now, there isn't anything else I can suggest. I hope we'll get government attention on this problem soon."

"What about yourself, sir?" asked Sergeant Ralph Ederly. "We all know that this killer is standing right here among us, listening. You're alone in your quarters and in your office a great deal of the time. Shouldn't you have a bodyguard?"

"I'm really not afraid, Sergeant."

"But sir, what's good for the goose is good for the gander, they say. You just said no man should be anywhere in this fort alone. I think we need to protect our commanding officer."

Many voiced their agreement with Ederly, urging Buckner to protect himself.

"And just whom would you appoint as my bodyguard, Sergeant Ederly? How many men in this fort are above suspicion?"

"Well, sir, if there is only one killer, you know he can't be Captains Claiborne, Donaldson, or McGuire or Corporal Tomberlin. By what you told us a few minutes ago, they were with you most of last evening. Couldn't one of these men stay with you?"

"Sergeant, I appreciate your concern for my welfare. But I would be safe only if there is only one killer. If he has accomplices, then who is to name them? As far as you or any of these other men know, even I could be a traitor. I assure you I will take necessary precautions."

When Ederly said no more, Buckner ran his gaze over the faces of the men and said, "If any of you see or hear anything suspicious, I want it reported to me immediately."

Buckner dismissed them and headed for the telegraph room. The men-in-gray moved about quietly, stunned by the news that at least one of them was a cold-blooded killer.

CHAPTER THREE

★

Brigadier General Ulysses S. Grant arrived at his command headquarters on the Mississippi River at Cairo, Illinois, in September 1861. Some five months before, the Senate Military Committee in Washington decided that the war in the western theater could well hinge on the control of the region's rivers. They would need to build a fleet of warships adapted to navigate the shallow, tricky waters.

The man who won the contract to produce the ships was James B. Eads, a veteran riverman, salvage expert, and hard-driving taskmaster. He would need to be a taskmaster, for the vessels had to be built quickly.

Eads and his associates faced enormous technical difficulties. The Confederates were actively constructing forts along the banks of critical rivers and equipping them with heavy guns. The Union ships would have to be strongly protected to withstand bombardment from the forts, and would have to carry cannon as heavy as the fixed artillery of the forts. Yet, the ships had to be capable of navigating in less than ten feet of water.

Eads's engineers and construction crews went to work. While

one crew rebuilt a five-year-old ferry known as the *New Era* into an ironclad, the others built larger ironclads from scratch. The contract called for seven identical ships, distinguished by colored bands painted on their smokestacks.

Each of the ironclads was to be 175 feet long and 51 feet wide in the beam. The casemate, its walls slanted at 35 degrees to deflect enemy fire, would be protected with iron plate 2.5 inches thick on the bow and sides. Each vessel would be armed with 13 big guns and powered by two high-compression steam engines.

Eads's construction crews swelled to four thousand men who worked night and day. By the last week of January 1862, ironclads *St. Louis* and *Carondelet* were anchored at Cairo, along with the smaller *New Era* which had been renamed *Essex*.

On Friday morning, January 31, 1862, Grant stood on the Cairo dock overlooking the broad Mississippi. Flanking him were Brigadier General John A. McClernand, Captain Henry Walke of the *Carondelet,* Captain Leland Timmons of the *St. Louis,* and Captain Douglas Oliver of the *Essex*. All three captains were under Grant's command.

A lash of cold lanced them as they watched the small, inno-cent-looking steamer *Lexington* chugging up the river from the south. Aboard her was another subordinate of Grant's, Brigadier General Charles F. Smith.

"Well, sir, we'll soon hear General Smith's expert opinion about Fort Henry," Captain Timmons said.

Grant, who was soon to turn forty, was a beefy man, and at five feet nine inches, was shorter than the other men who stood about him. He wore a full but well-trimmed beard and mustache and chewed on an unlit Havana cigar.

"I can already tell you what he'll say. I know the man too well. No matter how well-fortified the place is, he'll say we ought to go take it."

The *Lexington* was now veering toward the dock, and General Smith emerged from the cabin. He stepped to the railing and raised a hand to greet his fellow-officers, who stood half-frozen but smiling on the dock.

Grant held deep respect for Smith. The tough old Regular Army general had been commandant of cadets at West Point when Grant was a cadet there, and Grant had grown to respect Smith more than any man he knew. He still did. Though Grant was Smith's senior officer, Grant was inordinately respectful of him and found it difficult to give him orders. A professional to the core, Smith always sought to put him at ease.

Grant moved to the edge of the dock as the boat floated close. A deck hand tossed a rope to Captain Oliver from the bow. While Oliver wrapped the rope around a post, the generals grasped hands and Smith hopped onto the dock.

"Let's move on Fort Henry immediately, sir," Smith said.

Grant turned and smiled at Timmons, then said to Smith, "If they had ten thousand men and a hundred cannons, you'd still say, 'Let's move on Fort Henry immediately.'"

Smith looked down at his commanding officer and grinned. "Well, may be, but it's nothing like that."

The other officers closed in to hear the general's words above the wind that lashed at them off the cold, choppy surface of the Mississippi.

"Gentlemen, let's get our half-frozen carcasses inside before we hear General Smith's comments," Grant said.

General Grant had set up his headquarters in an old vacant house, which stood some two hundred yards westward from the riverbank. The Union officers walked briskly to the house with hardly a word passing between them. There an adjutant corporal was stoking the fire in an old pot-bellied stove as they entered the parlor, now the general's office.

Grant removed his hat and gloves, handing them to the corporal. "You're a good man, Corporal Bates. Since they don't allow sergeants to be adjutants, I'll make sure you never get a promotion."

There was a low rumble of laughter among the officers as they removed their wraps.

Corporal Albert Bates grinned and said, "May I take your coat, sir?"

Grant let his coat slip into the hands of the adjutant, then moved the cigar to the opposite side of his mouth with his tongue. "I want you to keep an eye on the river. The instant you see the *Cincinnati* steaming in, let me know."

"Yes, sir," Bates nodded.

Grant gestured for the officers to sit down around a large table opposite his desk, and took a seat at the end. "All right, General Smith, tell us what you saw down there."

"Well, since the *Lexington* looks like just any old steamer, I was able to get close and appraise the situation quite thoroughly...uh, without inviting myself inside for a better look, you understand.

"The fort encloses about three acres of ground in a five-sided earthwork parapet about eight feet high. I counted seventeen guns. There's a 128-pounder, two 68-pounders, six 32-pounders, and eight 6-inch cannon rifles. This may sound like they're ready for us, but the Confederates have made a grave mistake, General. They've built the fort on land that is too low. Right now, the Tennessee River is rising rapidly because of the heavy rains east of here. I think in another week, Fort Henry will be fighting its worst enemy—the river. If we move on them by, say, Thursday the sixth, most of their guns will be under water. A couple of those ironclads we've got anchored out there will make short work of Fort Henry."

Grant threw his chewed-up cigar in a wastebasket and said, "Then all I have to do is wire General Halleck in St. Louis and get his permission to attack Fort Henry next Thursday. I know he holds great respect for your opinion, General Smith. It's as good as done. However, instead of a couple ironclads, we'll go with four. As you know, Foote is coming down the Mississippi with his spanking new flagship, *Cincinnati*. That'll give us three big ones and your smaller *Essex,* Captain Oliver. We've got seventeen thousand men camped here at Cairo. I've already made arrangements for enough steamboats to come down from St. Louis to transport them. All they need is a day's notice. We'll hit that Rebel stronghold and capture it all on the same day. Once we've done that, we'll make a quick move on Fort Donelson. We don't want to give them time to fortify Donelson any more than it already is."

The Union officers all agreed with Grant's plan. McClernand was adding some suggestions of his own when the voice of Corporal Bates came from the other side of the room. "Excuse me, gentlemen. The *Cincinnati* is here."

The arrival of Flag Officer Andrew Hull Foote was the final ingredient in Grant's potent gunboat fleet. Like Grant, Foote was a stocky man who wore a well-trimmed beard, only without a mustache. He was in his early fifties and was military in every aspect. His fellow-officers found him amiable, yet blunt when it came to military matters. A devout Presbyterian, he crusaded passionately against the use of liquor in the Union navy. When he was commander of the *USS Cumberland,* he regularly gathered his crews on deck and preached hell-fire-and-brimstone sermons to them.

General Grant and the other officers welcomed Foote to Cairo, and he joined them at the table. After Grant explained the plan of attack against Fort Henry, the fiery flag officer spoke of his eagerness to put to use the fighting abilities of his new ironclad.

The meeting adjourned, and the navy officers returned to their ships, and the army officers to their quarters at the camp. General Grant told them he would wire General Halleck immediately and let them know as soon as he received a reply.

Within three hours after sending his message, Grant had Halleck's response. Grant was to begin preparations immediately for an attack on Fort Henry at dawn on Thursday, February 6. He was to use the steamboats from St. Louis to transport his seventeen thousand men down the river, preceded by the four ironclads, which were to bombard the fort heavily. Once General Tilghman's forces were sufficiently reduced, Grant was to swarm the fort and capture it. Once the task was completed, Grant was to advise Halleck by wire. Halleck would then tell Grant when he should move on Fort Donelson.

General Grant sent word to the officers to reconvene at his headquarters. He relayed General Halleck's message, then worked with the officers on the details of the attack. When every part and particle had been discussed and was clearly understood, Grant told them he wanted to set up temporary headquarters nearer the forts. Preferably, he would locate a farmhouse north of Fort Donelson and as near the Cumberland River as possible. This way, he could board the ships whenever necessary and steam toward Fort Donelson, which would be much harder to conquer than the smaller and less protected Fort Henry.

The meeting broke up, with the Union officers eager to return to their men and prepare them for the assault.

At the break of dawn on Sunday morning, February 2, Myrtle Crisp awakened with a start. The second-story bedroom of the old farmhouse had two windows, one in each outside wall. The east window gave a view of the slow-moving Cumberland River some seventy yards away, and the north window overlooked the front yard.

Myrtle rubbed her eyes, wondering what had jerked her awake. She raised up on an elbow and looked around the room. The dim gray light coming through the windows left heavy shadows lurking in the corners.

She heard horses nickering and blowing and realized it was the sound that had awakened her. Sitting up, she threw back the covers and swung her feet over the side of the bed. She stood up, gathered her robe from the back of a nearby chair, and padded across the hardwood floor to the north window.

While slipping into her robe, she put her back to the wall and slowly inched her way to the edge of the window. She looked into the yard. What she saw brought a chill to her spine and caused her heart to quicken pace. "Yankees!"

There was enough light that she could clearly make out the dark-blue uniforms of the dozen or more men who had dismounted and were gathering near the front porch.

The abrupt, heavy knock at the front door startled the old woman. Her mind was racing. What did Yankee soldiers want with her? She turned from the window and whispered, "Dear Lord, the enemy is at my door. Please help me!"

The pounding was repeated at the front door.

Myrtle knew if she didn't go down and open the door, the Yankees would break through it anyway. Shivering from the cold, she left the room and hurried down the stairs. Again she heard the pounding accompanied this time by a loud voice demanding whoever was inside to open up.

"I'm coming! I'm coming!" she half-screamed, hastening through the parlor, sliding the dead-bolt, and opening the door.

A husky sergeant filled the door frame. Myrtle could see three other soldiers directly behind him, and the rest clustered about the yard, looking on. "This is private Rebel property," she said stiffly. "There's nothing for you here. Please leave this instant."

The sergeant touched the bill of his cap and said, "Pardon me, ma'am, but General Ulysses S. Grant is here, and would like to talk to you."

The sergeant's courtesy gave Myrtle a little more courage. "I don't know any such man. And since he's in a blue uniform, I'm not interested in meeting him." She backed away and started to swing the door closed, saying, "Good day!"

The sergeant checked the door's motion with his boot. "General Grant is going to talk to you, ma'am."

General Grant pushed his way past and stood facing the elderly woman. Before he could say a word, Myrtle dashed to a corner of the parlor where an old flintlock musket leaned against the wall. Just as she brought it around, the sergeant was on her. Quickly but gently, he seized her wrists and said, "Please, ma'am. We don't want any trouble."

"Then you should go home and leave us Southerners alone!"

The sergeant slowly twisted the gun from her grasp. "It was the Southerners who fired the first shot, ma'am."

"Wouldn't have been any first shot if you blue-bellies hadn't been below the Mason-Dixon line at the time!"

The sergeant stepped back as his commander moved in to face the irate woman.

"I'm Brigadier General Ulysses S. Grant, ma'am," he said softly. "Neither I nor my men are here to do you any harm."

"Then what do you want?" she retorted, her bony jaw jutting.

"I need a house to set up temporary headquarters, and this one's perfect. My adjutant and I will be occupying it until further notice. I assume you have relatives or neighbors nearby who will take you in until we move on."

"And just what would you do if I said there's nobody who'll take me in?"

"I'd say you're not telling the truth, Mrs.—what is your name, ma'am?"

"Myrtle Crisp. I'm a widow."

"We'll be glad to transport you to wherever you'd like to go, Mrs. Crisp."

"I don't need your transportation. I can transport myself. But I shouldn't have to. You've no right to come busting in here and run me out of my own house."

"I understand that, ma'am, but this is war. Everybody's rights get stepped on in war."

Myrtle knew she was powerless to do anything about it. The hated Yankees were going to take over her house with or without her consent. Meeting Grant's level gaze, she said, "I suppose you'll eat up all my food and tear my place apart before you're through, won't you?"

"No, we won't. We have our own food, and I promise that no damage will be done to your property."

Myrtle threw her head back. "I could go to Fort Donelson and tell General Buckner you're here, y'know. How would you like to have a swarm of Rebels coming at you?"

"There's a reason you won't go to General Buckner and report our presence, ma'am," Grant said.

"Oh? And that is?"

"If those Rebels swarmed in here, before the battle was over this house would be nothing but a pile of broken glass and splintered wood."

Myrtle glared at him for a long moment. "You've got me no matter what, don't you?"

"Yes, ma'am."

"It'll take me a few minutes to get dressed and comb my hair," she sighed. "Am I allowed to do that?"

"Certainly. We'll wait right here."

Myrtle wheeled and started toward the staircase.

"Mrs. Crisp?"

"Yes?"

"I assume you live here alone. I mean, there isn't anyone else who calls this place home?"

"No. Just me."

"What about animals? Do you have some that will need feeding and watering?"

"Only one. My horse. When I'm through dressing, I'll hitch her to my wagon and be gone."

Twenty minutes later, Myrtle Crisp came downstairs to find that the Yankees had hitched her mare to the wagon and had it waiting at the front porch. Bundling up good, she moved toward the door and scowled at Grant, who stood with his hand on the knob. "If you Yankees have anything decent about you at all, you'll replenish my wood supply before you leave."

"That we'll do," the general assured her.

"And just how will you notify me when you're ready to go so I can occupy my home again?"

"Everyone in the area will know when we're gone, ma'am. When you hear that the Union has taken over Forts Henry and Donelson, I will have duty elsewhere."

Without another word, Myrtle moved outside. Her mare nickered at her as she stepped off the porch. A young corporal stood beside the wagon, ready to help her aboard, but as she approached she said curtly, "Don't you touch me."

The corporal looked at General Grant, shrugged, and stepped back. Myrtle hoisted her dress calf-high, climbed into the seat, and took the reins. "C'mon, Nellie. The air smells of blue-bellies around here. Let's go someplace where we can breathe." She drove away without looking back.

"I wish she was on our side, General," the sergeant said.

Grant grinned, ran a finger over his mustache, and said, "She's got spunk, I'll say that for her."

Though Clarence Clubson was busy running his own farm, he would drop by the Claiborne place whenever he could find the time and ask if anything needed attention. Everyone in the family knew his fascination for Linda Lee had a great deal to do with how often he came by.

At nineteen, Linda Lee was the youngest of the Claiborne children; Hannah Rose was twenty-one. Both sisters had long, thick chestnut hair and stood five-feet-five. Linda Lee's eyes were a soft blue, while Hannah Rose's were a vivacious emerald green.

The Claiborne sisters, however, were of a different makeup. Linda Lee was impetuous and sometimes made decisions on the spur of the moment. Hannah Rose was self-possessed and more careful about life in general.

The brothers—Britt, William, and Robert—loved their sisters dearly, but found Hannah Rose more approachable for sharing problems or heartaches.

Their father, Ewing Claiborne, had died suddenly of heart failure four years earlier. Their mother, Wilma Jean, was now bedridden most of the time from a long-term battle with tuberculosis. Dover's physician, Dr. Elmer Stutz, told the children their mother would probably live only another year or two at best.

Linda Lee did her part to care for her mother, though not with the level of compassion her sister showed. Often when both girls had offers for dates, Hannah Rose would decline and let Linda Lee go. She was not willing to let her mother stay home alone, though the ailing woman insisted she would be all right.

In mid-January, Britt's wife Donna Mae and William's wife Sally Marie gave up their apartments in Dover and moved to the six-bedroom farmhouse to help care for their mother-in-law. They were still close enough their husbands could visit them whenever they could get away from the fort. (The Claiborne farm was about two miles due south of Dover, putting it a little over five miles south of Fort Donelson.) Robert liked the arrangement because his sisters-in-law promised to cook him special meals whenever he could come home.

Three of the Claiborne women were sitting down to breakfast when they heard a wagon rattle into the yard and haul up at the back porch. Linda Lee started to rise from her chair, but Hannah Rose came into the kitchen carrying a tray— having just fed her mother breakfast upstairs— and said, "Don't bother, honey. I'll see who it is."

Hannah Rose laid the tray on the cupboard and hurried to the door. Parting the curtains, she peered through the window and said, "It's Aunt Myrtle. I wonder what she's doing here?"

Hannah Rose stepped out and met Myrtle at the edge of the porch. "Hello, Aunt Myrtle. What brings you here at this time of the morning?"

The elderly woman waved her hand toward the door and said, "Get yourself back in the house, child! You'll catch your death! I'll tell you inside. Go on...get in there!"

Myrtle greeted the women around the table, then took off her coat and hat and hung them on a peg next to the door. She moved near the welcome heat of the big kitchen stove and said, "First day we've seen the sun in awhile, but it's still colder'n a crock in a kraut-house out there." Her hands, opened palm out, almost touched the stove.

"Well, are you going to tell us why you're here and what the suitcase means?" Hannah Rose asked.

"If you've got an extra plate, I'll tell it while we're eating. If I can get these hands of mine thawed out enough to handle a fork, that is."

Moments later, the women were consuming bacon, eggs, grits, toast, and hot coffee as Myrtle told them about General Grant and his men forcing her from her home.

"Those Yankees think they own the world, don't they," Hannah Rose said. "Wish you'd had a houseful of Rebel soldiers waiting for them. That would've fixed General Grant's little red wagon."

"Sure would," Myrtle nodded. "But since I didn't, there was nothing I could do about it. I had to go. I told that buzzard I could go to Fort Donelson and tell General Buckner the Yankees were at my house, but he said if I did, and Buckner sent his soldiers to attack, my house would be destroyed in the battle. I figured he was right about that, so I gave up and came on over here."

"Well, you're perfectly welcome to stay here, Aunt Myrtle," smiled Hannah Rose. "You can take the room just east of Mother's."

"Thank you, dearie. Sure is wonderful to have family who care about me."

"Did you bring your Sunday clothes, Aunt Myrtle?" Sally Marie asked.

The elderly woman's hand went to her mouth. "Oh! I didn't even think of it! That...that General Grant had me so upset, I plain forgot." She gazed back and forth at the faces of the young women. "Who's turn is it to stay home with Wilma Jean?"

"It's my turn," Donna Mae said.

"Tell you what, honey"—Myrtle reached across the table to pat Donna Mae's hand—"you go ahead and go to church. I'll stay and look after Wilma Jean."

"You don't mind?"

"Of course not. It'll give us older girls a little time together. Wiley and I always said she was our favorite niece. Is Britt going to be able to get loose from his duties to go to church with you?"

"No, and William can't either. Even Robert has duty."

Myrtle looked at Hannah Rose. "So which one of your boyfriends is escorting you to church today? Let's see...what are their names? Jim and—Jim and—"

"Lanny," Linda Lee said. "Jim Lynch and Lanny Perkins. Only things have changed since we saw you last Sunday."

"How's that?"

"Well, Lanny finally noticed me and decided to let Jim pursue things with big sister here. Both were by on Monday on their way to town, and Lanny asked Hannah Rose if it would hurt her feelings if he dated me."

"Really? And what did you say, Hannah Rose?"

"I told Lanny it wouldn't hurt my feelings at all. I would've said the same thing if it had been Jim, too."

"You would've?"

"Aunt Myrtle, I'm just not ready to get serious with any man right now. Jim is very nice, but we're only friends."

"At least that's the way Hannah Rose sees it," Sally Marie giggled. "I've seen the way Jim looks at her. It's more than friendship to him."

"Oh, Sally Marie, don't be silly," Hannah Rose said, waving her off.

"So are Jim and Lanny coming to escort you two to church?" Myrtle asked.

"Yes," Linda Lee nodded. "They were both able to get free for this morning. They'll be here about nine o'clock to pick us up."

The women finished breakfast and Donna Mae led Aunt Myrtle upstairs, carrying her suitcase for her. Myrtle would get settled in her room, then look in on Wilma Jean.

Donna Mae returned to the kitchen to help clean up. When the dishes were done and the kitchen was sparkling, they went to their rooms to get ready for church.

At 8:45, they were all ready and waiting in the parlor. Sally Marie was wearing her hair in an upsweep, and had discovered an unruly lock of hair on the nape of her neck. While the others were seated, she stood at a large mirror and worked on the stubborn lock. The mirror reflected a front window. Turning, she walked to the window and looked out to make sure she had seen correctly.

"Are they here?" Hannah Rose asked, rising from her chair.

"No," her sister-in-law replied in a dismal tone. "It's Club."

"Club!" Linda Lee gasped, jumping up and dashing to the window. "Oh, no. Lanny and Jim will be here any minute. When Club finds out Lanny's taking me to church, there's going to be trouble."

CHAPTER FOUR

★

Club Clubson swung his wagon around the house and noted the horse and wagon parked next to the back porch. Hauling his own vehicle up beside it, he eased his massive frame groundward and headed toward the porch, eyeing the other wagon with suspicion. The door came open and Hannah Rose appeared.

"Good morning, Club," she said, trying to cover her nervousness.

Touching the bill of his cap, Club showed his buck teeth in a wide grin. "Same to you, Miss Hannah Rose. Had a little time this mornin', so I thought I'd come by and replace that broken hinge on the barn door."

"Oh, I appreciate that, Club. You might check the door at the back of the barn, too. I think the top hinge may be coming loose."

"Will do. Whose wagon?" Club threw a meaty thumb over his shoulder.

"Oh, that's Aunt Myrtle's. Seems the Yankees took over her house this morning to use as headquarters for General Grant. She came over here to stay with us till they leave."

"Grant, huh? I'd like to get my hands on him for five minutes. That's all I'd need. Five minutes."

Club's eyes fell on a broken ax handle that leaned against the house near a pile of cut wood. A new handle stood next to it. He grinned at Hannah Rose and shook his head. "Oh, yeah, the ax handle. I'll fix that, too. You want me to cut some more wood?"

"That would be nice." Hannah Rose rubbed her arms against the cold. "We sure appreciate your help."

"Glad to do it, ma'am. Uh...before I start workin', could I come in and see Linda Lee?"

"Well, we're about to leave for church."

"Oh, that's right. It is Sunday, isn't it?" Club turned toward the barn and saw the Claiborne wagon parked near the corral gate and the team behind the pole fence. "You goin' to church in your Aunt's wagon?"

"Ah...no, but I'd sure appreciate it if you'd unhitch the mare from the wagon and put her in the corral."

"Be glad to."

"Just park her wagon over there by ours and hang the harness inside the barn, would you?"

"Sure. You want I should hitch up the team to your wagon so's you can drive it to church?"

"You won't need to do that. We...ah...we have a ride."

"Oh?"

"A couple of soldiers from the fort are stopping by to take us in their wagon. Aunt Myrtle is going to stay with Mother so all four of us can go to church."

"Coupla army guys, eh?"

"Yes. They...ah...well, I've dated both of them before. Nice young men. They're kind enough to come out of their way and take all four of us."

Club nodded and said, "Well, I'll get my tools from the wagon and go to work on those barn doors. Tell my girl I'll see her later."

Hannah Rose wheeled and headed back inside. Before closing the door, she saw Club at the side of his wagon, reaching into the bed. "Maybe you ought to put Aunt Myrtle's mare in the corral before you start on the barn doors, Club," she called.

"Oh, sure. I'll do that."

"Thank you again for your help," she said, smiling.

"Oh, sis, what am I going to do?" Linda Lee was standing in the kitchen where Club could not have seen her. "Club's like a leech. I've told him over and over that I have no romantic interest in him, but he won't let go."

"I know, honey," Hannah Rose responded. "None of us want to hurt the big lummox. Maybe you'll just have to find the man you're going to marry and let him deal with Club."

"Hey, girls!" Sally Marie called from the parlor. "They're here!"

Jim Lynch and Lanny Perkins were all smiles as they mounted the steps of the front porch to escort the women to the wagon. When Jim did not see Hannah Rose, he asked, "Where's Miss Beautiful?"

"I'm right here," Linda Lee giggled.

"That's for sure," Perkins said with conviction, giving her his arm to assist her down the porch steps.

Donna Mae spoke up. "Since I assume you are referring to Hannah Rose, Corporal Lynch, she's upstairs making sure Mother Claiborne is all right before we leave. Our aunt is staying with her."

"Oh, so that's it," Lynch grinned. "When I saw the three of you come out the door, I was afraid maybe plans had changed and Hannah Rose was going to stay home this time."

Just then Hannah Rose came through the door, buttoning her coat. She greeted Lynch, and he gave her his arm.

Nobody noticed the pair of wide-set hazel eyes watching from the corner of the house.

Donna Mae and Sally Marie reached the wagon first. Corporal

Perkins hurried ahead and helped the married women up first so they could sit in the rear seat. For such occasions, two seats could be fitted in the wagon bed, allowing room for four extra people.

Corporal Lynch would be doing the driving, and planned for Hannah Rose to sit beside him. This left the middle seat for Corporal Perkins and Linda Lee. Lynch led Hannah Rose toward the front of the wagon to help her in, and Perkins took hold of Linda Lee's hand and led her toward the middle seat.

Linda Lee heard Perkins chuckling and asked, "What're you laughing about?"

"I just decided I'd put you into the wagon by picking you up instead of helping you in."

"Oh, you couldn't pick me up."

Even as she spoke, Perkins swept Linda Lee off her feet and cradled her in his arms. The others looked on with amusement.

Linda Lee giggled and clung to his neck. "Lanny, you're so strong!"

"Why, you're light as a feather. I just might carry you all the way into town!"

Hannah Rose was about to give her hand to Jim so he could help her into the wagon when she saw movement out of the corner of her eye. She looked and saw Clubson rounding the side of the house and coming on like an enraged bull.

Linda Lee saw the look on her sister's face and turned to see the oncoming Clubson. "Oh, no! Put me down, Lanny. Quick!"

By now, everyone was looking on as Club charged up, eyes blazing, and blared, "Put her down, soldier!"

Perkins took in Club's size and eased Linda Lee to the ground. "Who's this?" he asked her.

"He's a neighbor—Clarence Clubson, though everybody around here calls him Club."

"He have some kind of claim on you?"

"She's my girl," Club snapped, "and you ain't got no business holdin' her like you was!"

Perkins looked at Linda Lee. "Is this true? Are you his girl?"

"No, I am not! I've told you time and again, Club, I'm not your girl. You don't own me. You've been very kind to come over here and help us when we've needed things done, and I've tried to show you that I appreciate you, but when are you going to understand that it goes no further than that?"

Club's jaw was set. "I know you love me, Linda Lee. I've seen it in your eyes. You just don't want to admit it, yet. But you will. I'll treat you so good, you'll—"

"Club, you can't push yourself on her," cut in Hannah Rose. "She has a right to see any young man she cares to, and without interference from you."

"But she wasn't just seein' this soldier, Miss Hannah Rose. I saw him holdin' her."

Anger slashed through Perkins, reddening his face. "Since you have no claim on her, don't be telling me what I should have done! It's none of your business!"

Lynch saw a gathering fury in Clubson's face and stepped past Hannah Rose to confront him. "Best thing for you, Club, is to get back to whatever you were doing and let this incident die. We're about to take these ladies into town for church, and if we don't get going, we'll be late."

But Clubson was already blind with rage. His right fist lashed out, caught Lynch flush on the jaw, and flattened him.

Perkins rushed to his friend's defense. Club turned to face him, and Perkins landed a glancing blow to his jaw. Perkins's second punch landed solidly, but it hardly fazed the massive farmer. Club countered with a haymaker as a surprised Perkins backed away. The thick fist brushed past Lanny's chin. There was a sharp, popping sound as Perkins planted his feet and struck Club in the nose. Club roared like a grizzly and slammed home a punch to Perkins's ribs.

Club sensed Lynch coming and turned to meet him. Lynch lashed out with his right and caught Club square on the mouth, splitting his upper lip and staggering him backward. Lynch waded in, fists pumping. But Club grabbed him and threw him to the ground, knocking the wind out of him.

Perkins leaped on Club's back. Club roared like a wild beast and seized Perkins by the head. Bending forward, he flipped Perkins over his shoulder and slammed him to the ground.

Hannah Rose knew Club's reputation for whipping two or three men at a time. She moved up close and shouted, "Club, stop it! These are soldiers who fight for the Confederacy! You mustn't—" But her words fell on deaf ears.

Club spit blood, wiped the back of his hand across his cut lip, and sent a swift kick to Perkins's head. Club had both men down and was pounding and kicking them.

Hannah Rose realized there was no stopping Clarence Clubson. He was angry, and his size and strength were too much for the two soldiers. They were both going to be seriously hurt if something wasn't done. She darted away, intent on one thing. Reaching the rear of the house, she grabbed the new ax handle and ran back toward the front.

Perkins was stretched out on the ground, unconscious and bleeding from the mouth. Club had Lynch down, pounding his face with both fists as he straddled him on his knees.

The other women looked on wide-eyed as Hannah Rose moved up behind Club and swung the ax handle at his head. Wood met skull with a dull thud. Groaning, Club slumped on top of Lynch.

Lynch lay under Club's weight, gasping for breath, his strength spent. Helplessly he looked on through clouded eyes as Hannah Rose stood over Club, breathing in rapid, shallow breaths.

Club moaned, lifted himself to his knees, and turned and looked at Hannah Rose with blazing eyes. She bit down hard and swung again with all her might.

Club reeled and tried to fight off the effect of the blow, but his eyes rolled back in his head and he fell over backward. His legs lay across Lynch's waist.

The sisters-in-law scrambled out of the wagon, and Linda Lee hurried to Lanny Perkins, who was beginning to stir.

Dropping the ax handle, Hannah Rose lifted Club's legs by the ankles, allowing Lynch to roll free.

Sally Marie and Hannah Rose helped Lynch to his feet. He looked at Hannah Rose, blinked at a tiny trickle of blood flowing into his left eye, and said through swollen lips, "Remind me never to get on your bad side, lady! You really gave Goliath a couple of tough cracks on the head!"

"Well," Hannah Rose smiled, "I guess it's a good thing I didn't have my slingshot."

"I guess church is out for today," Sally Marie said. "We need to get you two into the house and tend to your wounds."

Holding a hand to his bleeding mouth, Perkins stood over Clarence Clubson and said, "What about him? He'll be coming around any minute. Maybe we ought to tie him up so he can't start this thing all over again."

"There's no need for that," Linda Lee said. "Y'all go into the house and see about those cuts. I'll talk to Club when he comes to."

Club's feet slowly moved, then he rolled his head from side to side and groaned.

"But what if he decides to take it out on you, Linda Lee?" Perkins asked.

"He won't. He would never hurt me. But you two better get in the house."

It took Club another three or four minutes to regain consciousness. Linda Lee helped him to a sitting position, and while he rubbed his aching head, she explained why Hannah Rose had been forced to hit him with the ax handle.

Club looked at her with glassy eyes and said, "I wouldn't have done what I did if that guy hadn't held you, Linda Lee. You're my girl, and no man should hold you like that."

Linda Lee sighed and looked toward the sky, shaking her head. What would it take to convince Club that she was not his girl? They had been over it so many times, she didn't know what else to say.

"Club, you're not mad at Hannah Rose for knocking you out, are you?"

"Them two guys had it comin', what I did to 'em. That shorter one had no business holdin' you like that."

"That isn't what I asked you. What I'm concerned about is you being angry at Hannah Rose and doing something rash to get back at her."

"Did you say a little while ago that she hit me because I wouldn't listen when she tried to get me to stop beatin' on those guys?"

"Yes, I did."

"I don't remember her sayin' anything to me about stoppin'." Club worked his way to a standing position and rubbed his head again.

"Well, she did. You were just so crazy with anger that you didn't hear her."

"Guess I was pretty mad."

"Club, if Hannah Rose hadn't knocked you out, you might have seriously hurt those soldiers, even killed them. If you had, the army would have come after you. My sister saved you from prison, maybe even execution, by knocking you out."

Clubson stared at her a long moment. "Yeah, I guess you're right. So I shouldn't be mad at her, huh."

"No, you shouldn't."

"Well, then, I ain't mad at her, okay?" A weak smile graced his thick lips.

"Okay," responded Linda Lee, relieved.

"So I better get to doin' the work I came here to do," Club said, looking toward the barn. As he spoke, he lifted both hands and massaged his temples.

"Club, maybe you'd better wait till you're feeling better."

"Yeah, I think you're right. Maybe I oughtta go home for awhile and come back later."

Linda Lee took hold of Club's muscular arm and guided him toward his wagon at the back of the house. He climbed up and settled on the seat. He released a weak grin and said, "G'bye. I'll be back later."

"Good-bye," she replied, and watched him drive away.

She entered the house through the back door and found the three women working on Corporals Lynch and Perkins. Their faces had been washed and now shone with salve smeared over the iodine spots that covered their cuts. Their bruises were beginning to turn purple.

"So what's he like now?" Hannah Rose asked.

"He's not mad at you. When I explained what kind of trouble he could have gotten into, he said he understood. He was going to go ahead and work, but I talked him into waiting. He's got a boomer of a headache, so he's heading for home."

"Well, I hope this'll be the end of it," Sally Marie sighed.

"I doubt it. Sure as he sees me with another man, he might go berserk again."

"Well, I'm not afraid to be seen with you again," Lanny said. "When I get a break from the fort, may I come see you again?"

Linda Lee smiled. "Of course."

"If we get a break," Jim said. "I think we'll be fighting the Yankees any day now. Our scouts tell us Grant is building up a fleet at Cairo. Who knows how long the battle will last when he brings those gunboats against us."

"Grant must be planning to come at you soon," Donna Mae said. "I didn't get a chance to explain why Aunt Myrtle is here. At dawn this morning, General Grant and a bunch of his soldiers rode up to her house and told her to leave. They're going to use her house as a headquarters. She lives only about a mile-and-a-half north of Fort Donelson on the Cumberland."

"Our scouts may know about it by now, but they may not. Lanny and I better head back and tell General Buckner."

"Yeah, he'd sure want to know if he doesn't already," Perkins said.

Lynch looked at Hannah Rose. "Could we talk in private before Lanny and I leave?"

"Of course. Let's go to the parlor."

When they reached the parlor, Hannah Rose guided him to a small couch. "Please, sit down."

"You first," he responded, smiling in spite of his battered face.

She sat down and followed Jim's face with her eyes as he eased down beside her.

"Hannah Rose, we've dated several times now and...well, I'd like to know if you'd be my steady girl. I really have strong feelings for you, and—"

"Jim," she cut in, speaking softly, "please let me explain something. You know that my mother is quite ill."

"Yes."

"I told you the first time we met that she probably doesn't have more than a year or two to live."

"Yes. I'm very sorry."

"I appreciate that." She cleared her throat and proceeded. "My first responsibility right now is to Mother. Until she...until she dies, I must do all I can to make her comfortable. There just isn't any room in my life for a steady boyfriend. I like you a lot, Jim, and I enjoy your company, but I'm just not ready to fall in love."

Disappointment showed in the corporal's eyes. Nodding slowly, he said, "I understand, Hannah Rose. And I will abide by your wishes. I must tell you, though, while we have this moment alone, that I love you, and I want to be the one you fall in love with, whenever the time comes. I realize you're free to see other men. All I ask is that I still be allowed to see you often."

She reached out and touched his forearm. "Of course you may, Jim. I appreciate that you understand. The Lord has a plan for your life, as well as for mine. If in His wisdom, He has planned for us to have a life together, He will work it out. So let's remain as friends until such time as the Lord leads differently."

"We can't miss if He's guiding our lives, Hannah Rose. I just want you to know I'll be praying that you'll fall in love with me."

Hannah Rose smiled. "That's in His hands, Jim. We'll leave it there. You're a fine man, and you'll make a good husband to whomever He has chosen for your mate."

Hannah Rose surprised him with a discreet kiss on his cheek.

"God bless you, Jim," she said quietly. "I'll look forward to the next time we can be together."

"Me, too," he replied, touching the place on his bruised cheek where she had kissed him.

CHAPTER FIVE

✦

I t was nearly noon when Corporals Jim Lynch and Lanny Perkins pulled up to the gate at Fort Donelson. The two privates who manned the gate eyed them carefully. While one swung the gate open, the other stepped close to the wagon and said, "Looks like you two must've run into some Yankees."

"Wasn't Yankees," Lynch replied.

"Meet up with some wild animal?"

"You might say that."

Lynch drove the wagon to the stables, and they unhitched the team and put them in the corral. As they were heading toward General Simon Buckner's office within the fort, they came abreast of Lieutenant Larry Faires. "What happened to you two?" he asked.

"We ran into a huge madman who thought Lanny was trying to take his girl away from him," Lynch replied. "We'd planned on going to church, but of course we didn't make it. But we uncovered some important news for General Buckner, and we're on our way to see him."

"Can you tell me what it is?"

"We found out that General Grant is occupying the house of a widow about a mile-and-a-half north of here. We figured the Yankees must be planning an assault mighty soon."

Faires frowned. "You're sure the information you have is reliable?"

"Absolutely," Perkins said. "The widow is staying with the women we were to take to church. She's their aunt."

"Sounds reliable enough to me. Don't let me detain you. I'm sure General Buckner will be eager to get your report."

Lieutenant Faires moved across the compound, greeting several men on the way. He was unaware that he was being followed.

Moments later, Faires entered the quarters he shared with Lieutenant Edgar Brinton. The room was vacant since Brinton was on the wall with the gunners, watching the river for any sign of an enemy approach.

Faires took off his coat, hung it on a peg, then took three steps back and tossed his hat at the peg next to it. He grinned when the hat settled on the peg. "Practice makes perfect, Larry ol' boy."

There was a knock at the door. "Come in!" he called across the room.

The soldier who stepped in was wearing a coat without insignia, so Faires could not tell his rank, though his face was familiar. "What is it, soldier?"

"Sir, I'd like to talk to you about the shooting of Colonel Parker and the escort, and the stabbing of Captain Sullivan."

Faires studied him with quizzical eyes. "Close the door."

"You know something about the killings?" Faires asked as the soldier stepped close to him.

"Yes, I do."

"Well, what is it?"

"I know who did the killin'."

Faires's eyebrows arched. "How long have you known this?"

"Since the killin's happened."

"Since they happened?"

"Yes, sir."

"Then why haven't you come forth with this information before now? You should have told General Buckner immediately!"

"I couldn't do that, sir."

"What do you mean? Why not?"

The soldier's hand suddenly came out of his coatpocket, wielding a knife with a nine-inch blade. Before Faires could react, the soldier plunged the knife into Faires's stomach and clamped his free hand over his mouth.

Faires's eyes bulged as the soldier yanked the knife out and stabbed him again, saying, "The reason I couldn't tell the general who the killer is, sir, is because it's me!"

Faires's knees gave way and a dark curtain descended over his brain. He felt the knife come out and strike his chest, piercing his heart. He was dead before the killer let him slump to the floor.

The assassin wiped the blade clean on Faires's shirt and put it back in his coatpocket. He did a quick check, making sure none of the lieutenant's blood had gotten on his coat.

He went to the nearest cot and pulled the covers down. Hoisting the body into his arms and being careful not to get any blood on him, he carried it to the cot. He laid Faires's body on its side and covered all but the top of his head with the blankets. It looked like Faires was sleeping.

"Won't they be surprised when they find you?" the assassin gloated. "Well, there'll be plenty more bodies before I get through." He stood a moment, admiring his work, then headed for the door.

He heard voices. Peeking out the small window, he saw Lieutenant Brinton coming his way, walking with Lieutenant Bruce Frye. The killer's heart quickened pace. As the two officers drew nearer, he flattened himself against the wall beside the door, knife at the ready. He cursed himself for not getting out of the room faster. This could end his deadly mission. If it didn't go right, he would be caught and executed.

Brinton and Frye paused outside the door. They were talking about the news General Buckner had just received about General Grant. While the killer waited, the officers discussed whether they thought Buckner should send a platoon upriver and try to capture or kill Grant.

The killer was relieved when Frye said, "Well, my friend, I'll see you in an hour or so."

"Okay," Brinton replied.

The man with the knife tensed as the door came open. Brinton stepped into the room, pushed the door shut behind him, and did a double-take when he saw his roommate on the cot.

"Hey, lazy bones! What're you doing in my cot?"

When Faires did not respond or even move, Brinton went to the cot, yanked the covers away, and saw the bloody shirt. Suddenly the killer drove his knife full haft into Brinton's lower back and clamped a strong hand over his mouth.

Brinton emitted a muffled cry and tried to break free. When the knife came out, he twisted around, trying to get a look at his assailant. He barely caught a glimpse of the man before he swung the knife over Brinton's shoulder and drove it into his heart. Brinton was dead when he hit the floor, the knife still in his chest.

Brinton's blood stained the front of the killer's coat. He dashed to the wall peg and found that Faires's coat was the same size as his. He quickly took his coat off, threw it on the floor, and slipped into Faires's. Nobody would ever know the difference; most of the men in Fort Donelson had identical government-issue coats without insignias, except for those worn by the generals and colonels.

He made his way to the small window and saw two soldiers walking by. When they were out of sight, he carefully opened the door, peered out, and found the coast clear. He looked back at the dead officers and whispered, "Well, at least you boys won't have to worry about General Grant and his gunboats." Moving outside, he closed the door and walked away humming a nameless tune.

It was just past one o'clock in the afternoon when General Buckner stood in the room where the two murders had taken place. Lieutenant Frye stood next to him, looking down at the bloody corpses. Captains Britt Claiborne, Ray Temple, and Nathan Willett were a few feet away, looking sick at heart, and a number of Rebel soldiers waited outside, trying to see through the half-open door and the small window.

Frye was pale as a ghost. He fought tears as he said, "The way the blood is drying, General, it had to have happened only minutes after I left Lieutenant Brinton. The killer must have either been in the room when he entered, or came in shortly afterward."

"Or killers," Temple said. "If Faires and Brinton were killed at the same time, they faced more than one man."

"I tend to believe it was one man," Claiborne said. "Looks to me like he killed Faires first, then when Brinton came in, he killed him."

"Why do you say that?"

"Well, for one thing, there's blood on this blanket where it touched Faires's back, but there's no hole in the blanket itself. The killer had to have stabbed him, placed him on the cot, and covered him up. But Brinton was left lying in a heap on the floor. If there were two or more killers, why did they bother to put Lieutenant Faires on the cot and cover him up, but just leave Lieutenant Brinton on the floor?"

"Good question," Temple admitted.

Turning to Frye, Claiborne said, "Lieutenant, you said when you came in the room, you found them exactly like we see them now. You didn't touch a thing, correct?"

"That's right."

"So Lieutenant Faires was not covered?"

"No, sir."

"Yet the evidence is quite clear—the blood on the bottom side of the blanket proves that he had been covered. So the way I see it, there was one killer. He was either waiting in the room when Faires entered or followed him in a little later. Either way, the killer took Faires by surprise and murdered him with the knife. For some reason—maybe a flare for the dramatic—he decided to place the lieutenant's body on the cot, cover it up, and make it look like he was simply asleep."

"Makes sense, Captain," Buckner said. "Proceed."

"Then maybe the killer heard Brinton coming and hid. When Brinton came in, his attention was on Faires. It's plain to see that Brinton was stabbed in the back first, which means he was most likely attacked from behind."

"I think you're right on the button, Captain," Buckner said. "So you think we're dealing with only one killer amongst us?"

"That's the way it looks to me, sir. But just because we proved that one sharpshooter took out Colonel Parker and his escort, and one assailant apparently killed Captain Sullivan, that doesn't mean they and the two lieutenants here were all killed by the same man. We could have two or three killers. I tend to think there is only one murderer, but we dare not assume it. We must remain alert and face the fact there could be more than one."

"Sir, we haven't heard from you about General Tilghman's reaction to your wire about the other killings," Temple said. "What's being done?"

"General Tilghman wired me back within an hour after I sent him the message. He said he would get through to General Lee about it as soon as possible. He's sure Lee will take necessary action to bring the killer—or killers, if there is more than one—to justice. I haven't heard any more from him. I will, however, wire him about these two deaths immediately."

"General?" said Captain Willett.

"Yes, Captain?"

"Have you decided what to do about blue-belly Grant's headquarters north of us in that farmhouse?"

"I wired General Tilghman about that, too. He said to sit tight until further notice, so we sit tight on it until further notice."

"Yes, sir."

"We've got to give these men a proper burial. Other than that, we need to ready ourselves for the assault that's definitely coming. I just wish I knew when."

On Monday afternoon, February 3, an armada of steamships moved down the Tennessee River from the north, carrying seventeen thousand Union troops. They were preceded a distance of five miles by Union gunboats *Essex*, *St. Louis*, *Carondolet*, and flag ship *Cincinnati* under the command of Andrew H. Foote. Drawing within six miles of Fort Henry, Foote anchored them for the night.

On Tuesday morning, General Grant rode across the marshy "land between the rivers" to a rendezvous point on the bank of the Tennessee and boarded the *Cincinnati*. From there they proceeded down the river to within several hundred yards of the fort and opened fire.

When the Confederate guns roared in retaliation, Foote's boat took a shell, then quickly scurried out of range. Grant noted where the Rebel shell struck the river. He would put his troops ashore just beyond that point the next morning.

Inside Fort Henry, General Tilghman stood beside Jesse Taylor, his artillery chief, as the cannons fired.

A large, husky man of fifty-five, Tilghman had a thick head of salt-and-pepper hair with a heavy mustache and goatee to match. A broad smile spread over his face when he saw the *Cincinnati* take the first shell. "Good shot, Captain!" he said with exuberance. "Give them another one!"

The walls of Fort Henry were lined with excited Rebels, and a rousing cheer erupted when they saw the Union flag ship take the hit. They continued to shout and shake their fists at the *Cincinnati* as it made a fast turn and retreated up the river.

Tilghman wired Buckner at Fort Donelson, informing him that the Union boat had fired on Fort Henry, and warning him to keep a sharp eye in case the Yankees decided to attack both forts simultaneously. He was expecting the Yankees to come full-force within a few hours.

At Fort Donelson, General Buckner was standing over the lifeless form of Captain Temple in the infirmary. Some soldiers had found Temple near the armory with a bayonet in his back, though still alive. Temple was quickly carried to the infirmary, where the fort's medical corpsman began working on him, but he died within minutes.

"This slaughter has got to be stopped!" Buckner said to Captain Claiborne.

"I agree, sir, but how?"

"That's the corker. I don't know how."

Several other officers had gathered in the infirmary. "General Buckner," Lieutenant Chet Nolan said, "we've got to come up with something. The way it looks to me, this maniac only has his eye on officers. I know those men with Colonel Parker weren't officers, but as I see it, they died only because they happened to be with him. There are plenty of enlisted men in this fort he could've murdered, but his other four victims have all been officers."

Just then Corporal Tomberlin came through the door. "General, a wire just came in from General Tilghman. Looks like the Yankees are about to launch their attack."

Buckner took the slip of paper from his telegraph operator and quickly read it. Lowering the paper, he looked around at the apprehensive faces of the men in the room and said, "The Yankees sent a gunboat down the Tennessee a few moments ago and fired on Fort Henry. General Tilghman is expecting them back with more gunboats for a full-force attack within a few hours. He thinks they might send armadas against both forts at the same time. Wants us to be on alert."

"I don't know what else we could do," Claiborne said. "Our lookout positions are all filled, and the artillerymen have been at their posts around the clock for weeks."

"Yes," Buckner nodded. "If those blue-bellies come steaming down here, we're ready for them."

Turning back to Temple's body , Claiborne sighed, "We can fortify against the Yankee army and navy, but how are we going to fortify against this?"

"Tough," Buckner replied. "He's either a deranged killer who has it in for officers, or he's a dirty Yankee murderer sent here to whittle down our staff."

"I assume, sir," spoke up Captain Leonard Billings, "that there's been no word from General Tilghman concerning his plea for help on this from General Lee."

"No. I'm sure if he'd heard anything, we'd know it."

"I suppose we should wire General Tilghman and advise him of Captain Temple's murder, sir," Captain Willett said.

"Not right now. General Tilghman's got his hands full with the pending Union attack. I'm going to wire directly to Richmond, advise them of the latest, and ask for at least one new captain, since we're down to six. I'll also remind them that we're waiting to hear from General Lee."

"Sir," Claiborne said, "may I suggest that you have another meeting with all the men? They're strung tight over these killings, and I think it would help if they heard from you that we're expecting some action soon."

"Good idea. I need to let them all know about what just happened at Fort Henry, anyhow, and alert them to the possibility that both forts may be attacked at the same time."

The meeting with all the fort's personnel was held thirty minutes later. General Buckner's words were relayed to those manning guns and lookout stations out of earshot. When the meeting was dismissed, Buckner was standing with his six captains and fifteen lieutenants near a wall of the enclosed yard, discussing the Union attack, when three sergeants approached, halted, and waited to be recognized.

"Were you men wanting to see me, Sergeant Weathers?" Buckner asked.

"Yes, sir. We've been talking, and we'd like to make a suggestion to you and the other officers."

Buckner smiled faintly and said, "I'm always open to suggestions. This is concerning what?"

"The officers being murdered in this fort, sir."

"Go on."

"First, sir, I'm sure not everyone here is acquainted with these two men and myself. This is Sergeant Ben Blanchard. This is Sergeant Ralph Ederly. And I'm Sergeant Randall Weathers."

There was a general nodding by the officers.

"So what do you men have to suggest?" queried Buckner.

"Well, sir, like everyone else in Fort Donelson, we're deeply concerned about our officers being murdered. We sort of put our heads together and came up with a way to possibly put a stop to it."

"We're listening," said the general.

"Well, sir, we would like to suggest that every officer be assigned a man to guard him."

Buckner looked down a moment, then looked at Weathers and said, "But one of those assigned men could be the killer, Sergeant. This would put the officer he's guarding in immediate jeopardy."

"Anticipating that you might say that, sir, we suggest then that there be two men assigned to each officer. And we suggest that the officers choose their own bodyguards."

"I appreciate this suggestion, gentlemen," Buckner said. "It will make things a little cumbersome and inconvenient at times, but it might just do the trick. I'm for anything feasible that'll keep another one of our officers from being murdered."

The other officers showed their agreement.

"We'll implement your plan right away, Sergeants," Buckner said. He paused briefly, then added, "However, such bodyguarding will be impossible in a time of combat."

"You're right about that, General," Ederly said, "but during combat, I'd think the killer would be too busy trying to save his own hide. Besides, it'd be pretty hard to murder an officer with men all around him in battle. Too easy to be seen doing it."

"Makes sense," Lieutenant Frye said. "I hope before too long, General Lee will do something so we won't have to worry about the killer anymore."

Buckner scrubbed a hand over his mouth. "I'll sure be glad when he's been caught and executed."

"So will the rest of us, sir," Lieutenant Boyd Diamond said. "And when he's buried, I'm going to dance on his grave!"

CHAPTER SIX

✦

L ate Monday afternoon, warm air flowed into northern Tennessee, and everyone welcomed the rise in temperature. By early evening, dark clouds rolled in, and by midnight the cloud-laden sky opened up. What would have been snow a few hours earlier came down in a torrent of rain.

It was still raining hard by morning, causing General Grant to postpone the assault on Fort Henry, including the landing of his seventeen thousand troops. They sat aboard their steamships some six miles north of the fort and watched the pounding rain drench the land.

The rain did not let up all day. It continued through the night, and rained hard until midafternoon on Wednesday, February 5. Though the rain eased up, it still did not stop. Fort Henry's greatest enemy, the Tennessee River, was rising fast. The swift current carried an immense quantity of driftwood, broken fences, tangled clumps of brush, trees large and small, and the bloated carcasses of cattle and horses.

General Tilghman stood on the highest ramparts of Fort Henry in the light spray from the low-hanging clouds and unhappily observed the floodwaters pouring inside the fort. He cursed the military engineers who had built the fort on such low ground. Already the water was over two feet deep.

Flanking Tilghman on either side were Colonel David Head and the fort's artillery chief, Captain Jesse Taylor.

"The way the water's coming in, General, those guns on the lowest level will be submerged in another couple of hours," Taylor said.

Movement on the choppy surface of the river northward caught Colonel Head's attention. "We've got more trouble, gentlemen," he said glumly, pointing that direction.

Four Union gunboats were dropping anchor just out of range of Fort Henry's guns.

"I'd say the Yankees are expecting the rain to stop soon," Taylor replied in a strained voice. "When it does, they'll come in, shooting."

"Even if it stops before dark, they won't come till morning," Tilghman said. "I doubt they want to start a fight with only a couple hours of daylight left. I'm sure this is a ploy of Grant's to make us nervous."

"You're right about that, sir," Head said. "As you know, I was a classmate of his at West Point. I know him well. He's a schemer for sure."

"I don't know about you gentlemen," Taylor said, "but if those gunboats are there to make us nervous, the ploy is working on me."

Tilghman grinned. "I don't like the looks of those gunboats, either, Captain. But if all they've got to throw at us are four ironclads, we can blow them out of the water, even if our lower guns are out of commission."

"But they have maneuverability, sir."

"Granted, but we've got more firepower than they have," Tilghman replied. "I'm going to wire General Johnston. Bowling Green isn't that far away. If he'll send us reinforcements just in case the Yankees have some land troops waiting to come at us from upriver, we can still win this fight."

Head and Taylor waited on the high wall and kept an eye on the enemy boats while Tilghman went below and wired General Johnston. His message carried a tone of optimism: if reinforced quickly, he had a "glorious chance to overwhelm the enemy."

A return wire moments later, however, caused Tilghman's heart to sink. Johnston regretted that he had no reinforcements to send. He had been trying to get Richmond to send more troops to the western theater, but the eastern theater was getting more of Jefferson Davis's attention, and therefore more men. Tilghman and his nearly twenty-six hundred troops would have to meet Grant's forces—no matter how large—on their own.

Head and Taylor were looking upriver when the general climbed to their perch on the wall. They gave Tilghman a dismal look. "We're done for, sir," Head said.

Tilghman looked to the river northward. His mouth went dry when through the light mist he saw the great fleet of Union troop transports coming down the turbulent river to join the ironclads. As far as the three officers could see, the course of the swollen Tennessee could be traced by columns of smoke from enemy smokestacks.

General Tilghman, face pallid, looked at the colonel and said, "You're right. General Johnston has no reinforcements to send. Just the troop ships we can see are enough to carry ten thousand men. We haven't got a chance."

"What are you going to do, sir?" queried Head as he wiped rain from his face.

Tilghman stared at the gathering armada for a long moment. "There's no reason to subject all our men to the inevitable pounding that's coming." He turned to Taylor and asked, "How many artillerymen would it take to man the higher guns, Captain?"

"Well, let me see...about seventy."

"And how many qualified gunners do we have?"

"Ninety-six, and twenty-eight others who can fill in if needed. They're just not as well-trained or experienced."

"Okay. Let's hope we can get seventy out of the hundred and twenty-four to volunteer."

"Excuse me, sir," said Colonel Head, "but I'm not following your line of thought, here. At least I hope I'm not. You're not thinking of sending the troops out of the fort and leaving seventy men here to man what guns are not under water...are you?"

"Precisely," nodded Tilghman. "If I can get seventy men to volunteer to bombard these Yankees when they come within range, we can cripple their fleet and take a toll on their infantry."

"We, sir?" blurted Head. "You don't mean that you plan to stay."

"I most certainly do. I'm not about to ask for volunteers to stay and fight it out, then leave, myself. If I get my volunteers like I believe I will, that'll leave just about twenty-five hundred men for you to lead on a dash for Fort Donelson."

"But sir, let me be the one to stay, and you lead the troops to safety."

"Can't do it, Colonel," Tilghman grinned. "Let's call a meeting of the gunners, including those who can work as substitutes. No man will be ordered to stay. If fewer than seventy volunteer, I'll make do. We can't just let the Yankees come in here and take the fort without a fight."

"I agree, sir, and I'm your first volunteer," Taylor said. "After all, this fight can't be properly carried out without your chief artillery man."

Tilghman grinned again. "Why am I not surprised that you're volunteering, Captain? I mean...there are three or four men who could lead the artillery if you were out of commission."

"Well, I'm not out of commission, sir," Taylor grinned back. "So you've got your artillery leader. Let's go see who else will stay and fight."

"Before we go, General," said Colonel Head, "I'm volunteering to stay here with you. I don't have to tell you, it's going to be a tough situation. You'll need me."

Looking the colonel square in the eye, Tilghman said, "I need you to lead the troops to Fort Donelson, so that's what you'll do. And that's an order."

The colonel knew it was useless to argue. "Yes, sir," he replied without enthusiasm.

Moments later, while special lookouts kept an eye on the enemy boats, General Tilghman gathered his regular gunners and those who qualified as substitutes in the rock-walled dining hall. He explained the hopeless situation and laid out his plan to make the Yankees pay for daring to attack the Confederate bastion.

"In a moment, I'm going to ask for volunteers. But before I do, I want to be sure all of you understand what you're facing. The enemy has at least ten thousand men on those steamers. Maybe we'll all die, or maybe some of us will live to be captured. But the more we cripple his attack force here, the less trouble General Buckner will have when Grant moves on to attack Fort Donelson. With an extra twenty-five hundred troops to bolster his forces over there, Buckner just might be able to beat them back."

A youthful corporal raised his hand for recognition.

"Yes, Corporal," nodded Tilghman.

"Sir, I'm Corporal Timothy Redmond. I joined the Confederate army in Nashville, because that's been my home for the past seven years. But I was born in Texas, and I just want to say that what's happening here right now reminds me of a mighty important historical moment that took place in my home state almost exactly twenty-six years ago."

Tilghman let a tight grin curve his lips. "You speak of the Alamo, Corporal."

"Yes, sir," nodded Redmond. "There was a principle to be fought for at the Alamo, and there's one to be fought for here. I'm volunteering right now to stay and fight."

There was a sudden eruption of voices as every man among them volunteered to stay and do what they could to cripple Grant's forces.

Overwhelmed at the sight, though not surprised, Tilghman fought back tears and said, "You're a great bunch of men. Since I only want seventy to stay behind, I'll keep the ninety-six regulars here. The rest of you are dismissed. We'll draw straws among the regulars and eliminate twenty-six."

Disappointment showed on the faces of most of the substitutes as they filed from the room. Within twenty minutes, twenty-six regular gunners filed out the door, also deeply disappointed that they were not among the "sacrificial company." Among those who remained to fight was the young Texan.

With an hour of daylight left, Colonel Head led the twenty-five hundred Confederate troops out of Fort Henry, moving eastward for Fort Donelson. The seventy-two men—including General Tilghman and Captain Taylor—prepared themselves for battle.

It was cloudy at the break of dawn on Thursday, February 6, but the rain had stopped. General Grant stood on the bow of the *Cincinnati* with Andrew Foote, the captains of the other gunboats, and his infantry leaders, Charles Smith and John McClernand.

Glancing at Fort Henry's big guns, Grant said, "All right, gentlemen, here's how it will go. The troop ships will remain out of cannon range, but go ashore as soon as the gunboats begin to move toward the fort. General Smith, you and your column will go ashore on the west bank, mount and secure the high points directly across the river from the fort. I want that bastion well-covered from your position."

"Yes, sir," nodded Smith.

Grant turned to McClernand. "And you, General, will go ashore with your column, make a circle around to the rear, and cut their escape route on that side. This way, if they try to escape by river or land, we've got them boxed in."

"Sounds good to me, sir."

"All right, you two get to your men and have them ready."

When the generals were gone, Grant ran his gaze over the faces of the navy men and said, "You gentlemen know what to do. Blast the devil out of those Rebels. I want that fort in our hands before dark."

Foote set determined eyes on the other naval officers. "You men know the procedure. I'll take the *Cincinnati* in first. Captain Walke, you'll be at my starboard side and sixty yards behind me. Captain Timmons, you'll be at my port side, the same distance from my stern. Captain Oliver, you will bring the *Essex* straight behind me at a distance of a hundred yards. This will give the Rebels headaches trying to figure out who to shoot at. All of us must keep our guns firing as rapidly as possible."

"I assume you will signal us to start firing by unleashing your own guns, sir," Timmons said.

"Correct," Foote nodded. Turning to Grant, he said, "Well, sir, it's time for you to go ashore. Could we pray before you go?"

Grant was not an atheist, but there was no room for the Lord of heaven in his life. He respected Foote and his faith, however, and removed his hat and bowed his head. The others followed suit, and stood quietly as Flag Officer Foote prayed loud and clear, asking God to give the Union forces victory over Fort Henry that day.

General Grant went ashore, joined his adjutant, Corporal Albert Bates, and mounted his horse. Grant and Bates rode to a high point about five hundred yards north of the fort on the west bank where they could get a good view of the battle. They were accompanied by a dozen mounted men who remained close to Grant at all times, following a special order made by President Abraham Lincoln.

It was twenty minutes before seven o'clock when Foote steamed down the choppy waters of the Tennessee River, with the other three ironclads positioned as he had commanded. When the *Cincinnati* was within seventeen hundred yards of Fort Henry, Foote ordered his gunners to open fire. Immediately the other three gunboats cut loose with a roar. The fort's big guns belched fire and smoke, and the battle was on.

Inside the fort, General Tilghman looked on as his chief artillery officer shouted commands at the gunners. The lower guns, as expected, had been completely covered by the flood waters during the night. The higher guns, however, were manned by gunners eager to unleash a hail of cannonballs on the four enemy vessels. Taylor had assigned each gun a specific boat as target.

The boom of cannons was deafening as the boats steamed steadily forward, the *Cincinnati* closing to within three hundred yards of the fort. The other gunboats were in their places, blazing away. Fort Henry's big guns rained cannonballs on the small Union fleet. A rising wind blew along the river southward, carrying the giant billows of smoke rapidly away.

One of the Rebels' big shells struck the *Cincinnati* like a thunderbolt. It ripped at her side timbers, showering splinters all over the deck. Though shell after shell pounded the flag ship, she did not slow down nor slacken fire.

The *Essex* had taken fourteen shots before a big shell plowed through the port casemate and burst her center boiler. The explosion opened a chasm of scalding steam and water. Inside the hull, men screamed and dove overboard through the port. Others clung to the casemate outside.

Captain Oliver was scalded by a blast of steam and threw himself blindly from a port. As he went into the muddy, turbulent river, one of his men caught him about the waist and lifted him out. In horrible pain, Oliver screamed wildly while another sailor helped lift him onto the narrow platform outside the casemate.

The larger ironclads continued to blast away at the fort. For the most part, their armor was giving excellent protection from the heavy artillery raining upon them.

Within half an hour, Fort Henry's two biggest guns had been disabled. The six-inch rifle received a direct hit, exploding with a deafening roar, killing the gunners instantly and scattering them in every direction. Almost simultaneously, the 128-pounder somehow fouled itself and would no longer fire. A quick examination by the crew revealed that it could not be fired without extensive repair. The two most effective guns were silent.

Moments later, two of the 32-pounders were struck almost at the same instant. Flying gun fragments and shrapnel killed every man at the two guns. One of the men to die was Corporal Timothy Redmond.

The Union gunboats' maneuverability gave them a distinct advantage over the fort's stationary guns. Cannon after cannon and crew after crew were rapidly disposed of. After one hour and ten minutes of battle, only four of the Confederate's guns were still in action.

Those four, however, fought back with fury.

In the first seventy minutes of bombardment, the *Cincinnati* had taken thirty-one hits. Her after-cabin and lifeboats were riddled with gaping holes, and her smokestacks were badly damaged. The top half had been blown off one of them. Two of her guns were disabled. One was struck by a Rebel 68-pounder directly on the muzzle, blowing it apart. The other took a 32-pounder in its side, destroying its firing ability.

The *St. Louis* and the *Carondelet* remained the least damaged and pounded the fort relentlessly. The *Cincinnati* still fired away, but the smaller *Essex* drifted slowly downstream. Her captain was hanging on for dear life on the narrow platform outside the casemate, being attended to by the two men who had rescued him. A number of her officers and crew were dead at their posts, while many others on deck writhed in agony from their burns.

As soon as the scalding steam dissipated, uninjured men explored the forward gun-deck. Both pilots had been scalded to death in the pilot-house. A sailor who was shot-man to the number two gun was found frozen in death on his knees. He had been in a kneeling position, taking a shell from its box to be passed to the load-man. The sudden blast of steam had struck him square in the face.

The *St. Louis* and *Carondelet* continued to fire without letup on Fort Henry, and the *Cincinnati,* though crippled and missing most of its guns, sent cannonballs hissing over the walls.

When the fort was down to two guns, General Tilghman stood beside his artillery chief under a shattered doorway, looked at the bodies strewn about, and said, "Captain, it's time to surrender. If we don't, the rest of us will die needlessly. We've inflicted plenty of damage to the boats, especially the smaller one. We've also battered their flag ship pretty good. Our fire power is almost nil. Tell your men to cease fire."

Captain Taylor looked toward the two crews busy reloading their cannons and shouted for them to cease fire and take cover.

Tilghman's features were stiff as he looked toward the flagpole and said, "Haul the flag down, Captain."

From his protective cubicle aboard the *Cincinnati,* Flag Officer Foote observed the Confederate flag being lowered. He knew it meant the Rebels were surrendering. He called for his men to cease firing, and signaled same to the *St. Louis* and the *Carondelet.* Suddenly there was silence.

Men aboard the Union boats—including the *Essex,* which had dropped anchor—lifted a rousing cheer.

Foote stepped onto the deck of his battered vessel and ordered his men to lower the only lifeboat that had not been destroyed. He commanded four men to row the boat through the flooded main gate of Fort Henry and invite whoever was in command to come aboard the *Cincinnati* for a formal surrender. He was hoping Tilghman was still alive and in charge.

Foote was pleased when he stood on the bow of his boat and observed General Tilghman emerge from the fort and board the small boat. When the boat drew up to the *Cincinnati*'s port side, Foote said, "Welcome aboard, General. I assume you wish to make a formal surrender."

Tilghman's face was grim as he stepped aboard the gunboat. "I don't want to, but I have no choice."

"Spoken like a true soldier," said Foote, extending his hand.

It galled Tilghman to shake the hand of his conqueror, but he did anyway.

When their hands parted, Foote said, "Come, General. You look hungry. Let's go into my cabin, and you can surrender while we have a bite to eat."

An hour later, General Grant wired General Henry W. Halleck in St. Louis, and Halleck wired Washington the same message: FORT HENRY IS OURS.

The meaning of the message was unmistakable. The Confederacy's Tennessee line had been breached, and the war in the western theater was starting to turn in the Union's favor.

CHAPTER SEVEN

★

On Thursday, February 6, Major General Henry Halleck wired Ulysses S. Grant that he was sending him ten thousand more troops. Grant was to wait until the troops arrived before moving across the twelve-mile neck of marshy land and launching his attack on Fort Donelson. The reinforcements were coming from a Union camp near St. Louis, and would arrive at Fort Henry by February 11.

Grant wired back that he would wait. Flag Officer Andrew Foote would need a few days, anyhow, to take his fleet upriver to Cairo for repairs. Both the *Cincinnati* and the *Essex* needed work before they would be ready for the assault on Fort Donelson.

Grant was eager to move against Fort Donelson. His handy victory over Fort Henry had put fire in his veins, and he was ready to do the same thing to Fort Donelson. The capture of these forts would not only clear two great rivers, but would cut the Confederate line of defense from Columbus to Bowling Green in Kentucky. This could force the Confederates to retreat to Tennessee.

On the same day, Major General Albert Sidney Johnston was joined at his Confederate headquarters in nearby Bowling Green by his newly arrived second-in-command, Brigadier General Pierre G.T. Beauregard. The handsome Creole had gained fame for his leadership in Confederate victories at Fort Sumter and at Bull Run.

Beauregard, a vain, touchy man, had quarreled with President Jefferson Davis over the conduct of the war, and Davis was only too glad to oblige Johnston, who had called for help, by sending the hotheaded general to be his second-in-command. The Louisiana Frenchman found General Johnston in a state of despair.

As they sat down at a table in Johnston's quarters, a puffy-eyed Johnston looked at Beauregard and said, "We're whipped in the western theater, General."

Beauregard stiffened. "I can't agree, sir. Just because you lost Fort Henry doesn't mean we're whipped. It looked like we were whipped at Manassas, too, but we just kept fighting with the determination that we were going to win. And it wasn't long till we had those Yankees splashing across Bull Run Creek and running for Washington. You mustn't allow the Fort Henry loss to defeat you, sir."

"I'm just being realistic," Johnston countered, rubbing his eyes.

Beauregard leaned on his elbows, stared at his commander across the table, and asked, "Are you not feeling well, General?"

"I'm all right," sighed Johnston. "Just tired. I haven't had a good night's sleep for a week. Got absolutely no sleep last night."

"I'm sorry, sir, but you mustn't let your weariness mar your judgment. We can still drive those blue-bellies out of Tennessee and Kentucky."

The older man shook his head. "There's no defense possible on those Tennessee rivers, General. When a Federal army can be landed, supplied, and reinforced against any position we might choose, we're whipped. After what happened at Fort Henry, it makes me think the Union gunboats can reduce Fort Donelson to rubble before Grant moves in with his land forces. He's got seventeen thousand at Fort Henry, I understand. We only have a little over five thousand to defend Donelson."

Beauregard ran his fingers through coal-black hair, which was dyed to cover the gray. "General Johnston...pardon me, sir, but if our men see you looking and acting defeated, it'll be like the measles. Your discouragement will spread throughout our ranks. If that happens, we're whipped for sure."

"Like I said, I'm just being realistic. When a man's got the chips down on him and refuses to admit it, he's a fool. Do you realize we only have forty-five thousand troops in Tennessee and Kentucky? I've begged Davis for more, but I can't seem to get his attention. Lee and Jackson can get all they ask for in Virginia, but it's like we don't exist here in the West."

"So we have forty-five thousand," said Beauregard. "How many's Grant got?"

"Well, I don't know exactly, but right here in Kentucky, Buell has about fifty thousand. Halleck has who-knows-how-many thousand in Missouri and Illinois. Probably forty, at least. And Grant's got seventeen thousand at Fort Henry. There's no question that the Federals have more than twice the troops we do."

"But, sir—"

"As soon as Grant has control of Fort Donelson, my position here and General Polk's position over at Columbus can be taken by the Yankees any time they choose. These are just the cold, hard facts."

Beauregard eased back in his chair. Clasping his hands together in a tight knot, he asked, "So what are we going to do?"

"The only thing there is to do—retreat."

Retreat was not in Brigadier General Beauregard's vocabulary. His irritation started with a frown, then as it grew in intensity, his face crimsoned. Rising to his feet, he banged the table with his fist and blared, "General Johnston, I didn't come all the way here from eastern Virginia to join in a retreat! I'll not be a part of turning tail and running from the enemy! If this is going to be your plan, then count me out! I'll head back for Virginia immediately."

Johnston fixed him with bloodshot eyes, now turned hot. "Don't speak to me that way, mister! Have you forgotten who's highest in rank here? Now, sit down and listen to me!"

Beauregard held his stiff posture before his senior officer, shoulders thrown back, and eased onto the chair.

Johnston leveled a steady look on Beauregard and said calmly, "Before Grant hits Fort Donelson, we'll abandon the fort, Polk's position at Columbus, and mine, here at Bowling Green. We'll move south into Mississippi."

"But, sir, you were sent here by General Lee with President Davis's sanction to rush to Nashville's defense if the Federals moved against it. With Nashville's important commerce and industry, it will fall into Union hands immediately if you pull out. There's got to be an answer, other than retreat."

"No," Johnston said. "In the long run, the retreat can teach Mr. Jefferson Davis a lesson. When Nashville falls, it'll get his attention. Davis has got to see the true peril here in the West. When he receives word that we've pulled out and that Nashville is in enemy hands, it'll force him to send men and arms where they're needed most."

"But, sir, the retreat you propose will demoralize our troops. They won't be worth their salt if that happens. They'll be no good as soldiers. Let me suggest that we mass our entire western army at Fort Donelson. We can smash Grant's seventeen thousand, then wheel back into Kentucky and take on Buell's army."

Johnston massaged his temples wearily. If Beauregard's words were not taking effect, his attitude was. He considered showing more fight by leaving a small garrison to hold Fort Donelson until he could withdraw the bulk of his army intact. It was either that or take Beauregard's suggestion and concentrate his forty-five thousand troops at the fort.

The Frenchman studied Johnston quietly, knowing his comments had produced a change in thinking. Just how much of a change he wouldn't know until the general came out with it.

After a lengthy silence, Johnston met Beauregard's steady gaze and said, "Tell you what, General."

"Yes, sir?"

"You angered me a little while ago, as I guess you could tell."

"Yes, sir."

"But sometimes a man has to be stirred up some to get his thinking gears turning."

"I'll agree to that."

"My mind tells me, General Beauregard, that the Fort Donelson situation is hopeless. But I have the heart of a soldier, and my heart—thanks to you—tells me to make a stand and fight."

"Yes, sir!" A broad smile spread across Beauregard's finely chiseled features.

Johnston sighed and scrubbed a shaky hand over his mouth. "We've got five thousand men at Donelson. I'll dispatch six thousand from here and six thousand from General Polk's camp over at Columbus."

"But, sir, that will only put seventeen thousand men at Donelson."

"Correct. I figure if we meet Grant's number evenly, we can still win the battle. Our men have more of a will to fight than the Yankees do. Look how you routed them at Bull Run."

"So what are you going to do with the other twenty-eight thousand?"

"Retreat to Corinth, Mississippi."

For a moment, rebellion and anger made a bleak battleground of the Creole's face. Johnston saw it, and fixed him with hard eyes.

"Don't say it, General," Johnston said, clipping his words short. "You wanted me to order a stand at Fort Donelson, and I will...with seventeen thousand men."

"But, sir—"

"That's final, General Beauregard. We'll take the remainder of our army and regroup at Corinth. Maybe, just maybe, President Davis will send us troops there, so we can make a full and proper stand. I'm sure I'll have his attention when Nashville is under the Union flag."

Johnston's words and the tone of his voice told Beauregard the issue was settled. "You're in charge, sir. As second-in-command, I assume you'll send me to work with General Buckner at Donelson?"

"No. You'll take charge of the camp at Columbus and lead General Polk and his troops to Corinth. I'll lead this camp."

"Me lead a retreat? Now wait a minute, General, I'm not cut out for leading retreats. My nature just won't let me. General Buckner will need leadership help at the fort."

"I'm aware of that," Johnston replied. "I'm sending General Pillow and General Floyd to bolster the leadership at the fort."

Brigadier General John B. Floyd, formerly governor of Virginia and secretary of war under President James Buchanan, was a politician, not a soldier. His political connections had landed him in uniform as a high-ranking general. Floyd lacked both training and talent in military affairs, shortages made worse by his vacillating nature. Before being assigned to the western theater, he had served long enough in Virginia to demonstrate his incompetence with stunning clarity.

Brigadier General Gideon J. Pillow was another politician who knew little or nothing about military matters. Pillow, a native of Tennessee, was a self-styled lawyer and public servant. He had served a short time in the Mexican War and received two minor wounds. Using his political clout, he convinced the powers that be that his brief military experience qualified him to be a premier soldier.

Floyd was higher in rank than Pillow, and both were higher than Buckner. Beauregard shivered at the thought of those two incompetents being in charge at Fort Donelson, but what could he say or do? General Johnston was his commanding officer, and Johnston's mind was made up. Though it galled him, Beauregard would have to lead the troops camped at Columbus, Kentucky, in a retreat to Corinth.

On Friday, February 7, 1862, General Buckner was seated behind his desk, discussing the fall of Fort Henry with Colonel David Head. Buckner was glad to finally have a colonel under his command to relieve him of some of the administrative load.

"I wonder how many of them are left alive," Buckner said. "If there are wounded men, I'm not sure what kind of treatment they'll get."

"Not very good, sir," said Head. "Those who are seriously wounded will probably die. The Yankees have recently opened a prison camp just outside of Chicago. That's probably where they'll be taken."

"Yes, I've heard that, too. Sure hate to think of General Tilghman and those brave men having to ride out the war in a prison camp."

"Yeah, me too, but every one of them knew he was facing prison or death when he volunteered to stay. I tried to talk Tilghman into leading the men here and letting me stay, but he would have none of it."

"Good man," Buckner said with conviction.

"The best, sir."

General Buckner adjusted himself on his chair and laid an arm on his desktop. "Up until now, there's been no time to talk to you about the killer in our midst, Colonel."

"I know General Tilghman wired Richmond about the problem. As far as I know, there hasn't been any response."

"I knew there hadn't been as of late yesterday," Buckner replied. "I sent a wire directly to General Lee myself, but haven't heard anything yet. We just set up a plan where every officer in the fort is to choose two men to accompany him at all times. I'll call for a meeting of the other officers who came with you and get them to do the same."

"Too bad we have to contend with such a thing. Since you've taken me into your quarters, will I need bodyguards at night? While we're sleeping, I mean."

"It'll just be you and me in the room. Door has a dead bolt." A grin curved Buckner's mouth. "Of course, I could be the killer as far as you know, Colonel. Maybe you'd rather have a couple men of your choosing sleep on the floor."

Colonel Head chuckled. "I'll take my chances on you, sir. There'll be no need for any extra men in those crowded quarters."

There was a knock at the door.

"Come in!" Buckner called.

The door came open, revealing the youthful face of Corporal Darrell Tomberlin. Smiling, he said, "I have two telegrams and a letter for you, General. One telegram is from General Johnston in Bowling Green, sir. The other is from General James Longstreet in Richmond. The letter came only moments ago by a special rider. It's directly from the office of general Robert E. Lee."

"Ah," Buckner smiled, "this must be in response to my plea for help in catching the killer."

"Would you like me to stay until you read the telegrams, sir?" Tomberlin asked.

"Please. I may want you to send return messages."

Buckner silently read the telegram from General Johnston. When he had read it through twice, he looked at Colonel Head and said, "General Johnston is going to send us twelve thousand men immediately—six thousand from his camp, and six thousand from General Polk's camp."

"Good," smiled Head. "We can use them."

"Says he and General Beauregard are going to lead the rest of the troops in retreat down to Corinth, Mississippi."

"I hate to hear that. We could use the rest of them right here, especially if Grant comes with a larger bunch than he's got at Fort Henry."

"There's more. General Johnston is also sending Generals Floyd and Pillow. General Floyd will be first in command, General Pillow will be second, and I'll be third."

Tomberlin's face screwed up. Head noticed it and said to Buckner,

"I know I'm not supposed to question the decisions of my superior officers, sir, but I think both the corporal and I are unhappy with this one. With all due respect to Generals Floyd and Pillow, you certainly are better qualified to command this fort, especially with a big battle coming. Floyd and Pillow are amateurs."

Buckner shrugged his shoulders. "Orders are orders, Colonel."

He unfolded the second telegram and read it silently. General James Longstreet was commander of Fourth Brigade, Confederate Army of Northern Virginia, presently stationed at Richmond.

Buckner was smiling when he finished reading the telegram. "I wired a request a few days ago for at least one new captain to be sent here. One is all I'm getting. I was down to six until you brought the eight with you, Colonel. I'll be glad to have this man from Fourth Brigade, too. Name's Wayne Gordon. General Longstreet says he'll be arriving on horseback in approximately a week."

"Would you like to dictate responses to the wires, sir?" queried Tomberlin.

"Briefly, yes."

Buckner took less than two minutes to give Tomberlin his return messages, then dismissed him. He picked up a letter opener and was about to open the letter from General Lee when Colonel Head rose to his feet, massaged the back of his neck, and said, "Sir, for some reason, I've developed a headache. Been having these quite a bit lately, and don't know why. I have some powders in my satchel at your quarters. Would you excuse me for a few minutes while I run over there and take them?"

"Of course," smiled Buckner. "However, Colonel, they are now our quarters."

"Thank you, sir," the colonel smiled back. "I won't be gone long. I'll be interested in hearing what General Lee has to say about catching the devil who's been killing your officers."

When the door closed behind Colonel Head, Buckner slit the envelope open, took out the folded sheet of paper, and read it carefully. A grim smile curved his lips as he opened a desk drawer, took a match from a small box, and struck it on the side of his chair. He let the flame flare up, then touched it to the bottom of the letter.

Colonel Head closed the door behind him and hurried along a narrow walkway toward the general's quarters. He was unaware of the man-in-gray who had been watching the office door and was now following him.

Head greeted several men along the way. He reached the door of the general's quarters, went inside, and closed it behind him. Crossing the room to his cot, he sat down and pulled a black satchel from underneath, and opened it. He took out a white envelope, went to the small table that stood against a windowless wall, and poured water from a pitcher into a tin cup.

Just as he set the pitcher down, there was a knock at the door. "Come in," he called.

A man entered the room and closed the door behind him. Finding the face unfamiliar, Head smiled and said, "You must be a Donelson man."

"That's right, sir," the man replied as he moved closer, one hand in the pocket of his heavy coat.

"Who are you, soldier?"

"Name's Woodley, sir. Jack Woodley. I'm a corporal."

"Well, what can I do for you, Corporal Woodley?"

"Die!" blurted the killer as he plunged the knife into Head's chest.

Shock showed on the colonel's face and his knees gave way. When he landed on the floor, the killer bent over, yanked the knife free, and stabbed him again. Head's body went limp and his eyes closed. The killer wiped the knife clean on the colonel's coat and headed for the door. Opening it a crack, he paused, then hastened away.

Colonel Head moaned and struggled to a sitting position. Gritting his teeth, he rolled to his knees and crawled toward the door. Twice he fell flat and had to force himself to a crawling position again. When he finally reached the door, his strength was nearly gone.

Try as he might, he could not lift himself high enough to reach the latch. Lying face-down, he attempted to cry out, but the sound wasn't loud enough to be heard. He was going to die, and he knew it. Rolling on his side, he used his forefinger to write a message in blood on the back of the door with shaky hand: CPL JACK WOODLEY.

The tail of the "Y" went all the way to the floor.

Colonel Head had been gone for nearly a half hour when General Buckner sent for Captain Britt Claiborne and told him to call a meeting of all the officers. He had received some important messages and wanted to tell the other officers about them.

A quarter-hour later, Buckner stood in the dining hall and watched as the officers filed in. When the last ones had entered, he scanned the faces of the group, looking for his new colonel, but didn't see him. Turning to Claiborne, he said, "Captain, I believe Colonel Head has been overlooked. He's aware of these messages, but he needs to be here for discussion. I forgot to tell you to stop by my quarters and advise him. He has a headache and may be lying down. Just stick your head out the door and send someone to fetch him."

"Since you won't want to start until he's here, sir, I'll go get him."

Britt made his way across the yard and turned down the stone-walled passageway that led to the officers' quarters. When he arrived at General Buckner's door, he tapped lightly and called, "Colonel Head...Colonel Head, are you in there, sir?"

There was no response. The captain thought possibly Head had fallen asleep, so he tripped the latch and opened the door a couple of inches. "Colonel Head. Meeting time for the officers, sir. General Buckner desires your presence."

When this did not bring a response, Claiborne pushed the door open further. The door struck something soft. Sticking his head and shoulders inside, he saw the body on the floor. "Colonel Head!" he gasped, turning sideways to slip inside.

As Captain Claiborne knelt beside the body, his eye caught the bloody scrawl on the back of the door. "Corporal Jack Woodley? Oh, dear Lord in heaven, he's identified the killer!"

Moments later, General Buckner stood in his own quarters and said to Britt Claiborne, "The name isn't familiar to me either, Captain, but it won't take long to find him, now. When Corporal Whiting gets back here with the roster, Jack Woodley is a dead man! I have power to execute spies or traitors. Whichever he turns out to be, he'll be dead before dark!"

While the other officers waited outside in the narrow corridor and dozens of curious enlisted men pressed close, Claiborne took a blanket off the dead colonel's cot and covered his body. He was just finishing when Whiting pushed his way past the press around the door and entered the room. Buckner wanted privacy for a moment, so he excused himself to the officers and closed the door.

Whiting carried the folder to the small table where the water pitcher sat. "This folder contains the list of corporals who were here before the Fort Henry troops came, sir," said Whiting, flipping pages. When he reached the Ws, he ran his finger down the list. There was no Jack Woodley.

Buckner and Claiborne were looking over his shoulder. Turning, he said, "I'm sorry, General, but we don't have any such corporal in the fort."

Buckner's face was livid. "Maybe he got the rank wrong. I want you to check every list in the place. Captain Claiborne and I will go to the records room with you."

Thirty minutes later, Buckner stood before the officers and told them about the name written in blood on the back of the door. There was no one named Jack Woodley in Fort Donelson, and none of the soldiers named Jack had a last name that sounded remotely close to Woodley.

Though greatly saddened by the violent death of his only colonel, Buckner went on to talk about the important messages he had received earlier in the day. There was already talk going around the fort about the letter delivered earlier that day by a Confederate rider on a puffing horse. Buckner told the officers that the letter was from General Lee advising him that Lee was taking steps to ferret out Fort Donelson's mysterious killer.

One of the lieutenants from Fort Henry raised his hand. When Buckner acknowledged him, he said, "Sir, I'm Lieutenant George Lamont, and I would like to ask what General Lee is doing to track down this murderer."

Officers all over the room voiced their agreement. They wanted to know exactly what was being done.

General Buckner quieted them and said, "Gentlemen, I'm sorry, but I am not at liberty to divulge General Lee's plan. It's possible that the killer could be an officer. We've had no reason to rule out that possibility. If he should be in this room at the moment, and I revealed how General Lee is planning to catch him, he would have opportunity to stay one step ahead of us. We must commence our bodyguard plan for you men from Fort Henry and keep it in effect for all officers until such time that the killer is caught and executed."

The officers from Fort Henry looked around at the Fort Donelson officers with wary eyes. Silence prevailed over the room.

"All right, gentlemen," Buckner said, "there's another enemy lurking about. We need to make plans for meeting Ulysses S. Grant's attack when it comes."

CHAPTER EIGHT

The sky was clear on Friday morning, February 7. Just as the sun was peeking over the eastern horizon, the two sentries at Fort Donelson's gate saw a wagon bounding their direction from the south. As it drew nearer, they could make out two young women on the seat.

Private Lester Dole turned to his partner and said, "Open the gate. I'll go out and see what they want."

Dole passed through the gate and the wagon team skidded to a halt. He smiled and said, "Good morning, ladies. How may I help you?"

The one holding the reins said, "I'm Donna Mae Claiborne, wife of Captain Britt Claiborne. This is my sister-in-law, Sally Marie, who is Sergeant William Claiborne's wife. There's been a death in the family. We need to see our husbands, please."

"I know them both, ma'am. You wait here. I'll bring them to you."

"There's a third Claiborne, Private," Sally Marie said. "Corporal Robert. Will you bring him too?"

"Sure will ma'am. Be back with them as soon as possible. Is...the deceased someone close?"

"Yes. Their mother."

"Oh, I'm so sorry."

Moments later, Britt, William, and Robert were at the gate, embracing Donna Mae and Sally Marie. They shed tears as Donna Mae told them how their mother had awakened Hannah Rose in the middle of the night, coughing and wheezing. Hannah Rose did her best to help her, but Wilma Jean died in her arms.

They had already contacted the family's pastor and the undertaker in Dover on their way to the fort. The funeral was scheduled at ten o'clock the next morning.

Leaving the others at the gate, Captain Claiborne went to General Buckner, asking for the rest of the day and all day Saturday to attend their mother's funeral and spend some time with the rest of the family. Buckner granted them three days, asking that they return on Monday morning.

There was a tearful meeting between brothers and sisters when the Claiborne wagon arrived at the house.

The funeral took place as scheduled, and members of the church brought food for the family. It was early afternoon when they sat down to eat, but no one had much of an appetite. They reminisced about their childhood and shared memories about their wonderful parents. The conversation then turned to the war and the brewing battle. They talked of Fort Henry's fall, and what the chances were that Fort Donelson could stand against the Union's attack, even with the additional twelve thousand men on their way from Kentucky.

The women wept out of fear for their men, who tried to comfort and encourage them. They were interrupted by a knock at the front door.

Robert jumped up and said, "I'll see who it is." Hurrying to the front of the house, he opened the door to find Club Clubson staring at him.

"Hello, Club. What can I do for you?"

"I'd like to see Linda Lee."

"She really isn't up to seeing you right now, Club."

"Yeah? Why not? I'm the guy who loves her. How come she ain't up to seein' me?"

"Our mother died yesterday, that's why! We just buried her."

Club blinked and his head bobbed. "Well, all the more reason she should see me. I can comfort her."

"All she needs right now is family, Club."

"I'll bet if that puny little soldier I caught holdin' her had knocked on the door, you'd let him in!"

"If I did, it wouldn't be any of your business! Listen, I appreciate what you've done to help my sisters here on the place, Club, but that doesn't give you the right to beat up on any man Linda Lee wants to see. You'd best get that into your head!"

Club stood like a post, boring holes in Robert with fierce, blazing eyes. "Ain't no man gonna have Linda Lee but me!" Club's voice carried all the way through the house to the kitchen.

Robert was a much smaller man, but when it came to defending one of his sisters, he would take on a dozen Club Clubsons. "My sister might have something to say about that! She has a right to choose who she spends her time with, and who she marries! If she doesn't choose you, then that's the way it is. Stay out of it!"

Club was about to make a sharp retort when Linda Lee moved up beside Robert. Britt and William were on her heels.

"That's enough, Club!" Britt said. "We've had a hard enough day without you coming around here making trouble. I heard the last few words between you and Robert, and I'm here to tell you right now that you don't have any claim on Linda Lee! I don't like at all what you did to Lanny Perkins and Jim Lynch."

"Perkins shouldn't have been holdin' Linda Lee!" Club boomed.

"Was she trying to get loose from him?" pressed Britt.

"No, and that made me mad, too!"

"Maybe she wanted Lanny to hold her. And if she did, that's none of your business."

"Well, I love her, and I don't want no other man anywhere near her. She's gonna marry me someday!"

William pushed his way to the front. "Is Linda Lee wearing your wedding ring, Club?"

The big man blinked. "No."

"Is she wearing your engagement ring?"

"No. But she's my girl."

"Has she told you she's your girl?"

Club looked at Linda Lee. "No, but she is."

"That's all in your head, Club," Britt said. "I don't want you putting that kind of pressure on my little sister. You embarrassed her something awful the way you acted with Lanny Perkins. She can't be living in your shadow, worried sick that the next time she has a caller, you're going to beat the daylights out of him. This business is going to stop here and now. Do you understand that?"

Club was growing angrier, and Linda Lee could see it. Laying a hand on Britt's shoulder, she said calmly, "Let me talk to Club alone, Britt."

The elder brother looked down at her, shaking his head. "I'm not about to leave you alone with him, the way he's acting. Who knows what he might do?"

"Then, at least step back so I can talk to him, please."

The three brothers retreated a few steps to find Hannah Rose, Donna Mae, and Sally Marie standing a few feet to the rear of the scene.

Moving closer, Linda Lee said, "Club, I don't want to hurt your feelings. You know that."

"Yes."

"Haven't I told you before that I'm fond of you, but I'm not in love with you?"

"Yeah."

"Do you understand what that means?"

"Sure, but it don't mean you won't one day fall in love with me."

Linda Lee sighed. "We've talked about that, too. Club, there's no future for us. There are many reasons for that. One of them is that you're not a Christian."

Club lifted his hat, ran splayed fingers through his tangled hair, and said, "I'll become a Christian if you want me to."

"No, Club, it doesn't work that way. It won't be real if you go through the motions just because you want to please me. I wish you'd become a Christian for your sake, not mine. But as I said, there are many reasons you and I cannot have a future together."

"But you'd learn to love me if you tried...and if your family would leave us alone."

"That's not true," Linda Lee said, stiffening at his mention of her family.

"It is, but you just don't know it."

Linda Lee was at her wits' end. She was trying to think of something to say that would make him understand, when suddenly Hannah Rose shouldered her way next to her and said, "Look, Club, I've listened to this conversation all I'm going to. Since you won't listen to reason, I now pronounce it over and done. You may leave now."

Club's tremendous body seemed to swell. His surly stare was a fixed and wicked pressure against the oldest and biggest of the Claiborne brothers. Barely moving his lips, he hissed, "If I'm of a mind to do it, Britt, I can beat you to a pulp."

Britt's jaw squared. "You might get yourself a meal, pal, but I'll get me a sandwich."

Club knew Britt was not afraid of him. Club was sure he could whip the smaller man, but the idea of Britt getting a "sandwich" in the scrap took away his will to fight. "I'll be goin' now," he grunted. "G'bye,

Linda Lee. I'll be back to see you later."

The family watched as the huge man climbed into his wagon and drove away. As he snapped the reins and put the team into a gallop, Club looked back toward the Claiborne house with malice. "If you don't fall in love with me, Linda Lee, I'll kill the man you do fall in love with. And that's a promise."

Late in the afternoon on Wednesday, February 12, General Ulysses S. Grant left the Crisp house with his adjutant and private bodyguards, and rode to Fort Henry. He was angry at General Henry Halleck because the ten thousand men Halleck had said would be there had not arrived. Eager to make his move on Fort Donelson, Grant decided to go without the reinforcements.

At Fort Henry, Grant assembled fifteen thousand troops and led them eastward toward the Cumberland River with Brigadier Generals Charles F. Smith and John A. McClernand flanking him. He had left two thousand men at Fort Henry under the command of Brigadier General Lew Wallace, just in case the Confederates sent in troops to recapture the fort.

The weather was mild, and the Union troops left their tents and overcoats at Fort Henry. With most of the fifteen thousand on foot, they crossed the marshy twelve-mile stretch and arrived within a thousand yards of Fort Donelson as darkness fell.

Grant told Smith and McClernand he would be back at sunrise to get a good look at the Rebel fortress. Andrew Foote's gunboat flotilla was in good repair and due to arrive at a designated spot on the Cumberland River. They would launch their attack once the ironclads were in place.

Grant set his troops in for the night and rode back to the Crisp house. He commented to his escorts how unseasonably warm it was. Corporal Albert Bates said it was too early for such warm weather. Certainly a cold front would soon be coming down from Canada.

At dawn on February 13, General Grant left the Crisp house and rode southwest, arriving where his troops were camped just as the sun's rays were spreading over the horizon.

Grant stood on a lofty knoll with Smith and McClernand and studied the fort in the light of the rising sun. From where he stood, the land rose quickly toward the river, topping out at the hundred-foot high bank. Fort Donelson frowned over the Cumberland River from that height, armed with powerful batteries. The land approaches were well-entrenched with rifle pits and protected by abatis, just as Grant's scouts had reported. Taking Fort Donelson would not be as easy as taking Fort Henry.

"It looks just as we had been told, gentlemen, so we'll proceed as in the briefing last night," Grant said.

General Smith's division was to fan out and cover any and all escape routes to the north of the fort, all the way to the river. General McClernand's division was to do the same on the south. Though Foote's flotilla had not yet come into view on the Cumberland, Grant told the generals to get their men ready.

From the knoll, General Grant observed the movement of the troops as they fanned out in a massive half-circle. He soon became troubled, however, when he saw that with both divisions stretched thin, General McClernand's unit did not reach the river bank on the south. This left the Confederates an escape route. He was anxious to close the gap, but knew he could not stretch the line any thinner. Since the ironclads had not yet arrived, he sent a rider to Fort Henry, ordering General Wallace and his troops to come immediately.

From their perch high atop the walls of Fort Donelson, the triumvirate of brigadiers observed the spread of Union troops. Nervously the garrison's gunners waited by their cannons and the bulk of the infantrymen lined the walls, standing by for action. Others were inside the fort being charged up for battle by their unit leaders, while still others were already outside the walls in the rifle pits, watching the Yankees fanning out around them just out of range.

The early morning wind stroked General Buckner's face as he scanned the river northward and said, "As sure as Monday follows Sunday, my friends, it won't be long till we see Union gunboats coming this way."

"You think they'll come with more than they brought against Fort Henry?" queried General Floyd, who though first in charge, was the least experienced in warfare.

"If they have them available."

"From what I know," General Pillow said, "the four they brought against Fort Henry did a pretty devastating job."

"We have more firepower than Fort Henry did," Buckner said. "If they only send those four, maybe we can blow them clear out of the water."

Within the confines of the fort, Captain Britt Claiborne was preparing the five hundred men under his command. "General Buckner is expecting the naval assault to begin first, men," he said. "Depending on how quickly the Yankees send in their infantry, we'll go into action. General Floyd will be the one to give the order for us to storm out of the fort to meet them. And don't forget the Rebel yell. From what I've been told, it curdles Yankee blood."

There was a round of nervous laughter. Britt let his eyes roam to his brothers, who were in his division. He had also chosen them to be his special bodyguards.

"I won't pull any punches with you, men. It's going to be a fierce battle. If it goes on long enough that our ammunition runs out, it'll be bayonets, knives, fists, and fingernails."

There was another round of laughter, but this time more subdued.

"How about it? Are you ready to go out there and show those blue-bellies how to fight?"

Fists and rifles were raised as the unit lifted a rousing cheer. Just as the excited voices were growing quiet, there was a loud commotion over by the latrines. Captain Claiborne dashed that direction, followed by his unit.

Several soldiers were gathered around a lifeless form in a lieutenant's uniform. Shoving his way through the press, Claiborne saw the young lieutenant lying on his back with a long-bladed knife buried in his chest. Looking around, he asked, "Who found him?"

"I did, sir," spoke up a private. "I was going into this latrine right here. When I opened the door, the lieutenant fell out."

Claiborne called for someone to fetch the three generals, then asked, "Anybody know who he is?"

"Yes, sir," a sergeant said. "He's Lieutenant Blake Matson. Belongs—belonged to Colonel Nathan Forrest's cavalry division. One of our men has gone after the colonel."

"Colonel?" squinted Claiborne. "I didn't know we had any colonels here since Parker and Head were killed."

"Well, sir, we were sent to Fort Henry when it first opened up...from General Polk's command in Columbus. Before we left, the general told Captain Forrest he was being promoted right past major to lieutenant colonel. The papers never came through to him at Fort Henry, but we started calling him 'Colonel' anyway. I'm sure it's official, even though he hasn't actually been told so."

"I see. I met Captain Forrest at the officers' meeting a few days ago. Seems like a good man."

"He sure is, sir. He's tough as nails, but we love him."

Just then the three brigadiers appeared, and the collection of soldiers cleared them a path. Right behind them came Captain Forrest, eyes wild. He pushed his way past them and swore as he knelt beside the dead man. Breathing hard, he looked up at the three generals and said heatedly, "It's bad enough that we have to send these men into battle to die, but when they die like this, it's insane! Something's got to be done! This bloody barbarian has got to be caught!"

"Captain Forrest, had Lieutenant Matson chosen his two bodyguards like he was supposed to?" General Buckner asked.

"I don't know, sir," replied Forrest, rising to his feet. "But I'll find out. If he had, and those men failed to stay close to him, they're in deep trouble."

Voice low, General Floyd said, "Captain Forrest, I owe you an apology."

"What for sir?"

"When I passed through the camp at Columbus, I was given an envelope to be delivered to you. General Polk placed it in my hand, saying it was important. I didn't know who you were until now. I just plain forgot I had it. Please wait here; I'll go get it."

Four men carried Matson's body away while Forrest, some of his men, and several officers waited for General Floyd to return.

"I bet I know what it is, sir," one of Forrest's corporals said. "It's your promotion papers."

Nathan Bedford Forrest, a tough amateur horseman, had joined the Confederate army at the beginning of the war. Because of his expert horsemanship, he was placed in a cavalry unit in Virginia, and soon was rapidly making himself a professional soldier. His adept handling of himself in battle gained the attention of General Robert E. Lee. Forrest was made a lieutenant, and by the time the war was six months old, he was promoted to captain.

General Floyd returned, apologized for forgetting he had the envelope, and handed it to Forrest. Forrest opened the envelope and found official papers declaring his promotion to lieutenant colonel, along with a letter of congratulations from General Lee. The other men gathered there offered their congratulations also.

Lieutenant Colonel Forrest then said to General Buckner, "I know you can't reveal General Lee's plan for catching this killer, sir, but can you at least tell us if it's being put into action yet?"

"I can tell you that necessary wheels are rolling, Forrest. I will be interested to learn whether or not Lieutenant Matson had chosen his two bodyguards."

"I'll let you know as soon as I can look into it, sir."

Nerves drew taut as the men in Fort Donelson were reminded afresh there was a cold-blooded killer loose in their midst and as they observed the enemy at the edges of the forests and in the fields, preparing for battle.

The brigadiers climbed back to their high perch and looked to see if any Union gunboats were coming down the river. So far there were none.

A gun crew stood nearby, leaning on their cannon. "General Floyd," called the shot-man, "how about letting us turn this gun around and blast those blue-bellies out there in the fields?"

"Can't do it. We've got to save our cannonballs for the gunboats."

"Are you sure they're coming, sir?" the powder-man asked.

"Without a doubt."

"We know it because the Yankee infantrymen haven't come at us," General Buckner said. "I have no doubt that General Grant plans to lay the fort in a shambles, then finish us off with the infantry."

Forrest moved amongst his men, questioning them about Lieutenant Matson, but none of them could tell him who the murdered lieutenant had chosen as bodyguards. Forrest ran his gaze over the faces of his men as they stood waiting to go into battle. He swore and said, "I have a hard time believing Lieutenant Matson had not sought protection! He had a good head on his shoulders. I think some of you know who his bodyguards were, but you're covering for them! I can't prove it, so I guess the matter dies right here. But if I somehow ever find out who Matson's bodyguards were, those two are going to wish they'd never seen a gray uniform!"

The soldiers in nearby units heard Forrest's outburst. Sergeant

Ralph Ederly detached himself from his group, approached Forrest, and said, "Colonel, I saw Lieutenant Matson heading for the latrine a few minutes before he was found dead, and no one was with him."

"You're sure?"

"Positive, sir. I just don't like to see a rift between you and your men, especially when we're about to go into battle."

"We'll handle it all right, Sergeant. Did you see anyone else around the latrines?"

"No, sir. Lieutenant Matson was alone."

"Not quite alone, Sergeant. The killer was there somewhere."

"Yes, of course, sir. But what I'm saying is that I saw no one else near the latrine when I noticed the lieutenant heading for them. Certainly if he had chosen his bodyguards, they would've been with him and waited at the door for him to come out. I really think, sir, that the lieutenant may not have taken the situation seriously. He just might not have picked himself any bodyguards."

Forrest rubbed his chin thoughtfully. "It's hard to believe, Sergeant, but you may be right. I'll make sure all my men know that I don't distrust a one of them."

As the morning passed, tension grew tighter inside the fort and in the rifle pits. The tension increased when the men of Fort Donelson caught sight of General Wallace and his men marching in from the west to join those already poised for attack.

CHAPTER NINE

✦

Pacing back and forth atop his lofty mound, General Ulysses S. Grant muttered angrily, blowing smoke from his cigar. The gunboats had not yet arrived, and it was two o'clock in the afternoon. Heavy clouds now covered the sun, and a north wind swept down the Cumberland River, dropping the temperature quickly. To make matters worse, Grant and his army had just witnessed a large influx of Confederate troops march down the west bank of the Cumberland and enter Fort Donelson. Grant and his generals estimated their number to be somewhere between ten and twelve thousand.

Swearing, Grant threw his cigar down, stomped on it, and said to his generals, "If those ironclads had been here when they were supposed to be, we'd have had the fort under fiery siege, and those new troops wouldn't have been able to get inside. What in the world is keeping Foote?"

"There has to be something wrong, sir," General Wallace said. "It isn't like Commander Foote to be late."

"I know, that's part of what's worrying me. I'm thinking that Johnston has pulled one on me. Maybe he figured out a way to blockade the river and keep our boats from getting through."

"If that's the case, we'll have to attack the fort with our infantry, sir," spoke up General Smith.

"You're right, but I sure hope we don't have to. Some of those big guns can be turned this direction, and they'd take an awful toll on us. We'll give Foote some more time. He's just got to get here and soon."

By nightfall, the ironclads still had not arrived, and Grant was fit to be tied. It was too late to turn back now. If Foote and his flotilla didn't show up by sunrise, Grant would have to send his troops against the fort and its big guns. If that happened, this was going to be the bloodiest battle Grant had ever seen. He wished for the ten thousand men General Halleck had promised, and wondered where they were.

All over the fields, Union soldiers rubbed their cold bodies, wishing they had brought their tents and overcoats from Fort Henry.

A dismal dawn came on the morning of February 14. The cutting north wind whined over the land, and the iron-gray sky was spitting snow. General Grant, his adjutant, and his bodyguards left the Crisp house and headed toward the fields where the Union soldiers waited impatiently to launch the attack.

The Cumberland River was nearly out of sight behind Grant and his companions when Corporal Albert Bates happened to cast a glance to the rear and saw pillars of black smoke rising toward the gray overcast. Hipping around in the saddle, he saw six gunboats, each flying the Union flag as they steamed down the river. "General, look!"

Grant and his bodyguards cheered when they saw the flotilla. Then the general wheeled his mount around and put it to a gallop. The others followed, lashing their horses to catch up. Grant reached the bank of the river and looked the boats over. Only two, the *St. Louis* and the *Carondelet*, were familiar from the force that attacked Fort Henry. There were two new ironclads, the *Pittsburgh* and the *Louisville*. They were flanked by two unnamed wooden gunboats.

The flag ship of the fleet was now the *St. Louis*, and it drew up to a high spot on the bank where the water was deep enough to carry it. Flag

Officer Foote appeared on the deck and raised a hand in greeting.

Agile for his age, Foote hopped off the boat onto the grassy bank and hastened to meet the general. "I'm sorry we're late, sir. We were slowed down and even stopped several times by debris on both rivers. Our worst problem was where the Tennessee and the Cumberland come together. It was blocked up real bad. Took us eight hours at that spot alone to maneuver the boats through."

Grant managed a weak smile. "I'm glad that's all it was. I was afraid the Rebels had waylaid you some way or the other. I see you have more boats."

"Yes, sir. My *Cincinnati* was battered up so bad, it's going to take a month to have it ready for service. The *Essex*...well, I'm not sure she'll ever be seaworthy again. They had the *Pittsburgh* and the *Louisville* ready at Cairo, so I asked for them. Thought I'd bring along the two wooden jobs, too. Gives us more firepower than we had going up against Fort Henry."

"Well, we're going to need it," sighed Grant.

"So what's the status?" The wind was whipping snow into their faces.

"We've been holding off the attack, waiting for you. I've got the troops fanned out around the land side of the fort, all the way to the river on both sides. There's no way they can escape."

"Good."

"I should tell you, though, the Rebs brought in an additional ten to twelve thousand troops yesterday. Even with the bombardment you're going to lay on them, we've got a tough scrap on our hands."

"I would say so," Foote nodded. "I assume you want us in attack formation."

"Correct. How soon can you be ready?"

"We've got some work to do first, but we should be ready by two o'clock."

"Two o'clock? Why so long?"

"Well, sir, we've needed every man on board to clear debris practically ever since we left Cairo. We need to fortify our decks against those Rebel shells."

Grant wanted to get the attack going—especially with snow falling—but he knew Foote wanted to be prepared before entering battle. "All right," he said with a sigh. "Just get ready as soon as possible. I want you to go in there with every gun on every boat blazing. I expect you to destroy Donelson's waterside batteries in short order. When those guns are silent, start lobbing shells behind the walls and blow the guts out of the place. Once I know all of their cannons are out of commission, I'll send the infantry in."

"We'll get the job done, General. I'll have men aboard the *St. Louis* keep an eye on shore, so if you send messengers, we'll see them."

"Good enough. Okay, Commander Foote, get going. I'll pass the word that you'll be ready to go at two o'clock."

"See you on the victory side," grinned the devout Presbyterian, and hopped aboard his flag ship.

Foote spent the morning getting the boats ready, piling the upper decks with heavy chains, lumber, and gunny sacks loaded with coal to protect them from bombardment. It took a little longer than he had anticipated. It was exactly 3:00 P.M. when the six Union gunboats steamed down the river in battle formation.

At 3:30, at a range of less than two thousand yards, the *St. Louis* opened fire, and immediately the *Louisville* followed suit. The gunners, high above the river in Fort Donelson's batteries, did not respond. They wanted the gunboats closer. Cannonballs exploded against the thick stone walls, showering the Rebels with bits and pieces of stone.

As the boats closed to about a thousand yards, the fort opened fire with its biggest guns, a 10-inch smoothbore Columbiad and a 32-pounder rifled cannon. The boats courageously came on until they were within four hundred yards. At that close range, all the Confederate guns could reach them. The Confederates were using mostly solid shot, hoping to do extensive damage by penetrating armor and plowing gaping holes in the decks.

The gunners shouted at the tops of their voices as their targets rocked and reeled in the choppy waters from one direct hit after another. The river rang like a giant forge with the sound of metal striking metal.

Out in the fields, thousands of Union soldiers listened and shivered in the cold. Some had asked their commanders to let them return to Fort Henry for their coats and tents, but permission was denied. Every man would be needed when Grant gave the command to attack.

While the cannon battle raged, the snow fell harder and the icy wind grew colder.

The Rebel guns were doing tremendous damage to the Union gunboats. Commander Foote's men, however, pushed their vessels against the river's powerful current under heavy fire and sent shell after shell at the fort. The Rebels continued to blow off smokestacks, batter decks and hulls, and kill Yankee crewmen.

Aboard Captain Henry Walke's *Carondelet*, a 128-pounder shell struck the anchor, which lay on deck, and smashed it into countless flying chunks of metal, wounding and killing crewmen and taking away part of the smokestack. Another Rebel shell whistled down, ripped at the iron plating, and fell in the river. Another struck and went through the plating, lodging in the heavy casemate. Another tore into the pilot house, ripping the plating to shreds, and sent sharp, spinning fragments into both pilots. One was killed outright; the other fell to the wooden floor, mortally wounded.

No matter how hard the Union boatmen fought, the Confederate shells continued to come harder and faster, taking flagstaffs and smoke-stacks, and tearing off the side armor as lightning rends bark from a tree.

High up in the parapets, the Confederates were taking heart as they beheld the damage they were inflicting on the enemy boats. The boom-ing of cannon on the walls and on boat decks was constant and deafen-ing, so that commands had to be given by hand signals.

An hour after the assault began, the first wooden gunboat took two direct hits in the lower part of the hull and began to sink. The captain commanded his men to abandon the doomed vessel, and dove into the icy waters as soon as the last crewman was gone.

The second wooden vessel was hit so many times, it had no operating guns. The captain gave orders to head back upriver. Before they could get out of cannon range, a huge shell struck the powder magazine. The exploding gunpowder turned the boat into a huge fireball, and left the entire crew dead in the water.

In desperation, Foote brought his ironclads in to point-blank range. He must destroy the waterside guns, which were taking such a horrendous toll on his fleet. Not until they were in close did Foote realize his mistake. The close position beneath the lofty wall forced the Union guns to fire at maxim elevation, and the arcing trajectories tended to completely overshoot the fort.

The ironclads were in a vulnerable position and taking a vicious pounding.

Daylight began to wane, and Foote attempted to withdraw his battered flotilla to safer waters. But the *Louisville* took a 10-inch solid shot in the starboard bow-port that demolished a gun carriage, killed three men, and seriously wounded four others. Another shell came shrieking in behind it, plowing into the forward starboard deck, blowing the rudder chains apart, killing one man, and wounding two. With the rudder chain destroyed, the boat could not be steered. It began drifting helplessly downstream.

Foote was in the pilot house aboard the flag ship *St. Louis* when a shell struck. It tore into the flag officer's left foot, killed the pilot, and carried away the wheel. Out of control, the *St. Louis* washed downstream after the *Louisville.*

The *Pittsburgh* took a shell low in the bow on the port side, and began to sink. Only when her captain shifted the heavy guns to the stern did the bow lift high enough to keep water from flowing in. Seeking to escape, the captain commanded the vessel to be turned sharply, but when it began the turn, it collided with the *Carondelet*, shearing her starboard rudder.

Captain Walke's boat was already heavily battered. This mishap dropped a cold blanket of discouragement over him. Frantically, he tried to rig emergency steering as the boat drifted downstream after the other ironclads. In the midst of the near-panic, Walke had enough presence of mind to keep his guns blazing away in hope that the heavy smoke would provide a screen from Donelson's relentless guns.

As darkness fell, the Rebels watched the boats drift helplessly downstream. During the entire battle, not one man in the fort had been killed, though a few had been wounded. A shout of exultation leaped from the lips of every man on the walls.

That night, General Grant, who had watched the debacle from the knoll, sent a wire to General Halleck in St. Louis. He told him of the Confederate victory over the gunboats and informed him that he was going in with the infantry the next day. He also complained that the ten thousand reinforcements had not arrived.

Inside the fort, the resounding Rebel victory did little to lighten the gloom that had settled over Generals Floyd, Pillow, and Buckner. During the afternoon's battle, they had agreed that the fort was a virtual trap and would cost them their army if they did not escape. Their pessimism had been bolstered by a somber telegraph message received late that morning advising them that General Albert Sidney Johnston had decided to take his troops to Nashville and fortify there. Johnston's message was: "If you lose the fort, bring your troops to Nashville if possible."

The three brigadiers were sure that with two of his boats sunk and the others severely damaged, General Grant would bring his infantry in full-force the next morning. They agreed on a plan. They would send their troops out of the fort like a flood at the crack of dawn, strike Grant's army with a sudden hammer blow of artillery and infantry, then make a fast break for Nashville, seventy-five miles to the east.

The Confederate commanders worked on their attack plan until nearly two o'clock in the morning, then went to their beds for a short sleep.

Snow continued to fall until about 4:00 A.M., then the sky began to clear. With the clearing came a howling, Arctic wind. Though the heartless wind knifed through their coats, the Confederates welcomed it because it covered their noise as they moved into attack position a few minutes before dawn. All was ready when dawn broke in a clear sky, showing the ground covered with fresh snow and skeletal tree limbs sheathed in ice.

Suddenly there was a crashing volley of cannon fire from the lofty parapets of the fort. At the same time, with a wild Rebel yell, over sixteen thousand infantrymen converged on the half-frozen, surprised Union troops.

Without overcoats or tents, the Yankees had spent the night huddled around small campfires and shivering against the cold. They fought back valiantly, but the surprise attack soon had those near the river bank retreating to the open fields to join their comrades.

The cannons roared on the walls for some time, then went silent as the battle spread across the fields and into the forests. Formal lines dissolved into separate skirmishes. Units on both sides quickly lost touch with each other, and soldiers waged countless individual fights, bitterly contesting each ditch, gully, mound, frozen bush, and ice-covered tree. Rifles barked and streaks of flame darted from the edges of the forest. Men ran from rock to rock and ditch to ditch on the open fields, threw themselves down, fired, and found shelter while they reloaded their guns.

Observing the battle from the walls, the three brigadiers realized things had not gone as planned. With the battle spreading out so much, there was no way the Confederate troops were going to be able to make a fast retreat. However, the battle seemed to be going in their favor, so the generals decided to let the fight take its natural course.

At the edge of a small forest, Corporal Jim Lynch was using a huge oak tree for cover while he shot it out with a Yankee soldier who was on his belly in a shallow draw. They had exchanged several shots, and both were reloading.

Unknown to Lynch, a second Yankee had noticed the contest and was working his way up behind him. Lynch finished reloading, dropped the ramrod, and cocked the hammer. Bracing the single-shot musket against the tree, he aimed it toward the draw and laid his finger against the trigger.

"C'mon, blue-belly," he whispered. "Just give me a little piece of target. C'mon."

Suddenly the Yankee's gun roared and the lead ball thwacked into the side of the tree, splattering bits of bark into Lynch's eyes. Blinking, Lynch fired directly at the spot where he had seen the powder flash. He pulled the trigger just as the enemy soldier raised up to see if he had hit his target. Lynch's bullet caught him at the base of the throat, and he fell back into the draw. It took him only seconds to die.

Lynch was thumbing bark from his eyes when a cold voice from the shadows behind him said, "Hey, Reb!"

He whirled around to find himself looking down the black muzzle of a .58 calibre musket. The Yankee squeezed the trigger, and Corporal Jim Lynch saw the flash an instant before the slug took his life.

In the fields and forests, the fighting continued. Late in the afternoon, ammunition began to run low on both sides. Soldiers took ammunition from the bodies of the dead to replenish their supply. By sundown, it was hand-to-hand fighting with bayonets, knives, rifle butts, and fists.

When darkness fell and a full moon began to rise, General Floyd ordered his weary men to return to the fort. Bedraggled Rebels helped their wounded comrades back to the fort from the forests and the fields. The temperature was plunging as the battered and bloodied Rebels gathered inside the fort.

Corporal Lanny Perkins, stumbling on tired legs and assisting a wounded private, came upon the body of Jim Lynch. Tears filled his eyes as he paused to look at him in the moonlight. Perkins wished he could carry the body to the fort, but he had to help the wounded man who was leaning on him. They stumbled wearily away, tears staining Perkins's cheeks.

The Yankees were just as weary. They regrouped and began to build fires at the edge of the woods a half-mile west of the fort. Confederate and Union bodies were scattered in the woods and on the open fields, their blood staining the snow a deep crimson.

While watching the battle, General Floyd had changed his mind about retreating to Nashville. He kept it to himself, wanting Buckner and Pillow to learn of it when he told the other officers. Gathering the officers in the dining hall, he noted that some were wounded and patched up, while others were missing. Two captains and three lieutenants were dead. Captain Leonard Billings and Lieutenant Bruce Frye had been seriously wounded and were being tended to in the infirmary.

Floyd looked at the exhausted men and said, "Gentlemen, General Pillow, General Buckner, and I observed the marvelous way our men took the fight to the enemy today. It was evident early on that our plan to strike hard, then run for Nashville wasn't going to be realized. No one could help it, but the battle spread too fast for a clean pullout. However, Generals Pillow and Buckner are as pleased as I am the way the battle went today. Our men really put it to them.

"In view of what I saw today, I've changed my mind about retreating to Nashville at all. I'm convinced that one more day of that kind of fighting will give us the victory. We can whip those Yankees."

There was a loud, startling knock at the door, followed by an excited voice. "General Floyd! General Floyd!"

"Come in!" Floyd called as every eye in the room swerved to the door.

Sergeant Cliff Nolan bolted into the room, face pallid, and gasped,

"Sir, we've got real trouble! There are a bunch of steamers pulling ashore upstream out of cannon range, and they're unloading thousands of Yankee troops!"

The officers left the room and dashed to the walls. Hearts sank as they observed thousands of men filing out of the boats onto the west bank of the Cumberland.

Somberly, they gathered back into the dining hall. General Floyd stood before them, face drawn, and said, "Gentlemen, this puts a whole new light on the situation. I'd estimate the Yankees have brought in easily eight thousand men...maybe more. We're vastly outnumbered now."

"We've only got one choice, sir," General Buckner said. "We've got to get out of this trap of a fort immediately. If we don't, they'll have us pinned in here and helpless by morning."

Colonel Forrest said, "I agree a hundred percent, General Buckner. This fort is nothing but a trap, and I say we'd better get out while the getting's good."

"But our men are too tired to strike out for Nashville," General Pillow argued. "Seventy-five miles is a long way in this weather. The bulk of us would never make it."

Pillow's words had a profound effect on most of the officers. General Floyd cleared his throat and said, "General Pillow is right. Our men are too fatigued to head out for Nashville tonight. I don't see that we have any choice but...to surrender."

"Surrender!" Forrest gusted. "You can't mean that!"

"None of us like the idea of surrender, Colonel, but General Pillow is right," General Buckner said. "We'd lose half of our men, or more, if we tried to make it to Nashville in this weather. All we can do is surrender."

"I hate the idea, too," Pillow said, "but there's no reasonable alternative."

Forrest swore, slammed his fist into his palm, and growled, "I can speak for my men. We would rather die attempting to make it to

Nashville than be locked up in a stinking Yankee prison camp!" Stomping to the door, he opened it, looked back and said, "My men and I will be leaving in a couple of hours. Anybody who wants to go with us is welcome."

When the door slammed, the brigadiers exchanged somber glances. The room was silent as a tomb.

Captain Claiborne broke the silence. "I'd like to say something, General Floyd."

"The floor is yours."

"I think you generals ought to give the men an opportunity to choose between staying and surrendering, or trying to make it to Nashville. If they want to gamble the journey, they ought to have that option."

"I'll tell you right now, Captain," said General Buckner, "the bulk of them will choose to stay. A Yankee prison camp is better than dying in the wilderness. As fatigued as they are right now, to attempt the journey will be nothing but suicide."

"I'm sure you're right, sir," Claiborne replied, "but I think each man should be given the choice."

"Fine. We'll let them choose," Floyd said. Turning to Buckner, he asked, "Are you determined to stay here and surrender, even if the bulk of the men choose to head for Nashville?"

"They won't, I assure you. But even if all we have left here is a handful, I'll stay and surrender with them."

"All right," Floyd said, "since you've stated your mind on it, I'll go with Colonel Forrest. Since I didn't have to fight today, I'm not fatigued. I can make it to Nashville."

"I can too," Pillow said. "I'll go along with you and Colonel Forrest."

The officers were dismissed to go to their men and offer the choice of surrendering or braving the winter weather.

When only the three generals were left in the room, Buckner said, "General Floyd, since you and General Pillow are leaving, I'll need both of you to formally pass the command of Fort Donelson to me...in writing."

"Okay. Let's go to the office."

When the necessary paper was written and signed, Floyd and Pillow left to make preparations for travel. General Buckner then sat down and wrote a proposal of surrender to be carried by messenger to General Grant.

On the battlefields and in the woods below, Union soldiers moved about in the clear light of the full moon, removing clothing from the bodies of dead soldiers—Union and Confederate alike—to help keep them from freezing during the night.

At the camp near the woods, General Grant welcomed his ten thousand new troops before retiring to the Crisp house for the night.

As midnight came, campfires winked against the silvery light that illuminated the countryside.

CHAPTER TEN

✦

His first sensation when coming to was that of bitter cold. He could hear the wind wailing about him like a wounded, dying beast, and the ice crystals that stung his face stimulated his senses and tore at the fog that webbed his brain.

The solid surface beneath him seemed to whirl and undulate. Suddenly aware that he was spread-eagled on his back, he slowly raised up on his right elbow and shook his head. A flash of blinding pain stabbed his left temple, and lights glittered before his eyes like a shower of meteors. His head swam and he tried to open his eyes. The right one cooperated, but the left one refused to come open. He caught a glimpse of a frozen landscape of white and shadow just before dizziness claimed him and an inky black curtain descended over his brain.

He stirred to consciousness again. His body was numb with cold. He recalled coming to before, but had no idea how long it had been. With effort he opened his right eye again. Looking directly above him, he saw the full moon hovering in a black, starlit sky. He felt around him and realized he was lying on crusted ice and snow.

Pain lanced his throbbing temple as he forced himself to a sitting position. Though he could see fairly well with his right eye, the left one stubbornly remained shut. He raised his left hand to find out why, and his fingertips touched a mat of clotted blood. He clawed at the clot until it was gone and he could see with both eyes.

He found that he was in a low spot on an open field. There was a stand of trees nearby, their ragged, naked branches resembling skeletal hands in the moonlight.

The pain in his temple caused him to probe with his fingertips till he found a long, slender ridge that burrowed horizontally along his temple and into his scalp. It was sticky with blood.

What could have caused this?

He looked down and discovered that he was clad only in long underwear and socks. No wonder he was so cold! Working against the stiffness of his joints, he forced himself to his knees. The silver moonlight showed him bodies strewn everywhere! Some were prostrate on their faces, some lying face-up, others crumpled. They had all been stripped of their outer clothing—their *uniforms.*

Yes, their uniforms! He was on a battlefield!

Now he knew what had caused the bloody ridge along his temple. A bullet had creased his head. He had narrowly escaped death.

He was on a battlefield, all right, but what battlefield? What war? Wait...the war between the states. The Civil War! Abraham Lincoln. Jefferson Davis. But...but *who am I?*

He could recall the names of Lincoln and Davis, of Lee and Jackson, of McClellan and Grant. But why couldn't he remember his own name? And where he was from? He was a soldier. But which side was he on?

He searched his memory for answers, but found none. He could remember nothing about himself except that he had come to consciousness some time earlier, then passed out again.

He struggled to suppress the fear welling up inside. He tried to calm himself, telling himself that soon he would remember everything.

The wintry wind lashed him with snow and ice. His eyes fell on a pair of boots lying a few feet away. Quickly, he crawled to them, sat on the frozen crust of snow, and pulled the boots on his aching feet. They fit. They were likely his boots.

With extreme effort, he worked his way to his feet and took a deep breath. A gust of wind hit him like a fist, knocking him off balance. Steadying himself, he fought off a wave of dizziness. When it cleared, he looked at the corpses that surrounded him. He moved among the dead soldiers and studied their faces. None were familiar. He couldn't even remember what his own face looked like. Another dizzy spell halted him in his tracks, and he swayed with both hands to his head. His breath puffed out in cones of frost. Crossing his arms over his chest, he tucked his freezing hands into his armpits.

When his head cleared once more, he continued moving amongst the dead. If he could remember the names of Lincoln and Davis, and even recall what they looked like, why couldn't he recognize the men he fought beside? The evidence around him was clear—the battle had been fierce, and there were dead soldiers from both sides. There should be men here that he had known. There had to be. Yet there was not one familiar face.

He groped among the dead, hoping to find one man who had not been stripped so he could don his clothing. Whoever had stripped the bodies must have thought he was dead. Or did they? Maybe they were the enemy, and just left him to die.

Cold! Yes, it's so cold.

This clothing search was getting him nowhere. Every man in sight had been stripped. He must get to a warm place, or he would soon freeze to death.

But where?

He rubbed his arms vigorously and continued walking, though still unsteadily. Try as he might, he could not make any of the white, moon-struck land look familiar. The fear that had been rising within him now threatened to become panic. "Why can't I remember who I am?" he cried out. "Or where I am?"

Directly ahead of him, he saw a wide river, shining like a silver ribbon as it reflected the brilliant moon. Following its trail off to his left, he saw the land rise up and top out at the edge of the river in a complex of square roofs, surrounded by a dark, looming wall.

A fort!

Abruptly he recalled that the war between the states was being fought on Southern soil. Then he was looking at a *Confederate* fort, and it was occupied, for he could make out movement atop the walls. He caught sight of winking campfires farther up the riverbank. It had to be a Union camp. Both sides were no doubt waiting for morning so they could resume the battle.

His heart quickened pace. There would be *warmth* in either the camp or the fort.

But which one was the enemy?

The panic within him surged. With effort, he strove to suppress it while his mind raced. If he went to the wrong place, he could be executed as a spy. Anyone captured in a battle zone out of uniform could very well be taken for a spy. If they believed he was a spy, he would be shot. There was no way he could prove otherwise. And even if they believed he was a soldier, if he didn't know which side he was on, certainly they could not either. They would have no choice but to incarcerate him for the duration of the war.

The truth came home. *Either* place was the wrong place. Yankees or Confederates would have to deal with him the same—shoot him, or put him in a prison camp till the war was over. He could not go to the camp, and he could not go to the fort.

Pain lanced through his head. Dizziness followed, and waves of nausea washed over him. He dropped to his knees and braced his hands against the crusted snow to keep from falling on his face. The wind took his breath. Soon the nausea was gone, and the dizziness eased off. If he could just get to a warm place and rest...

He decided to see if he could find a farm. In a barn or a shed he could get out of the wind. He dare not approach a farmhouse. This was Southern soil, and if the farmer chose to believe he was a Yankee, he could still be shot. A barn or shed would have to do for now, until he could thaw out and decide what to do.

He struggled back to his feet. Rubbing his hands together and whacking his upper torso with his arms, he headed back the way he came. There had to be a farm somewhere near. Threading amongst the dead, he moved as quickly as his legs would carry him. He recognized the stand of trees near the spot where he had first awakened, and another two hundred yards beyond them, he saw the beginnings of a forest. He would cut along the edge of the forest. Surely it would lead him to a farm...and warmth.

As he stumbled toward the woods, he noted for the first time that no weapons were in sight. Whoever stripped the bodies also took whatever guns, bayonets, and knives they could find. He was drawing nearer the edge of the forest when something off to the right caught his eye. He stopped, turning his head in that direction.

Something moved over there, didn't it?

Or was it a trick the wind and the shadows played on his confused mind?

He blinked against the wind, searching for further movement among the scattered corpses.

Then something else halted him. Was that a moan? It was hard to tell with the wind whining about him. He held his breath, straining, listening.

Then they came, both movement and sound at the same time. One of the men on the ground moaned and moved his legs, trying to raise his head.

The amnesiac breathed, "Oh, dear Lord in heaven, he's alive!" Even as he spoke, he stumbled toward the fallen soldier. "Lord, please let him know me! Please!"

He reached the wounded man and saw the broad spread of blood on the long underwear that covered his chest. Gripping the man's shoulder, he said, "Soldier, can you hear me?"

The moan stopped abruptly, the head quit rolling, and the bleeding man opened his eyes. Attempting to focus on the moonlit form above him, he gasped, "Who...who is it?"

"I'm a friend. Can you see me?"

"Yes."

"Do you know me?"

The soldier squinted, licked his lips, and replied shakily, "I...I can't...see you that good." He coughed, winced with pain, then said, "I'm hit bad. Can you...get me to the camp?"

The camp! He's a Yankee.

The amnesiac's thoughts jumbled, then cleared. If he took the wounded man to the camp, it would leave him in the fix he had pondered earlier. But this man was in bad shape. If there was a chance he could save his life, he must do it, no matter the risk to himself.

For a moment, he wondered at his willingness to sacrifice himself for a man he didn't even know, who might even be his enemy. Somehow it was a settled thing in his mind. He would carry the man to the camp.

"Sure, my friend," he breathed. "I'll get you to the camp. I assume there's a doctor there?"

"A medic," came the weak reply. A frown creased his brow. "But if you're a Yankee...you already know that."

No time to explain. He reached underneath the wounded man and surprised himself as he cradled him in his arms and stood up. Where had he gotten the strength to do this? The man had to weigh somewhere around two hundred pounds.

As they headed toward the camp, the wounded man looked at him with half-glazed eyes and said, "You're a Rebel, aren't you?"

"Yeah." No sense wasting breath.

"And you're willing...to carry me into the camp? You know they'll...take you prisoner."

"Yeah."

The wounded man was quiet for a long moment. Then he said weakly, "You're a Christian, aren't you."

"Yes, I am," he replied before he even pondered the question.

"I thought so. Only...only a man who...knows Jesus would do what you're doing."

His mind raced again. He couldn't remember who he was, where he came from, or even what army he belonged to, but he knew what a Christian was, and he knew he was one. His thoughts rushed to Calvary—the cross, the blood, the dying Redeemer with nails through His hands and feet. And he knew that this Jesus lived in his heart. This was not only a source of peace and comfort, it was also encouraging. Maybe his memory was already coming back!

The wounded Yankee coughed and spit up blood as they continued slowly across the battlefield. When he could speak again, he said with a voice that was growing even weaker, "I'm a Christian, too...my brother. I thought about it before we...attacked Fort Donelson. I wondered how many men...in that fort were my Christian brothers. Bad enough...bad enough for blood brothers...to fight each other, but even worse for...men in God's family...to be killing each other."

A sick feeling went through the amnesiac. He couldn't say if that awful thought had ever crossed his mind before, but he figured it was true.

His legs were growing weaker. They had traveled about a hundred and fifty yards when he said, breathing hard, "I'm going to have to put you down and rest a moment."

There was no response as he stopped and carefully lowered the Yankee soldier to the ground. The Yankee's eyes were closed and his mouth was sagging open. A quick check for a pulse revealed none. The man was dead.

There was a sudden piercing pain in his left temple, and with it came a rush of dizziness. His equilibrium gave way, and he found himself on the frozen ground next to the dead Yankee. The earth went into a spin and a black shroud began to overwhelm him. He was almost unconscious, but the sensation of spinning in a tight circle seemed to keep the shroud from blacking him out.

It took about three minutes for the spell to pass. When he felt he could stand once again, he struggled to his feet. The wind was easing some, though it still lashed his face enough to dispose of the sweat that beaded his brow.

He stood still for a moment waiting for his legs to quit shaking. Looking down at the dead man's face, he said softly, "I never asked your name, dear brother, and couldn't have told you mine. Well, now that you're in heaven, you can ask the Lord my name. He knows it, even if I don't."

He looked toward the hulking Confederate fort on the bank of the wide silver stream. "Fort Donelson, eh? Then that must be the Cumberland River." He paused, then said, "I can remember the name of the fort and the name of the river, but there's a fog bank when it comes to my own name."

He felt pain in his hands and looked at his fingers. They were deep purple. He feared frostbite. Breathing on his hands to warm them, he moved on unsteady legs toward the edge of the forest once again.

Turning slightly to follow the wooded rim, he felt another sharp pain in his temple. He staggered a few steps and fell. He clawed at his frozen surroundings, but was soon swallowed by a swirling black vortex.

When he came to, the moon had reached the western sky. He was chilled more than ever. His fingers were numb and so were his toes.

Forcing himself to a sitting position, he pulled off his boots and rubbed his feet until some measure of warmth returned. When his boots were back on, he breathed on his hands and rubbed them together until the stiffness left them.

His knees felt watery as he rose once again, but he forced himself to keep moving. If he didn't get someplace warm soon, he was going to freeze to death. He had been plodding along the edge of the trees for about fifteen minutes, scouring the moonlit landscape for some sign of a farm, when from within the woods, he heard the distinct blow of a horse.

He looked into the deep shadows and listened. Above the rush of the wind through the treetops, he heard the sound again. There was a horse amongst the trees, and not very far away.

He plunged into the shadows, using the solid trunks to steady himself. It took only seconds for him to find the horse, a bay gelding standing beside the crumpled body of its rider.

A few other bodies lay amid the trees, and none of them had been stripped. They were all clad in Rebel gray.

The horse nickered at him as he moved about, studying the dead men. He would take the uniform and coat of the man nearest his own size. He was already anticipating the warmth the clothing would give his shivering body. He finally decided the rider of the horse was closest in size.

The man had been a Confederate captain, and a single slug had plowed into the left side of his forehead, killing him instantly. There was a little blood on his hat, which lay next to him, and a small sprinkling of crimson on the left shoulder of his overcoat.

He hastily removed the outer clothing from the dead officer and put it on. The uniform fit him perfectly, even the hat, which he had to wear cocked to the right side because of the bloody furrow on the left. He touched the furrow and found that it was oozing blood. He must have reopened it when he fell the last time.

Searching the dead captain's pockets, he found a bandanna and tied it around his head. He then picked up the captain's gunbelt and strapped it on. As he was buckling the belt, he noted how natural it felt, even the heft of the revolver's weight against his hip.

Was he an officer? The very thought seemed right. But of which army?

The horse seemed a bit nervous as he prepared to mount. It nickered and danced about. Stroking the side of its face, he said gently, "It's all right, boy. I'm friendly, even if I'm a Yankee."

The soothing strokes and the low tone of voice settled the animal down. The amnesiac put his left foot in the stirrup, and with effort, swung into the McClellan saddle. This, too, felt natural.

A sudden wash of dizziness came over him, and his stomach experienced waves of nausea. Bending low, he waited for the nausea to pass, then with his head still spinning slightly, he nudged the horse forward. Soon they were out of the trees and moving across the body-strewn field. By the position of the moon in the low western sky, he knew he was headed south.

He kept the animal to a walk because of the pain in his head. He'd ridden but a short distance when he felt a warm trickle of blood down the side of his face. Drawing rein, he removed the bandanna, wrung the blood out of it, and tied it around his head tighter than before. Though his body welcomed the warmth of the captain's uniform and overcoat, he knew he must find help. Now that he was in a Confederate uniform, he could at least approach a farmhouse. Surely they would help a man they believed to be one of their own.

"Thank You, Lord, for letting me find a gray uniform. Since I'm in Tennessee, I'd be in grave danger in a blue one."

Dizzy spells came and went as horse and rider moved across the fields southward. It struck him that he had used his voice several times since finding himself on the frozen battlefield, but even it did not sound familiar. "Lord," he said in a half-whisper, "how could the loss of my memory serve any good purpose?"

Suddenly his mind was filled with a verse of Scripture. *And we know that all things work together for good to them that love God, to them who are the called according to his purpose.*

"Romans 8:28," he heard himself say. "I do love You, Lord. Bad as my memory is, I know that. All things work together for good, You say. All right. I'll accept that. It's in Your Word, so I believe it. But I sure don't understand this situation. Why can I remember some things but not others? As soon as that poor man back there identified the fort as Donelson, I knew it was on the Cumberland River, and that I was in Tennessee. But why can't I remember my own name, or where I'm from...or which army I belong to?"

He stayed on a southern course, unaware that the town of Dover was less than two miles off to his right behind a low line of hills. Between dizzy spells and intermittent waves of nausea, he racked his brain, trying to stimulate his memory.

Many names came to mind, all military or political. He recalled Richmond and Washington and knew they were the Confederate and Federal capitals, but frustration came over him because he could not remember where his own home was or the name he had lived with all his life.

All his life? How old was he? By the looks of his hands, he guessed himself to be somewhere in his late twenties or early thirties. Maybe. Why would he remember that hands change with age, but not remember his own age? Still, he was sure he was yet a young man. His body seemed strong and firm. In spite of his wound and the freezing cold, he had been able to lift the wounded Yankee and carry him in his arms.

Soon the moon dropped out of sight in the west, and was replaced by the breaking dawn. The early gray light showed that he was passing by a cemetery. He knew there would be names and dates on the grave markers. Strange. He knew he was in the Civil War, but could not recall what year it was, or even the decade.

Turning into the cemetery, he dismounted and studied the names on the tombstones, thinking that looking at some names might possibly jar his memory and tell him his own. He noted that the stone of a fresh grave indicated the deceased had died on February 3, 1862. He estimated the grave to be two, not more than three weeks old.

So it was February 1862.

He tried to recall the year he was born, but there was nothing. Nothing but that horrendous blank wall in his brain.

Once again, he was aware of blood trickling down the side of his face. A dizzy spell came over him. He leaned against the horse and clung to the saddle until it began to pass. He was about to mount up when the faint sound of water met his ears. He looked over the horse's back, through the trees, and saw a small ice-edged brook on the far side of the cemetery.

He led the horse around the cemetery's perimeter to the gurgling stream. He removed his hat and the blood-stained bandanna, knelt on the bank, and tossed the icy water into his face. It refreshed him and helped clear the thin fog that remained in his brain.

He washed the bandanna in the stream, squeezing out the blood, then broke off a piece of ice along the bank. Pressing the ice to his wound, he held it there with the bandanna for several minutes, hoping to stay the flow of blood. When he checked it, the bleeding had slowed. He broke off another piece and held it there until it appeared the bleeding had stopped. Soaking the bandanna in the stream and wringing it out, he tied it around his head once again and replaced the hat.

He was just rising to his feet when he heard his horse nicker, and a cold voice from behind him snapped, "Get your hands up, Reb!"

CHAPTER ELEVEN

★

Startled, the man in the Confederate captain's uniform whipped around to see two Union lieutenants on horseback, pointing their revolvers at him. Their faces were grim and full of determination.

The amnesiac's eyes bulged, and he recoiled as though he had been slapped in the face. Being in uniform would save him from a firing squad, but even the thought of the Yankee prison camp was repugnant. He thought of himself as a wild animal who had roamed free, suddenly cornered and about to be caged.

"I said get those hands in the air, Captain!" bawled the same man who had spoken before.

Slowly he lifted his hands, holding them at head level.

"Now, you just stay like that," the man said as he dismounted.

His partner kept his weapon trained on the man they believed to be a Rebel captain until the first man had both feet planted on the ground. Both Yankees were about the same age—late twenties—but the man on the ground was short and stocky, while the other was tall and thin. The stocky one held his gun on their captive while the thin one dismounted, then together, they moved toward him.

Halting about eight feet from him, the stocky one asked, "What brigade and division you belong to, Captain?"

"I...I don't know," he replied levelly.

"Don't play games with us, Reb!" the thin one snarled. "Answer Lieutenant Hovey's question!"

"I did. I have a head wound, as you can see. Bullet grazed me and I passed out. When I came to, I was lying up there on that battlefield near Fort Donelson. Somebody had stripped me of my uniform. I happened to find a dead Confederate captain, so I took his clothes."

"So what're you doing here?" Hovey demanded. "Why aren't you inside Donelson getting some medical attention?"

"Because I don't know whether I'm Rebel or Yankee."

The Union officers exchanged glances. Disbelief was in their eyes.

"That's the best cock-and-bull story I've heard in a long time," Hovey said. "Well, you're our prisoner now, Reb."

"But I might be a Yankee," protested the man-in-gray. "You wouldn't want to treat me as a prisoner if I'm one of your own."

"I'm sick of this claptrap," the thin one said. "Take his gun, Duane. I'll cover him." Lieutenant Hovey kept a wary eye on the prisoner as he moved up to take the gun from his holster.

Panic raced through the amnesia victim. He must not let them put him in a prison camp. Instinct took over. When Hovey was within arm's reach, the man-in-gray grabbed Hovey's revolver and wrested it from his grip. Surprised, Hovey swore and grappled with the prisoner for his weapon. The other Yankee raised his gun and took aim.

In one lightning-swift move, the amnesiac seized Hovey's coat collar with his free hand and used him as a shield just as the other Yankee fired. The bullet tore into Hovey's back. Still operating on instinct, the would-be prisoner lined Hovey's gun on the thin man's chest and fired. The slug went clear through him. Hovey, back arched, hit the ground barely two seconds before his partner did. Both men were dead.

The man-in-gray looked around to see if any other Union soldiers were in sight. He saw none, but thought there might be some close enough to have heard the shots. He dropped the gun, hurried to his horse, and leaped into the saddle. Sharp pain stabbed his left temple, but he tried to ignore it as he galloped out of the cemetery and once again headed south.

He kept the horse at a gallop for over a mile, while looking about him for blue uniforms. Soon he could ignore the pain no longer. He slowed the animal to a walk and pressed a palm against his pounding head. The sun was shafting a yellow fan of light on the eastern horizon when he caught sight of a farm up ahead.

For a brief moment, his mind went back to the two Yankee lieutenants he had just killed. His instincts were definitely honed for action. He had done that kind of thing before. What area of military work was he in? What kind of training would make him adept for a situation like the one he just faced?

Another question stabbed his mind. Had he killed foes or friends? The question faded from his thoughts as he drew nearer the farmhouse. It was a white, two-storied frame structure with a large porch. To the rear of the house, across a well-kept yard, stood a barn and several outbuildings.

The pain in his head was severe, and now a fresh fog was claiming his brain while the whole world seemed to go into a spin. Or was the horse dancing in tight circles? He had to grip the saddle to keep from falling off the horse as it carried him into the yard and up to the side of the house.

All the strength was leaving him. He was aware of a horse whinnying at the corral by the barn, and he heard his horse nicker back. He was bent low over the horse's neck and trying with everything that was in him to keep from passing out as the animal came to a halt.

He raised up to take a deep breath, and for a brief instant, his head cleared. He caught a glimpse of a female face at an upstairs window, then felt himself slipping from the saddle. He didn't even know when he hit the ground.

* * * * *

Some forty-five minutes earlier that morning, Hannah Rose Claiborne rose from her bed by the dull light of dawn and slipped into her robe. She lit the two lanterns that sat opposite each other on each side of the bed, then crossed the chilly room to the fireplace. Within a few minutes she had a blaze going, and stood before it, soaking up its pleasant warmth.

Soon there were soft footsteps in the hall, followed by a light tap on the door. Hannah Rose turned her back to the fire and called, "Come in, ladies."

The door opened, and Linda Lee entered first, carrying her Bible. Behind her came Donna Mae and Sally Marie, who also had their Bibles.

"You're early," Hannah Rose smiled. "I didn't get a chance to brush my hair."

"We'll forgive you this time," piped Sally Marie, "but don't let it happen again. You're so homely with unbrushed hair."

The others appreciated Sally Marie's attempt at a little humor. By their weary eyes, anyone could tell the four young women had not slept well. Immediately they began to discuss the battle that everyone in the area knew had taken place the day before at Fort Donelson.

Donna Mae's features were pale as she said with a tremor in her voice, "I hate this war. If those bullheaded Yankees had just kept their noses out of our business, there wouldn't have been any trouble at Fort Sumter. And the hundreds of our men and boys killed in these past ten months would still be alive."

"And we wouldn't be spending sleepless nights worrying over William, Britt, and Robert," Sally Marie added.

"And Lanny, too," Linda Lee said.

"Yes, honey," nodded Hannah Rose, patting her hand, "Lanny, too. You're becoming quite fond of him, aren't you?"

"Yes, I am," the younger sister said, apprehension showing in her eyes. "If God wills it, I believe Lanny and I will one day be married." Tears filmed her eyes, and her lower lip quivered. "That is, unless..."

"Unless what, honey?"

"Unless he was killed yesterday. Or he gets killed in some other horrible battle."

Hannah Rose moved to her little sister, put her arms around her, and said, "If God wills it, there's no *unless*. The Lord knows the end from the beginning. He won't plan for you to marry Lanny if He knows Lanny isn't going to make it through the war."

Linda Lee began to cry. Amid her sobs, she said, "The Lord just *has* to watch over Lanny, Hannah Rose. He knows I'm beyond being fond of him. I'm in love with him. Why would He let me fall in love with Lanny, then let him be killed?"

"Sometimes the Lord does things we don't always understand, honey. His thoughts are not our thoughts, and His ways are not our ways. Remember? And He tells us as the heavens are higher than the earth, so are His ways and His thoughts higher than ours. He often looks at things quite differently than we do.

"And that's where faith comes in. We not only must trust the Lord for our salvation by faith, but also for each day. And you know the Bible says without faith it is impossible to please Him. And we want to please Him above all things, don't we?"

"Yes."

"Well, that's why we're here right now—to read His Word and to pray for those men we love, trusting the Lord to answer our prayers and bring them back safely to us."

Linda Lee nodded, sniffed, and pulled gently away from her sister. While she went to Hannah Rose's dresser and picked up a handkerchief, she asked, "And what about you, sis? Are you falling for Jim?"

"Jim's a nice enough young man, and I like him very much...but no, I'm not falling for him."

"Now that Mother Claiborne is gone, Hannah Rose," Donna Mae said, "I think it's time you begin to think about yourself and your future for a change."

"I'll let the Lord take care of my future," smiled Hannah Rose. "And as for falling in love, that will happen when Mr. Right comes into my life. I'll let the Lord take care of that, too."

Hannah Rose now guided the Claiborne women to the Psalms, where they took turns reading aloud. They garnered strength for their hearts from the words of David, who trusted the God of Israel to deliver him out of all his troubles. When they finished reading, they knelt beside Hannah Rose's bed and prayed together, asking that God's hand of protection would be on Britt, William, Robert, and Lanny.

The sun's upper rim was about to peek over the eastern horizon as the four young women finished praying. They wiped tears, embraced each other, then returned to their rooms to dress for the day.

Hannah Rose quickly made up her bed, then changed from her robe and flannel nightgown into a simple cotton dress and topped it with a wool sweater for warmth. Sitting at her dressing table, she looked at her reflection in the mirror and began to brush her long, reddish-brown hair. She was almost finished when she heard the Claiborne family mare whinny three times in succession. When she heard a different horse softly nicker a reply, she knew someone was in the yard.

She hurried to the window. Pulling back the curtain, she saw a bay gelding with a Rebel officer slumped forward in the saddle. When the horse came to a halt below her window, the man in the saddle suddenly sat upright, looked toward her, then slumped over again. Slowly, he began to slide from the saddle, then fell to the ground and lay still.

Hannah Rose bolted through the door, ran down the hall, and bounded down the stairs. Her sister and sisters-in-law opened their doors just in time to catch a glimpse of her descending the stairs. All three stepped into the hall, exchanging puzzled glances. Sally Marie said, "Something's got her excited. We'd better go see what it is."

Hannah Rose burst through the front door of the house and dashed to where the man-in-gray lay crumpled on the ground. His horse nuzzled her as she knelt down beside him.

She knew by the insignias on his uniform that he was a captain. His hat had fallen from his head, and she saw the bloody bandanna that encircled his head. She made sure he was breathing, then rose to her feet and stretched out his legs and arms. She was checking him over for other wounds as the other three women arrived, out of breath.

"Oh!" exclaimed Linda Lee. "It's one of our soldiers!"

As all three pressed closer, Donna Mae asked, "How bad is he hurt?"

"Looks like the only wound is here on his head," answered Hannah Rose, pointing to the blood-soaked bandanna. "There's blood on the left side of his coat, and on the left side of his hat. Apparently the head wound has bled a lot. Let's get him in the house."

Together, the four young women carried the unconscious man inside the house and placed him on the bed in the first-floor guest room.

Working as a team, they removed the overcoat, then took off his uniform coat. Hannah Rose called for a pan of water, towels, washcloths, bandages, wood alcohol, iodine, and salve as she began removing the bloody bandanna.

The others scurried out of the room, and in a few minutes had placed everything she asked for on a small table beside the bed. Using two towels, she double-folded them and placed them under his head. As she began cleaning the wound, Hannah Rose spoke over her shoulder, "It would be a good idea if you ladies would fire up the kitchen stove and get breakfast started. Aunt Myrtle will be rising soon, and this young captain will probably be hungry when he comes to."

"Do you want one of us to stay here and help you?" Linda Lee asked.

"No, honey, I can manage. I would appreciate it, though, if you'd go put the captain's horse in the corral. Might as well remove the bridle and saddle, too. He's not going anywhere for a while."

"How bad is it?" Sally Marie asked, leaning close.

"Nothing life-threatening. A bullet creased his temple and cut a pretty good furrow, but I think he'll be all right. If that slug had been a half-inch to the right, it would've killed him. As it is, I'm sure he's got a concussion."

"You don't think he's lost so much blood that he might die?" Donna Mae asked.

"Well, there's no way to be sure, but his breathing is strong. I would think if he's exceptionally low on blood, his breathing would be more shallow."

"You should have been a doctor," Donna Mae said.

Hannah Rose took a moment to look up at her sister-in-law and smile. "I'm afraid it takes a lot more than having a little horse sense to be a doctor. Like being a *man*. You've never heard of a woman doctor, have you?"

"Well, there should be," Linda Lee said. "Who's to say that women can't be good doctors?"

"*Men*," chorused the other three together, then laughed.

"All right, ladies," said Hannah Rose, "get to work."

The room was quiet after the others had gone, and Hannah Rose proceeded with her task. First, she washed the left side of the wounded man's head with cold water, then she cleaned the wound with wood alcohol. Now she applied a liberal amount of iodine to kill any germs the alcohol might have missed. She knew the captain was deeply under when he did not even flinch. The wound began bleeding more freely when touched by the antiseptic, but Hannah Rose knew it was essential to kill the germs.

Working carefully and adeptly, she spread salve along the bloody furrow, then placed a thick bandage against it and wound white cloth around his head to hold it tightly in place.

That done, she removed the towels she had placed beneath his head earlier and replaced them with a pillow. She lay the towels on the table, went to the foot of the bed, and pulled off the captain's boots. Leaving him in his shirt and trousers, she drew the covers over him, then stood there looking down at him.

"Well, Captain," she said softly, "I wonder what your name is. Whoever you are, you appear to be in excellent physical condition. Everything's in your favor to come through this ordeal okay."

Hannah Rose found the man's angular features quite handsome. Complementing his good looks were his thick head of dark-brown wavy hair and neatly trimmed mustache. She told herself he had the polished look of an officer, and was probably a graduate of West Point. She speculated about the color of his eyes. "If I was a betting woman, Captain, I'd bet they're dark blue. Mmm, no, maybe dark-brown like your hair." Putting a forefinger to her cheek, she shook her head. "No, dark blue. That's it—I change my bet to dark blue."

Hannah Rose knew he had to have been in yesterday's battle at Fort Donelson. She wondered what part of the South he was from. Did he have a sweetheart waiting for him back home? Or maybe a wife? Children?

She sighed and half-whispered, "I hope you come out of it soon, Captain. I want to know who you are, and if you're acquainted with my brothers."

Presently, Aunt Myrtle appeared, and the women sat down at the breakfast table. They told Myrtle about their unexpected house guest, and she asked how he was doing. Hannah Rose showed concern in her eyes. "I think I've about got the bleeding stopped, but he's been unconscious for such a long time. I thought he would have come to by now. Maybe we ought to get Doc Stutz out here to look at him."

"I agree," Linda Lee said. "If someone will go with me, I'll drive into town and ask Doc to come."

"I'll go," Sally Marie volunteered.

"I'll go, too," Donna Mae said. "With all that's going on at Fort Donelson, it would be better if the three of us go together."

"Would you mind if I ride along?" asked the elderly aunt. "I just as well get something done while I'm staying here. I'd like to pick up some sewing materials and yard goods. Make me a new dress."

The four of them agreed to take the family wagon into town and return with Dr. Stutz, Dover's only physician. Hannah Rose would stay with her patient.

When breakfast was over, the kitchen cleaned up, and dishes done, it was only a short time until the wagon was on its way into town. Hannah Rose made a brief trip to the barn, then returned to the guest room. She sat in a chair beside the bed and watched the unconscious Confederate officer, praying that the Lord would bring him around soon.

Club Clubson was riding past the Claiborne place on his way to Dover. He eyed the house and wondered if he should stop and see Linda Lee for a few minutes. It was almost nine o'clock.

"Naw. They'll be cleanin' house about now. Linda Lee wouldn't have time to talk to me. I'll stop by on my way back."

His eye strayed to the corral behind the house and locked on the unfamiliar bay gelding standing with its head over the top rung of the split-rail fence. He drew rein and stared at the horse. Then he shrugged his bulky shoulders and concluded that one of the brothers had returned home.

Club nudged his mount forward, then drew rein again. Looking back at the horse, he shook his head. "Or," he said aloud, "that animal could belong to one of Linda Lee's suitors. If that's the case, he's here awful early in the day, and he's flirtin' with a broken neck."

Club rode into the Claiborne yard, breathing raggedly with the prospect of what he might find. No man—be he soldier or civilian—was going to stand between him and the woman he loved.

Reining in at the front porch, he left the saddle, mounted the steps, and knocked loudly on the door. When no answer came in what Club figured was a reasonable time, he banged on the door again, even harder. Presently he heard light footsteps, and the door came open.

"H'lo, Hannah Rose. I'd like to talk to Linda Lee."

"She's not here right now, Club," Hannah Rose responded quickly, annoyed that he was there.

"Well, where is she?"

"She's on her way into town."

"And who does that strange horse in your corral belong to?"

Hannah Rose looked him straight in the eye. "I don't like your tone, Club, and I don't like your attitude. It's really none of your business who that horse belongs to."

"Well, I just thought—"

"I know what you thought. You thought Linda Lee had a caller. She's not your property, Club. When are you going to understand that?"

He opened his mouth to speak, but she cut him off again.

"I don't have to explain anything to you, Club, but I will anyhow. That horse belongs to a Confederate captain who rode in here just before sunup. He was wounded in yesterday's battle at Fort Donelson. Passed out the instant he drew up to the house. Linda Lee and my sisters-in-law have gone to get Doc Stutz. Now, if you'll excuse me, I need to get back to my patient just in case he awakens before Doc Stutz gets here."

Club stared at her blankly for a moment, then asked, "Anything I can do to help?"

"No, thank you. The only help the captain needs now is the kind Dr. Stutz can give him."

"Oh...sure. Uh, in case I don't run onto Linda Lee while ridin' into town, tell her I was here to see her."

"I will," nodded Hannah Rose, stepping back to close the door.

"Tell her I love her."

"She already knows that, Club. I really must get back to my patient."

Hannah Rose moved briskly toward the rear of the house and entered the guest room. Her heart quickened when she saw the wounded man moaning and rolling his head.

He was regaining consciousness!

CHAPTER TWELVE

★

Hannah Rose rushed to the wounded man, whose eyes were fluttering as he rolled his head back and forth and licked his lips. She pushed the hair back from his forehead with one hand and dabbed at the perspiration there with a soft cloth in the other.

Finally, his fluttering eyes came all the way open. They were a bit glazed, but she congratulated herself when she saw them. They were dark blue.

As the brilliant sunlight struck his eyes, the amnesia victim felt a spasm of pain shoot through his head. Hannah Rose pulled her hands away and said quietly, "Don't open your eyes all at once, Captain. Go at it slowly."

He nodded and closed his eyes. After a few seconds, he opened them briefly, then closed them again. After he had repeated the action several times, his eyes began to adjust to the light and to lose their glaze. As his vision cleared, he saw that the woman standing over him had reddish-brown hair, and recalled seeing a female face in an upstairs window just before he passed out. This had to be her.

Hannah Rose smiled down at him. "Good morning, Captain. My name is Hannah Rose Claiborne, and I already know yours."

The man's hazy thoughts did not lay hold on her words at first. He noted instead her long chestnut hair, highlighted by the sunlight, which shone through a nearby window. He saw that her emerald-green eyes were warm and compassionate.

Suddenly her words sank in.

His heart pounded as he licked his dry lips and said excitedly, "You know me?"

Smiling, she replied, "Well, not really. But I know your name, and that you are a Captain in the Fourth Brigade, Confederate Army of Northern Virginia, temporarily assigned to Fort Donelson."

"I *am*," he gasped. "H-how do you know this?"

"From this letter," Hannah Rose replied, turning toward the night-stand. She picked up an envelope and pulled a folded sheet of paper from inside it. "I found it in your saddlebags. I hope you'll forgive me for opening it and reading it, but I felt I should know the name of the man I had taken in and patched up."

"Patched up?" he echoed, placing fingertips to the bandage that encircled his head.

"Yes. My sister and sisters-in-law helped me carry you in here and laid you on the bed. I cleaned your wound and bandaged it up. I think the bleeding has just about stopped. My sister and the others have gone into town to bring the doctor."

"Doctor?"

"I was worried because you had been unconscious so long. I thought it best to have Dr. Stutz take a look at you. I'm so glad that you've come out of it, but it's good that he's coming, anyhow. I'll feel better if he checks you over."

Managing a smile, the wounded man said, "You are very kind, Miss Claiborne—it *is* Miss, isn't it?"

"Yes."

"I can never thank you enough for what you've done."

"Just doing my patriotic duty," she smiled. "Being a true daughter of the South, I must do all I can to help us win this war. I saw one of our fine officers wounded and in trouble, so I did my duty and helped him. I have three brothers in the army, all attached over here at Fort Donelson. Two of them are married, and their wives live here with my sister and me. All of us feel the same way toward the Confederacy. We only wish we could do more to help."

"God bless you," he breathed. "You...you say you know my name?"

"Yes, it's here in the letter. Captain Wayne Gordon. The letter was sealed, of course, and addressed to Brigadier General Simon B. Buckner, commander at Fort Donelson. It's from Brigadier General James Longstreet, commander of Fourth Brigade, Confederate Army of Northern Virginia in Richmond. It introduces Captain Wayne Gordon as the officer requested by General Buckner. I was hoping you were already part of Fort Donelson's forces so you could tell me about my brothers, but according to this, you were just arriving here from Richmond, so you wouldn't know them. We've heard there was quite a battle at the fort yesterday."

He thought of all the bodies strewn on the moonlit battlefield. "Yes, ma'am. Quite a battle."

Looking at the letter, Hannah Rose said, "General Longstreet gives some of your military background and accomplishments, Captain. Quite impressive, I might say. But it doesn't tell where you're from, or anything about a wife and family."

He did not reply.

Feeling that possibly the captain did not want to talk about that part of his life, she said, "How...ah...did you get the wound on your head? You came very close to being killed, you know."

"Yes, I know. But, Miss Claiborne, I am going to have to be honest with you."

"Pardon me?"

"I'm not Captain Wayne Gordon."

"But this letter says you're Captain Gordon."

"Let me explain, ma'am. I don't know *who* I am. I know I'm a soldier, but I don't even know which side I was fighting on...whether I'm a Rebel or a Yankee. You see—"

"Now, wait a minute, Captain. You're not making sense. This letter says you are Captain Wayne Gordon, attached to Fourth Brigade at Richmond, Confederate Army of Northern Virginia."

"Please, ma'am...let me explain."

Hannah Rose went to a straight-backed chair near the window and carried it to the bed. Sitting down, she said, "All right. I'm listening."

"Ma'am, not only can I not remember my name, I can't remember anything beyond last night. Apparently when I was struck by that slug, it took my memory."

Hannah Rose's hand went to her mouth. "You mean you don't know anything about yourself—where you're from or who your family is?"

"That's right, ma'am."

"But even though your memory's gone, you have this letter. You're in a Confederate uniform. All we have to do is contact General Longstreet and his staff. We can have you reunited with your family—"

"No, ma'am. You still don't understand. Let me tell you the whole story."

"All right."

The wounded man told Hannah Rose his story, going back to the night before when he awakened on the frozen battlefield.

When he finished, Hannah Rose was staring at the floor. She pressed fingertips to her temples, shook her head, and said, "This is all so incredible, Captain." Then she raised her head and met his gaze. "Sorry. I don't know what else to call you."

"I guess you could call me ol' Blank Brain," he grinned. He was amazed at how relaxed he was in her presence, in spite of his dilemma.

"I wouldn't call you that," she smiled. "You...ah, you might be a Yankee. You don't have a Southern accent."

"Strange that I can remember this, ma'am, but many Southerners never develop an accent. In fact, yours is barely noticeable."

"Really? I've had many Northerners comment on how strong my accent is. Do you suppose you *are* a Southerner, and that's why my accent seems only slight to you?"

Hannah Rose saw a shadow of anxiety and a hint of panic in his eyes as he took a deep breath and sighed shakily, "This is all so...so nerve racking. Here I am in your home under your care, and I might even be your enemy. I can't go to the Rebels, and I can't go to the Yankees. If I'm a Yankee, there are no doubt men who know me over at that Yankee camp. If I'm a Rebel, there'll be men at Fort Donelson who will know me. But the problem is...if I chose the wrong place to present myself, at best I'd be locked up in a prison camp for the duration of the war. They might even think I'm a spy and stand me before a firing squad."

"They wouldn't execute you if you were in uniform, would they?"

"Well, I'm not sure. No matter which side I presented myself to, they might not believe my story. They might think I'm trying to pull the wool over their eyes. But even if they did believe my story, they couldn't put a gun in my hand. My memory might come back all of a sudden, and if I found myself amongst the enemy, I might start putting bullets in them. This has to be how they would think. So, either way—Yankees or Rebels—they'd have no choice but to lock me up. No thanks. No filthy, disease-infested prison camp for me."

"I can't blame you for that," Hannah Rose said, rising and laying a firm hand on his shoulder. "I want you to know, though, that you're welcome to stay here as long as you wish. I don't know anything about amnesia, but Dr. Stutz no doubt does. He'll be here soon. Maybe he can help."

The touch of Hannah Rose's hand on his shoulder was pleasant. There was something about this young woman that caused a gentle peace to settle over him. He thought her name fit her perfectly. Before he realized it, he was voicing his thoughts. "You're name fits you perfectly, ma'am," he said softly.

"In what way?" she asked, gently removing her hand from his shoulder.

"You're wholesome, like Hannah in the Bible, Samuel's mother. And...and you're tender and beautiful like a rose."

His words left her short of breath. "Why, Captain. I...I don't know what to say."

"You don't have to say anything, ma'am. I wasn't speaking flattery. I meant what I said very sincerely."

"I'm sure you did. Thank you." She paused, then said, "Captain, I'm surprised that with your amnesia, you can remember Scripture. I mean, about Hannah and all."

"Well, ma'am, I can quote whole verses, and even tell you where they're found. *For I delivered unto you first of all that which I also received, how that Christ died for our sins according to the scriptures; and that he was buried, and that he rose again the third day according to the scriptures.* That's First Corinthians fifteen, verses three and four."

Hannah Rose clapped her hands together. "That's wonderful, Captain! Are...are you a Christian?"

"Yes, ma'am. Bad as my memory is, I know that for sure."

Hannah Rose told the captain she had become a Christian when she was seven years old, and her sister and brothers had come to know the Lord in their childhood. Her sisters-in-law were also Christians.

When she finished, the wounded man said, "You know, while you were talking, a powerful thought hit me. The concussion of that bullet affected my brain but not my heart, the center of my soul. Maybe that's why the amnesia doesn't affect what I know about my salvation and why I can remember Scripture. Christ is in my heart, and His Word is in my heart, not just my mind. So the amnesia doesn't affect that part of me."

Smiling and shaking her head in wonderment, Hannah Rose said,

"I never thought of it like that, Captain. Maybe you were a preacher before you went into the war."

"I don't think so, ma'am. Not that the idea is repugnant to me, but somehow it just doesn't seem to fit. Of course, since I can't recall one little thing about my past, I could be wrong. But it seems to me that if I was a preacher, I would've gone into the army as a chaplain."

"Maybe you did. Since your clothing was gone when you came to, how would you know?"

He looked blankly at her for a moment. "Well...ah...I seem to recall that chaplains don't go into battle."

"Oh. Well, it was just a thought. Anyhow, you would make a fine-looking preacher."

"Well, thank you. I..." His eyes widened.

"What is it, Captain?"

"It just dawned on me. I don't know what I look like. Maybe if I saw my face in a mirror, it'd jar my memory. Might bring something back."

"It's worth a try. I have a hand mirror upstairs in my room. I'll go get it."

The wounded man had noticed the large mirror above the dresser on the other side of the room. "Wait a minute, Miss Hannah Rose. I can get a look at myself in that mirror over the dresser."

"I don't know about that, Captain. You've had quite a shock to your system, and you've lost a lot of blood. You shouldn't be trying to walk, yet."

"I can do it. Really."

"Are you sure?"

"Yes," he said, throwing back the covers. Sitting up, he twisted around on the bed and dangled his feet over the edge. His head went light, and the room started to spin.

Hannah Rose stepped close, touched his shoulder, and said, "You'd better lie down, Captain. Let me go get my hand mirror."

"No. No," he said, lifting a hand in protest. "I'll be all right. Just let me sit here a minute. Head's a little light, that's all. It'll clear up."

"Typical man," she said, placing a hand on her hip.

"What's that supposed to mean?" he asked, looking her straight in the eye.

"The male ego. My brothers have it. My father had it. My grand-fathers had it. The old, 'I'm a rugged he-man, and don't you forget it' routine."

He gave her a crooked grin. "Think you're pretty smart, don't you?"

"Doesn't take much smarts to figure you men out. Any woman of average intelligence can stay ahead of the smartest man."

The wounded man liked Hannah Rose. Not only was she beautiful, but she had a keen sense of humor. Repeating the crooked grin, he said, "Who's to argue with such a woman?"

As he spoke, he planted his feet firmly on the floor and, using the nightstand to steady himself, stood up. When he swayed slightly, Hannah Rose gripped his arm.

"You going to be all right?" she asked.

"Sure. I'll be fine. Gotta get over there and see what kind of face I've been living with all of my life."

Hannah Rose let go of his arm and stayed at his side as he headed slowly toward the dresser. He had taken four short steps when both knees buckled. Her strong hands took hold of his arm, stabilizing him. Swaying again, he blinked and said, "Didn't realize I was so weak."

"Well, I hate to say I told you so but...I told you so."

He grinned, looked back toward the bed, then toward the dresser. "Well, since we're just about halfway, I'll humble my male ego and ask you to help me to the mirror."

"Aha! Mark one up for the female of the species!" She put an arm around him and gripped his waist, then held the arm closest to her and guided him toward the dresser. When they reached it, he braced himself on its top.

Slowly he turned his eyes to the mirror. Hannah Rose stood close, watching him.

He was quiet for nearly a minute as he eyed the man who stared back at him, turning his head from side to side.

"Well?" she said.

"Don't know him. As far as I'm concerned, I've never seen him before in my life."

"I'm sorry," Hannah Rose said. "I was hoping you'd see something that would trigger a memory."

"I had guessed my age by looking at my hands. Judging by my face, I'd say I guessed pretty close."

"And what was that?"

"Late twenties or early thirties. Pretty close, wouldn't you say?"

"I was kinder than that. Before you awakened, I estimated twenty-eight or twenty-nine...but not yet in your thirties."

Still braced against the dresser, he awarded her another crooked grin and said, "Thank you. I hope you're right. And you're what? Nineteen?"

"I am not!" she said in mock indignation. "I'm twenty-one."

"That's what I really guessed, but I wanted to be as kind to you as you were to me."

"You're impossible, Captain," Hannah Rose retorted, laughing lightly. "I think we'd best get you back to the bed."

"I think I can do it on my own. I'm feeling a little stronger."

"Are we going to go through this again?"

Without replying, he let go of the dresser and took a step toward the bed. Suddenly his knees gave way, and he started to go down. Hannah Rose leaped in front of him and caught him in her arms. "Feeling stronger, huh?" she chided.

"Well, I thought I was."

She eased her hold on him and moved back slightly. He was eight or nine inches taller than she, but their eyes met and locked for one magical moment. There was dead silence between them. Both of them felt the magic, but neither one let on.

Hannah Rose broke the spell. "All right, Captain Whatever-your-name-is, get a good hold on me, and we'll have you back to bed in no time."

He marveled at her strength, and figured it came from doing her share of the work on the farm.

When they reached the bed, she helped him onto it. Working his way to the center and lying flat on his back, he heaved a big sigh and said, "Remind me to listen to you next time."

"I'll do that," she laughed, covering him up. "Are you hungry?"

"Yes, definitely."

"You look a little pale after your little walk. No nausea?"

"No, thank the Lord, but I sure feel weak. I think some food will help. I have no idea when I ate last."

Bending over him, Hannah Rose said, "Lift your head."

When he did, she picked up the pillow, fluffed it good, then placed it under his head. "There. Comfortable?"

"Yes, thank you," he replied, lifting a hand to the bandage.

"Pain?" she asked.

"A little."

Looking closely at the bandage, she said, "I think I see blood seeping. I hope your jaunt to the mirror hasn't started it bleeding again."

"I hope not, too. Guess I'd better take it easy till I'm feeling stronger."

"Now you're making sense, Captain," she smiled. "My sister and the others should be back shortly. Well, that is, unless Doc is extra busy.

All we can do is wait. Whenever he gets here, I'm sure he'll work on that wound. You lie still and rest, now, and I'll be back with something to eat. Do you feel like breakfast, or are you in the mood for lunch? We're a little closer to lunch time, but I can make you either."

"Whatever's easiest, ma'am. Just don't go to a lot of trouble."

"Whatever I do won't be any trouble, Captain, I assure you. After all, the kind of sacrifice you soldiers make for us, we could never repay you."

"Even Union soldiers? I could be one, you know."

"I know," she said, moving toward the door. When she reached it, she stopped and said, "If all Union soldiers were like you, Captain, there wouldn't be any Civil War."

"And if all Confederate women were like you, ma'am, there wouldn't be any men in the North."

Hannah Rose batted her eyelashes coyly. "Why thank you, kind sir. That's the nicest compliment I've had all day. Or even yesterday and today put together."

She was almost out the door, when he called, "Miss Hannah Rose, I...don't know how I'm going to repay you. You didn't happen to find any money in those saddlebags, did you?"

"No, I didn't. But don't you fret about paying me back. It's not necessary, and besides, I wouldn't let you if you had money falling out your ears."

He watched her walk away, then laid an arm on his forehead and looked heavenward. "Dear Lord, whatever I may forget, please don't let me forget Hannah Rose Claiborne."

CHAPTER THIRTEEN

✦

annah Rose returned with steaming food on a tray and found her patient lying flat on his back with both hands covering his face. He brought his hands away when he heard her light footsteps and the swish of her skirt.

"Are you all right?" she asked, moving toward the bed.

He squinted tightly, then opened his eyes wide. "Just having another dizzy spell. It's about gone now."

"I decided to fix you breakfast. I've got grits and gravy, scrambled eggs, bacon, and coffee. Are you having any nausea?"

"No. No nausea. Grits and gravy, eh? Now I must be a Southerner, Miss Hannah Rose. That sounds awfully good to me."

"Could be just because you haven't eaten for so long," she said, setting the tray on the nightstand. "Think you can sit up?"

"Yes, ma'am. Smells delicious. I'm so hungry I could eat an elephant."

Hannah Rose helped him to a sitting position. "Sorry, but I don't cook elephant. Too hard to get them in the oven."

He grinned. "Shucks, I was hoping to have baked elephant for supper."

"Supper? Don't they call it *dinner* up north? I'm beginning to believe you're a son of the South, Captain."

"The thought is not unpleasant to me, ma'am. You may be right. Trouble is, I don't know how to find out."

She picked up the tray and set it on his lap. "Well, for sure we're not going to find out in the next few minutes. Might as well go ahead and eat."

He bowed his head and audibly thanked the Lord for bringing him to the Claiborne house, and for the kindness and care shown him by Hannah Rose. Then he started eating.

"You'll probably choke on it."

He looked at her, chewing a mouthful of scrambled eggs, and raised his eyebrows. "Hmm?"

"You thanked the Lord for everything but the food."

He grinned and shook his head. "Guess I'm getting a little forgetful."

Hannah Rose enjoyed his sense of humor. She laughed and said, "I don't think this latest forgetfulness is from your head wound. I think you're just a bit over-appreciative of my services."

"Well, I appreciate what you're doing, ma'am. More than you'll ever know."

Hannah Rose sat in the chair beside the bed, and they talked while he ate. He was almost finished when the sounds of people entering the house met their ears.

"Oh, they're back," she said, jumping up and heading for the door. "I hope they have Dr. Stutz with them."

Hannah Rose disappeared for a moment, then returned with the women and Dr. Elmer Stutz, who had followed them from town in his one-horse buggy. The women were glad to see their house guest awake and alert, as was the physician. Introductions were made, then Hannah Rose stayed in the room while Dr. Stutz prepared to work on the patient.

Laying him flat on his back, he lit a lantern and used its light to examine his eyes. Nodding, he handed the lantern to Hannah Rose and said, "Concussion, all right. That bullet really did a job on you, Captain."

"It would've done a bigger job if I had been standing a half-inch farther to the left."

"Might say that," grinned Stutz. "Let's get this bandage off, and let me see just how bad the wound is."

When the bandage was off, Dr. Stutz complimented Hannah Rose on the excellent job she did in cleaning and dressing the wound. It had bled some since she had bandaged it, but was not bleeding any longer.

When the wound was dressed once more and wrapped with fresh gauze, the physician said, "Now, Captain, I want to hear the story you told Hannah Rose after you came around. About all she told me in the parlor was that you can't remember anything about your past, where you are from, or even what your name is."

The women returned at Hannah Rose's call and stood by while the amnesia victim told the doctor his story. When he finished, the doctor said, "Captain—I guess it's all right to call you that—what you have is known as *selective amnesia*. While it leaves the victim with partial memory, it usually steals his identity, resulting in a blank concerning his name and anything about his past. It also leaves a blank in regard to his family and those he is close to. It doesn't change his personality or his values. A real mystery to say the least, but this is how it works nearly every time."

"Is there anything you can do that would help me get my memory back?"

Stutz shook his head slowly. "I'm sorry, but there isn't. Medical science is baffled by amnesia, especially the selective kind. There's just no medical cure for it." Pausing, he grinned and said, "Of course, experience with amnesia has taught us that sometimes a second jolt to the head will bring the entire memory back. But I don't recommend letting somebody whack you over the cranium with a club, or worse yet, having some crack-shot marksman zing another bullet along your temple."

"You don't have to worry about that," the patient chuckled. Then in a somber tone, he said, "I've got a real problem, Doctor. I know I'm a soldier, but as I mentioned in my story, I don't know of which army. The worst thing a soldier can do is run away. I don't want to be a deserter, but I can't report to either side. There's a 50 percent chance it would be the wrong side."

"You really are in a pickle, son. Tell you what. I know this Claiborne family well. The three brothers are fine men. Sooner or later, they'll show up here. Since Britt is a Confederate officer, he can give you proper advice on what to do."

"But what if it's weeks or even months till he comes home? I don't want to wear out my welcome here."

"You'd have a hard time doing that," Hannah Rose assured him. "Besides, once you're feeling up to it, we'll put you to work around here. We'll make you earn your keep."

"Besides, in the meantime your memory could come back," the doctor said.

"It could?"

"Yes. Quite often the memory will suddenly return all at once, for no apparent reason. And there have been a number of cases where the memory returned a little at a time."

"And probably a great number when it never came back at all," the patient said plaintively.

"Yes. That, too. There's really nothing you or I can do to make a difference. Only time will tell."

Dr. Stutz said he needed to get back to town, and closed up his medical bag. When the patient explained he had no money to pay him, Stutz told him there was no charge. The good doctor said he would be back to check on him in a few days and headed for the door. Linda Lee walked him to the front of the house and watched him drive away.

When she returned to the guest room, she found Hannah Rose

doing what she could to make the patient comfortable. Sally Marie said, "Since this gentleman is going to be our guest for awhile, what are we going to call him? We can't just call him 'Captain'."

The guest chuckled. "Especially when you don't even know that I *am* a captain."

"Well, since the real Wayne Gordon is dead, we could call him by that name," Linda Lee said.

"Why not?" said Aunt Myrtle. "It's a nice enough name."

"I agree," said Donna Mae.

Hannah Rose turned toward the bed and asked, "How's that sound to you?"

"Well, it's better than Herman Schmohauser or Leonardo Finklestein."

"Well, then," Hannah Rose said, "until further notice, our guest's name is Wayne Gordon."

Wayne Gordon rested the remainder of the day and got up to eat the evening meal with the Claiborne women and Myrtle Crisp. His meal earlier in the day had definitely improved his strength. At one point during supper, a dizzy spell overtook him, but it lasted only a few seconds.

When the meal was over, Hannah Rose escorted Gordon to his room. When he was back in bed, but sitting up, she told him she would return after the dishes were done and the kitchen was cleaned up.

As she turned to leave, he asked, "Miss Hannah Rose, would you have a Bible I could borrow?"

"Yes, of course," she replied, opening the top drawer of the nightstand and pulling out an old black Bible. It was well-worn, and the lettering on the leather cover was faded. Its pages were frayed on the edges. "This was my father's. As you can see, it's had a lot of use. Daddy loved God's Word and taught us from this old Book every day."

"He must've been a great man."

Tears filmed her eyes. "Yes, he was. I still miss him terribly."

When Hannah Rose was gone, Gordon opened the Bible and angled it toward the lantern that glowed on the nightstand. In the flyleaf, he found that the Bible had been a gift to Hannah Rose's father from her mother on his fortieth birthday, January 9,1844. Soon he was carefully leafing through it, noticing the underlined verses and notes in the wide margins.

Suddenly Romans 8:28 stared him in the face. It was underlined in red, and Ewing Claiborne had written beside the verse, *It's still in here!*

Wayne Gordon smiled and laid his head back against the bedstead. He looked up and half-whispered, "According to Your purpose, Lord. All things work together for good to them that love You, who are the called according to Your purpose. This amnesia. My coming to this house. Is this part of Your plan and purpose in my life? If that bullet hadn't stolen my memory, I would never have come here. I would never have met—"

"Are you comfortable, Captain Gordon?" Myrtle Crisp asked from the open door.

"Yes, ma'am," he replied with a smile, looking her direction. "Quite comfortable, thank you."

"May I talk to you for a moment?"

"Yes, of course. Please come in."

Myrtle was a pleasant little woman, and her wrinkled face displayed the warmth of her personality. Sitting down in the chair beside the bed, she said, "When you were telling your story to Dr. Stutz, you mentioned that you could remember such names as Robert E. Lee and Ulysses S. Grant."

"Yes, ma'am."

"So you know that Grant is our enemy."

"Yes, ma'am."

"The dirty dog is living in *my* house."

Wayne Gordon wasn't sure whether to believe her. Certainly if Grant was commanding the Union forces battling it out with the

Confederates in Fort Donelson, he would be housed somewhere near. He decided to test the waters. "I, ah, I thought you lived here with Hannah Rose and the others, ma'am."

"Oh, heavens no. I live several miles north of here. On the Cumberland River. Just north of Fort Donelson, in fact. That no-good Useless S. Grant just marched himself up to my front door one Sunday morning and ran me out of my house. Ornery skunk! I've had to stay here ever since. Whenever he's gone, and I can go home, who knows if I'll even have a home to go to?"

Just then Hannah Rose came through the door. Smiling, she said, "Oh! I see my dear, sweet aunt has taken a shine to you." She drew up to the bed and patted the elderly woman's shoulder. "Now Auntie, dear, Wayne is too young for you to be flirting with."

"Aw, Hannah Rose, I wasn't flirtin'. I was just tellin' this nice young man about General Useless Grant a-runnin' me out of my house."

Wayne looked to Hannah Rose for confirmation of Myrtle's claim. She understood and nodded.

"I sure hope General Grant doesn't harm your property, ma'am," he said.

"He'd better not, or I'll..."

"You'll what, Auntie dear?"

"I don't know," she replied, rising from the chair, "but I'll find some way to make him pay. Sure hope you don't turn out to be a Yankee, young feller. Sure would be a disappointment."

Nonplused, Gordon swung his gaze to Hannah Rose, who hunched her shoulders, then patted Myrtle's shoulder and said, "It's almost your bedtime, Auntie. Goodnight."

Myrtle nodded and said, "Goodnight, dear." Then to Gordon, "Goodnight to you, and pleasant dreams...unless you're a Yankee."

"Since I don't know whether I am or not, ma'am, I'll try not to dream at all."

"Well, if you ever find out that you are a Yankee, there's one thing you'd better do."

"What's that, ma'am?"

"Ask God to forgive you!" With that she wheeled and headed out the door.

Wayne Gordon looked at Hannah Rose and said, "She's a fireball."

"Quite," Hannah Rose said, easing onto the chair. "Rebel to the bone."

"Person ought to go whole-hog for what he or she believes in."

"I'll say amen to that."

There was a lengthy silence, then Hannah Rose said, "You commented earlier that you don't think you could've been a preacher. Said it just didn't seem to fit."

"Mm-hmm."

"Any hint at all about what you might have been before the war?"

He started to say no, then checked himself.

Hannah Rose caught it. "There *is* something. Tell me about it."

"I just remembered something," he said quietly, looking into her emerald eyes. "Early this morning—not long before I showed up here—I was at a small stream, washing the blood off my face and trying to slow the bleeding with ice. All of a sudden there were two Yankee lieutenants behind me, holding their guns on me. They were going to take me prisoner. I tried to explain my problem, but got nowhere. They thought I was lying."

"So what happened?"

Gordon scrubbed a hand over his face. "Well, Miss Hannah Rose, I figured I just couldn't let them take me and put me in a prison camp. So I...well, it was like...my natural instincts went to work. Before I knew it, I'd taken the gun from one of them, and a couple of seconds later, they were both dead. It was...well, it was like I'd done the same thing, or at least something akin to it, many times before."

"But it bothered you that you had to take their lives, didn't it?"

"Yes, ma'am. Especially when I thought there was a 50 percent chance I'd killed men from my own army."

"Well, if you're that good at hand-to-hand fighting, I'd say you're probably a veteran of some kind, maybe even an officer and a graduate of West Point. You've been trained to fight, so it's natural to do so."

Wayne thought about her suggestion for a moment, then said, "The West Point idea is possible, but to be a veteran, I would've had to fight in the Mexican War. I don't know if I'm old enough to have done that. When was that war?"

"I'm not sure. Let's see...I remember being about eight or nine years old then, so it must have been 1846, 1847. Let's say that you're thirty, though I think you're shy of that by a year or two. That would mean you were born in 1831 or 1832, so you would've been only fourteen or fifteen during the Mexican War. You're definitely not a veteran of that war."

"Maybe I've just been in enough hand-to-hand battles since this war began to develop some natural instincts. How long has this war been going on?"

"It'll be a year in April."

"That must be it. Maybe I'm part of one of those ranger groups in the Confederate army."

"My brothers haven't said anything about any rangers at Fort Donelson, but that doesn't mean there aren't any. Oh, I hope you are a Southerner."

Their eyes met, and before Hannah Rose looked away, he held her soft gaze and said, "I do too."

Hannah Rose met his eyes again and expressed another hope, this time only in her mind. *Oh, Wayne, I hope you don't have a wife and family.* She silently asked the Lord to forgive her selfish thoughts, and said as she rose from the chair, "Well, Captain, I think it's time for my patient to call it a day. Is there anything I can get you before you go to sleep?"

"No, thank you," he smiled. "I'm fine."

"All right, then I'll say goodnight." She extinguished the two lamps in the room and walked to the door.

"Goodnight, Miss Hannah," Wayne Gordon said warmly. "Thank you for taking in this wounded wayfarer."

"You are entirely welcome, Captain. I hope you rest well."

She closed the door, leaving him in almost total darkness. As he lay there, he marveled at the effect she had on him. He thought of that moment when their eyes locked, and wondered if she felt the same thing he did. Then he pondered the possibility that he might have a wife somewhere, maybe even children.

He tried hard to conjure up some scrap of memory, but there was only the familiar blank wall. Perspiring heavily, though the room was cool, he asked himself, *Am I married? Widowed? If I am married, what is she like? If I'm a father, what are my children like? If I have a family, will I ever see them again? Are they somewhere out there tonight, praying for my safety?*

His thoughts came back to Hannah Rose. There was no mistaking that though he had known her only a few hours, she stirred him in the depths of his heart. He lashed himself. If he had a wife, he had no business letting himself be attracted to another woman. He must keep his vows. He must keep himself only unto his wife, even in his thoughts. Especially as a Christian.

But was he married? For now, there was no way to know. Since there was a chance he was, he must not allow his heart to reach for Hannah Rose.

"Oh, dear Lord," he prayed, "You know all about me. You know who I am, where I'm from, whether or not I have a wife. Please...help me."

Lying in the darkness, he clenched his fists and held his breath, straining, trying to force his brain to reach back into the past, seize something—*anything*—and bring it to the fore. But it was like dipping a bucket into a dry well. He could recall nothing.

He lay there for a long time, weary but wide awake. His thoughts ran to Hannah Rose. He struggled to prevent it, but soon could resist it no longer. It was not until he let his mind return unhindered to her, picturing her beautiful face and remembering the tender touch of her hand, that he was able to relax and drop off to sleep.

CHAPTER FOURTEEN

✦

At the same time the amnesiac was putting on the captain's uniform in the forest, Brigadier General Charles F. Smith rode up to the house owned by Myrtle Crisp and dismounted. The moon was slanting westward in the starlit sky, and the four sentries who guarded the house came off the porch, collars turned up and greeted him.

"A bit nippy tonight, isn't it?" said Smith.

"Quite, sir," nodded one of the sentries. "Unless you have something urgent for General Grant, we must ask you to come back at sunrise. Right now, he's asleep."

"What I have is *very* urgent, Corporal," responded Smith. "Believe me, if he's not awakened immediately to see what I have for him, he will have your hide."

"Yes, sir. Let me take you inside at once."

When they stepped into the house, Smith felt the warmth of the pot-bellied stove in the parlor. Lying on the couch under a blanket was General Grant's personal physician and friend, Dr. John H. Brinton. The doctor sat up immediately.

"Sorry to awaken you, Doctor," the sentry said, "but General Smith has something urgent to show General Grant."

"I wasn't asleep, Corporal. I was up only a minute or two ago stoking the fire. Hello, General."

"Glad to see you, Doctor," Smith nodded, removing his hat and gloves.

Dr. Brinton rose from the couch and said, "I'll go awaken General Grant."

The sentry went back outside, closing the door behind him. Smith removed his overcoat and hung it on a clothes tree next to the door. Then reaching inside his uniform coat, he pulled out a sealed white envelope and held it in his hand while edging up to the pot-bellied stove. Warming his backside, he waited for General Grant to appear.

Presently, a sleepy-eyed Ulysses S. Grant entered the room, followed by his physician. Tousle-haired, Grant was in his boots and trousers, a pair of wide suspenders looped over his shoulders. The upper half of his body was covered only by his long-johns. Blinking and scratching his beard, he looked at Smith and said, "I hope this is good news."

"The best, sir!" Smith replied, smiling broadly and extending the envelope toward him. "See for yourself."

Brinton turned a lantern to full flame as Grant moved toward it and sat in a straight-backed chair beside a small table. Yawning, he ripped the envelope open, pulled out the folded sheet of paper, and angled it toward the flame.

"Why don't you read it aloud, sir?" suggested Smith. "That way Dr. Brinton can learn of it right away, too."

Grant eyed Smith. "I see it's from General Buckner, but it was sealed. How do you know its contents?"

"The Rebel lieutenant who delivered it under a white flag told me its contents, sir."

Grant nodded, then read the message aloud:

Headquarters, Fort Donelson
February 16, 1862
General Ulysses S. Grant, Sir:

In consideration of all the circumstances governing the present situation of affairs at this station, I propose to the Commanding Officer of the Federal forces the appointment of Commissioners to agree upon terms of capitulation of the forces and fort under my command, and in that view, suggest an armistice until 12 o'clock today.

I am, sir, very respectfully,

Your obedient servant,
S.B. Buckner
Brigadier General, C.S.A.

When he had finished reading the message, Grant sat silently, reading it over again. Smith and Brinton exchanged glances, but said nothing. Both men knew that Grant and Buckner had gone through West Point together, and after graduation had served together in the Regular U.S. Army. They had great respect for each other and had become good friends.

When Grant looked up, General Smith said, "This has to be difficult for you, sir. I mean, seeing that you and General Buckner are friends."

"Better than you even know," Grant replied solemnly. He thought briefly of the money Buckner had loaned him when he was in desperate need following a business failure.

"So, what are you going to do?" Dr. Brinton asked.

Grant thoughtfully stroked his beard for a long moment, then replied, "I can't let sentiment warp my thinking, here. This is war. The Confederates broke the law by seceding from the Union. They're traitors, and therefore so is General Buckner. He wants to come to terms for his surrender, but this cannot be allowed." His face crimsoned. "No terms with traitors!"

General Grant went to his valise and produced paper, pencil, and envelope. Sitting down at the small table again, he dashed off his reply:

Headquarters Army in the Field
Camp near Donelson
February 16, 1862
Brigadier General S.B. Buckner
Confederate Army

Sir: Yours of this date, proposing armistice and appointment of Commissioners to settle terms of capitulation, is just received. No terms except an unconditional and immediate surrender can be accepted. I propose to move immediately upon your works.

I am, sir, very respectfully,

Your obedient servant,
U.S. Grant
Brigadier General, U.S.A.

Grant folded the paper, placed it in the envelope, and sealed it. Handing it to Smith, he said, "Have this delivered to General Buckner immediately."

Under a westering moon, Colonel Nathan B. Forrest was preparing to lead his cavalry unit out of Fort Donelson, along with some four thousand footmen who had chosen to take their chances of making it to Nashville rather than surrender.

General Buckner had sent Lieutenant John Carmody on horseback to the Union camp with his surrender proposal an hour earlier, and was expecting him back with General Grant's reply momentarily. In the meantime, Buckner watched as some four hundred wounded men were being crammed into thirty-two large wagons.

Captain Britt Claiborne had volunteered to take the most seriously wounded men to the hospital at Clarksville, Tennessee. General Buckner had expressed his hope that General Grant would allow those who surrendered to remain at the fort until the weather warmed up. He would even ask in the terms of surrender that medical help be given those wounded men who stayed. He thanked Claiborne for being willing to take the most seriously wounded on to Clarksville, for they needed the help only a hospital could give. If they didn't get medical attention soon, most of them would die. Claiborne planned to drive one wagon himself, and his two brothers, Corporal Lanny Perkins, and other volunteers would drive the other wagons.

Generals Floyd and Pillow were ready to ride with Forrest to Nashville. They looked on as Captain Claiborne studied a map of Tennessee spread out on General Buckner's desk. By lantern light, Claiborne showed Buckner that his wagons would head southward with Colonel Forrest, skirt around Dover, and follow the west bank of the Cumberland River as it curved southeast to Bear Spring, about nine miles south of Fort Donelson. The river widened out at Bear Spring, making the water shallow enough to drive the wagons across. Colonel Forrest and those who followed him would go on southeast toward Nashville.

Once the wagons crossed the Cumberland, it was twenty-eight miles northeast to Clarksville. General Buckner's haggard face and tired eyes showed the strain he was under. He looked at Claiborne and said, "I wish there were more wagons and horses so you could take all the wounded men to the hospital, Captain."

"I do too, sir."

Buckner rubbed the back of his neck. "When you first came to me about this venture, Captain, I warned you that if Grant has scouts in the area, you could be in real trouble. I don't know but what he might send troops to run you down. If he does, you're doomed."

"My men and I realize the risk we're taking, sir," Claiborne replied evenly. "Grant's scouts might not realize that we're transporting wounded men, and even if they do, I'm not so sure Grant would hold back, even then. He might consider it a feather in his cap to wipe out four hundred of us in one sweep. I know what we're up against, sir, but my volunteers and I are determined to get these wounded men to Clarksville."

"All right, Captain, I wish you the best." Buckner paused, then asked, "You're not planning to take your men on to Nashville afterward, are you? Not in this cold weather?"

"I figure to, sir," Claiborne nodded. "We'll report in to General Floyd there."

"I think it'd be wise just to hole up in Clarksville till the weather warms up. It's a long way from Clarksville to Nashville."

General Floyd spoke up. "Captain Claiborne, as your commanding officer, I'll give you an order."

"Yes sir?"

"The way things were shaping up in central Tennessee when I left there, I really don't think General Johnston will be in Nashville long. A number of our troops are being marched down to Corinth, Mississippi. I believe that's the direction General Johnston will eventually take the troops that are in Nashville. Looks like there may end up being a major battle somewhere near Corinth. So when you've delivered the wounded men to the hospital at Clarksville, take your men and the wagons straight south to Corinth."

"Is that an order, sir?" Claiborne asked.

"It is. I'll take full responsibility for sending you down there."

"I'd like to ask that you put the orders in writing, General, just in case something happened to you."

"Of course. I'll do that right now."

At 2:30 A.M., General Buckner stood at the main gate of the fort and watched Generals Floyd and Pillow ride away with Colonel Forrest. Directly behind them were the wagons loaded with wounded soldiers, and behind them were some four thousand footmen. He breathed a prayer that they would make it without being detected by Union scouts. Remaining with Buckner were nearly twelve thousand men who preferred to take their chances with the Federal army rather than strike out for Nashville.

The long line had barely passed from view when Lieutenant Carmody came riding in with General Grant's reply. When Buckner read it, anger welled up within him. He sat down and penned his reply.

Headquarters, Fort Donelson
February 16, 1862
General Ulysses S. Grant, Sir:

The distribution of the forces under my command, incident to an unexpected change of commanders, and the overwhelming force under your command, compel me, notwithstanding the brilliant success of the Confederate arms yesterday, to accept the ungenerous and unchivalrous terms which you propose.

I am, sir,

Your very obedient servant,
S.B. Buckner
Brigadier General, C.S.A.

Carmody was given the letter to deliver to Grant, and rode away while Buckner stood at the gate and watched. When Carmody was out of sight, Buckner sighed and returned to his quarters. Once again, he breathed a prayer that Claiborne and his men would make it safely to Clarksville.

By the time the sun was up, General Buckner and his men were in enemy hands. Within an hour, they were being herded northward toward Camp Douglas, a Union prison camp near Chicago.

General Grant, upon occupying Fort Donelson, realized that a great number of Confederate troops had left the fort some time earlier. He sent out several dozen patrols to scour the countryside and hunt down as many escapees as possible.

Northern newspapers picked up on the surrender, reporting Grant's harsh approach to the Rebels at Fort Donelson. They made a play on his initials, dubbing him *U*nconditional *S*urrender Grant. They reported over nine hundred Confederates killed in the two-day battle, and nearly fifteen hundred wounded. With regret, they also reported over one thousand Federals killed and twenty-one hundred wounded.

The Federal victory at Fort Donelson touched off exuberant celebrations all over the North. When President Lincoln received word of the victory, he immediately issued orders that Grant be promoted to major-general. Lincoln sent a wire, congratulating Grant on the victory and informing him of his promotion.

Word of the defeat reached General Johnston in Nashville by mid-morning. In turn, he wired General Beauregard, who was in Alabama on the Tennessee River, awaiting orders. Johnston advised Beauregard of the Confederate defeat, then ordered him to take his troops to Corinth, Mississippi. Johnston explained he had word that Union General Don Carlos Buell was marching his forty-five-thousand-man army toward Nashville from Bowling Green. This would give Johnston only five or six days to evacuate his troops. He would meet Beauregard in Corinth.

After breakfast on February 17, Wayne Gordon shared a time of Bible reading and prayer with the women of the house. Gordon's dizzy spells had stopped, and his strength was quickly returning. Since he was feeling better, he decided it was time for a bath and shave. When Gordon had finished, he carried the bath water outside, dumped it in the yard, then hung the galvanized tub in its place on the back porch. He found the women busy in the sewing room.

Leaning on the door frame, he folded his arms and said, "Well, ladies, you'll be able to stand my presence easier now, I'm sure."

Hannah Rose looked up from her sewing, smiled and said, "The house smells better already."

Gordon gave her a sly grin as everyone laughed.

"Did you have any trouble washing around the bandage?" Hannah Rose asked.

Placing fingertips to the bandage, he replied, "A little. Got it wet along the edge while I was washing my face and neck. I'll be glad when I can wash my hair."

"A few more days," she said.

"You ladies do a lot of sewing?"

"Oh, I guess we haven't told you," Hannah Rose said, holding up the half-finished dress in her hands. "We make dresses for a clothing shop in Dover. This is how we've been making our living since the war started and there's been no one to work the farm."

"I see. Tell you what...I'm feeling like I need a little exercise. Any work I can do for you?"

"Are you sure you're up to it?"

"Well, I couldn't do real heavy work yet, but something light would be good for me."

"We haven't pitched hay down from the hayloft to the horses yet. Think you could climb into the loft and do that?"

"Sure."

"How about working the lever on the water pump?"

"No problem. I can even clean the barn for you, if it needs it."

"Let's not get carried away, Captain," Hannah Rose said. "If you do well with the feeding and watering today, we'll see about more work tomorrow. Oh, the horses will need some oats, too. I'll come out and show you the feed bin."

"No need," he said, throwing up his palms. "I'll find it. How much should I give them?"

"You'll find a hand scoop in the bin. Two of those for each horse, including yours."

"Okay, I'll get to it. See you ladies later."

Going to his room, Gordon donned his overcoat and hat, then strapped on his gunbelt. He pulled the .45 caliber revolver from its holster, broke it open, and checked the loads. Smiling, he said to himself, "Well, you've definitely worn a handgun. Checked the loads almost without thinking."

He moved out into the frosty air and went to the barn. It took him only ten minutes to complete the assigned chores. However, in pitching the hay, he found that the head of the pitchfork was loose. A little searching brought him to a small tool room within the barn, and he spent some twenty minutes repairing the loose handle.

He was about to take the pitchfork back up to the loft when he heard the barn door open and close. He noted with some amusement and curiosity that his hand went instinctively to his revolver. He moved through the door of the tool room and saw Hannah Rose looking about.

"Ah, there you are," she said, smiling. "I was getting worried about you."

"Oh. Well, while I was pitching hay, I noticed the pitchfork needed some repair. I was just going to take it back up to the loft." He reentered the tool room, came out with the pitchfork, and headed for the ladder that led to the loft.

While he was climbing the ladder, Hannah Rose said, "I'm sorry about the fork. Club usually fixes things like that."

Halting halfway up, he looked down and asked, "Who's Club?"

"A neighbor. Big as a mountain. He's been doing whatever heavy labor and repair work we've needed done around here since my brothers entered the war. Seems he overlooked the pitchfork."

"His name is *Club?*"

"Well, it's actually Clarence Clubson. As a kid growing up, he was always bigger than boys three and four years older than him. Sometimes, I guess, he got kidded about his size, and often beat up the kidders. 'Club' sort of naturally became his nickname. He...ah...he's got a powerful crush on Linda Lee, but she wants nothing to do with him. Club has the idea no other man ought to come near her, and he's been rough on some who've shown an interest in her."

"Seems to me if she's not interested in him, he ought to let her be."

"I know, but getting that across to Club is like trying to reason with a grizzly bear. In fact we had a problem over this not long ago, and come to think of it, Club hasn't come by to do any work since."

Climbing on to the top, he leaned the fork against the wall of the loft, then started back down the ladder. "Well, for a while, at least, you've got ol' whatzizname here to do the work for you. And I do mean *whatzizname.*"

As he reached the floor, Hannah Rose said, "I appreciate your willingness to do the work, Captain, but you mustn't overdo it."

"I'll pace myself, but I must also earn my keep around here."

"Just so you don't push yourself too hard and have a relapse. I'd feel terribly guilty if that happened."

Wayne Gordon felt his heart reaching for Hannah Rose. Before he realized it, he was saying, "You have the most beautiful eyes I've ever seen, Hannah Rose. They're like shining emeralds."

Hannah Rose was battling her own heart. This man stirred things within her she had never felt before. She wished he would take her in his arms and kiss her. Fighting off the feeling, she said, "Now, Captain, how can you possibly say mine are the most beautiful eyes you've ever seen? You can't *remember* all the eyes you've ever seen."

"Well, I *forgot* that I can't remember all the eyes I've ever seen. But I can tell you something for sure."

"What's that?"

"Even though I can't remember them, I still know yours are the most beautiful. Don't ask me how...just take my word that it's so."

Hannah Rose looked down at the barn floor. "Thank you," she said softly. Then slowly raising her eyes to meet his, she said, "Captain, I think it would be good if you came back into the house to rest. I'm afraid if you push yourself too hard too soon, you might have a relapse. Concussions aren't something to toy with."

"All right," he said, grinning. "I'll do that."

They entered the house, and Hannah Rose walked down the hall with him. When they reached the sewing room, she turned into it and said she would check on him later.

He entered his room, hung up his overcoat and hat, and glanced at the stranger in the dresser mirror. Then he laid down on the bed. He was tired, but thankful there had been no more dizzy spells. Hannah Rose was right. He shouldn't push himself too hard, or they could come back.

Hannah Rose. What a lovely name for such a lovely young woman. He scolded himself for what he had said about her eyes. If he had a wife...

It was almost an hour later when Wayne Gordon was awakened by the sound of male voices coming from the front part of the house. One was more predominant than the others, but none were friendly. Tiptoeing to his door, he turned the knob as quietly as possible and peered into the hallway. There was no one in his line of sight. Everyone was in the parlor. The predominant voice said, "Whether you like it or not, ma'am, we are going to search this house."

Hannah Rose half-screamed, "You Yankees have no right to come in here and search through our house! We're not harboring any Confederate soldiers! Now, Sergeant, take your two privates and get out!"

"Like I told you, ma'am," the sergeant boomed, "Fort Donelson is now in our hands. We are part of a patrol sent out by General Grant to track down Rebel soldiers. I have my orders, and I will obey them! Now, you ladies stay right here. Don't move. Okay, fellas, you search the second floor. I'll take this one."

Wayne Gordon could hear the two privates thundering up the stairs and closet doors being opened and closed on the first floor. It was only a matter of time till the sergeant entered the guest bedroom. Closing the door, Gordon hurriedly stuffed his overcoat and hat into a bureau drawer, along with his shaving mug and razor. He could hear the heavy footsteps overhead as he squeezed into the closet, along with some old coats. He slid down in the corner and pulled out his revolver, earing back the hammer. He was well-hidden, but if the Yankee decided to probe deep, he would find more than he bargained for.

Gordon sat there with mixed emotions. If only he knew which army he belonged to. If they found him, they would take him for a Rebel captain, and he would have no choice but to shoot his way out. His greater fear was that if there was gunplay, the women could get hit.

There was still rummaging going on overhead when the door of the guest bedroom came open, followed by the sound of heavy boots. Gordon tensed, aimed the .45 toward the closet door, and held his breath. His heart drummed his ribs as the door jerked open. A meaty hand pushed the clothes on the hangers back and forth impatiently, then the thudding footsteps left the room and faded up the hall.

Gordon squeezed out of the closet, dashed to the open door, and eased up to the frame, listening. He could hear the other two Yankees coming down the stairs, announcing that the second floor was unoccupied.

"Same down here," the sergeant said. Then Gordon heard him say, "Grandma, I want you to go upstairs and find something to do. The boys and I want to get a little better acquainted with these lovely young things."

Myrtle Crisp's voice cut the air sharply. "Oh, no you don't, you filthy pigs! You're not about to touch these girls!"

Gordon heard the sergeant swear at the elderly woman, followed by a loud pop. Something hit the floor. Gordon knew the man had slapped Aunt Myrtle and knocked her down. All four of the young women were screaming at him.

Gordon knew he had to intervene before the situation got any worse. He had hoped the Yankees would just quietly leave, but the women were too much of a temptation for them.

Gun-in-hand, Gordon ran down the hall and into the parlor, surprising the Yankees. Hannah Rose and her sister were bending over Aunt Myrtle. Donna Mae and Sally Marie were backing away from the two privates, moving close to the other women. Holding his gun cocked and aimed at the sergeant's head, Gordon spat, "All three of you! Play statue!"

"Don't move, boys. He'll blow my head off," the sergeant said.

"You got that exactly right, big boy!" huffed Gordon. "Now, you ladies go back to the kitchen and close the door. I'll handle this."

Suddenly a wave of dizziness washed over him, followed by another. The Yankees did not recognize it, but Hannah Rose did. She tensed. The threat of violence hung like a thick cloud over the room. Gordon blinked, shook his head, and the dizziness was gone. "Hurry, ladies."

It took the women a full thirty seconds to move out of the parlor, pass through the large dining room, and enter the kitchen. When the door clicked shut, Gordon glowered at the sergeant and hissed, "You know what I think of a man who hits a woman? I think he ought to have his nose shot off."

The sergeant's head bobbed and his face went dead-white. This Rebel captain just might be angry enough to do what he was thinking.

All three Yankees had leaned their carbines against the wall by the front door. None of them wore sidearms. The Rebel had them cold. The sergeant kept his fearful eyes on the muzzle of Gordon's .45, while the two privates looked at each other, wondering what to do.

Gordon nodded toward the front door and said, "Outside."

"Now, wait a minute!" the sergeant gasped. "War is one thing, Captain. Murder is something else."

"What do you call slapping an old woman? Is that your idea of war? Or how about what you had planned for the other women? Is that war?"

The sergeant swallowed hard and said nothing.

Gordon knew the only thing he could do was send them on their way. It wasn't in him to just shoot them down, and there was no Confederate installation to take them to. He thought about tying them up in the barn, but when they didn't report to their unit leader, there would be more Yankees coming around looking for them. All he could do was make them get on their horses and ride. He knew if he did, they would be back with more troops. But what choice did he have?

Through a front window, Gordon could see the three Union horses. Motioning toward the door with his chin, he said, "Let's go. When you get on the porch, I want one of you at a time to get on his horse and ride.

I'll say who goes when."

The Yankees looked at him as if they couldn't believe their ears. "You...you mean you're just gonna let us ride away?" one of the privates gasped.

"That's right. What's your name, Private?"

"Helms. Elbert Helms."

"Well, Private Helms, I want you to mount up first." Looking at the other private, he asked, "What's your name?"

"Bob Finch."

"You'll go second, Finch. But only when I tell you."

Fear was still on the sergeant's face. "Don't believe him, fellas. He's gonna shoot us in the back."

"I'll blow your nose off right now if you don't get out that door!" Gordon shouted.

Licking his lips nervously, the sergeant opened the door and led the way. Helms and Finch were on his heels. The man in the Confederate uniform followed them onto the porch, holding his gun on the sergeant.

Gordon felt dizziness coming on as he said, "All right, Helms, you first. Get on your...horse and...ride."

The sergeant heard the waver in Gordon's voice and looked at him over his shoulder. Gordon was fighting the swirling of his brain. The sergeant had wondered how extensive the head wound was. When he saw a glaze come over Gordon's eyes, he lunged for him.

But Gordon's instincts were still honed sharp. The sergeant was making a mistake that would be his last. The hammer of the .45 slammed down and the gun roared. The sergeant took the slug in his heart, and was dead before he fell over the edge of the porch.

Helms grabbed Gordon's wrist with one hand and the revolver with the other, but the man in gray fought back. Finch made a lunge for the gun, also, but he was a second too late. Gordon had already broken Helms's hold and had the revolver free. Swinging almost blindly, Gordon caught Helms on the temple. Helms's knees buckled. He staggered help-lessly and fell down the porch steps, sprawling on the ground.

Now Finch was on Gordon, wrestling for control of the gun. Breathing heavily, they went round and round on the porch. Gordon gal-lantly battled two enemies—the dizziness and Bob Finch.

While the life-and-death struggle continued on the porch, Helms staggered to his horse where a spare carbine rested in its boot. A stream of blood ran down his face from the gash on his temple.

Gordon and Finch stumbled off the porch, hit the ground, and continued to wrestle for control of the gun. The fall made Gordon's dizzi-ness momentarily worse, giving his opponent the advantage. Finch was not able to wrest the weapon from Gordon's grasp, but he eared back the hammer and began twisting the muzzle around to bring it to bear on Gordon's face.

Both men grunted and hissed through their teeth, knowing that one of them was going to die. Their hands quivered, meeting strength for strength.

Helms moved unsteadily toward the combatants, working the lever of the carbine. One clear opportunity and he would end the fight.

Unexpectedly, Gordon's dizziness began to vanish, and a fresh surge of strength rushed through his body. Unaware that Helms was trying to get a clear shot at him, he surprised Finch by reversing the direction of the muzzle.

Finch's eyes bulged with terror as Gordon turned the black bore of the .45 toward his forehead. The hammer snapped down, the gun fired, and Private Bob Finch was in eternity. Just as Finch's lifeless body hit the ground, Wayne Gordon jerked and staggered as the sound of an army carbine being fired assaulted his ears.

CHAPTER FIFTEEN

✦

Wayne Gordon steadied himself as he saw Private Elbert Helms land on his back. The weapon fell from his fingers and clattered to the frozen ground. Looking the other way, Gordon was shocked to see Hannah Rose Claiborne standing on the porch with a smoking carbine in her hands. She had used one of the Yankees' guns to save his life.

Her lower lip was quivering as she stammered, "He...he w-was going to shoot you. I...I had t-to stop him."

Gordon took one quick look at Helms to make sure he was dead. Turning back, he holstered his .45 and opened his arms. The emotion of the moment was too much. Hannah Rose dropped the carbine, bounded off the porch, and they were in each other's arms.

Hannah Rose was weeping as Wayne held her tight, whispering, "You saved my life, little gal! You saved my life."

Suddenly the other women poured out the front door of the house and gathered around the couple. Warily they eyed the lifeless forms of the three Yankees and praised Wayne Gordon for protecting them.

"I did my best, ladies," Gordon said. "But if it weren't for Hannah

Rose's courage and fast thinking—not to mention straight-shooting—I'd be dead."

A wagon came rolling into the yard and squeaked to a halt. The elderly man who held the reins was alone. Looking around at the corpses, he said, "I was headin' toward town and heard the shootin'. What's goin' on here?"

"It's kind of a long story, Mr. Manning," Linda Lee replied. "You probably know that Fort Donelson has fallen into Union hands."

"No, I didn't know."

Gently pulling free of Gordon's arms, Hannah Rose led him by the hand to the wagon, and said, "Mr. Manning, this is Captain Wayne Gordon. Captain Gordon, this is our neighbor to the south, Walter Manning."

Wayne extended his hand and said, "Glad to meet you, sir."

"Same here," grinned Manning, gripping Gordon's hand solidly. "You took out these scummy blue-bellies all by yourself?"

"Not exactly, sir. Miss Hannah Rose saved my life by taking out this one over here. He was about to shoot me in the back."

"Well I declare, Miss Hannah," Manning said. "I didn't know you were such a crack shot."

"I'm not really, and I hope never to have to use a gun like that again. But I think we're going to need your help, Mr. Manning. Something will have to be done with these bodies." Hannah Rose quickly explained Captain Gordon's situation and what had happened with the Yankees.

Manning grinned at Gordon and said, "I appreciate you tyin' into them no-good blue-bellies, Captain. Took courage for one man to take on three."

"Had to be done, sir," Gordon replied. He noted that Hannah Rose had wisely left out the fact of his amnesia. If Manning thought he might be a Yankee, it would only complicate things.

The old man wrapped the reins around the brake handle and climbed down. "The best thing for us to do is take these Union horses into the woods a good distance and turn 'em loose," he said to Gordon. "If you'll help me load these Yankees into the wagon, I'll get a couple of neighbors to help me bury 'em someplace where the Federals can't find 'em."

After they loaded the corpses into the wagon, Manning said, "You're lookin' a little peaked, Captain. Best you go in and lie down for a while. You catch some shrapnel in your head?"

"No, sir. A bullet grazed the left side. If I'd zigged instead of zagged, I'd be dead."

"Close one, eh? Well, let's tie these horses to the back of the wagon, and I'll take 'em a few miles and let 'em loose somewhere."

When it was done, Manning climbed up into the seat, took the reins in hand, and said, "Good luck to you, Captain. Get back in the war as soon as you can and help whip the tar outta those blue-bellies!"

"Yes, sir," Gordon nodded. He watched the wagon pull out of the yard, then worked quickly to cover the blood spots on the snow-glazed ground. More Yankees would be around looking for their missing comrades. They must not find evidence of the shootout.

When Gordon returned to the house, Hannah Rose was waiting for him in the parlor. "You're pale, Captain. Time for another rest. I'll come get you at lunch time."

Gordon's knees were watery. He didn't argue.

Lying on the bed alone, his mind replayed the moment he held Hannah Rose in his arms. It felt so right. If he had a wife, could he feel this way about Hannah Rose? How could anyone answer such a question?

The kitchen smelled of cornbread as the women prepared lunch. Only one subject occupied their conversation: the fall of Fort Donelson.

Had their men been killed? Wounded? Captured? If they were alive but in a Yankee prison camp somewhere up north, how would they ever know where they were?

Linda Lee, like the others, was concerned about her brothers, but also voiced her concern for Corporal Lanny Perkins. The women agreed that all they could do was trust the Lord to take care of their men.

Donna Mae was working at the counter in front of the window that offered a view of the back yard, corral, and outbuildings. Suddenly her eye caught movement between the barn and a small storage shed. She stared at the spot where she was sure something had moved. There was movement again, but this time she saw a man—then another...and another.

Donna Mae sucked in a deep breath and held it. The other women looked at her and saw her staring out the window with her mouth wide open. "What is it, Donna Mae?" asked Linda Lee.

"It's them!" she cried and dashed for the back door.

"It's who?" Hannah Rose called, hurrying after her, with the others following.

"Britt, William, and Robert!" Donna Mae shouted as she sprang off the porch and into Britt's arms.

Tears flowed as the happy reunion began. When Linda Lee left the porch, her eyes fell on young Lanny Perkins. She screamed his name and dashed into his arms. There were hugs and kisses all around. Finally, Britt told the women that Yankee patrols were all over the area. They needed to get inside and out of sight.

Everyone hurried into the house, and the four tired men sat around the kitchen table while the women added to what was cooking on the stove so there would be plenty for all. The women wanted to know all that had happened, so Britt began the story of Fort Donelson's fall, and the other three put in their bits and pieces. They were describing taking the wounded men to the Clarksville hospital when the amnesia victim appeared at the door that led from the kitchen to the hallway.

All conversation stopped, and the four soldiers rose to their feet. "Who's this?" Britt asked.

Hannah Rose moved to her guest and said, "Britt, William, Robert, I want you to meet Captain Wayne Gordon. Captain Gordon, these are my brothers. And this man over here is Corporal Lanny Perkins."

It was evident that Britt did not know him, but as they shook hands, Gordon watched the eyes of the other three men to catch any hint that they might recognize him. There was nothing.

Gordon was offered a chair next to Britt, and as he sat down, Hannah Rose stood behind him and said, "I have quite a story to tell about the captain, here. Let's get the food on the table, and I'll tell it while we eat. That is, after we hear the full story from our men, whom the Lord has brought back to us safely."

When the meal was ready and everyone was seated around the table, Britt gave thanks for the food and for bringing them safely back together.

As they began to eat, Britt continued on with their story. He explained that General Floyd had ordered the thirty-two wagon drivers to go to Corinth, Mississippi, where a great part of General Albert Sidney Johnston's troops were already gathering. Britt had put a lieutenant in charge of the wagons and sent them on to Corinth, advising the lieutenant that he, his brothers, and Corporal Perkins were going to make a quick trip home to let their family know they were all right, and where they were going.

They had stashed their wagons and horses in the barns of a couple of farmers near the Cumberland River. The farmers were old friends of the Claiborne family, and were glad to help. Britt told the farmers that he, his brothers, and Lanny Perkins would hole up at the Claiborne place for a few days until the Union patrols tired of searching for Rebel escapees, then they would pick up the wagons and head for Corinth.

Linda Lee looked at Lanny and said, "I'll be so glad when this horrible war is over, and we can all get back to living normal lives."

"Yeah, me too," agreed Perkins. Then turning to Hannah Rose, he said, "Before you tell us Captain Gordon's story, I think I should tell you about Jim Lynch."

Hannah Rose knew by the tone of his voice that the news was bad. Meeting Lanny's gaze, she said cautiously, "Oh, no. Don't tell me..."

"Yes, ma'am. I came across his body on the battlefield. We got separated during the fighting, and when I was heading back to the fort, I found him." Tears surfaced. "I sure will miss him."

"I'm so sorry," Hannah Rose said quietly. "He certainly was a fine man. A dedicated Christian, too. Thank the Lord we know Jim's with Him."

Everyone was quiet for a few minutes, then Hannah Rose said, "Well, let me tell you about our friend, Captain Gordon." As she told her part of the story, Wayne Gordon filled in the gaps. He told about coming to on the battlefield with his memory gone and taking the uniform and horse from the dead Confederate captain.

The men asked pointed questions, and soon understood that Gordon had no idea who he was, where he was from, whether he was married or not, and what he had done for a living before the war.

Linda Lee then told the men about the three Yankee soldiers who had come to the house that morning, and how Gordon had protected the women from them.

Britt smiled at Gordon and said, "I want you to know, my friend, how much I appreciate what you did." The other men expressed their appreciation, also.

"I just did what any man would do in such a situation," Gordon said.

"Any decent man, that is," Britt added.

"Well, thank you...and you're welcome. But can you appreciate the dilemma I'm in? I don't know which army I belong to, or even what to do to find out.

"Something in my heart tells me you're a Confederate, Captain," Hannah Rose said.

Gordon smiled at her. "I hope so." Then he said to Britt, "Dr. Stutz said whenever you showed up, as an officer, you could advise me what to do."

Britt carefully chewed his bite, laid his fork down, and wiped his mouth with his napkin. Finally, he said, "From what I've heard here, it sounds to me like you're an officer, whichever army you belong to. If so, and your memory will cooperate, you might be able to quote portions of the army manual. As an officer, I know the Confederate manual by heart. I've also seen the Union manual, and it is quite a bit different. If you can quote even a portion of the manual you learned, we'll know whether you're Rebel or Yankee. What do you think? Is it worth a try?"

"Yes, of course." Wayne Gordon's fingertips were at his temples as he concentrated. A smile broke across his face. "I think I can quote it!"

"All right, lets' hear it."

There was tension around the table as Gordon closed his eyes and began quoting from his army manual. By the time he had quoted most of Section One, Britt smiled and said, "Welcome back, sir! You're definitely a Confederate officer."

Hannah Rose jumped up from her chair and flung her arms around Gordon's neck. Suddenly she realized what she was doing, and backed away. "Oh, I'm sorry. I...I'm just so glad to know you're not a Yankee."

Gordon stood up and took her hand. "Don't be sorry, Miss Hannah Rose."

"We're all glad you're not a Yankee!" said Linda Lee, clapping her hands. Her action spurred the rest of them, and they all broke into applause. Wayne and Hannah Rose smiled at each other, then they both sat down.

"All right, Captain Claiborne, now that we know I'm a Confederate officer, what shall I do?"

"Do you think you'll be up to some travel in a day or two?"

"I'm sure I will."

"All right. We'll take you with us to Corinth. General Floyd gave me written orders to take my men and report in down there. He was certain that General Johnston—Are these names familiar to you?"

"Floyd's name isn't, but the name of General Albert Sidney Johnston sure is. He's the big gun in the western theater, isn't he?"

"Sure is. Anyway, General Floyd is certain that General Johnston will find it necessary to abandon Nashville and regroup all of his western Tennessee forces in Corinth. Since we were under General Buckner's command, and he's now a prisoner of war, we'll be assigned to existing units there in Corinth. We'll present you to whoever is in charge, tell him about your amnesia...and go from there. If General Johnston isn't there yet, it'll probably be General Beauregard."

Gordon's eyes lit up. "Beauregard! Yes, the Little Creole! I remember him all right!"

"Good!" laughed Britt. "Maybe you'll begin to remember more as time passes. What did Dr. Stutz say about it?"

"Well, he admitted that medical science knows very little about amnesia. He said my memory could come back a little at a time, all at once, or not at all. It's in the Lord's hands, and I'll have to leave it there. He allowed this to happen to me for a reason. That's what Romans 8:28 says, so I'll have to let Him work it all out."

"And God doesn't always hurry, does He?" piped up Robert.

Gordon smiled. "No, He doesn't. Unless it's to save a lost soul."

"We've been praying that the Lord will give him his memory back," Sally Marie said. "I'm sure He will in His own time."

"Well, at least we'll get you back into service at Corinth," Britt said. "Who knows? Maybe there'll be somebody amongst all those troops down there who'll know you."

Things were quiet for a few minutes as they finished their meal, then Robert said, "Britt, I've been thinking about those murders at the fort. If the killer is amongst those men who headed for Nashville with Colonel Forrest—and if they all end up at Corinth—we could have more officers getting murdered down there."

"Murders?" Donna Mae gasped. "What murders?"

Robert told how several Confederate officers had been murdered by some unknown assassin. As Robert talked, Hannah Rose noticed the rapt attention Wayne Gordon was giving him.

When a break came in the conversation, Hannah Rose said, "Captain, I couldn't help but notice your keen interest in this story. Are you getting some kind of memory flashbacks?"

Gordon nodded slowly and said, "There's definitely something, ma'am. The mention of these officers being murdered triggered something in the back of my mind, but I can't identify it."

"Well, you found yourself on that battlefield at Fort Donelson," Robert said. "You may have been among the newest reinforcements, and were told of the murders when you got there. Perhaps you're remembering being told about them."

"You're probably right, Robert," Gordon said.

"But wouldn't you men have seen Captain Gordon at the fort if he'd been part of the reinforcements?" Donna Mae asked.

"Not necessarily," Britt said. "You have to bear in mind, honey, that there were seventeen thousand men at the fort just before the battle. There were hundreds of men who never saw each other."

"Oh, I hadn't realized there were so many men there."

The meal was finished, and while the women cleaned up, the men sat in the parlor discussing the war. Frequently, one of them went to a window to see if any Union patrols were in sight. They knew the possibility was good that a search party would be looking for the three Yankees who had been killed in front of the Claiborne house that morning.

After a while, Britt and William wanted to spend time with their wives, and Lanny sat in the kitchen talking with Linda Lee. Gordon went to his room to rest, and Hannah Rose and Aunt Myrtle busied themselves in the sewing room.

The afternoon passed without any sign of patrols. After supper that evening, they all sat in the parlor enjoying the warmth of the fireplace and talked together of the war and how it was going for the South. After awhile, Aunt Myrtle announced that she was going up to bed, and shortly thereafter, the married couples retired to their rooms. Lanny was assigned a room, Robert went to his, and Linda Lee went to hers.

Wayne and Hannah Rose wanted to stay up and talk, so he threw more logs on the fire, and they sat on the floor in front of the fireplace, leaning back against the front of the couch.

They both sat and stared at the dancing flames for a few minutes, then Wayne said, "A penny for your thoughts."

When she didn't turn toward him, he leaned forward so he could see her face and saw tears in her eyes.

"What is it?" he asked.

She looked away, then down at her hands. "It's just that...you'll be leaving in a couple of days, and...and I may never see you again."

"Now, that's just not so. As soon as possible, I'll be back."

Hannah Rose sniffed and brushed a tear from her cheek. "Not if you get to Corinth and meet someone who knows you. If that happens, the first thing you'll do—which is natural—is go home. And...if you have a wife there, you'll have no reason to ever come back here."

He took hold of her hand and said, "But I may not be married, Miss Hannah Rose."

Looking him directly in the eye through her tears, she said, "I hope with all my heart that you aren't."

He swallowed hard, bit his lower lip, and choked out the words, "I hope with all my heart I'm not either, because..."

There was yearning visible in Hannah Rose's eyes. "Because why?"

Gordon struggled with his feelings. He knew he shouldn't tell her, but he was like an overloaded dam, attempting to hold back a force too great. The words gushed out. "Because I love you!"

Tears streaming down her cheeks, Hannah Rose said, "I realize we've known each other such a short time, but...is love a captive of time? Can't love be real and genuine in spite of shortness of time? It has to be so, for I've fallen in love with you, too!"

Suddenly they were in each other's arms, enjoying a sweet velvet kiss. When their lips parted, he held her close for a long moment, and neither one spoke. Finally, he eased back, looked into her eyes, and said, "I don't know what to do. My thinking is that if I have a wife, the Lord wouldn't let me fall for you like this...but I just don't know."

Hannah Rose looked at him in the firelight with adoring eyes. She reached above the bandage that encircled his head and stroked his thick locks. "You're such a good man, Capt—Wayne—oh, I don't know what to call you. You're such a good man, *darling*. I guess I should tell you I'm sorry to complicate your life like this, but I'm not. If I can have your love only for a few days, I will accept it."

He kissed her again, then said, "Even with my shadowed memories, Hannah Rose Claiborne, I know one thing for sure. There has never been a woman so sweet and wonderful as you. It's just impossible for me to believe that I have a wife out there somewhere. How could I feel so much love for you, if—Oh, Hannah Rose, this has to be the hardest thing I've ever faced."

"You have such a true and honest heart," she whispered. "If it should turn out that you are married, you and I both know the only right thing before the Lord will be for you to return to your wife."

He closed his eyes and held Hannah Rose tight. Throat constricted, he choked, "The only right thing for me to do, Hannah Rose, is to get out of your life so you can forget me quicker."

"Forget you? How can I forget you? I know my heart. I will always love you. I know for now we mustn't let things get any stronger between us, but until you have to leave, please let me at least have you near me."

Wayne blew out the lantern in his room a little while later and settled his head on the pillow. He knew what Hannah Rose had said was right. They must not allow what they felt for each other to grow any stronger. They would keep proper distance until and unless they learned that he did not have a wife. He stared into the darkness and prayed that he would find out soon.

CHAPTER SIXTEEN

The next day, Hannah Rose and Linda Lee drove into town to deliver four new dresses to the clothing store and to pick up some groceries. When they returned, they pulled the wagon up to the back porch, and the men started out the door to carry in the groceries. Linda Lee waved them back in, saying in a hushed voice, "Stay inside! We just saw a Yankee patrol!"

When Hannah Rose and Linda Lee entered the kitchen with the first load of groceries, everyone gathered around.

"They're about a mile north of here," Hannah Rose said. "They passed within a hundred yards of us. They looked our direction, watched us for about half a minute, then went on."

"I hope they keep going," Myrtle said.

"Oh, and Aunt Myrtle," said Linda Lee, "we were told in town that General Grant has left the area. I hope you still have a house."

"Well, ol' Useless S. Grant promised they wouldn't do any damage, but who can believe anything a stinkin' Yankee says?"

"We'll go with you and check it out," Hannah Rose said.

"'Tain't necessary," said the oldster, shaking her head. "I'll drive on home after lunch. If there's any problem, I'll be back."

"We'd be glad to go with you," said Donna Mae.

"You just stay here with your husband, dearie," said Myrtle, patting her arm. "He'll be leavin' soon enough. You two need all the time you can get."

"If it weren't for the possibility of running into a patrol, us fellas would take you, Aunt Myrtle," William said. "I just don't like the thought of you driving home by yourself."

"Hey, boy," Myrtle chuckled, "I've been drivin' myself around for a long time. If I run into one of them Yankee patrols, they ain't gonna mistake me for a Rebel soldier, are they?"

"Well, no, but—"

"It's settled, then. I'll head for home right after lunch. Like I told you, if my house ain't livable, I'll be back. If you don't see me in a couple of hours, you'll know everything's okay."

Hannah Rose turned to the amnesia victim and said, "Captain, I saw Dr. Stutz on the street. He asked if you could come into town tomorrow and let him check your wound and change the bandage. He suggested you borrow some civilian clothes from Britt—since you're about the same size—and ride in with a couple of us girls. If a Yankee patrol stops us, you're a friend of the family who's been injured, and we're taking you to the doctor."

"Guess that'd work," nodded Gordon. "And I'm sure it's best that Dr. Stutz checks this wound. I don't need blood-poisoning, along with everything else."

When Aunt Myrtle had not returned by mid-afternoon, Hannah Rose decided she would not rest until she knew everything was all right. When she announced that she was going to drive over to check on Aunt Myrtle, Linda Lee volunteered to go with her.

The sun was lowering in the western sky when Hannah Rose and Linda Lee started for home. They had found Aunt Myrtle cleaning her house, which General Grant had not harmed in any way. The wagon swung onto the road that led to Dover, and headed for the Claiborne farm, about two miles in the distance. At the same time, they saw Club Clubson coming from town on horseback. He stood up in the stirrups and waved his hat.

"Brace yourself, honey," Hannah Rose said. "Here comes Romeo."

"Well, I'm not Juliet," Linda Lee sighed.

It took Club only a few seconds to trot his horse up beside the wagon. "Hello, Linda Lee...Miss Hannah Rose," he said, smiling.

Both women nodded a greeting.

Hannah Rose held the reins and kept the wagon moving. Keeping pace, Club asked, "Where ya been?"

"Aunt Myrtle's," Hannah Rose answered.

"Goin' home, now, huh?"

"Yes." Again it was the older sister who spoke.

"Cat got your tongue, Linda Lee?" asked Club.

"No," she said, looking up at him, "but Hannah Rose is capable of answering your questions."

"I s'pose you heard about the Yankees takin' Fort Donelson."

"Yes," replied Linda Lee. "Our brothers escaped. They're at the house right now."

"Oh. So you don't need me doin' any work while they're there, huh?"

"No."

Club was thoughtfully quiet for a moment, then said, "One good thing about the fort bein' captured by the Yankees."

"What could be good about that?" Linda Lee asked.

"There ain't no soldiers gonna come around your house wantin' to court you."

"Even if they did, it wouldn't be any of your business."

"Linda Lee, when are you gonna quit talkin' that way? Of course it's my business. I'm plannin' to marry you some day. Just as soon as you figger out—"

"Clarence! I've tried to be nice to you, but you won't listen to reason. I'll court whoever I want, and you can't do anything about it."

"Well, I *can* do somethin' about it! I can crack the skull of every man who shows up on your doorstep! And I will, too! You belong to me, Linda Lee. The sooner you figger that out, the better it's gonna be for both of us!"

With that, Club gouged the sides of his horse and galloped away. Looking back twice, he burned Linda Lee with blazing eyes.

"Oh, sis, when am I going to be rid of him?"

"Like we've said all along—not until you meet the right man and marry him. That man will have to make Club understand he's to leave you alone."

"I have met the right man, sis," Linda Lee said, turning toward her on the seat. "I know Lanny and I will have to wait till this dumb war is over before we can get serious about marriage, but he's in love with me, and wants to marry me. He said so."

"Well, if he's the Lord's choice for you, honey, it'll all work out."

"Yes, I suppose you're right," Linda Lee sighed as they drew near the Claiborne house.

That evening, Hannah Rose and Wayne Gordon were careful not to be alone together. When the rest of the family decided it was time to call it a day, they went to their respective rooms. No one in the house knew it, but both lay in their beds, staring into the darkness, wishing they could be together.

The next morning, Gordon put on Britt's civilian clothes and hitched the horses to the wagon. He helped the Claiborne sisters aboard, then drove toward town. Purposely, they arranged for Linda Lee to sit between Wayne and Hannah Rose.

They saw no Union patrols while driving into town, for which they were thankful. As they turned onto Main Street and headed for Dr. Stutz's office, they were not aware that Club Clubson happened to see them through the barbershop window. He focused on the stranger who was driving and noted that Linda Lee was sitting next to him.

Wrath boiled up inside him. *Who's this new man Linda Lee has attached herself to? She's gone and dug herself up some dandy wearing a wide-brimmed hat cocked sideways.* Cursing under his breath, Club paid the barber and stepped onto the boardwalk. He moved into the street so he could see where Linda Lee and Hannah Rose were going with Linda Lee's new suitor. When the wagon pulled up in front of the blacksmith shop, he rolled his massive shoulders, set his jaw, and headed that direction.

There was no place to park in front of the doctor's office, so Wayne parked across the street in front of the blacksmith shop. He set the brake, then hopped down. Looking past Linda Lee, he said, "I'll help her down first, Hannah Rose, then I'll come around that side and help you."

Linda Lee was wearing a new pair of low-cut shoes, and the soles were slick. She placed her right foot on the metal step on the side of the wagon, then let Wayne support part of her weight with his hands as she lifted her other foot over the side. Suddenly her right foot slipped, and she fell straight down, raking her ankle on the metal step.

"Oh!" she gasped as Wayne caught her in his arms. He backed a couple of steps from the wagon and eased her onto her feet "I'm sorry," he said. "Are you all right?"

Hannah Rose climbed down from the wagon and hurried toward them.

"It wasn't your fault, Captain," Linda Lee said. "The soles on these shoes are just too slick. I...I scraped my ankle."

Hannah Rose bent over and lifted her sister's skirt high enough to assess the damage. "Oh, dear," she said, "you really scraped it bad, honey. Can you walk okay?"

Linda Lee took a step and winced, sucking air through her teeth. "It hurts pretty bad, but I can make it to Doc's office."

"No need for that," said Wayne. "I'll carry you."

"That's kind of you, Captain, but I can—" Even as she spoke, he bent over and swept her off her feet.

Just then, Hannah Rose looked up the street and saw Club Clubson coming on the run.

"Oh-oh," she said. "We've got trouble."

Wayne and Linda Lee, who had her arms around his neck, turned to see the huge man bearing down on them.

"What's his problem?" Gordon asked.

"That's Club Clubson," Hannah Rose said. "I told you about him."

"Oh, the guy who has a crush on little sister here."

"And doesn't want any other man to come near her."

"He'll want to fight you, Wayne," Linda Lee said with a quiver in her voice. "Don't let him push you into it. He's dangerous."

Club drew up with rage bulging his eyes. "Put her down, mister!"

Wayne Gordon could remember nothing about his past, but Club's insolence stirred within him some primal, bred-in-the-bone desire to resist. He found no trace of fear for the man who was much bigger than he. He met Club's gaze with icy eyes and asked, "Why should I?"

Clarence Clubson was not used to being defied. Men had always cowered in his presence. The bold impudence of the smaller man fired his temper even more. His cheeks went darker, and he seemed to swell in size. "I told you to put her down!"

A crowd was gathering. The people of Dover had seen Club in temper tantrums before.

Ignoring him, Gordon said to Hannah Rose, "Let's get her to the doctor," and he started across the street.

Club leaped in front of Gordon, barring his way, and bellowed,

"Put Linda Lee down! She's my woman!"

Hannah Rose stepped between them, facing the giant, and said in a calm voice, "Club, Linda Lee hurt herself climbing down from the wagon. This man is carrying her because she's in pain. He's taking her to Dr. Stutz."

"She was sittin' next to him in the wagon! I saw it!" Looking past Hannah Rose, Club growled, "If you don't put her down, I'll beat you to a pulp!"

Purposely blocking Club's path, Hannah Rose said over her shoulder, "Go on, Wayne. Get her into the office."

Club cursed and slammed Hannah Rose aside with his massive arm. The crowd gasped when she tumbled to the street. Two men dashed from the side of the street to help her up.

Gordon regarded Club with eyes of venom and said through clenched teeth, "You wait right there."

Club knew he had the fight he wanted. Any man who rivaled him for Linda Lee's affection had to be disposed of. This wouldn't take long.

Still carrying Linda Lee in his arms, Gordon went to Hannah Rose and asked, "Are you hurt?"

Her hair was disheveled and there was dust on her face and dress, but she assured him she was all right.

"He's going to pay for that," Gordon said. "But first, let's get sis into the doctor's office."

Both sisters begged Wayne not to fight Club, but their words fell on angry, deaf ears. He carried Linda Lee to the door of the office where he found Dr. Stutz waiting.

Setting her down, Gordon said, "Take care of her, Doc. I'll let you check me and change my bandage later."

"Don't do it, son," Stutz pleaded. "With your concussion, it could be very dangerous."

Hannah Rose had fear in her eyes. "Doc's right, Wayne. Club's vicious! He'll—"

"That sorry excuse for a man knocked you down, and I won't stand for it. I don't care how big or vicious he is."

Leaving those words to hang in the air, Wayne Gordon set his gaze on the yellow-haired giant. Removing Britt Claiborne's wide-brimmed hat and coat, he handed them to the nearest man and said, "Hold these for me, please."

"Sure," the man nodded, wondering if this tall, slender stranger with the bandage encircling his head would ever need the coat and hat again.

Club felt better already with Linda Lee out of the man's arms. He flexed his bull-like shoulders and massive arms, pleased that a large crowd was looking on. He heard a woman ask her husband to get the town constable. A man standing near said, "Somebody already thought of that, Mrs. Jenkins. Constable Herrick is out of town."

Club laughed within. Constable Dale Herrick had given him trouble in the past for beating up men in his town. There would be no interference this time.

Gordon halted six feet from Club and regarded him with contempt. "Man who roughs up a woman is the lowest form of man there is."

"She got in the way. If you'd put Linda Lee down the first time I told ya, it wouldn't have happened."

Gordon's instincts told him to get in the first lick. He took a quick step forward, aiming a fist at Club's jaw. Club tried to dodge it, but he was too slow. The punch landed solidly and his head snapped back. On the rebound, Gordon popped him with a stiff left jab, then followed quickly with another right to the jaw. Club staggered sideways. Before he could stabilize himself, Gordon gave him a hard shove with his foot. Club stumbled and fell on his face.

The crowd cheered and applauded, which made Club angrier than ever. He was cursing a blue streak as he raised up on his hands and knees. He was just about to stand when Gordon planted his boot on his backside and shoved him again. All balance gone, Club went face-down, reduced to a clumsy, scrabbling buffoon. Swearing more than ever, he came up in a crouching position and pivoted so he could see his opponent. The curse that left his lips was a low, strangled growl.

Humiliated as the crowd continued to cheer, Club rose to his feet, breathing heavily, more from anger than exertion. Gordon was making a fool of him. This was too much. Club would kill the man right here in front of everybody.

Ejecting a beastly growl, Club went after Gordon. Gordon caught him with a glancing blow, but Club slammed him with a meaty fist flush on the jaw. The impact sent a shower of stars through Gordon's head, and a name seemed to echo against the walls of his brain. He felt his feet leave the ground. The brilliant midday sun blinded him for a second, then he rolled over in the dust and started to get up. Club kicked him in the ribs. The breath gushed from his lungs, and a fiery streamer of pain shot through his body. A wave of dizziness washed over him, and he felt a touch of gloom. If he went dizzy now, he was done for. There was murder in Club's eyes, and Gordon doubted that anyone would try to stop the man if he went for the kill. Hannah Rose might, but what could she do?

Club attempted to kick him again, but Gordon dodged the hissing foot, grabbed the man by the ankle, and gave a savage twist. Club howled and landed on the wagon-rutted street with a heavy thump.

Gordon leaped to his feet, ignoring the pain in his ribs. He waited for Club to get up, then charged him, landing four quick punches to Club's face. Club staggered, but came back strong, though he limped on the injured ankle and his lip was split.

The brassy taste of blood fueled Club's fire. He moved in and landed a glancing haymaker to Gordon's temple, enough to send more stars rushing through his head and let him hear the name he had heard earlier.

Gordon was sure the blows to his head were giving him some kind of flashback. It was a blow to the head that robbed him of his memory, and now some powerful blows had made a name echo through his mind.

He tried to focus on it, but there wasn't time.

He noticed his bandage was loose. He knew if the wound opened up, he was in deep trouble. Countering quickly, he landed a hard punch to Club's wide nose. It made the big man blink and filled his eyes with tears. Gordon smashed the nose two more times, then felt a dizzy spell coming on. He staggered, swaying, and took a hard blow to the left cheekbone. He felt as if he were falling through an endless black hole, but was aware of the crowd shouting for him to finish Clubson off.

The name came again: *Julie*. It echoed through his mind over and over. He rolled to his feet, and became aware that they were now fighting at the wide doorway of the blacksmith shop.

The dizziness was subsiding again as Club came at Gordon. He took a couple of backward steps and bumped against the door frame. He could feel a trickle of blood flowing down his face from beneath the loosened bandages. Club closed in and threw a right jab that Wayne ducked in the nick of time.

Club's fist banged against the solid wood. He howled in agony, grabbing the fist with his other hand. His wide face was now smeared with blood from his mouth and nose.

Jerry Spaulding, the blacksmith, had deserted his shop and joined the crowd as they pressed into the middle of the street, not wanting to miss the finish, whenever it came. Inside the shop, two draft horses that were there being fitted for shoes were becoming increasingly nervous with the combatants fighting so close behind them. They whinnied, fought their bits, and struggled against the leathers that kept them tied to the posts.

Gordon got in another good punch, popping Club's head back, then the giant blindly swung his wounded right fist. Gordon ducked as before, and the big doors rattled with the impact. Club let out a wild howl.

Club threw his weight against Gordon, knocking him off balance. Suddenly the Confederate officer found himself wrapped in a vise from behind. His feet were off the ground. Club had broken his right hand and could no longer punch with it, but he had Gordon in a deadly bear hug, bearing down with all his might.

Gordon felt the breath leave his lungs. His already damaged ribs ached as Club did his best to crush him. Gordon caught a glimpse of Hannah Rose in the crowd. Her disheveled hair reminded him of what Club had done to her. His fury grew like a prairie fire in a high wind. Gritting his teeth, he threw both hands back and jabbed his thumbs in Club's eyes.

Screaming wildly, Club whirled and threw Gordon fifteen feet through the air. Gordon rolled toward the two horses, striking his head on the side of the firepit. He was barely aware that the massive animals were whinnying and kicking blindly behind them. The deathly hooves of the closest horse missed his head only by a couple of feet.

The jolt of striking the firepit sent another meteor shower through Gordon's head, but immediately upon the heels of the shower, he saw the image of a young woman and heard the name *Julie* come from his lips.

Suddenly he saw Club shuffling toward him, wielding a five-foot steel bar he had found leaning against the wall of the shop. Spaulding was silhouetted against the stark sunlight in the wide door, shouting at Club to stop. Those outside stood wide-eyed.

But Club paid no attention to the blacksmith. He was coming for the kill, and Wayne Gordon knew it. Scrambling to his feet, he met Club head-on, gripping the steel bar. With his brute strength, Club swung Gordon around toward the door, breaking his hold on the bar. Gordon staggered backward. Club gripped the bar at one end and rushed at his opponent, swinging the deadly thing wildly. Gordon's back was against the door frame again, and he ducked the hissing bar as it came at his head. The horses, eyes bulging, were neighing with fear and dancing about, still fighting the leathers that held them to the posts.

The bar struck the door frame with a deafening bang, showering splinters in every direction. The sound echoed down the street like the crack of a rifle. Catching Club off balance, Gordon planted his feet and landed a solid blow to his jaw. Club staggered, but did not go down. Nor did he let go of the bar.

Club swung the bar wildly and missed, throwing himself off balance. His ponderous body went full-circle, plummeting him toward the terrified horses. Club's feet tangled, and he fell forward, slamming into the rumps of both animals. Suddenly the powerful hooves were up and kicking blindly at the object that had bumped them. Two hooves found Club's head, caving in his skull. When he fell dead, the terrified animals continued to whinny and kick the lifeless body.

Wayne Gordon, still fighting dizziness, staggered toward the door and collapsed. Still conscious, he was carried by two men into Dr. Stutz's office and laid on the examining table. While Hannah Rose stood close by, the kindly physician checked the head wound and found, surprisingly, that it had not been severely damaged. He cleaned it up, dressed it good, and put on a new bandage. There were no serious injuries. Hannah Rose embraced him, relieved that he had not been maimed or killed.

Linda Lee's ankle had been bandaged up, and according to Stutz, would heal without any further complications. Together, the weary amnesia victim and the two women boarded the wagon and headed for home.

Linda Lee and Hannah Rose thanked Gordon for standing up to Club. Though Club had been a pest in her life, Linda Lee was sorry he was dead. She told herself if only he had listened to her, he would still be alive.

CHAPTER SEVENTEEN

★

A week passed, and Wayne Gordon was back to full strength. Twice during that time he had been checked by Dr. Stutz, and the second time, the bandage came off. There were no more sightings of Union patrols, and on Tuesday, February 25, Britt Claiborne announced it was time to leave for Corinth. They would head south at sunrise the next morning.

When supper was over on Tuesday night, the married couples bundled up and took a walk in the light of a half-moon, as did Lanny and Linda Lee. Robert, Hannah Rose, and Wayne Gordon were in the parlor, sitting in front of the fireplace. The flickering shadows from the fire danced on their faces. Wayne and Hannah Rose sat at opposite ends of the couch, and Robert was between them on the floor. The conversation centered on the war and the departure of the men in the morning. Hannah Rose was having trouble disguising her feelings of dread.

Robert knew his sister well. Looking up at her, he said, "Sis, you and Wayne are making a good try at it, but it's obvious you're losing the battle."

"What are you talking about?" asked Hannah Rose.

Robert grinned from ear to ear, glanced up at Wayne, then looked at his sister and replied, "Come on. We've all talked about it when you two weren't around. You're so much in love, a blind man would know it."

Wayne and Hannah Rose exchanged quick glances.

"We all understand," said Robert, rising to his feet and looking down at them. "Wayne may have a wife and children somewhere. You two have faced the possibility, and are doing your best to keep from getting any more attached to each other. Am I hitting the proverbial nail right on the head?"

Wayne stood up, shoved his hands in his pockets, and said, "I didn't realize we were so obvious. But you're right, Robert. Even though we've only known each other a short while, your sister and I have fallen head-over-heels in love."

"So when we pull out of here in the morning, you both know it could be the last time you ever see each other."

"It'll have to be, if I get to Corinth and find someone who knows me...and that leads me to a wife. No matter how I feel about Hannah Rose, the only right thing is to go back to my wife."

"It's hard for me even to imagine what you're going through," Robert said with compassion in his voice. "But...well, we've talked about Romans 8:28. The Lord certainly could have prevented that bullet from taking away your memory. He didn't, so this has to work out for your good. It has to be part of His plan and purpose for you."

"You're right," Hannah Rose said, rising from the couch. Embracing Robert, she said, "I love you, big brother. Thank you for caring. Wayne and I need a lot of prayer right now."

Robert gave his sister a tight squeeze and said, "You also need a little time together. Morning will come all too soon." With that, he turned and left the room.

Wayne and Hannah Rose stood looking at each other by the light of the fire. A long moment passed, then he said, "I guess I better go to my room."

Hannah Rose was fighting tears. Lips quivering, she nodded, "You need to get a good night's rest."

Wayne had not told Hannah Rose about the flashbacks that had come to him while fighting Club Clubson. Even as he stood there, he could clearly picture the face of the young woman named Julie. Who was she? An old girlfriend? A fiancée? His wife?

Hannah Rose was fighting her own battle. She had fallen in love with this man the very day he entered her life—the man without a name, the man who very possibly belonged to another woman. This man was going to ride away tomorrow and maybe never return.

Wayne told himself he would rather be on the front line of battle facing enemy guns than the torment ripping at his insides. When he saw the tears trail down Hannah Rose's cheeks, it was more than he could bear.

Through her tears, Hannah Rose half-whispered, "I love you so much."

The barrier they had tried so hard to erect suddenly crumbled. They rushed to each other and embraced.

"The thought of never seeing you again is driving me wild!" Wayne said, choking on the words,

Hannah Rose broke into heart-wrenching sobs and hung on to him as if her very life depended on his presence.

When their emotions had settled, they sat together on the couch, holding hands and staring into the fire.

Soon the other couples returned. Lanny and Linda Lee announced they had become engaged and would marry as soon as the war was over. Everyone rejoiced with the young couple and congratulated them. No one said anything about the dilemma Wayne and Hannah Rose faced, though everyone wondered how the announcement of the engagement affected them.

Soon the heartsick couple found themselves alone once again. They sat together on the couch, staring silently into the dying embers. Holding Hannah Rose's hand, Wayne looked into her emerald eyes and said, "I know we both need to get some sleep. I was just thinking of what the Bible says in Proverbs 3:5 and 6. It really fits our situation."

Hannah Rose squeezed his hand and nodded. "I know the verses well."

"Let's pray and ask the Lord to help us to do our part—to trust Him—so He can direct our paths," Wayne said.

Hannah Rose was fighting tears again as together they knelt beside the couch, clasping hands. Wayne poured out his heart, saying, "Lord, both of us want to do what is right. If I have a wife waiting for me somewhere, then please help me find her somehow. Lord, You've allowed all of this to happen for a purpose. Help us both to acknowledge You in all our ways, and not to lean to our own feeble understanding. As You direct our paths, please help us to accept Your will as You reveal it to us. And...if it isn't Your will for us to have a life together, please give this wonderful woman the man You have for her."

He was about to close when Hannah Rose said, "Lord Jesus, You know my heart better than I do, but I know it well enough to say for sure that if this man I'm holding onto is not to come back to me, I can never love another man. Give me the grace, then, to face the future as I trust in You with all my heart. Amen."

Wayne was overwhelmed. Tears filmed his eyes as he helped Hannah Rose to her feet and folded her in his arms. Then he walked her to her room, kissed her goodnight, and waited till she closed the door. He went downstairs to his room and spent a restless night.

The next morning, Wayne Gordon donned his Confederate uniform and saddled his horse. He would walk with the other men, leading the horse, until they reached the farms where they had stashed the wagons and teams. Then he would ride with them south for Corinth.

Tears were shed as the Claiborne women told their men good-bye. Hannah Rose promised Wayne she would pray for him every day. He promised the same, adding that with the uncertainty of the war, there was no way he could say when she might hear from him or see him again. They would have to leave it in the Lord's hands.

When all the good-byes had been said, Wayne kissed Hannah Rose in front of everyone, told her he loved her, and joined the other men.

The women stood in front of the big white house and watched their men until they vanished from sight, then turned and went inside.

The surrender of Fort Donelson was an unmitigated disaster for the Confederacy. Morale was low when Brigadiers John Floyd and Gideon Pillow arrived in Nashville with Colonel Nathan Forrest and their four thousand troops. They found Confederate commander General Albert Sidney Johnston packing up his troops, ready to abandon the city and head for Corinth, Mississippi.

Johnston—happy to see that so many men had escaped the fort—explained that thirty-five thousand Union troops were headed for Nashville from Bowling Green, Kentucky, under the leadership of General Don Carlos Buell. Nashville was doomed to fall into Federal hands.

Forrest told Johnston his men needed to rest before striking out on the long journey to Corinth. Since it would still be several days before Buell and his army arrived, Forrest advised Johnston to take his troops and start south. Forrest and his men would follow within a couple of days.

With the month of March came heavy rains, but Johnston's troops and thousands of Confederates commanded by General Pierre G.T. Beauregard braved the weather and headed for Corinth.

Johnston had chosen Corinth because it was a strategic rail junction for the Mobile & Ohio and Memphis & Charleston Railroads. If Corinth fell to the Union, Memphis would be cut off from its supply lines on the Atlantic coast, and Mobile—which was vital for supplies coming in from the Gulf of Mexico—would lose its communication link into the vastly important Tennessee valley.

By the time the prisoners from Fort Donelson arrived at Camp Douglas, Illinois, Union commander General Henry Halleck had received important news at his headquarters in St. Louis. Federal spies within the Confederate army were reporting that General Johnston was planning to move nearly his entire force to Corinth.

Halleck went to work and drew up a plan. He would send a massive force to Corinth, wipe out the Rebels, and take the strategic railroad junction for the Union. This would cripple the Confederate cause in the western theater and help bring an end to the war.

In his plan, Halleck would let General Buell, commander of the Union Army of the Ohio, capture Nashville, then take four of his divisions to Corinth, leaving two to hold the city. He would also send General Ulysses S. Grant and his Union Army of the Tennessee and all six of his divisions to join forces with Buell. This would give the Federals an approximate strength of sixty-seven thousand men. From what Halleck knew of Johnston's army, all four corps could not total more than about forty thousand.

Halleck figured to have his troops near Corinth and ready to attack the Confederate stronghold by early April.

General Johnston knew that sooner or later, the Union military leaders would make the rail center at Corinth an objective for capture. With Nashville in Federal hands, it would probably be sooner. What better place than Corinth for Johnston to mass his troops and be ready to launch a devastating counterattack against the boldly aggressive Yankees?

Confederate troops streamed into Corinth from every direction. Among the converging Rebels were five thousand men of First Division, I Corps under Major General Leonidas Polk, who marched from

Columbus, Kentucky. Under General Johnston's orders, Polk had sent the five thousand men of Second Division to defend Island Number Ten, a fortified piece of real estate that blocked the Mississippi River near New Madrid, Missouri. The Confederacy could not afford to leave Island Number Ten unprotected.

Also among those streaming into Corinth were fifteen thousand men of II Corps under Major General Braxton Bragg. Bragg and his Second Division commander, Brigadier General Jones M. Withers, came with ten thousand from Pensacola, Florida, and First Division under Brigadier General Daniel Ruggles came with five thousand from New Orleans.

The Claiborne brothers, Corporal Lanny Perkins, and the man who called himself Wayne Gordon arrived at the Confederate army camp on Saturday, March 8. They had spotted two Union patrols along the banks of the Cumberland River just before they reached the first farm where they had stashed horses and wagons. They had holed up for a few days to make sure travel was safe, and heavy rains had also slowed them. They were immediately assigned to II Corps, Army of the Mississippi, commanded by General Bragg. Bragg placed them in First Division under General Ruggles.

The Claiborne brothers and Perkins were pleased to see a number of men they knew from Fort Donelson, including John Carmody, who had carried the messages between Buckner and Grant at the time of Fort Donelson's surrender. Carmody told them that when he returned to Fort Donelson with Grant's message demanding unconditional surrender, he took advantage of the opportunity to escape, and rode hard to catch up with Colonel Forrest and his troops. He was glad he did, since General Buckner and the nearly twelve thousand men who stayed were now in a Yankee prison camp.

While the Claibornes and Perkins greeted men they knew, Wayne Gordon watched to see if anyone recognized him. There was no sign that anyone did.

Captain Britt Claiborne then introduced Captain Wayne Gordon to General Bragg and told him they needed to talk with him and General Ruggles about a serious problem. Bragg, who was a soldier's soldier, said that whatever the problem was, it needed to be dealt with. He called for General Ruggles to appear at once. In Bragg's large tent, the generals listened to Gordon's story with keen interest. Gordon also showed the generals that he could quote the Confederate army manual almost perfectly, and Britt vouched for Gordon's integrity and ability to handle himself in threatening situations.

Thinking on it for a few moments, General Bragg decided the amnesia victim would come in as a captain and remain Wayne Gordon, since the real Wayne Gordon was dead and not known in the Army of the Mississippi. Gordon would be in Ruggles's First Division, along with Captain Claiborne. Bragg thought it best that Gordon not try to hide his amnesia, but to let the men in the camp find out as occasion dictated. Bragg would put Captain Claiborne in command of a company, and let Gordon work closely with him until he had proven himself in battle. Once Bragg received a satisfactory report, Gordon would be given a company of his own.

That night at supper, the Claibornes, Gordon, and Perkins learned from Captain Waldon McGuire that First Division II Corps had some two thousand men in it who had been at Fort Donelson and had followed Colonel Forrest to Nashville.

When the meal was over and they sat around their chosen fire drinking coffee, Britt eyed McGuire in the orange light between them and said, "Captain, I hate to ask this, but have there been any more officers murdered?"

"No, thank God. Many of the Fort Donelson men and I have talked about that since we arrived here. It looks like the assassin was either killed in the Fort Donelson battle or allowed himself to be captured and taken to the Union prison camp. If he was, as we suspect, a Union plant, it won't be hard to get himself out of the camp."

"Well, if I could vote on it," William Claiborne said, "I'd vote him killed in the battle and say good riddance."

Sergeants Cliff Nolan and Randall Weathers had been standing nearby and now joined them.

"Excuse us, gentlemen," Nolan said, "but Randall and I couldn't help but overhear your discussion."

"Sit down," gestured McGuire, adjusting his position to allow room for one man to sit next to him. The others followed suit, and the two sergeants sat down.

"Randall and I have talked about this with many of the men from Donelson," said Nolan, "and like Sergeant Claiborne here, we all hope the bloody fiend is dead."

Weathers slid his cap to the back of his head and spoke to McGuire. "Captain, we only got in on part of the conversation. Did you explain to these men that General Johnston has already advised the commanding officers to spread the word throughout the camp about what happened at Donelson?"

"I hadn't gotten that far," McGuire replied, pulling at his droopy mustache. Running his gaze over the faces of the new arrivals, he said, "Everybody is being warned that the killer could be amongst us and simply biding his time. There's been no move to institute the bodyguard program we had at Donelson as yet."

"Probably because General Johnston deep down believes the killer is dead," Weathers said. "We had a lot of men killed at Donelson. He sure could've been one of them."

Britt had been watching Gordon since the conversation about Donelson's assassin started. Gordon showed definite interest, but at times seemed preoccupied. Britt was about to question him about it when Nolan spoke to Gordon and said, "I saw you with these men earlier today, Captain, but didn't get to meet you." Extending his hand, he said, "I'm Sergeant Cliff Nolan."

"Wayne Gordon," smiled the amnesia victim, giving Nolan a firm grip.

Weathers introduced himself and shook Gordon's hand. "I don't remember seeing you at Donelson, Captain. I assume since you came in with these men that you were there."

Wayne glanced at Britt, then looked at Nolan and said, "I was there, Sergeant. Took a head wound in the battle. Of course, with some seventeen thousand troops there, no doubt a lot of us never got a real look at each other."

"What division were you in?" Weathers asked.

"I don't know, Sergeant."

"You don't know?"

Gordon removed his campaign hat, exposing the scar that ridged the left side of his head. "As you can see, I missed death by a fraction. However, the bullet jolted my head so hard, it stole away my memory."

"Amnesia?" Nolan asked.

Gordon nodded.

"I've heard of amnesia, but I've never met a person who had it." Nolan said.

Gordon knew he might as well tell his story. He took a half hour, giving every important detail, including his stay at the Claiborne farm. He left out the part about falling in love with Hannah Rose.

When it was time to turn in, Britt and Wayne found that they shared a tent. Lying in the darkness after putting out the lantern, Britt said, "Wayne?"

"Yes?"

"I noticed again your rapt attention when we were talking tonight about the Donelson assassin—like it meant something to you. Were you remembering something?"

"I...I don't think you could call it that. I wasn't getting any mental pictures. But the subject of an assassin killing Confederate officers seems familiar."

"That's all?"

"That's all."

"Well, maybe it'll come clearer as time passes. You know, like Doc Stutz told you. Maybe your memory will come back a little at a time."

"I hope so," Wayne responded, feeling a sharp pain in his heart. He thought of Hannah Rose and wondered if he would ever see her again.

As March went into its second week, General Johnston continued building up his forces at Corinth. Since the railroad was so vital, it would be patrolled and protected along the eighty-five-mile stretch all the way west to Memphis, and the sixty-five-mile stretch east to Florence, Alabama. General Ruggles's II Corps First Division shared with other units in patrolling the section to the west.

As soon as the patrolling started, small units of Federal troops began harassing the patrols. There were skirmishes every day.

On Friday, March 14, Captain Claiborne and his company of three hundred men were assigned a fifteen-mile stretch to patrol. Claiborne had ridden along the tracks that morning as he distributed his troops, assigning sections of track to patrol. Gordon rode with him.

Claiborne and Gordon stayed at the extreme western end of their assigned section until mid-afternoon, then headed back toward Corinth. There had been no sign of Yankees all day, for which Britt was thankful. They had been in a skirmish once a day for the past three days, and Gordon had shown himself quite adept. He was deadly accurate with both revolver and rifle.

The sun was throwing long shadows when Claiborne and Gordon neared the eastern end of their section. Both of them noticed a group of their men collected at the edge of the woods some thirty yards from the railroad track. They were standing in a circle and looking at something on the ground.

"I've got a feeling something's wrong," Britt said.

Both men put their horses to a gallop and quickly closed in. When the soldiers saw them coming, they broke the circle, revealing a man in an officer's uniform lying amid the long shadows of the trees.

Lieutenant Shawn O'Leary, face devoid of color, hurried to Claiborne as he was dismounting and said with shaky voice, "It's John Carmody, sir. He's been murdered!"

Without a word, Claiborne dashed to where Carmody lay face-down, a ten-inch knife protruding from his back.

"We haven't touched him, sir," O'Leary said. "I wanted you to see him just as we found him."

Claiborne felt the loss of Carmody deeply. Looking around at the men, he said in a tight voice, "This knife came from the cook shack at camp. The Fort Donelson assassin is still with us."

CHAPTER EIGHTEEN

★

When Lieutenant Carmody's body was brought in draped over his saddle, word of his murder spread rapidly throughout the camp. The men who had been at Fort Donelson were sick at heart to learn that the killer had only been lying low.

Captain Claiborne questioned the men of Carmody's unit, but not one of them had seen anything that could give a clue as to whether the assassin was even a part of their unit. Since the murder had taken place at the edge of the woods, the killer could have been any one of a number of men-in-gray who were moving about the area.

That night, General Johnston gathered the troops and instructed the unit commanders to begin the bodyguard plan that had been used at Fort Donelson. Johnston ordered each officer present to choose two bodyguards. Since all the officers shared tents at night, they agreed to choose their bodyguards in the morning. The bodyguards would stick as close as possible to the officers from sunup to bedtime every day.

The meeting broke up, and the men prepared to retire for the night. Captain Thomas Sundeen of Second Division II Corps shared a tent with Lieutenant Billy John Axel. Sundeen visited one of the latrines at the edge of the camp, then threaded his way amongst milling men, tents, and campfires to his own tent. Carrying his lantern inside, he pulled off his boots, removed his uniform, and slid into his bedroll. Soon things were quiet, and Sundeen knew that just about everybody except the sentries had retired for the night. No more voices could be heard.

Where was Billy John Axel?

Sundeen waited another five minutes, and when Axel still had not appeared, he left the bedroll, pushed the flap aside, and stuck his head out. Campfires all around were dwindling to embers. He could vaguely make out sentries patrolling the edge of the area. But there was no sign of the young lieutenant.

Worry scratched at the back of his mind as Sundeen put his clothes on and left the tent. He was hoping to find a cluster of men in conversation somewhere, but there were no men to be seen but the sentries. He approached the sentries one by one, asking if they had seen Lieutenant Axel. None had.

He decided if Axel was not at the tent by now, he would report him missing to Colonel Aaron White, commander of their regiment. When Sundeen arrived at the tent, Axel had not shown up. He picked up his lantern and went to the colonel's tent. White was disturbed at the news and ordered an immediate search.

All the men of Second Division were rousted from their tents, and began searching about in small groups. Men of other units soon joined the search. After nearly a half hour, Sergeant Ralph Ederly and Corporal Donald Yockey approached a gurgling brook swollen from the recent rains. The brook was a few yards from the edge of the woods that encircled the camp, winding its way amid the trees. Several men had already entered the woods at other places and were moving along the banks of the stream.

Suddenly Yockey pointed through the trees. "Look, Sergeant!"

Hastening together, the two soldiers came upon Axel's lifeless form. He was face-down on the bank, his head submerged in the water.

Ederly and Yockey shouted to the other searchers and were soon surrounded. Standing over the body, which was well-illuminated by lanterns, Colonel White pointed out the signs of struggle on the bank. A canteen lay nearby. Apparently the young lieutenant had gone to fill his canteen before going to bed and was followed by the assassin. He was attacked from behind and overpowered by the killer, who forced his head under the water until he had drowned.

By the time Axel's body was carried into the camp, all the officers were up, including every one of the generals. General Johnston swore that when the killer was caught, he would be sorry he had ever been born.

Before the officers returned to their tents, a number of enlisted men sought them out and offered their services as bodyguards. The officers said they would make their choices in the morning.

Wayne Gordon lay in his tent, listening to Britt Claiborne's even breathing and wondering why the assassin's deeds picked at his brain. There was something familiar about the situation, but it just wouldn't surface. Soon his thoughts turned to Hannah Rose, and he recalled an old saying: *Absence makes the heart grow fonder.* He could vouch for that. He missed her greatly, and the love in his heart was growing.

He was about to drop off to sleep when he remembered the face of a beautiful young woman, whose name apparently was Julie. He could still picture her features clearly, but he could not recall who she was nor how she fit into his life.

Bringing his thoughts back to Hannah Rose, he finally drifted off to sleep.

Dawn came at the Claiborne farm on Saturday morning, March 15. Hannah Rose awakened and found that the man she loved was on her mind. This was the way it had been since Wayne Gordon had left. He was on her mind continuously through every day. Tears spilled down the sides of her face as she lay on her back, raised her eyes heavenward, and said, "Dear Lord, I need Your help. Please strengthen me. You know all about Wayne and his past. If...if it turns out that he has a wife, I'm going to need Your grace to see me through the heartache."

* * * * *

After breakfast on Saturday morning, March 15, the officers in the Confederate camp at Corinth, Mississippi, chose the men they wanted as bodyguards. Captain Claiborne picked out two men he knew well and trusted—Sergeant Weathers and a corporal named Derek Wilson. Captain Gordon chose Sergeant Nolan and a private who had impressed him during one of the skirmishes. The private was a young man from Dayton, Tennessee, named Saul Hendley.

Around seven o'clock that morning, Captain Claiborne and his company of three hundred reached the starting point of their assigned fifteen-mile section. A third of the men were left at that point, and the others moved on west. When they reached the ten-mile point, the second hundred fanned out along the track, and the remainder moved on with the two captains.

Claiborne and Gordon rode slowly allowing the footmen to keep pace. As they rounded a bend, Gordon looked north and saw black smoke billowing up above a stand of trees some eight or nine hundred yards in the distance. "Looks like we've got a train coming our way."

"Supply train from Memphis," Claiborne said casually. "General Bragg said something yesterday about one due in sometime soon."

They kept moving north, watching for sight of the train on the tracks. Soon the smokestack appeared, belching black smoke, then the rest of the engine came into view, and the sound of its chugging reached their ears. Four boxcars followed the coal car. When the train was within a hundred yards of them, it started to slow down.

Gordon glanced at Claiborne and asked, "Why would they be stopping?"

"I don't know. Has to be some reason."

Motioning for his men to halt, Claiborne pushed his horse ahead of the troops to talk to the engineer when the train stopped. Gordon stayed right beside him. Clouds of steam boiled from the sides of the engine as the big steel wheels began to squeal against the tracks.

Suddenly, Gordon saw the barrel of a rifle flash in the sun, followed by another. "Look out!" he shouted, leaping from his horse and knocking Claiborne out of the saddle. They had not hit the ground yet when the air seemed to explode with gunfire.

The four cars were loaded with Yankees. Some were firing from the train, while others piled out and fired from the ground.

Claiborne's men quickly returned fire, though several had gone down in the first volley. Britt looked around amid the bedlam, looking for a place to lead his men. If they stayed where they were, they were easy targets.

Off to the west was a deep gully, lined with naked-limbed bushes. The gully would offer some protection. Shouting above the roar of battle, Claiborne commanded his troops to head for the gully.

Just as Claiborne issued his order, Gordon put a bullet into the man who had commandeered the big engine. The Yankee grabbed his chest and tumbled to the ground.

The first volley of return fire had driven most of the Yankees back into the cars, or under them. This gave the Confederates a slight reprieve, and they darted to the gully for cover. Once over the edge, they began firing back through the bushes.

Yankee bullets hissed through the bushes, and Rebel bullets chewed into railroad cars and ricocheted off the engine. Both sides took numerous hits.

The battle area soon was enveloped in drifting clouds of smoke and dust. Claiborne told Gordon and his two bodyguards to remain where they were. He was going to take Weathers and Wilson and move a few yards to the left. Three Rebels who had been fighting from that spot now lay dead. Just as they raised up to shift positions, a Yankee slug tore into Corporal Wilson. He went down and lay still. There was no time to check on him. Bullets buzzed over the edge of the gully like angry hornets.

Claiborne and Weathers reached the spot and continued firing toward the train. Off to Gordon's right, another gap formed in the line when two Rebels went down. Quickly, Gordon commanded Nolan and Hendley to fill the gap. They were reluctant to leave him, but knew they must obey. Soon they were firing from that position. Gordon could barely see them through the thick pall of dust and smoke.

Gordon felt the breath of a bullet as it hummed by his left cheek. He returned fire, taking out another Yankee, who was firing from the coal car. Gordon ducked down to reload, but as he did, a Yankee private, wild-eyed and screeching, charged at him through the brush, bayonet poised for the kill. Gordon dodged the deadly blade. The Yankee stumbled past him, slid to his rump, then whirled about, ready to charge again.

Gordon had no time to load his revolver. He threw it at the Yankee's face as hard as he could. It struck him square between the eyes, knocking him backward down the slope. Gordon hastened after him, grabbed the rifle from his loosened grip, and plunged the bayonet into his heart.

Gordon wheeled and picked up his empty revolver. There was a deep gouge in the bank of the gully three steps away. He dived into it for cover and reloaded his gun.

Claiborne and Weathers were still fighting side-by-side several yards to Gordon's left, and now, quite a ways above him. Weathers dropped down to shove another cartridge into his carbine. When the cartridge was in place, Weathers looked both ways along the gully. The men to his left were some distance away, hidden by smoke and dust. He looked quickly to the right and saw no one where Gordon and his bodyguards had been. His eye caught sight of Wilson's crumpled form on the dusty slope, but the dust and smoke further along the gully completely hid Nolan and Hendley from his view.

Weathers smiled to himself. The perfect moment had come. He would aim his carbine at Claiborne's head, then call out to him. When the captain turned, Weathers would squeeze the trigger. He would then rush to the men off to his left and tell them the captain had taken a Yankee bullet in the face.

Down the slope, Gordon snapped the cylinder shut, cocked the hammer, and raised up to climb back to the crest of the gully. Just as his head came up, the smoke cleared, and he looked toward the spot where Claiborne was firing away. For a second, he couldn't believe his eyes. Sergeant Weathers was flanking Claiborne and aiming his carbine at his head.

There was no time for anything but action. Gordon took aim and fired. The slug tore through Weathers's head at an upward angle, splattering Claiborne with blood. The impact of the slug threw the carbine's muzzle off target just enough to miss Claiborne's head when it discharged. Weathers went down like a brain-shot steer.

Claiborne turned and saw Gordon and the smoking revolver in his hand. Then he looked to the would-be assassin who lay at his feet. His ears were ringing.

There was a sudden whoop of elation from his men along the line. All firing stopped at the train, and when Claiborne turned to see what was happening, a smile broke across his face. The men he left at the ten-mile point had heard the gunfire and had come on the run. They were now closing in, guns ready for action, but the reduced unit of Yankees had lost their will to fight. They were throwing down their guns and raising their hands in surrender.

Claiborne took another look at the dead man at his feet and said to Gordon, "I owe you for my life twice today."

"Just doing my duty," Gordon grinned.

The captains hurried through the bushes together, and Britt Claiborne led in the capture of a hundred and fifty-nine Yankees, forty-four of whom were wounded. Thirty-one were dead.

A quick tally showed thirty-nine Rebels dead and thirty-five wounded. Claiborne found a man amongst those who had just come to the rescue that knew how to run the engine. They loaded the dead in the last car, the unscathed prisoners into the third car under guard, and all the wounded in the first and second cars. The train moved off toward

Corinth, and the remainder stayed to patrol what stretch of the track they could reasonably cover.

While the men stood in a circle around them, Claiborne and Gordon discussed the shooting of Sergeant Weathers. Everyone was shocked, but none more than Claiborne. "Randall was one of the men I chose to be my bodyguard," he said. "I trusted the man with my life."

Blanchard and Ederly, who had been close companions to Weathers, assured Claiborne they were in a state of shock also. They never dreamed Weathers could be a Union plant.

"No offense to Corporal Wilson, sir, but I'm surprised you didn't ask for your brothers to be your bodyguards," one of the men said.

"Well, as you know, William and Robert have been assigned to another company. I suppose I could've requested that they be reassigned so they could play bodyguard for me, but I had no reason to distrust Wilson or Weathers. Well, at least there won't have to be any bodyguards anymore, thanks to Captain Gordon here." The men whistled and applauded.

"Just doing my duty," Gordon said with embarrassment.

There was elation throughout the camp that evening when the news of the assassin's death was announced. Now everyone could concentrate on the upcoming battle with the Union army.

That night Gordon lay awake for some time, his emotions stirred, as he thought of the two times he had saved Britt Claiborne's life. He was amazed that he had reacted so naturally, especially when he had but a second or two to make the decision to shoot Weathers. There seemed to be absolute confidence that he would do it successfully. Wondering once again what he had been before the war, he soon fell into slumber.

He found himself standing in a large yard, surrounded by towering trees, bushes, and flower gardens. A young woman was running toward him, arms open and smiling. It was the same face he had seen in the flashback. Julie. She was in brilliant sunlight with a large white, two-story house in the background.

Julie was coming closer and her features growing plainer. She was about to wrap her arms around him when he woke up.

Gordon sat bolt upright in the dark, breathing hard. His heart was pounding. He could hear Claiborne's soft, even breathing beside him in the tent. Cold sweat beaded his brow. The dream had been so real, so incredibly real.

Lying back down, he stared into the darkness and relived the dream over and over again. Julie. Beautiful woman. My wife? Or maybe just a girlfriend? Fiancée? My sister? No, the look in her eyes was not sisterly.

The big white house. The yard. Familiar? Yes.

Gordon strained to make the picture broaden and give him more. But no matter how many times he went over it in his mind, there was always the large yard, surrounded by tall trees, thick with branches and heavy with green leaves. Cottonwoods. Yes! And oaks. And the bushes were...lilacs! Flower gardens. Small and beautiful, placed in strategic spots of the yard. Julie, coming toward him off the porch of the big white house. The house. He tried to picture what it looked like inside— upstairs, downstairs, the kitchen, the parlor. But nothing would come. What he could see was plain and clear. He had lived that scene in his life, possibly many times.

Yes. Julie had bounded off the porch many times and run toward him, smiling, open-armed, with lovelight in her eyes. This was not just a dream. These were memories.

But there was nothing more. Nothing for him to cling to but brief, haunting, shadowed memories.

There were continual skirmishes along the railroad line until the beginning of the fourth week of March. Suddenly no more Yankee troops were seen in the forests or fields that skirted the tracks. The Federals, who knew that General Johnston was gathering troops by the thousands at Corinth, were moving that direction for a giant assault. General Grant had directed the establishment of a Union camp at Pittsburgh Landing,

Tennessee, a transfer point for goods and supplies shipped from the Tennessee River to Corinth, twenty-two miles to the southwest. In command at the Pittsburgh Landing camp was Brigadier General William Tecumseh Sherman, a close friend of Grant.

When Grant arrived on the scene on Thursday, March 27, he established his headquarters at Savannah, Tennessee, a river town eight miles north of Pittsburgh Landing. Grant moved into a large southern mansion, forcing the family to go elsewhere.

The next morning, Grant steamed down the river in his command boat, the *Tigress*, and met with Sherman. Grant looked the area over and liked the terrain. Sherman had bivouacked his army on a rough plateau that rolled westward from the high bluffs overlooking the Tennessee River. The encampment was protected, not only by the Tennessee, but by its tributaries, Owl and Snake Creeks in the north, and Lick Creek to the south, all of them in flood stage and twenty-five feet deep in places.

The terrain was heavily forested, dotted with farmland and orchards, and slashed by deep, narrow ravines.

Sherman had set up his headquarters on a wooded hillside a short distance away in a one-room log building known as "Shiloh Church." It had been erected long before by the Methodists, but was seldom used. A small settlement nearby had been named Shiloh, taking its name from the church.

Little did Grant and Sherman realize the irony of the place they chose to establish the Union camp. The Confederates were thought to be demoralized after the Fort Donelson defeat, and neither man expected to be attacked by them. Their plan was to establish the camp within a day's march of Corinth and launch an attack on the disheartened Confederates. Surprisingly, the Confederates were the ones to carry the battle to the Federals at their encampment. One of the bloodiest battles of the Civil War would take place at Shiloh, "the place of peace."

CHAPTER NINETEEN

✦

A t Corinth, Generals Albert Sidney Johnston and Pierre G.T. Beauregard were working feverishly to shape the incoming troops into a working army. There was little time to spare. Johnston had roughly forty thousand men. He was fully aware that General Don Carlos Buell was on his way to Shiloh with somewhere around thirty-five thousand troops. Scouts reported that Buell and his army were delayed by bad weather, but were expected to arrive at Shiloh on Sunday, April 6.

Johnston knew Grant had about forty thousand troops at Shiloh, and once Buell arrived, the Confederates would be outnumbered two to one. Johnston and Beauregard knew what their strategy had to be: *strike Grant before Buell reaches Shiloh.*

Since Beauregard had proven his skill at military organization, Johnston assigned him to assemble the Army of the Mississippi into four corps, each with two or more divisions. The officers appointed as corps commanders were distinguished men. Major General John C. Breckinridge, who headed a corps of sixty-four hundred men, had been vice-president of the United States under James Buchanan. Major General Leonidas Polk, an Episcopal bishop and a graduate of West Point, commanded a corps of ninety-one hundred men.

Major General William J. Hardee, whose corps had sixty-eight hundred men, was a capable military tactician who had served as commandant of cadets at West Point. The fourth commander was the rough-and-ready Major General Braxton Bragg, a West Pointer who had served with distinction in the Mexican War. Bragg led the largest corps, a crack unit of just under eighteen thousand men. On March 31, Captain Wayne Gordon was given command of a company of three hundred men, under Bragg. Captain Britt Claiborne, given troops to replace those killed during the railroad skirmishes, also commanded a company of three hundred.

Late in the third week of March, General Johnston had sent for Major General Earl Van Dorn, who had been given command of the Confederate forces in northern Arkansas on March 3. Van Dorn had led his troops into battle against the Federal forces at Pea Ridge, Arkansas, on March 7 and 8. The Yankees outmaneuvered them, and on the second day of battle, Van Dorn found it necessary to withdraw and head south. The Federals did not pursue them, and Van Dorn led his troops to a spot east of Little Rock to regroup.

The rider who had carried Johnston's message to Van Dorn returned to say that Van Dorn would begin the march the next day. In his message to Johnston, he estimated their arrival at Corinth on April 1 or 2.

At Shiloh, Grant was still complacent about the enemy forces camped just twenty-two miles away. This was reflected in the haphazard arrangements of the army's campsites. Five of the six divisions were located in the narrow plateau-like triangle of land between the creeks which extended southwest from Pittsburgh Landing.

These five divisions were commanded by intelligent and well-seasoned men: Major General John A. McClernand, Brigadier General W.H.L. Wallace, Brigadier General Stephen A. Hurlbut, Brigadier General William T. Sherman, and Brigadier General Benjamin A. Prentiss. The remaining division, commanded by Major General Lew

Wallace, was posted five miles north of Shiloh at Crump's Landing.

(Lew Wallace was a practicing attorney before entering the U.S. Army to fight in the Mexican War. He also was a poet, a playwright, and an author, and was known to be an unbeliever and skeptic. He often spoke against the Bible and took a humanistic approach to life. After the Civil War, he returned to Indianapolis and resumed his law practice. Shortly thereafter, Wallace met a preacher on a train and maligned him for his "blind faith" in the Bible and for believing that Jesus Christ was virgin born. The preacher gave Wallace a Bible, daring him to read it. Wallace took the dare, and within a matter of weeks, wrote to the preacher, telling him that he had put his faith in Jesus Christ for salvation. The lawyer-soldier-writer had successfully published historical novels in the past. While governor of New Mexico [1878-1881], Wallace wrote a biblical novel on the earthly life and crucifixion of Jesus Christ, titled *Ben Hur*.)

General Grant had employed no system in arranging his camps. The divisions of Sherman and Prentiss, made up of the rawest recruits, occupied the most vulnerable positions. Sherman's camp constituted the right flank of the advanced line and covered the main approach to Pittsburgh Landing from Corinth. Prentiss's division—so raw they had just drawn their muskets—was situated to Sherman's left, the most exposed if an attack came.

Neither Grant nor any of his generals expected an attack, however. Camp Shiloh was not fortified at all. Some young recruit suggested to his commanding officer that they dig trenches for protection just in case. He was disdained for such thinking. Early in the Civil War, entrenching for battle was considered cowardly. The Union generals at Shiloh were in one accord with Grant—entrenching would ruin the morale of their men and convey an impression of weakness to the enemy.

At Corinth on the evening of April 2, General Johnston paced the sod floor of his command tent. General Van Dorn had not arrived with his sixteen thousand men, and he couldn't wait much longer to launch the attack. Word had come that day that Buell's troops had cleared the worst obstacles caused by the heavy rains and were marching rapidly to join Grant.

Johnston wondered if it was raining heavily in eastern Arkansas.

He heard footsteps outside his tent, then Beauregard's voice. "General Johnston, sir!"

Moving to the flap, Johnston pulled it open and saw General Bragg with Beauregard. He stepped aside to allow them entrance. "Come in, gentlemen," Johnston said. "I know why you're here."

"Good, sir," said Beauregard. "General Bragg and I have been talking. We're going to have to move toward Shiloh at dawn, whether Van Dorn and his troops are here or not. Buell could put his men to a trot and get to Grant early. We must strike *now*."

Johnston nodded and rubbed his chin. "I'd sure love to have those extra sixteen thousand men, but I was about to call for the two of you. We must hit Grant at dawn day after tomorrow."

Orders to corps commanders were drafted by Johnston immediately. They were to be ready to march at dawn. One day's march would put them in position to attack the Union camp at Shiloh at dawn on April 4.

Beauregard had devised the plan of attack. He called the other three corps commanders to join Bragg and himself in his tent. Beauregard did not take the time to write out the orders. While Breckinridge, Polk, Hardee, and Bragg stood before him by lantern light, Beauregard explained an intricate pattern of march to accommodate the heavy traffic of infantry, artillery, cavalry, and supply wagons on the two roads that led to Shiloh. The infantry and artillery would take the road on the west; the cavalry and supply wagons the one on the east. The roads converged seven miles from Camp Shiloh at a crossroads known as Mickey's, named after a house that stood there. The army was to rendezvous at the crossroads, then move up under the direction of the corps leaders and form battle lines.

Beauregard's scheme was for three corps to attack the Union camp in three successive lines, each spread evenly across a three-mile front. Hardee's corps would attack first, followed by Bragg and Polk. Breckinridge's corps would remain in reserve for service wherever they were needed most once the battle was under way.

The next day, when the Confederate army was converging at Mickey's crossroads, Hardee's corps of sixty-eight hundred were not there. The army was stalled. Beauregard was told that Hardee had refused to move his men from Corinth because the army manual stated that orders for an attack must be given in writing. He would not move toward Shiloh until he had written orders from Beauregard.

Angry at Hardee's obstinacy, Beauregard quickly wrote out the orders and sent them back to Corinth with a rider. The sun was setting by the time Hardee's corps arrived. There was not enough time to move the rest of the way and set up for the attack at dawn. Beauregard pushed back the attack date to April 5. The forty thousand men, their animals and equipment, spent the night bivouacked in farmers' fields.

A cold rain began to fall in torrents and continued heavily all the next day. The roads became vast pools of water and pockets of mud. The attack would have to be delayed yet another day.

The skies cleared during the night, and on the morning of April 5, the sun shafted its cheerful light over the soggy fields where the Rebels huddled under wagons and trees, anywhere they could find shelter. The sun's cheer failed to reach the men-in-gray, who were soaked to the skin and chilled to the bone.

After a breakfast of cold rations, the corps leaders made preparations to move out. Though it was only seven miles to where they would make ready to launch the attack the next morning, they knew the going would be slow. Cannons and wagons sank to their hubs in the mire, and infantry units, trying to help out, became separated, resulting in commands intermixing.

By the time the Confederates reached the staging area, the sun was setting. Weary as they were, General Johnston knew they dare not wait.

The attack would be launched at dawn the next morning, Sunday April 6, 1862.

Strict silence was the code in the Confederate camp that night. All talking must be done in low tones. Captain Wayne Gordon lay on a damp, grassy mound, glad for some rest. Since his company had been positioned next to Britt Claiborne's company, the two captains lay side-by-side on the mound. Next to Britt were his brothers, who had been assigned to his company.

While the stars twinkled overhead, Britt said softly, "Wayne, this is going to be a huge battle. If you make it through and I don't...will you get a message to Donna Mae for me?"

"Don't talk like that, Britt. You're going to make it."

"But if the Lord sees fit to take me..."

"If He does, what would you like me to tell her?"

"Just that I love her."

"But she already knows that."

"Tell her anyway, okay?"

"Okay."

From Britt's other side, William spoke up. "Wayne?"

"Yeah, I'll tell Sally Marie that you love her," Gordon said in a kidding manner. Without lifting his head, he said, "Robert, who should I tell for you?"

"Just my sisters and sisters-in-law."

All was silent for a few moments, then Britt said, "Wayne?"

"Yeah?"

"Just in case it would be you who didn't make it...any messages?"

"Yes, one."

"Hannah Rose?"

"Who else? Tell her I died with her on my mind...and in my heart."

"I will," Britt whispered, and fell silent.

In the middle of the night, Gordon sat up on the mound, his breath coming in short spurts. He had experienced the same dream again. The big yard, towering trees, flower gardens, the white house...and Julie running toward him, eyes full of love, smiling, arms outstretched. Again he had awakened just before they touched.

Lying back down, he told himself Julie was only an old flame and not his wife. He hoped it was true. He was in love with Hannah Rose, and he wanted to live through the war and spend the rest of his life as her husband.

Lying under a mulberry bush, General Beauregard was about to drift off to sleep when he heard the sound of a harmonica nearby. Sitting up, he swore under his breath. Beauregard whispered to his aide, "Corporal, find that man and tell him to shut that thing off. And bring his name to me!"

"Yes, sir," Jimmy Watts said, and hurried away toward the sound.

The general waited, and the harmonica kept playing. It was still playing when Watts returned.

"Didn't you tell him to shut up?" Beauregard hissed.

"No, sir. I'd have to go into enemy territory to do it, sir."

"What? What are you talking about?"

"The man playing the harmonica is in a Union camp just across that shallow gully over there, sir."

The general was stunned. He had no idea the two armies lay so close together.

Incredibly, the southernmost Union camp did not know that forty thousand enemy soldiers were lying on the cool, damp ground just beyond their picket line.

The surprise attack never happened.

At 3:00 A.M. on Sunday, April 6, Union Colonel Everett Peabody was awakened by Major James Powell of the Twenty-fifth Missouri Brigade. Peabody was a thirty-one-year-old Harvard graduate who commanded a brigade in General Benjamin Prentiss's division. With Powell was Lieutenant Frederick Klinger, also of the Twenty-fifth Missouri.

Klinger, a young German with pale blue eyes, had been awakened ten minutes earlier by a youthful private who had decided to desert. The private had slipped out of camp just after midnight, and losing his sense of direction, had gone south instead of north. When he had passed the southernmost Union camp, he came upon the great mass of men spread out in the fields. He could make out the Confederate flag on a staff attached to a supply wagon.

Suddenly he couldn't find it in himself to desert. He returned to the camp and awakened Klinger.

Peabody asked in anger who the soldier was, but Klinger had had to promise the soldier anonymity before he would tell why he had awakened him. Klinger felt the Colonel should honor his promise in light of the news he was bringing.

Peabody wasn't sure he believed the anonymous private. He wanted word that he knew was reliable. Powell volunteered to make a reconnaissance mission and see for himself. Peabody approved it, but told him to take three hundred men with him. Just before dawn, Powell, Klinger, and the three hundred men drew near the Confederate camp.

The Rebels were already up, preparing to launch their surprise attack, and the Yankees ran into Major Aaron Hardcastle's Third Mississippi Infantry Battalion, the advance guard of General Hardee's Third Brigade. Hardcastle's troops opened fire and fell back. The Federals answered with a volley of their own and moved forward. A long line of Rebels kneeling on bushy high ground just ahead opened fire on the advancing Yankees, and Lieutenant Klinger went down, the first man to die in the battle of Shiloh.

Powell and his men took cover and began to fight back. It was the beginning of what General Sherman would call "the devil's own day."

Hearing heavy firing, the Yankees in the adjacent camp scrambled for their weapons. Farther back, Peabody ordered the long drum roll, calling the Union soldiers to get out of their bedrolls, grab their weapons, and form a battle line. By the time they reached the front, the whole Confederate line was moving, thousands upon thousands of men advancing at once. The Federals fell back, sounding the alarm to their sleeping comrades in nearby camps.

General Johnston commanded Beauregard to stay in the rear and direct men and supplies as needed, unwittingly relinquishing control of the battle to Beauregard. Johnston rode forward amongst his troops, shouting, "Onward, men! We'll water our horses in the Tennessee River tonight!" The long day of battle was under way.

Around Johnston, long lines of grim, silent men marched through a heavy gray mist that hovered at the tops of the trees. Soon the sun began to burn off the mist and a perfect Tennessee spring day was in the offing.

Grant heard at his headquarters the dull roar of cannon. He cut short his breakfast to steam down the Tennessee River on the *Tigress*. On his way, he stopped at Crump's Landing and ordered General Wallace to hold his division in readiness. Grant, who had been so sure the Rebels would not attack, was still not sure he had a battle on his hands. Wallace told Grant his men were ready now. Grant told him to sit tight.

It was just before 9:00 A.M. when Grant got his horse ashore and put it in a trot toward the sounds of battle. As he reached the front, he found Prentiss's line on the verge of collapse. A Confederate bayonet charge, sent in by General Beauregard, swept across three hundred yards of open field and pushed Prentiss's Sixth Division back to their camp. Peabody, bleeding from four wounds, rode his horse in a gallop among the tents, attempting to rally the battered Yankees for another stand. A swarm of Rebels attacked from the nearby woods, and a bullet struck Peabody in the head, killing him instantly. Prentiss's division held briefly in the camp as the Rebels came on, then broke and scattered.

Fresh Union troops moving up encountered the men of Sixth Division as they scattered. Prentiss's men, wild-eyed, were screaming,

"The Rebels are coming! They'll cut you to pieces! Run! The Rebels are coming!"

The panicked troops clogged the road and infuriated the troops trying to advance. The newcomers shouted at the fleeing soldiers, calling them cowards and traitors, but nothing could stop them from running for Pittsburgh Landing. The number of Yankees hiding at the river's edge grew all morning, running into the hundreds.

The Shiloh battlefield soon stretched over a line three miles in length. Along the Confederate artillery lines, officers shouted "Shrapnel! Canister!" to the loaders and gunners. Deep-throated cannons thundered and howitzers roared as the morning breeze carried thick clouds of blue-white smoke over the bloody, body-strewn fields.

When the Yankees wheeled in their artillery to fight back, the cry was heard along the Rebel lines, "Double shrapnel! Double canister!" The Confederate cannons fired with such rapidity that the separate discharges were blended into one continuous roar.

On an adjacent open field, opposing infantrymen moved toward each other in tight phalanxes, their gunfire sending forth a sheet of flame and leaden hail that elicited curses, shrieks, groans, and shouts. Men and mere boys dropped like flies, some dead before they fell, others dying within seconds. Still others lay in pain and agony, mortally wounded.

By 9:30, all of General Breckinridge's Rebel reserves had been called into action. Every Confederate man on the field was engaged in the battle. Johnston and Beauregard were still looking for Van Dorn's troops to show up.

Except for Wallace and his division, who were still at Crump's Landing some five miles north, Grant had every Yankee soldier in the battle. He was unhappy the way the battle was going, but expected to see Buell and his men coming in from the north at any time.

The horrid work of death was underway in the fields and thickets and along the creek banks that surrounded the little settlement called Shiloh.

As the sun moved slowly upward, the din of battle carried across the rolling hills. There was the steady *pum-pum* of the big guns, the roar of the howitzers, the shrieking of the shells, and the thunder of their explosions. Punctuating all of this ear-splitting noise was the steady rattle of musketry, the shouting of soldiers, and the cries of the wounded and dying. Great masses of men hurled death into each other's faces, lost in the blaze, the thunder, the excitement, the frenzy of combat.

In the midst of the battle, Gordon noticed a farmhouse some three hundred yards down the road. He could see the farmer, his wife, and young son standing on the porch, clinging to each other as they beheld the fire, smoke, and carnage of battle. A few minutes later, a half-dozen Yankees broke from the battle area and ran toward the farmhouse. Gordon knew the farmer and his family were in trouble. The Yankees would hole up in the house and use it as a fort.

"You two stay here and keep shooting!" Gordon shouted to Sergeants Ederly and Blanchard, who were on either side of him.

"Where you going?" asked Ederly, ducking as a Yankee slug chewed into a rail above his head and whined away angrily.

"Some Yankees heading for that farmhouse over there! I saw the family on the porch a few minutes ago. I'll pick up some men along the line so as not to leave a gap anywhere."

With that, Gordon crawled for several yards, then leaped to his feet and, bending low, tapped men on the shoulder as he ran along the line.

At the farmhouse, Eldon Coffman shoved his wife Mary and eight-year-old son Danny into the parlor closet. "Get down on the floor! Be quiet and don't move, no matter what!" he told them.

Mary's lips trembled and fear filled her eyes as she cried, "Eldon, they'll kill you!"

"Maybe not, honey. Maybe they'll take what they want and leave.

Please, don't move or make any sounds." He started to close the door, checked himself, and said, "Danny, you hold your mother's hand. Take care of her. Okay?"

"Yes, sir," nodded the frightened boy.

Coffman thought of the handgun he kept in the desk drawer in the parlor, but he knew he was no match for the six Yankees running across the field toward his house. He could only hope they would take what they wanted and move on.

He moved to the front door and stepped out on the porch. The sounds of battle rolled across the fields as the soldiers ran onto the porch, gasping for breath.

"What do you want?" Coffman asked, running his gaze over their young faces. They were all under twenty and without rank.

The one who seemed to be their leader said, "We want your house, and we're takin' it."

"What for?" Coffman asked.

The leader looked toward the door. "Your family inside?"

"No. They're away visiting relatives."

"Let's go see," he said gruffly, shoving the farmer toward the door.

When they entered the parlor, one of the soldiers said, "You look healthy enough to me, fella. How come you ain't in a gray uniform?"

"Farmer exemption," replied Coffman, irritated. "Somebody has to provide food for the army."

The leader, Kent Frye, barked an order for the others to search the house. As they scattered through the one-story frame structure, Frye looked Coffman in the eye and said, "I sure hope you didn't lie to me, mister. If we find anyone else in the house, you die!"

The sounds of soldiers stomping into room after room, opening and slamming doors, filled the house. Coffman trembled inside and hoped they would overlook the closet in the parlor.

Soon the five searchers were back. "Guess he's tellin' the truth, Kent.

Nobody here," one of them said.

"Better check the outbuildings. We just don't need any surprises."

Coffman's heart pounded like a mad thing in his chest. They wouldn't find anyone in the barn, sheds, or privy, but if they took over the house, they would find his wife and son sooner or later. His only hope was to admit he had hid them, and ask the Yankees to let the three of them go. They could have the house.

Drawing a shuddering breath, he said, "No need to search the outbuildings, private. My family is here. I hope you...can understand that a man's natural duty is to protect his family."

Frye's angry eyes bored into the farmer. "You lied to me, southern man."

"I just didn't want my family harmed!"

"Where are they?" Frye demanded.

"You can have the house, private," Coffman said. "Just let me take my family and leave. Okay?"

"Where are they?"

"You haven't answered my question."

Frye's face reddened. "You die!"

"No-o-o!" Mary Coffman cried as she flung open the closet door and burst into the room. She had covered Danny with clothes and told him to lie still.

All eyes followed Mary as she dashed to her husband, flung her arms around him, and screamed at the enemy soldiers, "Leave him alone! He's no threat to you! Like he said, you can have the house! Just let us go!"

"We know that, lady," Frye said, looking her up and down, "but he lied to me, and I told him he'd die if he did. I ain't goin' back on my word."

Frye pulled an officer's pistol from under his belt and said, "Grab her, Alex."

Coffman's arms were around his wife. Jerking her from Alex's reach, he blared, "Don't you touch her!"

Frye's eyes blazed as he cocked the pistol, placed the muzzle against the farmer's temple, and barked, "Let go of her!"

Reluctantly, Coffman released Mary from his arms. She was shaking all over and her lips were quivering as Alex took hold of an arm and pulled her aside.

Frye grinned malevolently, backed up several steps, and leveled the gun on Coffman's chest. The farmer said shakily, "You have no reason to kill me. If I was in a gray uniform it would be different, but I'm no threat to you. What kind of man are you?"

"Shut up, you stinkin' Tennessee plowboy! You lied to me." Narrowing his eyes, Frye said, "Besides, you said *family*—where's the rest of them?"

"There aren't any others. That's just my way of referring to my wife." Even as the words left his mouth, Coffman knew he had made a grave mistake. The soldiers had been in Danny's room. They knew at least one boy lived in the house.

"He's lyin' again!" one of them said. "There's a boy's bedroom back there."

Frye cursed Coffman and raised his revolver. Just before he fired, Coffman ducked, and the bullet struck him in the upper left shoulder. The impact turned him halfway around before he fell to the floor. Mary screamed, jerked loose from Alex, and threw herself at Frye, raking his eyes with her fingernails. He howled and yelled for the others to get her off him. Five Yankees converged on Mary, trying to pull her loose, but she was fighting like a wildcat.

Suddenly the front door burst open and Wayne Gordon bellowed, "That's enough. Leave the woman alone."

The Yankees looked around to see the room filling with gray uniforms. Alex also had an officer's revolver under his belt, and he jerked it out and brought it to bear on Gordon. Rebel guns boomed, and Alex went down.

At the same time Alex was going for his gun, Frye cursed at the gray blur before his wounded eyes and raised his revolver, cocking the hammer. Gordon's pistol roared, drilling Frye through the heart. He was dead before his body slumped to the floor.

The other four Yankees threw their guns down and raised their hands, begging the Rebels not to shoot.

Gordon motioned toward them and said to his men, "Get them out of here!"

Mary was kneeling beside her bleeding husband, checking his wound. A trembling voice came from the closet, "Mama!"

Mary looked around. The Rebel captain was standing over her, and the prisoners were being ushered outside with their hands in the air. Frye and the one called Alex lay dead on the floor.

Calling toward the closet, Mary said, "You can come out, Danny!"

Quickly the boy dashed from the closet, eyes wild with fear, and knelt beside his mother. She wrapped an arm around him, pulled him close, and half-whispered, "It's all right, honey. The Yankees won't hurt us now."

Danny looked at the two dead men-in-blue, then at his father.

"Papa's all right, son," the farmer assured him.

Danny looked to his mother for assurance. "It's only a shoulder wound, honey," she said softly. "Papa will be all right."

"Will you need some medical help, ma'am?" Gordon asked.

"I don't think so, Captain, thank you," she replied, looking up at him and trying to smile. "The bullet appears to have gone through cleanly, and there's not a lot of bleeding. I have some medical training and some supplies here in the house. I'll take care of my husband. He'll be fine."

Nodding, Gordon looked around at the few men who remained in the room and said, "All right, men. Get these bodies out of here. We'll bury them later. Let's get back to the battle."

CHAPTER TWENTY

The battle raged as the morning wore on. The ear-piercing Rebel yell and the defiant shouts of the men in blue rose and fell with the tide of battle. Soldiers made a mad rush in tight-knit lines across the fields, firing muskets and carbines. Cannons laid down a raking storm of shrapnel and canister, littering each field with the dead and dying. All through the long morning hours, this dance of death went on...and continued as the sun reached its apex and started westward.

A fierce battle raged about a mile due east of Shiloh Church. Some five thousand Federals had established themselves in a ten acre thicket, dense with brush and tall oak. It was a natural bastion, with a sunken road running along one side, the crest of a low hill on another, and wide open fields forming the other two approaches. Confederates coming across those fields faced heavy artillery.

General Braxton Bragg discussed the Union fortress with Johnston and Beauregard, and asked for permission to pull some seven thousand of his men from other fields and launch an attack. Permission was given, and the Yankees soon faced an onslaught of yelling Rebels.

Captains Britt Claiborne and Wayne Gordon and their men, along with many other companies, were sent to attack the Union stronghold from the side that skirted the hill. Bragg sent another unit against the position along the sunken road. He sent two entire brigades across the open fields. As the Rebels reached the 150-yard range, the Federal guns opened up, raking them with canister in a crossfire, right and left. The long lines rippled like tall grass in the wind as the shot cut through. Many went down, but still the swarm came on.

Soon, Bragg's troops surrounded the Yankee position and began to infiltrate. In some places, they were fighting hand-to-hand. In desperation, the Federals wheeled their cannons around and began firing into the woods behind them, sometimes killing and wounding their own men.

In spite of the artillery fire, the Confederates were undaunted, and the fighting continued heavy into the afternoon. Everywhere, wounded men cried and whimpered. Bodies lay in piles.

At about two o'clock, a Confederate soldier came stumbling out, needing ammunition. He approached a Confederate ammunition wagon and said to the men, "It's a hornet's nest in there!" From that moment, the bloody area was known as the Hornet's Nest.

While the Confederate soldier was unwittingly naming what would become a famous part of the Shiloh battle, deep in the Hornet's Nest, Captain Gordon's company was battling it out with the Yankees. Many of Gordon's men had been killed, and others lay wounded. Others had gotten separated from their comrades amid the smoke of battle.

Gordon had just shot a Yankee who came at him with a bayonet when he realized that he was alone. Only moments before, Sergeants Ben Blanchard, Cliff Nolan, and Ralph Ederly had been fighting next to him, along with a number of other men in his unit. Now they were somewhere out there amid the clamor and roar and smoke of the battle.

Gordon saw two Yankees rushing his way and ducked behind a bush. A few feet away, he saw a Confederate captain down on one knee, aiming his revolver through the brush. The revolver roared once, then again, and both men-in-blue fell dead on a bed of dried leaves.

"Good shooting, Captain!" Gordon said.

"Thank you," the man nodded, breaking his revolver open to reload. Neither man had looked closely at the other.

Gordon peered through the brush for sign of more Yankees. "Looks like you got separated from your company like I did."

"Yeah, you're right."

When the other man snapped his cylinder shut, Gordon looked back at him, and their eyes met.

The man's eyes widened. "Cliff Barrett, is that *you?*"

Gordon blinked at him, nonplused.

"Don't you know me?" the man asked. "We were roommates at West Point. Certainly you haven't forgotten your ol' pal, Mark Haverly!"

Wayne Gordon's heart quickened pace at the captain's words. Cold little needles pricked his spine, running its length. Reaching blankly into his memory, he echoed, "Mark Haverly."

Hearing his name on his old friend's lips, Haverly thought his former roommate recognized him. "Sure is good to see you, Cliff! We haven't seen each other since the day after graduation when you went home to Richmond to marry Julie. I still can't believe I came down sick with influenza and couldn't be your best man. Remember?"

Gordon was speechless, trying to think of a way to explain.

Haverly studied him quizzically and asked, "So how's Julie? I bet you've got a passel of kids by now! How many boys and how many girls? I sure hope the girls look like their mother. What a beauty!"

Gordon's mind was spinning. He was about to blurt out his predicament when three Yankees materialized from the smoke a few yards away, saw them, and raised their muskets to fire. Gordon brought his revolver up and fired. His bullet struck the lead one in the chest. The other two fired into the bush, and one of the slugs hummed by his ear. Gordon shot a second one, and before the third one could bring his bayonet to bear and charge, Gordon put a bullet through his heart. All three lay dead.

Whipping around, Gordon found Haverly with a bullet through his forehead. His heart sank. Here in the midst of battle, he had found a close friend from his past, a man who could give him some answers and... Wait, he had!

Haverly had told him he was a graduate of West Point, that his name was Cliff Barrett, that he was from Richmond, and that...he had married a girl named Julie.

Julie. So his flashbacks and his dreams were accurate. The name that had echoed through his head was correct. Cliff Barrett had married Julie *somebody*. He closed his eyes and saw her once again, as in his dreams, running toward him with love in her eyes, arms outstretched to embrace him.

Suddenly his thoughts turned to Hannah Rose. His insides were churning. "Hannah Rose," he breathed shakily, "this can't be happening! I love you! I don't want to lose you!"

"Captain!" came a loud voice from behind him. "You all right?"

Pivoting, the man who now knew his name was Cliff Barrett focused on the face of Sergeant Ederly. Blinking, he replied, "Yes. Yes, I'm okay." Dropping his gaze to the dead man at his feet, he said, "This was Captain Mark Haverly."

"We missed you, sir," Ederly said. "The bulk of our company is over here a ways."

As Cliff Barrett started to leave, he paused a few seconds and looked at Haverly's face again. They had to have been close friends. Mark was to have been the best man in his wedding.

Thank you, my friend. If I live through this war, I can go to Richmond and find out all about Cliff Barrett. God bless your memory.

It was nearly 3:00 o'clock when General Johnston's attention focused on a peach orchard just to the south of the Hornet's Nest. The orchard was in full bloom, a glory of pink petals that came down like snow as flying shrapnel and bullets slashed the trees. The rear of the orchard was on the sunken road that ran past the Hornet's Nest, and Federal troops held a line toward its front. Johnston was determined to break that line. He ordered a charge into the orchard by a single brigade of General Breckinridge's corps, and told Breckinridge he would lead it.

Johnston's aide in the Shiloh battle was Tennessee's governor, Isham G. Harris. He had left Nashville with Johnston and accompanied him to Corinth. When the general-in-chief was about to leave Corinth for Shiloh, Harris volunteered to go along as his aide. Honored, Johnston gave him a horse and took him north for the attack on the Union camps.

Leaving Harris in a safe place, Johnston led the charge with Breckinridge at his side. The Yankees offered stiff resistance for about twenty minutes, but the wild charge finally sent them scattering back through the orchard to the safety of the sunken road, where the sounds of fierce battle could still be heard coming from the Hornet's Nest.

Returning to Governor Harris, Johnston said from the saddle, "Governor, they came very near putting me out of the fight in that charge. Look at my boot."

Harris looked down and saw that the general's left boot sole had been sliced off by a bullet and was dangling from the toe. Eyeing it closely for blood, Harris asked, "Are you in pain, sir?"

"No," Johnston said, shaking his head. "Bullet came plenty close, though, didn't it?"

"I'd say so," nodded the governor, noting a couple of places where Johnston's uniform had been nicked. "Any pain there, sir?" he asked, pointing them out.

The general hadn't noticed. Looking down, he rubbed a hand over them and said, "Guess there were a couple of close calls here, too." Johnston's hand went to his forehead, and he seemed to sway in the saddle.

"General, are you sure you're all right?" Harris asked.

Johnston looked down at his right leg, which was opposite from where the governor stood. "Oh, no," he gasped.

Harris, worry etched on his face, hurried around to the horse's right side. It was then that he saw the bullet wound in the bend of Johnston's right knee. The pantleg was soaked with blood, and it was running down into his boot.

"Yes, and I fear right seriously," replied Johnston, about to topple from the horse's back.

Harris reached up as the general started to fall, and eased him to the ground. He called for help, and some nearby soldiers aided him in carrying the wounded general to a tree, where they sat him down so he could lean against it.

Harris told a soldier to run and find a surgeon. But before the surgeon could be found, Albert Sidney Johnston was dead. When the surgeon arrived shortly thereafter and removed the boot, it was full of blood. The bullet had severed an artery and somehow numbed the knee and leg. Johnston had bled to death, not knowing he was hit.

General Beauregard immediately assumed command of the Confederate Army of the Mississippi and ordered that Johnston's body be shrouded for secrecy and that the bad news be suppressed lest it demoralize the troops.

He then turned his full attention to the Hornet's Nest, where the fiercest fighting was going on.

Beauregard found General Bragg riding back and forth along the Hornet's Nest, shouting commands. Beauregard thought it only right that Bragg be informed of General Johnston's death. The bad news infuriated Bragg, putting more drive in him to finish the job at the Hornet's Nest. He conferred briefly with his new commander, then went back to the battle. Within another hour, the end was in sight for the defenders of the Nest. Union withdrawals on their left and right had exposed their flanks, and the furious Rebel infantry charges had hammered their flanks backward until their battle line was in the shape of a horseshoe. With the renewed thrust to Bragg's attack, the Federals were breaking up and pulling out of the open end of the horseshoe.

The battle looked bad for the Union. Grant had sent for Wallace in the early afternoon, but the sun was setting, and the Crump's Landing division had not yet appeared. The Hornet's Nest had crumbled, and all its able-bodied soldiers had made a run for the safety of Pittsburgh Landing.

As the sun dipped below the western horizon, the fields and woods were so full of smoke that hardly anything could be seen. Artillery batteries still pounded away, but most of the cannons were Southern. A struggling Union army, still firing but disheartened at the way the day had gone, moved back toward the landing.

Beauregard pushed his troops in a final effort to drive the Yankees all the way into the Tennessee River. Then suddenly he called for cease fire and ordered his army to fall back quickly. By dusk's faint light, the general had caught sight of Buell's Army of the Ohio marching down the west bank of the Tennessee River.

Darkness fell, and with it came the cries of the wounded from the Hornet's Nest, the surrounding woods, and the open fields. The Federal troops had left their wounded behind with their dead.

Weary and hungry Confederate soldiers denied their own needs until they had carried their wounded into the camp. There were thousands, and very few medics to help them. Acting as angels of mercy, the unscathed Rebels carried water to their wounded comrades.

After the troops were finally able to eat, they sat around the campfires and talked about the battle, wondering what would happen on the morrow. Van Dorn had not arrived with his men, but Buell was at Pittsburgh Landing, adding his sizable force to Grant's otherwise whipped army.

At one campfire, the man who had been called Wayne Gordon sat with the Claiborne brothers, Lanny Perkins, and Sergeants Blanchard, Nolan, and Ederly. The wide-eyed men listened as Gordon told them of meeting Mark Haverly and what he had learned before Haverly was killed.

To Captain Cliff Barrett's friends, the facts were in. He was married to a woman named Julie, and she was most likely waiting for him in Richmond. But all agreed that Cliff wouldn't know for sure until he could get to Richmond and find out for himself.

There was jubilation at Pittsburgh Landing. Don Carlos Buell had arrived with a fresh army of thirty-five thousand, and Lew Wallace and his troops had shown up at 7:00 P.M. Wallace had been delayed because of a mix-up in orders which sent him down the wrong road. Regardless of the delay, Grant was glad to see them. Things would go differently tomorrow.

General Beauregard set up his battle lines the best he could at dawn on Monday, April 7. By eight o'clock, the conflict was once again under way on battlefields already strewn with so many bodies it was difficult for both infantries to maneuver.

With his great numbers, General Grant formed a powerful counterattack, and almost immediately the tide turned for the Union. In spite of the overwhelming odds against them, the Confederates fought back valiantly.

Late in the afternoon, Captain Cliff Barrett's company—now down to 203 men—was fighting in a wooded area near Shiloh Church. Some thirty yards to his left, in the same woods, Captain Britt Claiborne and his company of 197 men were battling it out with a greater number of Union troops coming at them from two sides. The Yankees were in the open fields, inching their infantry steadily closer.

There was heavy brush in the woods, especially along the edges, where the Rebels were doing their fighting. Captain Claiborne was hunkered in thick brush, firing across the open field with his revolver. Flanking him were Nolan and Ederly and two corporals, one of them Lanny Perkins. William and Robert Claiborne had been sent deeper into the woods to carry a wounded lieutenant to a safer place.

A sergeant of Claiborne's company came dashing up, saying he needed help further down the line. Claiborne asked how many men he needed, and the sergeant said at least five. Britt ordered Nolan and Perkins to go with the sergeant, and told them the names of three other men to pick up on the way back down the line.

Claiborne turned back to the battle at hand and found his revolver empty. Dropping low to reload, he broke the gun open and punched out the shells. As he slid the last cartridge into the cylinder, he saw Ederly move away from him a few feet and bring his cocked rifle to bear on him.

Claiborne looked at the rifle, then at Ederly. "What's this?" he asked.

"The last few seconds of your life, Captain," Ederly sneered. "You southern fools thought there was only one killer at Donelson. I'll just tell 'em the Yankees got you, and they'll still think Weathers was the only assassin."

"Drop it, Ederly, or your dead!" boomed William Claiborne, who stood among the trees, his carbine trained on Ederly's head. Beside him was Robert, who also had him covered.

Ederly grimaced and let his weapon drop to the ground. They tied him up with his own belt and shirt, and Britt told his brothers what Ederly had told him.

Ederly was kept flat on the ground while the battle continued. Captains Claiborne and Barrett moved up and down the line periodically, encouraging their men to keep fighting. The Confederates stayed in the battle despite the overwhelming odds. General Beauregard's tactics proved efficient once again. However, as the sun was going down, it was evident that the Federals were taking control. Morning could bring a bloody defeat of the Rebel army.

The weary Federals withdrew to Pittsburgh Landing, and word was passed along the Confederate lines for everyone to sit tight. The generals would send word shortly about their plans to the division and company leaders. If the decision was to abandon the fight, they would pull out under cover of darkness. The men had not been told of General Johnston's death.

The sky was still light in the west when the Confederates in the woods collected into small groups and made themselves comfortable for the night. They didn't bother to regroup into companies, since they had fought in mixtures all day.

Captain Claiborne collected with his brothers and Lanny Perkins in a private spot. Perkins was shocked to learn about Ralph Ederly, who was still tied hand and foot, sitting on the ground. Soon Ben Blanchard appeared, carrying his carbine and wearing an officer's gunbelt. He had a second revolver jammed under his pants belt.

William Claiborne eyed the handguns and said, "Collect some souvenirs, Ben?"

"Might say that," Blanchard nodded, leaning his carbine against a tree. "Took 'em off a couple dead Yankees. Figured they didn't need 'em no more."

At that instant, Blanchard noticed Ederly. "What's this?" he asked.

Britt Claiborne gave a quick explanation of what had happened earlier.

"I'm shocked, Captain," Blanchard said, glaring at Ederly. "Man doesn't know who he can trust any more, does he?"

"That's for sure."

"What are you going to do with him?" Blanchard asked.

"I'll turn him over to General Bragg once he and the other generals are through with their conference. The general will most likely stand him before a firing squad here, or wherever we are by sunrise."

The group decided it was time to eat supper, such as it was. They had a few rations between them, but not enough.

"Guess it would be all right to go lift some rations off the dead ones, wouldn't it?" asked Robert Claiborne.

"I don't see why not," Britt said. "Let's all go, and we can collect enough real quick."

"What about your prisoner here?" Blanchard asked. "He might just work his way loose while we're gone."

"I think he's pretty secure," Britt said.

"Well, I'll feel better if he's watched," Blanchard said. "I'll just stay here and keep an eye on him."

"Suit yourself," said Britt, hunching his shoulders and turning away.

Ben Blanchard could not afford to wait any longer. Though they were in a private spot in the woods, someone could come along any minute. As soon as the backs of the four men were turned, he whipped out both revolvers, snapped back the hammers, and said, "You can stop right there! Throw your guns down!"

The Claiborne brothers and Perkins halted and turned around, eyeing Blanchard with puzzlement.

"Ben, what're you doing?" Britt asked.

"Takin' you as my prisoners," Blanchard replied coldly. "I said throw those guns down."

When each man's gun was on the ground, Blanchard jerked his head at Robert Claiborne and said, "Untie my partner."

Britt's eyes widened. "Ben, what th—"

"You're smart, Britt. C'mon, now. Figure it out."

Robert stooped to untie Ederly, who was grinning from ear to ear.

"*Three* Union plants?" Britt asked.

"Yep. And it's time for Ralph and me to get back with our own kind. We're takin' you boys to Pittsburgh Landing. That'll make U.S. Grant happy. He'll get us back safely and pick him up a hotshot Rebel captain to boot. These others will just be puddin' to go under the cherry."

"So you two and Weathers were all doing the killing at Donelson."

"Yep. At Corinth, too. And it was me who took out Colonel Parker and his little group of escorts. Some shootin', eh?"

Ederly sprang to his feet, picked up Britt Claiborne's revolver, and said, "Okay, Ben, let's get going before somebody comes along."

"You were fighting against your own men in these battles," Britt said. "You could've taken Yankee bullets at any time. Weren't you taking an awful chance?"

"Sure, but no more'n if we were on the other side of the fight. War's always a gamble. But we've done away with a whole bunch of Rebel officers, and while you plowboys weren't lookin', we've been feedin' information to our military leaders."

Stalling for time, Britt said, "So when you guys were in these battles, you were making sure you missed when you shot at the Yankees."

Blanchard grinned evilly. "See, I said you were smart, didn't I?"

"C'mon, Ben," Ederly said nervously, "let's get outta here!"

"Nobody's going anywhere!" came a sharp voice from the shadows. "Drop those guns!"

Startled, both Union men pivoted to fire in the direction of the voice. A shot rang out and Blanchard went down dead. Ederly's gun fired, but a second shot from the shadows put a slug in his heart, and his bullet went wild.

Every eye was fastened on the figure that emerged from the shadows. It was Cliff Barrett. As the group scrambled to pick up their guns, Barrett broke his revolver open to reload it and said, "I decided to let Blanchard shoot off his mouth as much as possible before I moved in. Looks like this clears up the whole thing."

Word came before midnight from General Beauregard that the Confederate army was going to withdraw and head for Corinth. They would pull out two hours before dawn. Since the fighting was over, Beauregard released the bad news that General Johnston was dead.

The weary Rebels laid down to get what rest they could, relieved that they wouldn't have to go up against the Union's much larger numbers in another day of battle. All over the camp, words of sorrow were spoken over their beloved leader's death.

When Beauregard's message reached the Claiborne and Barrett companies, Cliff said to Britt, "Captain, since we're backtracking to Corinth, I'm going to see if General Bragg will let me have some time to go to Hannah Rose and tell her what I know about myself, then make tracks for Richmond. If he'll permit it, I can clear up this awful blank in my life."

"Well, let's go see what the man says," said Britt, laying a hand on his shoulder. "If there's any chance I can have you as my brother-in-law, I'd sure like to see it happen."

Barrett and Claiborne sought out General Bragg. When they found him, Cliff told the general about learning who he was and laid out his request for time to clear up the vital matters in his life.

Bragg, a crusty old soldier, rubbed his scraggly beard and looked at Barrett. "I'm glad you found out your name, and that you're a West Point graduate, Captain. I'm sure it's good for you to know where you're from, too. But this is war. And in war, a man's personal life has to take a back seat. We've got to get this army to Corinth and make ready to fight again. Permission denied."

Cliff's heart sank. He looked at Britt, then said softly, "I understand, General. Thank you for your time."

The captains turned and walked away. They had gone some twenty yards when General Bragg's voice cut through the night air. "Captain Barrett!"

"Yes, sir?" Cliff said, halting and turning around.

"Come here a minute."

Britt waited while Cliff hurried back to the general.

As Cliff drew up, Bragg said, "Wasn't it you who killed that Donelson assassin...what was his name?"

"Randall Weathers, sir. Yes, sir."

"And you saved Captain Claiborne's life when you did it, right?"

"Yes, sir, and...well, Captain Claiborne can tell you that there were actually three assassins. I killed the other two, also."

"*Three?* You did?"

"Yes, sir."

Looking toward Britt, the general called, "Captain Claiborne! Come, please!"

Britt moved swiftly past other soldiers who were milling about. "Yes, sir?"

"Tell me about these other two assassins Captain Barrett killed."

Britt quickly told Bragg about the incident with Ederly and Blanchard, explaining how they had admitted that they and Weathers were Union plants. He flourished it good when he described how Blanchard and Ederly were going to take several of them to the Union camp, and how Captain Barrett moved in and shot them down.

Smiling, Bragg looked at Barrett and said, "Tell you what, Captain. I've changed my mind. You've earned a little time off. We won't be in another battle for a while, I'm sure. I'll write up the order. You can have three weeks, then you must report to me at Corinth."

Smiling broadly, Captain Barrett said, "Thank you, sir!"

Bragg quickly scribbled the order and put it in Barrett's hand. "See you in Corinth on April 30, Captain."

CHAPTER TWENTY-ONE

The Claiborne women cleaned up the kitchen after breakfast on Thursday morning, April 10, and sat down at the table to pray for their men. They had learned the day before about the bloody battle at Shiloh, Tennessee, and they knew Britt, William, Robert, Wayne, and Lanny would be in the thick of it.

Their neighbor, Walter Manning, had brought them a copy of the *Dover Sentinel* at midmorning on Wednesday. The paper had given what details were available, explaining that many hundreds had been killed and wounded on Sunday, and the battle was continuing as of Monday morning. Sunday's battle had gone decidedly well for the Confederacy.

Hannah Rose had gathered the others into the kitchen on Wednesday to thank the Lord that things had gone well on Sunday and to pray for their men.

As they sat around the table on Thursday morning, Hannah Rose laid her Bible on the table and said, "Before we pray, I want to read a passage that came to mind as I was lying in bed last night. I read it first thing this morning, and in my private time with the Lord, I claimed it for our men. It's in the Ninety-first Psalm."

The others began flipping pages in their Bibles. Hannah Rose looked around to make sure everybody had the passage before them, then she began to read:

"He that dwelleth in the secret place of the most High shall abide under the shadow of the Almighty. I will say of the Lord, He is my refuge and my fortress: my God; in him will I trust. Surely he shall deliver thee from the snare of the fowler, and from the noisome pestilence. He shall cover thee with his feathers, and under his wings shalt thou trust: his truth shall be thy shield and buckler.

"Thou shalt not be afraid for the terror by night; nor for the arrow that flieth by day; nor for the pestilence that walketh in darkness; nor for the destruction that wasteth at noonday. A thousand shall fall at thy side, and ten thousand at thy right hand; but it shall not come nigh thee."

"That's wonderful," Donna Mae said. "I've read this passage more times than I can count, but I'd never thought of these verses, especially five and seven, speaking about men at war. But there it is—the arrow that flieth by day. Thousands of men falling in the battle, but certain ones being protected."

Sally Marie wiped tears and said, "Oh, Hannah Rose, we must claim these verses for our men."

"Yes, I agree," Hannah Rose nodded.

With their Bibles open before them, the four women bowed their heads and prayed around the table, each asking God to protect the men they loved and to bring them back safely one day. Each one asked that the Lord give them the faith to claim the passage they had just read for their men.

They were all weeping and dabbing at their noses with hankies when the last amen was said. Suddenly there was a knock at the front door.

"I'll get it," said Linda Lee, pushing back her chair and hurrying through the house.

She opened the front door to find elderly Walter Manning with a sad look on his face, holding a folded newspaper.

"Good morning, Mr. Manning. Is there bad news?"

"'Fraid so, honey," Manning replied, handing her the morning edition of the *Sentinel*. "Looks like we got whipped at Shiloh after all. General Johnston got killed on Sunday, and after the Yankees brought in massive numbers of troops Sunday night, General Beauregard led our men to fight them anyhow on Monday. We were whipped bad, Linda Lee. What's left of our army is on its way back to Corinth. Paper says we put up a great fight, but they flat outnumbered us. They don't have any idea how many have been killed and wounded, but looks like it's gonna be up in the thousands."

At that moment the other three women appeared. "It's all there in the paper," he said, pointing at the folded newspaper in Linda Lee's hand. "Well, I gotta get home to my missus and break the bad news to her. See y'all later."

The Claiborne women went to the kitchen, and leaning over the table together, spread the newspaper before them. The headlines read:

THOUSANDS KILLED AT BLOODY SHILOH!
Army of Mississippi, Vastly Outnumbered Puts Up Gallant Fight. Retreats to Corinth!

Saddened by the news, the four women prayed around the table again, asking God to give them the faith to lay hold of the Scriptures they had just read and to believe that their men were still alive.

It was late morning and the women were working in the sewing room, when they heard a knock at the front door.

"I'll get it," Linda Lee said, laying down the blouse she was trimming with lace and dashing out the door.

Her jaw slacked when she opened the door and saw the familiar face of the man in the captain's uniform. "Wayne!" she gasped. Turning to call over her shoulder, she shouted, "Hannah Rose! It's Wayne! Wayne's here!"

Cliff Barrett entered the parlor just as Hannah Rose ran in with her sisters-in-law on her heels. "Wayne!" she cried, rushing into his arms.

While Hannah Rose clung to the man she loved, weeping and thanking the Lord for his safe return, the others pumped him for answers about their men.

Holding Hannah Rose close, Cliff told them that Britt, William, Robert, and Lanny had all come through the battle unscathed. The women filled the room with praises to the Lord, shedding tears of relief and thankfulness. Then they sat down and listened as the handsome young captain told them every detail of the Shiloh battle, including the shooting of the Donelson assassins. The women fired questions at him right and left, and he answered each one as accurately as he could.

When they were satisfied that their men were safely on their way to Corinth, Barrett reached inside his uniform coat and produced four battered, folded pieces of paper. "I must apologize for the awful condition of these letters, ladies," he said, smiling, "but this paper's all we had to use."

There were shrieks of joy as the captain handed each woman her letter. Robert's letter, he placed in Hannah Rose's hand.

Looking around at her sister and sisters-in-law, who clutched the letters to their breasts, Hannah Rose said, "I know you will want to read your letters in the privacy of your rooms, so let me first read Robert's to you, which is addressed to all of us."

When Robert's letter had been read, evoking more tears and "God bless hims," the three young women went to their rooms, leaving Cliff and Hannah Rose alone.

When they had embraced once more and kissed each other soundly, Hannah Rose stroked his cheek and said, "Oh, Wayne, I'm so thankful you've come back safely. But there's one thing I don't understand."

"What's that?"

"How come you're able to be here, but my brothers are on their way to Corinth?"

"Because of you," he said, rising from the couch.

"Me?"

"Yes. General Bragg is aware of my amnesia. You see, Hannah Rose, I...I learned who I am during the Shiloh battle."

Hannah Rose sprang off the couch, gasping, "You did? You did? And you're back here? That means—"

"Not so fast," he said, raising his palms toward her. "There's a lot to tell you."

"Well, before we get into how you found out, and who you are, I have to know—are you married?"

"I don't know yet," he sighed. "Sit down, please, and let me tell it to you in some semblance of order."

While the man she loved remained on his feet, Hannah Rose eased down on the couch without taking her eyes off him. "Before you start, could I at least know your real name?" she asked.

"Of course," he said, smiling. "It's Cliff Barrett. Probably Clifford Barrett. And I'm from Richmond."

Staring at the floor, Hannah Rose tested the name on her tongue. "Clifford Barrett. Cliff...Cliff." Raising her eyes to him, she said, "Yes, that fits you better than Wayne. I like it. The last name, too."

"Thank you," he smiled.

"Now, I'll be quiet. Tell me all about it."

A bit shaky, Cliff Barrett first told Hannah Rose about the flashback he had experienced during the fight with Club Clubson. Just that much brought a cold, heavy feeling to Hannah Rose's heart.

He told her about the dreams in which he saw the yard, the big white house, the trees, the flowers, and the young woman running toward him with arms outstretched. He had been sure without a doubt that her name was Julie.

Hannah Rose's heart grew heavier.

He described his chance meeting with Mark Haverly, who identified him as Cliff Barrett, his old friend and roommate at West Point, and that Cliff had left immediately after graduation to go home to Richmond and marry a girl named Julie.

Hannah Rose was feeling a bit faint, but covered it. Inside she prayed, *Lord Jesus, give me strength. I can't face this without Your help.*

Cliff told Hannah Rose that Haverly had been killed before he could find out more, but what he had learned was a good beginning, for which he had thanked the Lord. Proceeding, he explained that General Bragg had given him a three-week leave to come see her and to make the trip to Richmond to clear up the mystery of his past.

When he finished, Hannah Rose was biting her lip and trying not to cry. "Oh, Wayne—*Cliff,* I'm scared. Scared that you'll go home and find Julie waiting for you."

Taking her hand, he helped her off the couch and folded her in his arms. He held her close and half-whispered, "I'm scared, too. Maybe *frightened* is a better word. I get cramps in my stomach just thinking about going home. But...I have no choice."

"I know. It's just that...I'm not sure I can stand it if you don't...don't come back to me."

The emotion of it all was too much for them. They clung to each other and cried. Fighting the awful ache in his heart, he said, "I have to keep telling myself that Romans 8:28 is still in the Bible. And...I keep quoting Proverbs 3:5 and 6 to myself, over and over."

"Me, too," said Hannah Rose, looking up at him.

"We don't always understand God's ways," Cliff said softly, "but this whole thing is in His hands. We must trust Him, believing that He never does wrong, He doesn't make mistakes."

Hannah Rose nodded, then laid her head against his chest.

After a long moment, he said, "If...somehow it turns out that I'm not married, I'll come back to you as fast as I can. After we marry, I'll have to report back to General Bragg at Corinth. I'm due to report in on April 30."

Hannah Rose clung to him silently.

Cliff went on, his voice choking. "If I am married...I guess all I can do is write and tell you so...and never return."

Hot tears coursed down Hannah Rose's cheeks. All she could do was nod and press her head tighter against him.

"Hannah Rose," he said past the lump in his throat, "this whole thing is so unfair to you. If it turns out that I'm married, you've wasted all the love you've poured out on me. What a horrible thing for you to—"

Her forefinger was pressed hard against his lips. "Don't," she whispered. "My love for you, Cliff Barrett, knows no bounds. I would rather have had what little time we've known together—and had your love, at least for a little while—than to have loved anyone else. I mean that, darling."

"Oh, Hannah Rose, you're the most wonderful woman God ever made. I'm so sorry you have to face—"

Again her finger was pressed to his lips. "Listen to me," she breathed softly. "I will be waiting for you...or your letter. Just remember that I love you with all my heart."

He kissed her forehead. Then silently, Cliff Barrett and Hannah Rose Claiborne walked out onto the porch together. His horse nickered at the sight of them. They held each other for a long, painful moment, and kissed fervently. Then Cliff wheeled, hurried off the porch, and swung into the saddle.

Tears streamed down Hannah Rose's cheeks as she moved to the edge of the porch and dropped down to the first step, steadying herself with the banister.

The horse danced about nervously, bobbing its head as if it felt the emotional strain in the air. Cliff looked at Hannah Rose tenderly. Her lovely chestnut hair was shining in the sun, framing her tear-stained face. He felt as though his heart was bleeding. The silence between them was excruciating, but there was nothing more to say. He pulled the horse's head around, put the animal into a canter, and rode away.

He did not look back.

On Monday, April 14, Captain Cliff Barrett arrived in Richmond, Virginia, by rail, having brought his horse in a flat-bedded stock car. When the animal was unloaded, he saddled it and rode toward the center of town. He had decided to hunt up the town constable's office. The constable would surely know Cliff Barrett, and could tell him where to find Julie or his parents...or both.

Traffic was heavy in Richmond as Barrett rode slowly along the main thoroughfare. He saw many men-in-gray milling about, which made him feel better. His presence would not attract attention. Richmond was his hometown, according to Mark Haverly, but nothing looked familiar to him. It might as well have been a town in some foreign country.

It didn't take much effort to locate the constable's office. A sign hung over the door, freshly painted, that read:

Richmond Constable's Office
Tom Berry, Chief

Hauling up, Cliff dismounted and wrapped the reins around the hitch rail. He was vaguely aware of an older couple who had just walked passed and were looking back at him. "Sure enough, it *is* Cliff, honey," the man said.

The amnesia victim thought about hurrying after them, but decided he should talk to the constable. Crossing the boardwalk, he found the door partially open and stepped inside.

Sixty-year-old Tom Berry was at his desk, working over a stack of papers with his head bent low.

Papers. Boring papers, Cliff thought, then wondered what put such a thought in his mind.

"Chief Berry?"

Berry's head jerked up. Focusing on the tall man, he said, "Sorry, son, I didn't hear you come in."

"Interesting stuff, eh?" Cliff said, noting that the man showed no recognition of him.

Dropping the pencil in his hand, Berry said, "Boring's what it is."

Same word I used, Cliff thought. Aloud, he said, "I'm Cliff Barrett."

A smile broke on the lawman's face. Rising quickly, he extended his hand and said, "Well, I do declare! I sure have heard enough about *you,* young fellow! Folks around here think you hung the moon!" Looking him over, he added, "Uniform looks good on you. Better than what we law officers wear, eh? Some change for you, I'd say. A *good* change, I mean."

"I'm...not sure I follow you," Cliff said.

"I, uh...was comparing the clothes you wore when you had my job with those you're wearing now."

Suddenly Cliff realized why he had the instincts that had cropped up so often when he needed them. He was a lawman!

"Ah...Chief," he said, "would you have a few minutes to talk to me?"

"Sure, my boy," Berry grinned. "Be better than this paper work. It's like watching grass grow."

Both men took a seat, and Cliff told him the story of his amnesia, bringing him up to the moment. Accepting it without question, the older man explained that Cliff was Richmond's chief constable up until the war started. He had resigned to reenter the army. Another man had followed Cliff, but was killed in the line of duty just three weeks ago. Berry had come from Roanoke to take the job. He had two deputies that were out of town on errands.

"I realize you're new here, Chief," said Cliff, "but would you happen to know a woman named Julie Barrett?"

Berry pursed his lips, then shook his head. "No, can't say that I do. But come to think of it, I remember somebody telling me that your pa is Reverend Micaiah Barrett, pastor of Richmond's First Baptist Church."

Though the information brought back no memories, it did explain why he had such a thorough knowledge of the Bible.

Rising from his chair, Cliff said, "Chief Berry, you've been a great help. Just one more thing. Could you direct me to the home of Micaiah Barrett?"

"No problem. Your ma and pa live in the parsonage, which is right next to the church. I...ah...haven't been inside the church because I'm a Presbyterian, you understand."

"Well, my memory may be bad, Chief, but I don't think those Baptists would bite the nose off a Presbyterian if he visited their services."

Berry chuckled. "Probably not. I just might do it some time. I hear your pa is quite the preacher. Hurry on home now, and see those parents of yours."

"I will when you tell me where to find the church and parsonage."

"Oh, yeah! That'd help, wouldn't it? You probably noticed you're on First Street."

"Mm-hmm."

"Well you go south two blocks to Third Street, then turn left and go two blocks to Oak Street. Church is right on that corner."

Thanking the lawman for his help, Cliff Barrett rode south to Third Street, turned left, and headed east toward Oak. His stomach was in his mouth and his heart drummed his ribs. The drumming became more intense when the steeple on the church building came into view, its lofty point showing above the treetops. As he drew closer, he saw the sign in front of the glistening white building, identifying it as First Baptist

Church, and Reverend Micaiah Barrett as pastor.

He was nearing the corner where the church stood when an elderly man called to him from the front porch of a house. "Hey! Cliff Barrett! Welcome home!"

Cliff lifted a hand in a friendly gesture, but said nothing.

"Tell your pa I was sick Sunday, Cliff, but I'll be back in church this Lord's Day!"

"Will do," Cliff nodded and waved.

Crossing the intersection, he veered his horse toward the church yard when the parsonage came into view, standing elegant and white in the brilliant sunshine. Giant cottonwoods towered over it, casting shade on the roof and the flower gardens that adorned the base of the front porch. Bushes and trees, interspersed with smaller flower gardens, surrounded the large yard. Though he did not remember the place from the past, he most certainly recognized it from his dreams. It was exactly as he had seen it.

The house sat back some distance from the street. Cliff's mouth was dry as a sandpit when he skirted the church building and headed for the house. He saw movement at a first-floor window, then the front door flew open and the woman he had seen in his dreams darted across the porch, down the steps, and opened her arms.

Julie.

He dismounted, and she met him with tears in her eyes, crying, "Oh, Cliff, darling! You're home! You're home!"

Cliff mechanically took Julie in his arms. How could he be a husband to a woman he didn't even know?

But he knew that he must. It was only right that he return to his role as Julie's husband and the father of his children, if he had any. It was he who had changed. Not Julie and the children. They were innocent and should not be made to do without him because of his love for Hannah Rose. And it would not be right before God.

While Julie wept and he embraced her dutifully, he saw a mental picture of Hannah Rose. But the picture was growing dim. He could feel her slipping away. He would never see her again. Never hold her again. Her sweet lips would never—

"Clifford!" a woman shrieked.

He looked up to see a lovely fiftyish woman descending the porch steps with a man about the same age following her...a man Cliff imagined he would look like in about twenty-five years. This was his father, all right. No question about it.

Julie released Cliff so he could embrace the older couple, who were shedding tears of relief and delight to see him.

Looking down at them, Cliff smiled and said, "It's so good to see you, Mother. You too, Dad."

Both of them looked at him askance. Grace Barrett frowned and said, "Clifford, dear, you've always called us Mama and Pop. Are you all right? Is something wrong?"

Cliff nodded gravely with a haunted look on his face. "Yes, something is wrong. I have amnesia. I...don't remember you and Pop. I don't remember Julie, either."

The three people were stunned.

Laying a hand on his shoulder, Micaiah Barrett said, "Son, I...let's all go in the house. This has us rather confused."

Cliff Barrett sat in the large parlor with Julie and his parents and told them the story of his amnesia, going all the way back to that frosty night when he came to on the battlefield under the shadow of Fort Donelson. He explained about his flashbacks, how Julie's name came to his mind, and of seeing her and the house in the dreams that followed. He said nothing about his feelings for Hannah Rose.

As he spoke, he knew something was awry. His parents kept sending strange glances at Julie, and she turned pale and looked at the floor.

When Cliff finished, Julie would not meet his gaze. Micaiah Barrett stood up, wringing his hands, and said, "Clifford, we are sorry that this has happened to you. And we'll be praying that the Lord will restore your memory. But...well, I'm sure you're assuming something here that isn't true. You need to be filled in on the facts.

"Of course your mother and I remember you telling us about your good friend Mark Haverly. But since Mark was ill and couldn't come for the wedding, there was something he didn't know."

Grace Barrett pulled a hanky from her sleeve and dabbed at her eyes. Julie interlaced her fingers, squeezing hard enough to turn them white, and only stared at the floor.

Rising from the couch to meet his father's gaze, Cliff said, "Go on, Pop."

Amazed at how much he and his father resembled each other, Cliff listened intently as the godly man told him that during the weeks he was home from West Point during Christmas of 1855, he and Julie became engaged. They had gone together since high school. Cliff was to graduate the following May, and the wedding was set for the first Sunday in June. However, during those months from December to May, Julie had met a handsome, dashing army officer and let him sweep her off her feet. She had run off with him the very day Cliff had left West Point to come home.

Cliff was devastated to learn what Julie had done. He pulled himself together, however, and reported for army duty at a military installation near Winchester, Virginia. With no action, he soon found army life dull. While visiting home the following summer, he was on First Street in Richmond when a gang of five hoodlums tried to break one of their friends out of the town jail.

Cliff was in his lieutenant's uniform and wearing his service revolver. He jumped in to help the town's constable, who was facing the gang alone. In the fracas, the chief was killed after cutting down one of them, but Cliff cut down two more and captured the remaining two.

Because of the way he had handled the situation, the townspeople asked Cliff if he would resign from the army and become their chief constable. Cliff liked the idea and took them up on it.

As Richmond's chief constable, Cliff proved himself a capable lawman. He was especially good at tracking down and capturing criminals. When the Civil War broke out, Cliff re-enlisted as a lieutenant, but soon was promoted to the rank of captain.

Cliff had fought in the battle at Rich Mountain, Virginia, on July 11, 1861. During that battle, several Rebel soldiers deserted and hightailed it into the Blue Ridge Mountains to hide out. Because of Cliff's reputation for tracking criminals, General Robert E. Lee commissioned him to go into the mountains and track them down.

Cliff missed the battle at Bull Run because he was on the trail of the deserters. He was successful in tracking them down, but had to kill a couple of them in the process. Shortly thereafter, General Lee sent him to track down nearly a hundred deserters from the Bull Run battle. He was kept busy as a tracker until late January 1862. He caught the last of them hiding in the woods just east of Charlottesville, Virginia, and turned them in to the army post at Charlottesville.

Micaiah showed his son a letter he had sent home from Charlottesville, dated February 1. It told how some inside assailant was murdering officers at Fort Donelson, Tennessee, and that because of Cliff's reputation as a proficient lawman, Lee was sending him to Fort Donelson to see if he could ferret out the killer.

The letter capped off the picture for Cliff Barrett. He had left Charlottesville upon posting the letter and headed southwest into Tennessee. He had arrived at the fort while the battle was raging, and a Yankee bullet had creased his head, knocking him down and out.

While Julie wept, Micaiah explained to his son that Julie's marriage had not been a pleasant one. She had learned the first week that she had made a grave mistake. She was still in love with Cliff. But since she had made the mistake, she told herself she would have to live with it. Julie's husband was a major in the Confederate army, serving under General

Pierre G.T. Beauregard. He was killed at Bull Run.

Just six weeks ago, Julie had returned to Richmond and had come to the parsonage. Micaiah had been her pastor, and she wanted counsel from him and to talk to him and Grace about her horrible mistake.

She told them of her bad marriage, and of her husband being killed, and asked their forgiveness for jilting their son. They readily forgave her. Julie's parents had moved to Atlanta a year previously, so she asked if she could stay with the Barretts until Cliff came home, which he was bound to do sooner or later. She wanted to admit her mistake, tell him that she still loved him, and ask his forgiveness. If Cliff still loved her, things just might work out between them.

Julie sat on the chair, sniffling and dabbing at her eyes during the entire time Micaiah told her story. When Micaiah finished, he looked at his son and asked, "Can you find it in your heart to forgive this precious girl for what she did?"

Cliff Barrett's mind was awhirl. He was not married to Julie! He was free to marry Hannah Rose!

"I have no problem forgiving Julie," he managed to say.

"Wonderful!" exclaimed the preacher.

"I knew you'd forgive her, son," Grace said.

Cliff knelt before the young woman with the red, swollen eyes, and said in a tender tone, "Julie, all of us are human, and we can make some awful mistakes at times. You made a big one, I agree. But I want you to know that I forgive you."

Julie burst into sobs and lunged to embrace him. He avoided her grasp and stood up. As she rose to her feet, looking at him with puzzled eyes, he said, "Please don't misunderstand, Julie. Forgiving you doesn't mean I want you back. There is someone else in my life, now."

While Julie stood in stunned silence, Cliff turned to his parents and said, "Remember I told you about Hannah Rose Claiborne taking me in and nursing me back to health?"

"Yes, of course," his father said.

"During that time, we fell in love. We tried not to, but it happened anyway. She's waiting to hear from me. If I found out I was married, I was to write her a letter saying so, and we would never see each other again. She loves me enough to wait for me...and to marry me if I'm free to do so."

"Is she a Christian, Clifford?" asked Grace.

"Yes, Mama!" responded the happy man. "The best! Oh, praise the Lord! Romans 8:28 is still in the Book! All things do work together for good to them that love God! If that bullet hadn't given me amnesia, I would never have met my wonderful Hannah Rose!"

Julie had slipped away to her room while Cliff was telling his parents about Hannah Rose. Looking around for her, he said, "I'll talk to Julie before I leave in the morning. I'm sorry her marriage was bad, but I'm sure the Lord has someone for a young widow like her."

"Do you have to go so soon, son?" his father asked.

"Oh, yes, sir. I can't keep Hannah Rose waiting. I wish you could perform the ceremony, but I'm going to marry her, then head for Corinth to report to General Bragg. When this horrible war is over, I'll bring your wonderful daughter-in-law home for you to meet. I know you'll love her! She's the sweetest, most wonderful woman the Lord ever made!"

CHAPTER TWENTY-TWO

★

I t was midmorning on a bright sunny day, and Hannah Rose Claiborne was home alone, working on dress orders. Linda Lee, Donna Mae, and Sally Marie were visiting Aunt Myrtle.

Glancing at the calendar on the wall of the sewing room, Hannah Rose sighed, "April nineteenth. It's been nine days. Oh, Cliff, what has happened?"

As each day had passed, the melancholy young woman had marked it off the calendar, and yesterday her hopes had begun to die. While no letter had come telling her Cliff was married, neither had the man she loved returned.

Sighing, Hannah Rose decided to go outside and get a breath of fresh air. It was spring in Tennessee, and the dogwood was in bloom, filling the air with its lovely aroma. She settled on the old swing, idly pushing against the porch with her foot.

She inhaled deeply of the dogwood and recalled the conversation at the breakfast table that morning. Linda Lee and her sisters-in-law had told her that she just as well face it. The war was slowing the mail, and the letter Cliff had sent would be a long time coming. Cliff Barrett was a married man, and Hannah Rose would never see him again. She might as well start looking for another man.

Clearly she recalled her reply. If she couldn't be Cliff Barrett's wife, she would be an old maid.

Hannah Rose's eye caught movement on the grassy hills to the east. A lone rider on horseback was coming her way. They were too far away for her to identify the rider, but the horse was the same color as Cliff's— the horse he was falling from the very first time she saw him.

She left the swing and made her way to the edge of the porch. She shaded her eyes with her hand and watched intently, almost not believing her eyes as the rider drew closer.

Her heart hammered in her breast, and a lump formed and lodged in her throat.

It was Cliff!

Lifting her long skirt calf-high, she flew off the porch and ran toward him, her long chestnut-colored hair flying in the breeze. When they were some twenty yards apart, Cliff slid from the saddle and ran to meet her, taking her in his arms.

"Oh, Cliff!" she cried, tears streaming down her face. "You're not married to Julie!"

"No, darling, I never was. I've never been married to anyone! There's only one woman God made for me, and I'm about to kiss her like she's never been kissed before!"

EPILOGUE

✮

After "Bloody Shiloh," the bruised and battered Confederate Army of the Mississippi stumbled back to Corinth. Though the battle was considered a Union victory, both sides suffered horrible losses. Shiloh was the scene of the first epic bloody land battle in the West, and one of the fiercest combats in the history of American arms. It was a cruel baptism of fire for the soldiers of the West on both sides, with nearly 24,000 casualties. Of those, the *U.S. Official Records* lists 1,754 Yankees and 1, 728 Rebels killed.

The most notable casualty was General-in-Chief Albert Sidney Johnston, leader of the Army of the Mississippi. He holds the distinction of being the highest ranking officer during the entire Civil War to meet his death in battle.

Union and Confederate hospitals were jammed, and urgent calls for nurses and doctors were sent out. In addition to the nearly 3,500 killed, an estimated 16,000 men, who a few days before were hale and hearty, now faced amputations, festering wounds, and disease that would eventually account for many more deaths. Doctors reported that eight out of every ten amputations ended in death. There were no drugs to combat tetanus and gangrene, and supplies of chloroform were quickly exhausted.

Workers at every hospital had to dig huge holes to bury massive numbers of amputated limbs.

General Earl Van Dorn's long-delayed army never arrived at Shiloh. The weather and many other obstacles held them up. They finally appeared at Corinth in early May, weary, worn, and footsore.

The outcome of Shiloh pointed the way to a long and bloody conflict ahead. The situation appeared extremely grim for the Confederacy in the West. Not only had they been driven from Shiloh, but they lost Island Number Ten at the same time to the Union naval and land forces. The loss of the highly effective batteries located on the island meant the opening of the Mississippi River to Union gunboat traffic.

After the success at Shiloh, Major General Henry W. Halleck consolidated the Union's western forces into an army of 128,000 and marched them from Pittsburgh Landing toward Corinth to engage what remained of the Confederate Army of the Mississippi. However, the difficulty of assembling such a massive army and marching it even a relatively short distance, kept the Union forces from arriving at Corinth until the last of May. By that time General Pierre G.T. Beauregard's army had withdrawn from the area.

The Battle of "Bloody Shiloh" remains one of the most horrendous in Civil War history. In the days that followed, as Northern and Southern newspapers published the facts and figures, along with photographs taken of the battlefield the day after, the populace was stunned. The details of horror and bloodshed left readers appalled, especially when they read of the Hornet's Nest. Reporters wrote that the bodies of Union and Confederate soldiers were so numerous that one could walk over the entire Shiloh battlefield and never set foot on the ground.

Brigadier General James A. Garfield served in the Twentieth Brigade, Sixth Division, Army of the Ohio, and later became the twentieth president of the United States. Although he was not present at Shiloh, he reflected on it shortly thereafter with these words: "No blaze of glory that flashes around the magnificent triumphs of war can ever atone for the unwritten and unutterable horrors of the scene of carnage."

AN EXCERPT FROM

Beloved Enemy

If you enjoyed the love story of Cliff Barrett and Hannah Rose Claiborne, you'll also want to read **Beloved Enemy.** *The following excerpt begins as Jenny Jordan approaches a Union checkpoint, set up to ferret out Confederate spies.*

It was almost three o'clock that afternoon when a nervous Jenny Jordan rode along the edge of the Union camp and headed for the bridge that spanned the Potomac. A small group of soldiers huddled at the bridge. Jenny eyed the camp with its long rows of tents, and noted the old barn and the two sheds that stood in their midst. She figured there once must have been a farmhouse on the site.

The sun danced on the rippling waters of the Potomac as Jenny approached the bridge. Soldiers who milled about stopped to look at her. She wore her black riding boots, a black split skirt, and a ruffled white blouse. On her head was a small black hat, topping off the upsweep of her thick, dark hair. A sergeant left the group and strode toward her.

Jenny's heart skipped a beat as she drew rein. Struggling to mask her fear, she painted on a warm smile.

"Good afternoon, Miss," said the sergeant, touching his hat brim and smiling in return. "It isn't often we see a young lady traveling alone. Are you a Northerner or a Southerner?"

"Half-and-half," she replied, maintaining the forced smile. "I live in Washington, but I was born in Virginia. I'm on my way to visit an ailing aunt in Fairfax Courthouse."

"You'll be returning yet today, I assume, since you're carrying no luggage."

"That's right, Sergeant. I'm only planning to stay an hour or so."

"Well, ma'am, I hate to detain you, but with all the spy activity of late, you'll have to be searched."

Fear formed and settled in Jenny's stomach. "Searched? Do I look like a spy, Sergeant?"

Scratching at an ear, the sergeant replied, "Well, ma'am, I wouldn't take you for one, but I'm really not sure what a spy looks like. All I know is, somebody's been carrying classified information to the Confederate army. General McClellan has laid down strict orders to search everybody who crosses from the Union to the Confederate side. No exceptions."

Jenny's face blanched. She ran her gaze over the men who stood around and said loudly, "Well, just who is going to make this search, sergeant?"

The sergeant blushed. Shaking his head, he said, "Oh, I'm sorry, ma'am. We have a farmer's wife just over that hill behind you who searches the women for us."

Jenny saw an officer detach himself from the nearby group and move toward her and the sergeant. Running his gaze between the two, he asked, "Is there a problem, here, Wilkins? The lady sounds upset."

"It's my fault, sir," said Wilkins. "I told her she would have to be searched, but I forgot to explain that Mrs. Harrison would do the searching."

Smiling up at Jenny, the officer touched his hat brim and

said, "I'm Major Donald Sparks, Miss—"

"Jenny Jordan. My father is Lieutenant Colonel Jeffrey Jordan." Jenny hoped possibly this would spare her the search.

"I've long been an admirer of your father, Miss Jordan," said Sparks. "He made quite a name for himself in the Mexican War. I was pleased when President Lincoln made him military adviser for the Senate Military Committee."

"Thank you, Major," she nodded. "May I be allowed to resume my journey now? As I told the sergeant, I'm on my way to visit my sick aunt in Fairfax Courthouse."

"As soon as Mrs. Harrison searches you, ma'am. I'm sorry for this delay, but I'm under strict orders. Everyone who crosses this bridge must be searched. General McClellan made it clear that there are to be no exceptions."

Jenny had no choice but to submit to the search. If she told them she had changed her mind about visiting her aunt, they would immediately suspect her. If she wheeled her horse and galloped away, she would not get far. There were horses in the camp. They would ride her down. Besides...they knew who she was now. If she ran for it, they would soon have her in custody. She could only hope that the farmer's wife would not think to look in her hair.

The farmer's wife was summoned. Jenny was taken into the old barn, and in a private cell, she allowed Mrs. Harrison to search beneath her skirt and blouse.

When nothing was found there, Mrs. Harrison said, "I'll have to ask you to remove your boots, honey."

When the boots were cleared, the woman asked Jenny to remove her hat. While Mrs. Harrison ran her nimble fingers beneath the brim on the inside of the hat, Jenny felt a trickle of cold sweat run down her back.

Mrs. Harrison smiled and handed the hat back. "Okay, honey, you're cleared. Sorry to put you through this, but you understand."

"Of course," nodded Jenny, inwardly breathing a sigh of relief. "We must do all we can to stop this Confederate espionage."

As Jenny raised the hat to her head, Mrs. Harrison gazed at the thick folds of carefully upswept hair. "Just a minute, Miss Jordan," she said. "I just realized I didn't do as thorough a job as I should have. I'll have to ask you to let your hair down."

Jenny's nerves were suddenly taut and screaming. She was caught.

With shaky hands, she unpinned her hair. When the folded slip of paper fell out, Mrs. Harrison grabbed it. Jenny let out a tiny whine of mounting dread as the woman quickly read it and called for the soldiers.

Sergeant Wilkins and Major Sparks entered the small cubicle to find Jenny with her hair undone and her hands covering her face. She whimpered fearfully as Sparks read the message intended for General Thomas J. Jackson, grunted disgustedly, and handed it to Wilkins to read. Sparks turned to Jenny and said, "If you are really Jeffrey Jordan's daughter, Miss, this is going to bring great shame to him. His own daughter a Confederate spy."

Jenny's heartbeats felt like club blows in her chest. She could hardly breathe. Her mind was racing. Would this lead to her father's capture? What would Buck think of her? Jenny knew the president's edict concerning spies. She would face a firing squad and die without ever knowing the answers to these questions.

Excusing Mrs. Harrison, Major Sparks said, "Young lady, according to Federal law you must be executed within twenty-four hours. Nothing can alter that, but you could at least die with a clear conscience. How about telling me who the other spies are?"

Jenny lifted her tear-stained face and looked Sparks in the eye. She thought not only of her father, but of John Calhoun, Rose Greenhow, and Rose's girls. There was no way she would turn the Yankees on them. Moving her head slowly back and forth, she released a shaky, "Never."

"I thought so," Sparks sighed. "You will be locked in this compartment, ma'am. I'll see that you have water. It's really a shame, you know, for a beautiful young woman like you to have to face a firing squad. I'm sure glad your execution won't be on my shoulders. Our new commander will be here about supper time, and it'll be up to him to set the exact time of your execution."

Sparks and Wilkins left the cubicle and secured the door with a steel bolt. Jenny sat on the small cot in the gloomy cell. The terror that gripped her seemed to steal her breath, which was coming in short, painful gasps. She feared for her father's life, wishing somehow she could let him know she had been caught. Her mind then turned to Buck. Breaking down completely, she buried her face in her hands and sobbed Buck's name.

Jenny's weeping was interrupted by a young soldier who brought her a bucket of water and a tin cup. She said nothing, but stared at him while he set the bucket on a crude table, placed the cup beside it, and moved back to the door. Pausing, he looked at her with compassion and said softly, "I wish Mr. Lincoln hadn't set such a hard-and-fast rule about Rebel spies. It ain't gonna be easy to find men in the camp who will want to be part of the firing squad."

Jenny continued to stare at him, but said nothing.

"Well," the soldier said, "my prayers will be with you, ma'am."

When the steel bolt was shot home and the place was quiet, Jenny clenched her fists and said in a shaky voice, "Lord, You know I've hated living deceitfully before Buck. I didn't want to. I didn't ask for this awful war, and I didn't ask to be a Southerner living in the North. I...I don't want to die, Lord. Please let me live! And please, please don't let Buck hate me! I want to live...and to be his wife. Oh, God, please don't let them kill me!" Jenny broke down again, sobbing.

Word spread quickly through the camp that a Confederate

spy had been caught at the bridge, carrying classified military information to General Jackson, and that the spy was a beautiful young woman. Major Sparks had told Mrs. Harrison and Sergeant Wilkins not to tell anyone that the spy was Jeffrey Jordan's daughter. He wanted to keep that kind of information confidential until Colonel Brownell arrived and decided what to do about it.

Some of the men-in-blue gathered around Major Sparks, concerned that they were going to have to execute a woman. Sparks ran his gaze over their faces and said, "Gentlemen, I admit this has me mighty shaky, myself. But this is war. Nobody is forced into becoming a spy. The lady knew what she was doing when she rode in here carrying that message for Jackson. We all know the army regulations about the fate of spies. The responsibility for the execution lies on the shoulders of First Brigade's commander. And I don't mind telling you, I'm glad I'm not in Colonel Brownell's boots. Putting a woman to death—especially one as pretty as she is—will wrench his insides, I'll guarantee you."

"Major," said one of the soldiers, "how will the colonel choose his firing squad?"

"He won't get any volunteers, that's for sure. He'll have to choose them, making it an order."

"Is it true, sir," asked another, "that the execution has to be done within twenty-four hours of the time she was caught?"

"That's right. When the president sanctioned the rule, he meant for the execution to be swift and without mercy. The rule is known far and wide, even in the South. Mr. Lincoln made it so to discourage enemy personnel from becoming spies."

Another soldier spoke up. "Major, I guess if Colonel Brownell chose me for the firing squad and I refused, I'd be in trouble, wouldn't I?"

Every eye was on Sparks as he nodded slowly and said, "You sure would, Corporal. Then you might be facing a firing squad. Not a man of us would volunteer to kill this woman, but the law says it must be done. Some kind of welcome for our new commander, eh?"

Inside the large shed adjacent to the barn, nine of the thirteen Confederate prisoners were making plans to escape. They had been working on a plan previously, but when they heard about the female spy who was to be executed within twenty-four hours, they accelerated those plans. When supper was brought to them, they would overpower the guards, seize their weapons, and take them as hostages. They would demand the release of their four comrades in the other shed, and the release of the woman spy.

They would then head deep into Rebel country, taking the woman and the guards with them. The Yankees would be warned that if they pursued them, the guards would die. If there was no pursuit, the guards would be held as prisoners of war.

As the sun was lowering toward the western horizon, Buck Brownell saddled his horse for the ride down the river bank to his new command. From the corner of his eye, he saw General McClellan coming his way. Grinning to himself, he made as if he was having trouble with the cinch.

Drawing up, McClellan frowned and asked, "Got a problem, Colonel?"

"Yes, sir. It's this weird saddle. Whoever designed it must've been half-asleep at the time."

The general's brows knitted together and his mouth pulled tight. "I'll have you know, Colonel, I designed that saddle!"

Feigning ignorance, Buck said, "Oh, no! Is that why they call it a McClellan saddle, sir?"

The general saw that Buck was joshing him. He broke into a hearty laugh and said, "You just about had yourself a court-martial!"

The two officers laughed together, then McClellan said, "I want to thank you for a job well-done, Colonel. You've really sharpened up the troops with your training. Next time they face the Rebels, they'll be ready for them."

As the general spoke, he looked past Buck to see General Tyler riding in, accompanied by a pair of adjutant lieutenants. Spotting McClellan and Brownell, Tyler excused the lieutenants and beelined for them. "Gentleman, I've got some mighty good news!"

As Tyler was dismounting, McClellan said, "I'm sure we can use some of that kind of news, General. What is it?"

"Unbeknownst to everyone except Generals Scott and McDowell, the president hired Allan Pinkerton and his agency to hunt down the Rebel spies he suspected were working within the Capitol. It paid off. Three Rebel spies were caught and arrested today. One of them was a genuine shock to Mr. Lincoln."

"Someone in high places?" queried McClellan.

Tyler hitched up his pants by the belt. "You might say that. Lieutenant Colonel Jeffrey Jordan."

The name hit Buck Brownell like the kick of a mule. His scalp tingled, and his mouth went dry. "Jordan?" The word left his lips before he was aware he had spoken it. "Jeffrey Jordan?"

"I'm afraid so," said Tyler. "You sound like you might know him personally."

"I do, sir. It...it just doesn't seem possible. Jeffrey Jordan a Rebel spy. This is going to hit his daughter awfully hard."

"Who were the other ones?" asked McClellan.

"John Calhoun, a clerical worker in the Senate Chamber, and a woman named Lola Morrow who is employed in the U.S. Patent Office. Or I should say was employed there."

"How'd they catch them?"

"Lincoln hired a Pinkerton detective to work undercover as assistant to Calhoun. He saw Calhoun acting suspicious with Jordan, whom we all know was military adviser to the

Committee. Following his suspicions, the detective caught Calhoun passing a slip of paper to the Morrow woman and confiscated it at gunpoint. It was a message to Confederate military leaders, divulging classified information about an upcoming Union move on Rebel territory. The handwriting was Jordan's."

Buck was feeling sick all over for Jenny.

"So," proceeded Tyler, "the three of them are to die the moment the sun goes down. General Scott is overseeing the execution, and he told me that Pinkerton says there are definitely more spies in the ring...but all three refuse to name them."

Buck's mind was racing. He wanted to be by Jenny's side, though it was too late to get to her before the execution. What an awful thing for her to have to endure alone.

Looking at his superior officers, Buck said, "General McClellan...General Tyler...I need to ask something of you. I said a moment ago that I know Jordan. Actually, I know his daughter better. The fact is, I'm in love with her, and she feels the same way about me. This has to be an awful ordeal for her. I would like permission to ride into Washington immediately and be there to comfort her."

Tyler looked at McClellan. The field commander shook his head. "I'm sorry, Colonel, but you must be at your post down river as scheduled. For the young lady's sake, I wish I could let you go, but you are in charge of the camp down there, and you must go immediately."

"Yes, sir," Buck replied, trying not to show his disappointment. "I'm on my way now."

Buck rode south along the bank of the Potomac and watched the sun go down. Jeffrey Jordan and his two espionage companions were now dead. Buck vowed to go to Jenny as soon as possible. She would understand why he could not come to her immediately. Another thought came to mind. At least one good thing could come of this dreadful situation. With Jenny's father gone, they could have each other. Once she was over her grief, he would propose. He had no doubt she would accept the proposal.

Twilight was hovering over the camp when Buck rode in. Major Sparks was there to meet him when he moved past the sentries.

"Good evening, Colonel," said Sparks as Buck dismounted. "I was getting a bit worried about you."

"Had a slight delay in getting away," Buck replied.

"I have your tent ready, sir. It is the same one that Colonel Keyes occupied."

"Fine. Have the men had their evening meal yet?"

"No, sir. Ordinarily we would have, but we had some excitement around here. We're about ready to eat now, though."

"I would like to meet with you and the rest of the officers right after supper, then," said Brownell. "What was the excitement?"

"You remember when you brought the thirteen Rebel prisoners in, we put nine of them in that larger shed over there, and the other four in the small one."

"Yes."

"Well, sir, the nine in the large shed made an escape attempt about a half hour ago. They grabbed a couple guards to use as hostages and demanded to take the other four with them, along with a woman spy we caught this afternoon. Our marksmen went into action and took out all nine. The guards didn't get a scratch."

Buck's eyebrows arched. "A woman spy?"

"Yes, sir. She was carrying classified information to General Jackson. I'm sure you know what the regulation manual says about spies."

Buck felt a hot spot in his stomach knowing he would have to oversee the execution of a woman. "Yes, Major, I am fully aware of my responsibility. Executions are to take place at sunrise or sunset, but within twenty-four hours of the time the spy is caught. Executing a woman—even an enemy spy—is a distasteful thing, but it must be done. The execution will be at sunrise in the morning."

"Yes, sir."

"Major, I want you to pick out seven of our best marksmen for the firing squad. I have some news to tell you about captured spies, too, but it'll wait until later this evening when I meet with you and the other officers. Right now, I want to talk to this woman and see if I can get her to tell me more about the spy ring."

"All right, sir. I'll take you to her."

Sparks led his commanding officer through the big barn door, past several cubicles, and halted at one in a corner. Lantern light glowed through the cracks between the boards. "We've already given her supper, sir. I didn't want her to have to sit in the dark, so we brought in a lantern."

"Good gesture," nodded Brownell.

Sliding the bolt, Sparks said, "She's a pretty one, Colonel. You'll see that for yourself."

Buck waited for the major to pull the door open and step in ahead of him. Sparks moved inside the cubicle with Buck on his heels. "Miss Jordan, this is our camp commander, Colonel Brownell."

Buck saw Jenny sitting on the cot at the same instant he heard Sparks call her "Miss Jordan."

Their eyes met.

Jenny was stunned, but the horror that slammed into Buck was so powerful, it knocked the breath from him. A roaring began in his ears, red spots danced madly before his eyes, his flesh crawled. The cubicle seemed to swirl and heave around him.

OTHER COMPELLING STORIES BY AL LACY

Books in the Battles of Destiny series:

☞ *A Promise Unbroken*

Experience the heartache and victory of two couples battling jealousy and racial hatred amidst a war that would cripple America. From a prosperous Virginia plantation to a grim jail cell outside Lynchburg, follow the dramatic story of a love that could not be destroyed.

☞ *A Heart Divided*

Ryan McGraw—leader of the Confederate Sharpshooters—is nursed back to health by beautiful army nurse Dixie Quade. Their romance would survive the perils of war, but can it withstand the reappearance of a past love?

Books in the forthcoming Journeys of the Stranger series:

☞ *Legacy* (available April 1994)

Can John Stranger, a mysterious hero who brings truth, honor, and justice to the Old West, bring Clay Austin back to the right side of the law...and restore the code of honor shared by the woman he loves?

Available at your local Christian bookstore